# THE NIGHT SITTER

ALSO BY RUSSELL GILWEE:

*Shady Creek*
*Tess's Revenge*
*Sorcerie*
*Here Lurk Monsters*

# THE NIGHT SITTER

RUSSELL GILWEE

Author Disclaimer

This is a work of fiction. Names, characters, businesses, places, events, and incidents are either the product of the author's imagination or used in a fictitious manner. Any resemblance to actual persons, living or dead, or actual events is purely coincidental.

Copyright © 2022 Russell Gilwee

All rights reserved.

ISBN-13: 9798402334861

# DEDICATION

This book is dedicated to my wife, Lauraleen, and our goldendoodle, Sophie; family and friends; and to you, Dear Reader. My deepest gratitude.

# 1.

THE EMPTY CITY STREETS seemed, despite their sentry of street lamps, darker and colder without people. Maybe it was simply all those storefront neon signs turned dark and the restaurant windows black. Then again, maybe it *was* the absence of people. As if people themselves somehow imbued the city with their very own light, reminding Emily, in an admittedly childish and silly way, of lightning bugs. Rather like the little flying critters she'd chased on her grandparents' farm down there in North Carolina on hot muggy summer nights, the long grass pleasantly cool under her bare feet as she toted about a mason jar with tiny holes punched in the tin lid, gleefully snatching and stuffing the little flying critters by the handful into the jar until the jar blinked and glowed with the *soft golden light* emitting from their tiny translucent bottoms.

She'd then sit beneath a large oak tree in the dark. Her back to its trunk. There at the very outskirts of the property. Just inside the wooden split-rail fence. Peering closely into the mason jar. Twisting the jar this way and then that way. Peering at all those beetles fluttering about. Those trapped soft-bellied fluttering beetles.

Blinking and glowing inside the thick glass.

Resisting the urge to shake the jar. To make those buggers really dance. To make them all suddenly glow at once. To make them all light-up in the heavy darkness. And cast her completely in their *soft golden light*. As if she were somehow in the jar with them.

As if she were somehow *glowing herself.*
Resisting the urge even as she knew she'd not be able to resist the urge forever. Knowing she'd eventually shake that jar. Knowing she was helpless to stop herself. It being the reason she'd collected the bugs in the first place. Needing to be swallowed by all that *soft golden light.* To feel as if she were imbued *with her very own light.*
If only for but a brief, if glorious moment.
Imbued with a most *magical golden light.*
And not lost in all that darkness.
She sighed with the thought now, her grandparents long gone, the property subdivided into tract homes, as she stared out at those empty city streets, somehow darker and colder without people.
The sentry of street lamps somehow dull, too.
Dull and rather sleepy without them. The people.
As if the street lamps were gradually fading to black.
Rather like a panoply of guttering candlelight.
Certain to wink out. With dawn an eternity away.
Amid all those dark storefront neon signs.
And all the restaurant windows black.
Emily hugged herself. Shivering. Her teeth chattering quietly. The night cold seeping beneath her wool coat in the back of a slow-moving bus. The bus empty but for her and the driver.
She could see her breath hanging in the air. Small evaporating little clouds. Despite her fashionable nod at protective face-wear.
A scarf wrapped around her nose and mouth.
Perhaps, in retrospect, she should have inserted unused coffee filters inside the scarf as the CDC recommended. Despite her fear of being unable to breathe. A silly fear seemingly under the circumstances. Claustrophobia. But there it was all the same.
The fear of being smothered. Suffocated.
She tried breathing out more slowly, but it did little good. Her breath still in the air. Appearing briefly like cartoon bubbles.
This was how it spread. The awful virus that had closed down the entire fucking world in a matter of only weeks. In the air. Or so the experts vehemently insisted. Droplets. Moving about. Expelled by coughing. Sneezing. By simply having a conversation. Droplets breathed in by others. Landing on things, too. Lingering. Awaiting an unsuspecting hand that might touch a face. A nose. A mouth. An eye. Like an invading alien race. A tiny microscopic alien race. Patient and potentially deadly. These infected little droplets.

# THE NIGHT SITTER

The terrible virus had initially gone by an innocuous-sounding alpha-numeric designation (SARS-COV-X9) before the increasingly frightened public rebranded it *The Reaper Virus*. It was a novel virus that managed to overcome the immune system in days and was not discriminating. Striking down the young and the healthy as well as the old and infirm. Early rumors suggested it had maybe originated in a small province in China. A zoological event. But this interpretation was quickly dismissed by the computer models that suggested the virus had somehow seemingly appeared everywhere at once. Almost as if its arrival had been purposeful. Coordinated.

A terrorism event, perhaps. (Or worse.)

Regardless, its arrival produced an invention of terms. Terms now ubiquitous across the globe within only a short month.

*Mask-up. Social-distancing. Stay-at-home. Stop-the-spread. Shelter-in-place. Alone-together.*

The amount of National Guard on the streets suggested it was only a matter of days, if not hours, before Martial Law. The troops were already preparing to erect giant sawhorse barricades at strategic intersections. Coils of razor-wire standing at the ready. Soldiers dressed in inky-black combat gear with Darth Vader-like protective masks, turning their owners from human into something else altogether -- something *decidedly less human*. Something more automaton, frankly. As if anything might soon be required of them. Something requiring the mind of a machine rather than of a thoughtful thinking man. Or a thoughtful thinking woman for that matter.

A most terrible dark war from *within*.

Emily wasn't yet certain if she was sick herself. It was only too very easy to confuse a minor cough or sniffles, a stress-headache or the evening chills, to the preamble of the virus. And then there was the disquieting fact a certain percentage of the population appeared to be asymptomatic, if still capable of spreading the virus.

One tended to regard others with suspicion.

And take great pains to maintain six feet distance.

Not that six feet appeared to be any insurance.

Given the startling rate of infection.

Emily felt a nagging cough coming on now, burning inside her chest, probably just allergies, molds and whatnot, maybe the pollen from a tree that had mistaken the warm weather a few days ago for the beginning of spring only to be shocked back into reality by another cold snap. She did her best to suppress the cough.

Still, she found the bus driver staring at her.

Staring at her in his observation mirror. As if sensing her need to cough. Or maybe just watching all those breath clouds. Judging her. Perhaps meaning to report her.

He was wearing his own mask. A camo hunting mask made of neoprene. The mask covering his entire head, but for his dark eyes. Dark eyes watching her intently from dark oval-shaped holes.

The bus suddenly drifting on the empty street.

Drifting toward one of those dull street lamps.

Flickering on an approaching corner.

She gagged softly in an attempt to fight back the cough, only to subsequently feel it gather like hellfire in her chest. Her eyes beginning to water terribly. Tears eventually spilling down her flushed cheeks. Before she gagged again and finally *coughed*. *A world-beater of a cough.* And once she began coughing beneath her dreary scarf, she could not stop. The itchy wool only adding to the grievous tickle in the very back of her dry throat. All of her spasming. Every muscle and fiber of her unfortunate being in a terrible earthquake with the tears now spilling more furiously down her flushed cheeks, and her miserable fashionable scarf slipping, skewing off to the side.

The droplet flying from her mouth.

Harboring those microscopic alien invaders maybe.

Spilling out into the cold air before her.

She tried to cover her mouth with the inside of her thin elbow as she'd been shown on the television, but it was too late, the droplets suddenly in horrible flight. Some landing immediately and quite noticeably. Making wet the seat fabric in front of her. Others flinging rudely forward and riding-out on invisible air currents.

Spreading. Disseminating. Contaminating.

The bus driver's dark eyes went wide.

First at her. Then at that arriving lamp post.

He stamped down hard on the bus's air brakes (the air brakes sounding like hissing dragon's breath) while simultaneously tugging on the steering wheel. Swerving the bus to avoid hitting that lamp post. A large tire grazing the sidewalk curb. The long giant bus jolting and rocking before finding the empty street again.

Emily returned the scarf to her face, having to hold it over her face until she could tighten the dumb knot behind her head.

The bus driver staring at her once again.

Staring at her most balefully now.

# THE NIGHT SITTER

Stifling his own cough behind his camo mask.
Those dark baleful eyes already accusing her.
Already accusing her of being *contagious*.
As if he might somehow exhibit symptoms of the horrible infection in only just a few seconds after such an exposure.
He hit the bus brakes again.
If slightly more reasonably this time.
Slowing the bus at the next corner.
He reached for the lever that opened the bus doors. The front door and the mid-bus door. The opening doors made more dragon breath noises as they folded open, allowing the uncomfortably frigid night air to flow inside the bus. Like cold rushing water.
Emily's intended stop was several blocks away.
But she understood to disembark the bus.
She stood in the aisle a beat, however, staring at the bus driver over her scarf, if not to implore him, then to reassure him. To reassure him that *she was not sick*. Not that she could know such a thing. Not with any certainty, anyway. Not without a test. Tests that were few and far between. And not always reliable in the end.
He coughed again. Still staring.
Glaring. With those dark baleful eyes.
It was understandable to be afraid. The death rate for infected individuals was nearly thirty percent, at least according to the most recent reports. Still, it was a cold night and her suitcase was heavy. One of the tiny rubber wheels had fallen off in the past before this awful madness. Another tiny rubber wheel had gone stiff, refusing to turn, grabbing the ground and yanking the suitcase off course, threatening to dump it, insisting she carry the insipid suitcase. Her shoulder and back ached most terribly from having gotten it to the bus stop. And here she was still blocks from her destination.
She had watched this bus pass by her window for weeks now. Empty. Bouncing along the empty streets. Until tonight. The man behind the camo mask almost hadn't stopped for her. Perhaps not seeing her in the darkness. Perhaps not wanting to see her.
She doubted he would ever stop again. For her. Or for anyone in the near future, assuming public transport wasn't just ended with the almost certain Martial Law order in the coming days. Hours.
She offered the poor driver one last nod.
A human-to-human nod. Good luck, the nod said.
He blinked. Those dark eyes. Looked away.

She exited the bus via the mid-bus door, lugging her suitcase, huffing and grunting, her stupid scarf askew again, hiking down the short flight of steps, entering the dark and cold night. Nowhere to go but onward. Onward out into this dark and cold night.

Whatever it might eventually invite for her.

She had the address in her pocket. And directions. Written out in her ragged penmanship. Not trusting to save it on her phone just in case technology was the next to go. There was already talk about that. Amongst so very much unsettled talk. A desperate stab at censorship by the government to quell this untamable hysteria from its large restless flock of sheep growing ever more restless.

There were so many hideous rumors.

That the stated death rate was *higher* than thirty percent. Much higher, in fact. That experts in the scientific community were warning the government a vaccine would be very difficult to produce, if not impossible, given the virulent characteristics of the virus.

That there was evidence it was *already mutating*.

Becoming even more infectious. Even more virulent.

In a matter of only weeks. This terrible novel virus.

That perhaps this was part of its elegant design.

That the virus had, indeed, been *man-made*. Or, at the very least, procured somewhere in nature, then manipulated by man.

A gruesome Pandora's Box. Now open.

Emily shook her head and got moving. Her shoulder and back smarting as she lugged the suitcase through the cold darkness.

Her scarf falling down about her neck.

She passed by the dark storefronts. Restaurants.

An abandoned fluttering banner, also hanging askew, screaming: CONTACTLESS TAKE OUT FOR YOUR SAFETY.

A burger joint. A poster with a big fat juicy cheeseburger next to a plastic basket of French fries and a frothy chocolate shake. She could smell the grease and oil. Or at least she convinced herself she could if she closed her eyes. Her mouth instantly watering.

*When was the last time she'd eaten anything?*

*Yesterday morning? Had it been that long ago?*

*That stale bagel with an old packet of cream cheese?*

She thought it just might have been.

The grocery stores suddenly closing and her not heeding the rumors such a dire thing was actually coming in this once bountiful country of three hundred million souls. National Guard foodstuffs still working out the distribution kinks. Implying it could take days. Others suggesting it might even take weeks. Or months. The daunting logistics still unannounced.

She imagined those Darth Vader-looking soldiers clad in their combat black with their ugly rifles slung over their shoulders arriving on doorsteps across the entire country, sea-to-freaking-shining sea, with large cardboard boxes of tasteless nonperishables.

Powdered milk and juices.
Dried fruits and vegetables and meats.
Nuts and flours and other milled products.
Toiletries and medicines and vitamins.
Probably all of it laced with sedatives. Psychotropics.

She set the suitcase down a moment on the sidewalk. Stretching out her screaming back, shoulder. Re-securing her scarf.

She watched the bus in the night. The narrow taillights fading into the darkness. Blinking once, then twice. Dully. Before slipping around a corner. Vanishing past a darkened Whole Foods.

But that wasn't what held her attention.
Rather, it was what she saw in the distance.
Or what she imagined she could see.
Past swirling layers of low-hanging gray fog.

She thought she could see razor wire in the distance and a wall of those sawhorse barricades beneath what looked like the glow of floodlights. And in the glow of those floodlights, the automatons in all their inky-black combat gear closing down this dismal world for good. Finally. Inevitably. Inexorably. Locking it all down.

Voluntary action replaced with compulsory.
A euphemism for turning the world into a prison.
A freaking prison for who knew how long.

Conveniently for her, Emily was not heading in that direction, but east. Hefting her suitcase with a whimpering groan, and earning what felt like an ice pick stabbing at the back of her neck, a terrible pain that radiated down both her arms and made like tiny splinters in her otherwise numb fingers, she stumbled past a small hardware store with a busted display window staring-out at her vacantly. The jagged edges of broken glass offering a mimicry of razor-sharp eyelashes as she rounded a hibernating hair salon and left behind the dark and lonely midtown commercial district for a quiet residential neighborhood populated with massive Victorians, Tudors, and Colonials standing behind a silent line-up of large dark elm trees.

Faltering along, Emily followed her directions. The directions written out in her ragged penmanship now pulled from her pocket. Squinting at them in the night as she moved slowly past--
Drawn curtains and locked doors.
Shadows moving behind those curtains.
The only evidence of any life in this place.
Cars slumbering in narrow driveways.
Yellowing front lawns in need of mowing.
Bushes and such in need of trimming.
Porches and such in need of sweeping.
Even the birds unusually muted here seemingly.
Or maybe it was just the rather late hour.
Only the crickets appearing happy.
Chirping in all that yellowing unruly grass.
Greeting her as she faltered along.
Or perhaps just whistling derisive things at her.
Judging her. Chastising her *for being out.*
There were deserted swing sets in side yards. Forlorn.
A dirty basketball come to rest in the street. Abandoned. The name BOYD scribbled on one of its synthetic leather panels.
A ceramic garden gnome crouched below a mailbox, its pudgy little red-cheeked face crushed by a rock. Its one good eye contemplating her suspiciously as she passed by it in the night.
*Where do you think you're going, young lady?* Or so it seemed to ask of her, the gnome with its one good eye. *Stop-the-spread. Stay-at-home. Shelter-in-place. Alone-together. You stupid little fucking nitwit. You unforgivable spreader. Diseased! Diseased! Stop her! Stop her! Stop her!*
She could understand why someone might've had the impulse to grab a rock and heave it at the detestable little thing. Staring-out at her like it was. Berating her in such a manner. She'd half-a-mind to find another rock and just blind the ugly little troll.
Instead, she kept moving. Moving.
Lugging. Grunting. Groaning. Whimpering.
Turning off 47th Street and onto Washington Irving Way, then bumbling past a small playground surrounded by fluttering yellow caution tape. The playground looking like an abandoned crime scene. A swing set, jungle gym, slide frozen in the darkness over a bed of dirty sand as if trying to blend into the shadows. Looking rather guilty for its clumsy efforts behind a PARK CLOSED sign.
She took a left onto Sleepy Hollow Road.

# THE NIGHT SITTER

The wide sidewalks eventually faded away. Replaced with narrow gutters. The large homes suddenly much older-looking and not the silly modern reproductions she had just left behind her.
Venerable homes that had withstood time.
As opposed to offering mere caricatures of it.
She continued following her directions.
She passed a NO THROUGH ROAD sign.
Circled into a deep and dark cul-de-sac.
A large Victorian sat at the back of the cul-de-sac.
A dark gothic dollhouse of a Victorian.
Rising and disappearing into the night darkness.
Beneath a dull thumbnail-sliver of moon.

It was at least three stories tall, looming over the cul-de-sac as if the Victorian were somehow leaning forward. Dark wood siding complemented dark scalloped shingles that only too closely resembled oily reptilian scales. A giant slumbering asymmetrical monster of a beast with decorative lattice trim and whimsical brackets, dentil molding, ornate spandrels, and beaded rails beneath a steep multifaceted roof with a series of gables facing in many directions over a long and deep wraparound porch. But the spooky Victorian's most defining quality, perhaps, was its host of tall dark rectangular multipaned windows that stared down at her blindly like black eyes.

She checked its address in her hand.
Written out in her ragged penmanship.
43 SLEEPY HOLLOW ROAD.

She could just decipher as much on a mailbox standing at the end of the driveway. A narrow metal box on a rather crooked post, the front flap of the metal box flung open. As if the mailbox were sticking out its black tongue at her. Revealing a dark throat.

As if the mailbox might just jump out at her.
Bite her. Swallow her into its long narrow gullet.
As if it might be able to squeeze her down.
Breaking each of her bones like a python.
Turning her insides into a soft jelly.
As it greedily sucked her deep inside it.
Into a most horrible cold darkness.

She paused here and *almost turned around, as if the mailbox with its black tongue were speaking to her silently without words, warning her she'd no business exploring this any further than from the street,* but felt that ice pick stab harder, sending that terrible pain down that highway of nerves from her neck into her splintery hands. And yet, *she still almost turned around* even though she had nowhere else in this world to go.

Not since that boy had been put in the ground.

A small coffin. Henry. All of nine years old.

Six feet down into that cold black hole.

The boy's family hadn't blamed her necessarily, not after nearly a year of service, but they'd been only too quick to provide her a severance check and hush their goodbyes. Their eyes averted above their masks, scarves, and other face-coverings in a gloomy gray rain amid a congregation of old and fresh graves beneath an audience of red cedar trees with wind-twisted trunks in the cemetery beside that deep river at the far corner of town. The river pushing along silently. Indifferently. Muddy and dark and unquestionably deep.

That had been two long weeks ago now.

She'd spent the two long weeks quarantined in a tiny shit-hole motel apartment. A veritable rat's nest with stained threadbare carpet and tattered curtains and a mini-fridge with a noisy compressor screeching to life every hour of the freaking night and day beneath a filthy window staring-out toward a desolate drive-in theater next door with trash blowing around in endless circles. The trash unable to escape that wretched drive-in theater's rusty chain-link fence in a rather miserable waltz of the discarded and the forgotten.

The placement agency had contacted her last evening. Darcey. Working from home these days. She hadn't many details. Only that the position needed to be filled immediately. ASAP. And intimating Emily had been asked for by name. A *referral* it would seem, though not offering any elaboration. Working from home these days. Distracted by her children. A barking dog. Her husband.

She'd provided Emily a contact number.

Emily had called it. ASAP. Left a message.

She had almost burned through her severance. Referral or not, it seemed an act of providence. So many of the other girls had been laid off. So many of the other girls without any prospects.

Girls with far sunnier dispositions than she.

Girls who hadn't buried a poor child.

A small coffin. Henry. All of nine years old.

Six feet down into that cold black hole.

She'd received back a curt text moments later.

A time and date for an interview. An address.

And lastly, a name. *Ms. Vivian Dancemore.*

# THE NIGHT SITTER

A rather delicious-sounding name for all that. This name. This Ms. Vivian Dancemore. A name that almost sounded made-up. Rather like something pulled, perhaps, from the credits of an old black and white movie. Or right out of the Victorian age itself. Arriving her here now on this cold night. Here to the very end of this dark cul-de-sac. Here to the very edge of the world seemingly. With nowhere else in this world to go. In this world come so very undone. The suitcase now on the sidewalk beside her. Sitting there like a quiet companionable dog. Leaning against her leg. Also weary as her eyes were slowly drawn to a welcome sign on the long and deep wraparound porch. The sign leaning against the exterior wall beside an obsidian black front door and beneath a suspended antique ceiling lantern buzzing softly with a flurry of black and white moths. The sign wrought-iron. And reading in gothic-calligraphy:

*Luke 10:5 Whatever house you enter,*
*First say: 'Peace be to this house.'*

Emily, with a final exhausted grunt, gathered her suitcase with both hands, and holding it in front of her now, the thing bouncing against her knees, labored up a narrow flagstone walkway.

The flagstones rather slick in the night.
The house seeming to loom over her even more.
A dark shadow against the dark night sky.
With its host of many black-eyed windows.
Black-eyed windows that now seemed awake.
Watchful. No longer just staring blindly.
Tall. Dark. Rectangular. Multi-paned.

The tall dark rectangular multi-paned windows dark *not because* it was necessarily dark inside the house, Emily realized, but because the windowpanes were black. As black at that front door. Perhaps tinted. Then again, she couldn't see any obvious tinting. Rather, the windows appeared to be *naturally* black. Setting her mind to wonder what might *naturally darken glass* in such an inveigling manner.

Obscuring anything beyond them.
Only reflecting the dark night sky above her.
The shadow-glow of that thumbnail-sliver moon.
While containing all else within its walls.

Once again, she almost turned around. Maybe it was all those dark windows. Staring down at her silently. So solemnly.

Maybe it was how the house loomed. Loomed so heavily over her in the cold night. As if leaning forward to embrace her. Perhaps she had a sense of it even then. In the very beginning of things. That once she passed into this strange house there could be *no turning back*. There could be *no turning around* ever again. But her suitcase was so heavy. Her back aching. Her poor shoulder smarting. Her feet sore. And she was expected after all. Expected. Here. With nowhere else in this world to go. In this world come so very undone.

# 2.

THERE WAS A BRASS KNOCKER. Black. Nearly invisible against the thick black door. Emily vaguely remembered reading somewhere that a black door should face north. She seemed to recall it had something to do with *Feng Shui*. That such a bold and elegant door as this black door should face north in order to bring a peaceful and productive energy to the space that resided beyond it. Emily bit down on her bottom lip, standing silently at its threshold, and wondered if this black door faced north, and what it might portend for what lay beyond it if the door did not.

She sighed. Reached for the knocker. She could not locate any doorbell. Perhaps such old homes eschewed them, she considered. Such silly and banal trappings of modern convenience.

The knocker made a deep hollow sound.

Echoing into the thick walls of the old house.

The tall black windows offered little greeting. Still dark even at this close vantage. Almost as if the home were abandoned. Almost as if the home were hollow. A funny thing to consider, perhaps. To think of it as abandoned and hollow. Filled with only a most terrible darkness. Despite the fact she was expected after all. As if the house itself had somehow summoned her. So it would not have to be so alone. The job offer merely a most clever charade.

And Darcey its unwitting accomplice.

A useful, if already forgotten go-between.

The deep hollow knocker sound faded into a heavy silence inside the old house. And yet, Emily took a step back in anticipation. As if the door might suddenly open *of its own accord.* Suck her right into that most terrible darkness. As if the black door, moving all by itself, magically so, of its own accord, might produce a malevolent undertow. A dark riptide from which she might not escape.

But the black door stayed predictably still.

And the house beyond it deafeningly quiet.

Emily blinked. Sighed again. Standing beneath the porch lantern buzzing softly with that flurry of black and white moths. Swiping away the insects with one hand, then the other. Their feathery wings in her face. Sticky little bodies tangling in her hair.

She stepped over into the shadows.

If only to escape their harmless torment.

There was a suspended porch swing, its rusted chains creaking in a listless breeze. A wrought-iron bistro table with four wrought-iron chairs. A company of dark window-boxes and hanging baskets displaying a mélange of rather weedy-looking, if fragrant herbs and wildflowers. But most interestingly, perhaps, was the large cast iron bell that hung on the wall in the darkness. Its mounting shaped like a sleek black dragon, featuring detailed wings and scales.

Emily peeked inside the black dragon bell.

And was pleased to find it still had its clapper.

She imagined what a racket the bell might make in this deafeningly quiet neighborhood if she took to clanging the thing.

All those shadows behind all those curtains.

In all those houses pushing down the dark street.

All those shadows suddenly pulling back all those curtains and peering out with terrible alarm at the bell's most robust sound.

The bell sounding like the end of the world.

Echoing, perhaps, the horn of the rapture itself.

Which drew her attention back to that sign. The wrought-iron sign beside the black door. Propped against the house wall exterior under the porch lantern. Offering in gothic-calligraphy:

*Luke 10:5 "Whatever house you enter,*
*First say: 'Peace be to this house.'*

And that was when she heard *footsteps*. Footsteps on the other side of that black door. Dark little echoes in all that stillness.

Like the hooves of the four horsemen.

Stamping across a world forsaken.

# THE NIGHT SITTER

And once again experienced the most terrible urge to just *turn around* and run. To leave her suitcase behind on this porch with the mad flurry of fluttering black and white moths. To just run off into the dark night even with nowhere else in this world to go.

But then the thick black door was *opening*, revealing beyond it a dull hazy light interrupted by deep pockets of dark shadow.

*Through which a mysterious figure appeared.*
*A small female form. A young girl.*
*Momentarily lost in a tendril of dark shadow.*
*Before she slipped into the dull hazy light.*
*And revealing, not a young girl at all.*
*But rather, a grown woman in the end.*
*As if Emily had witnessed the undoing of a curse.*
*Or, at the very least, a peculiar enchantment.*
*In that transition from shadow to light.*

*Still, hadn't the woman seemed to skip just as she'd opened the door and spilled that dull hazy light interrupted by deep pockets of dark shadow? Like a child might skip for no reason whatsoever? For no other reason than it felt good to do so? To lift oneself into the air and spring forward? Hands lifting momentarily beyond her hips? Had she actually done that? This woman?*

*As downright silly as all that seemed now?*

Emily thought not. It seemed much too ridiculous to contemplate, though she would wonder about it again later. Later when the strangeness of this charge had finally been revealed to her.

But, for now, it was only too easy to assume it a mischievous trick of the light and shadows. Only just too easy at that.

For the woman standing before her possessed a very un-child-like stiff and restrained bearing. An austere demeanor further complemented by a long muted black dress fashioned with a black puritan stand-up collar that managed to conceal most of her long pale neck, a button-front bodice with small white pearlized buttons fastened with thin fabric loops over a traditional modesty panel, and a sleek gathered-skirt with a sheer black overlay that fell from a narrow seamed-waistline and down over a pair of small black slippers embroidered with a geometric pattern of dark red roses.

Her long dark hair featured a clean middle part and was tied back tidily in a simple bun, presenting a stern and pale face without a hint of make-up or humor, her razor-thin lips pursed as if in anger, chapped and waxen. Her eyes gray and expressionless.

A countenance as if in perpetual judgement.

Perhaps it was for this reason Emily was reminded to pull her scarf back over her nose and mouth and take a step back to maintain the polite six feet of social-distancing. This despite the fact the woman was not wearing any protective mask of her own.

She waited a moment for the woman to speak.

When the grim woman did not do so--

Emily cleared the night cold from her throat, if still sounding rather embarrassingly hoarse as she managed to mutter:

"Vivian Dancemore, if you please, miss."

Not wanting to just simply presume.

As if this woman could be anyone but her.

The woman just stared at her, however.

Stared at her with those expressionless gray eyes.

And for a moment Emily was quite certain she had the wrong home. Had somehow scratched down the wrong address and managed to knock on the wrong door. That the strange woman clad in the gothic black dress was a mute and unfamiliar to callers.

Emily offered her name. Surname.

Suddenly realizing she'd not yet done so.

"I'm expected," she attempted next.

Nodding down at her suitcase beside her.

As if that might better explain things.

The woman in black blinked, though it was more of a sudden eye-twitch. Both gray eyes blinking hard at the same time. An affectation Emily would grow accustomed to over the coming days.

If not over the coming nights, anyway.

"I'm Vivian Dancemore, miss," the woman finally said to her. Her voice a cold whisper of wind rustling a scrum of dead autumn leaves. *Perhaps even in endless circles like all that trash in that desolate drive-in theater. In that miserable waltz of the forgotten and the discarded.*

Emphasizing the word *miss*. This woman.

Perhaps because Emily had said it moments before.

*Vivian Dancemore, if you please, miss*, she'd said.

Perhaps it had sounded rather snotty. Perhaps it had sounded rather dismissive. Perhaps this was a correction of behavior.

Emily blinked. Wondering if she'd only imagined such an emphasis. It wasn't beyond her to imagine such rebukes.

Assuming they were only to be imagined.

Emily actually felt herself do a little ridiculous curtsey now. As if she were standing before the fucking Queen of England.

"Please to make your acquaintance," she said.

Her voice muffled beneath the scarf.

The scarf pulled back over her nose and mouth.

And felt another cough bubbling in her chest.

The scarf wool fibers tickling her throat.

The woman nodded. Stepped aside. Presumably inviting Emily inside and out of the night. This Ms. Vivian Dancemore. Into all that dull hazy light. Into those deep pockets of dark shadow.

Emily, however, hesitated on the front stoop.

Not because she felt that need to *turn around*. *To turn around and maybe run madly back out into all that cold unwelcoming darkness.*

But because of a more practical concern.

"Should I just leave the suitcase, then?" she said.

Meaning to leave it outside the thick black front door. Thinking perhaps the woman might want her to sanitize it first.

She'd packed Clorox wipes. Hand sanitizer.

"You may leave it at the bottom of the staircase," the woman said. Nodding at thin carpeted risers ascending into darkness.

And for a moment Emily though she might've detected a resignation in the woman's voice. A whisper of surrender.

Not that it was uncommon these days.

The grim acceptance any control was illusory.

"Thank you," Emily said, and finally stepped into the house, lugging her suitcase the final few feet before dumping it next to the staircase where it leaned against a newel post. The suitcase seeming to shrug, then offer an exhausted sigh. The newel post as old as the house. A carved black walnut. Fluted with ribbed columns.

Emily found herself in a small foyer. The foyer fronting a low narrow hall. The low narrow hall pushing into a house divided into many small rooms, and reminding her once again of a dollhouse. A maze of a dollhouse. And imagined it possible to get lost in such a place even as she quickly dismissed the idea away as absurd.

The walls wood-paneled. Dark and thick.

The many odd doorways also low and narrow.

It was also cold in here. Colder seemingly than outside, if one could imagine such a thing. And yet the air rather stale-tasting. Unstirred. As if the door perhaps hadn't been opened in ages.

The woman, her black dress dragging on a hardwood floor in need of a fresh coat of varnish, led her slowly down the low narrow hall and into a small sitting room made to feel even smaller, a peculiar curiosity of the house, with plush overstuffed antique furniture, pictorial tapestries and landscapes, long dark window draperies, and an impressive, if suffocating collection of antique knickknacks. Including marble sculptures and figurines. Porcelain bowls. And large spelter statues with French engravings (e.g. *Mestais* and *Le Sauveteur*). As well as an assortment of Victorian table lamps displaying ornamental bronze scroll designs and elegant dark glass globes harkening back to a long-ago-lost bygone era of oil and candlelight. Even their modern low-watt lightbulbs seeming to flicker softly.

As if time had been turned back on itself.

As if that erstwhile era had returned.

Top hats, bonnets, and long frock coats.

A time of horse carriages and muddy streets.

The city air filled with soot and smoke.

The effect was only further complemented by a small fireplace in the near corner in which a small fire crackled contently.

In addition, drawing and confusing the eye, making dizzy the head, Emily found the room, as she would find many of the other rooms in the home, adorned with medallions and arches and ovals. Garlands and wreaths. Chintz china and large house plants.

Still, despite this congestion of things--
She found it all rather cozy and charming.
Rather cozy and charming for all that.

If a bit stiff and restrained like Ms. Vivian Dancemore herself. Though Emily had the growing sense the woman's taciturn bearing was only just a carefully manufactured façade, perhaps, intended to conceal something less calm lurking beneath the surface.

Something less cozy and charming maybe.

Something less cozy and charming for all that.

An admittedly somewhat *prescient* thought Emily would drearily reflect upon later after this woman had revealed what she would eventually reveal to her inside this rather cozy and charming, if stiff and restrained small sitting room inside this quiet house.

Inside this very much too-quiet house.

With only the tick of a grandfather clock.

The grandfather clock stood proudly in the far corner of the room. Marquetry accented with fleur-de-lis and its large brass pendulum swinging sleepily back and forth. Sleepily back and forth like a metronome. As if it were slowly trying to hypnotize her.

*Tick, tock, tick, tock. Tick, tock, tick.*

# THE NIGHT SITTER

As if time could somehow be reduced here.
Somehow shrunk down to its smallest tiny bits.
Paused and manipulated, perhaps. Time.
Perhaps even reversed in the end. Maybe.
That brass pendulum reversing course.
Moving in the opposite direction.
*Tick, tock, tick, tock. Tick, tock, tick.*
The idiotic spell was broken by that awful tickle reemerging in the back of her throat. Emily breathed in deeply, hoping to clear it, only to feel it turn into a dust feather thanks in no small part to the scratchy wool of her scarf. The scarf still over her nose and mouth. That tickle quickly burning inside her tightening chest. And Emily realizing with mortification there would be no stopping it. Her entire body shaking violently once again in a terrible earthquake. Still, she'd the presence of mind to cough into her thin bent elbow while managing to keep her stupid scarf in place this time. Albeit her eyes watering despite her best efforts. Tears spilling out. A few dribbling down her cheeks, only making the coughing fit worse. Gasping, she tried to apologize only to begin coughing yet again with that ticking grandfather clock seeming to keep time with her awful fit. She focused on that *tick, tock, tick* and it seemed to calm her spell.
As if moving time forward or backward.
She felt her heaving lungs finally settle down.
And blinked away the remaining tears.
She expected the woman, Ms. Vivian Dancemore, might very well wear a horrified expression and motion Emily back to the narrow hall and her suitcase and back out the black front door.
But the woman did none of these things.
She merely sat on a short chenille sofa and gestured for Emily to settle in a facing fuzzy blue velvet armchair. A low marble coffee table with short gold-trim walnut legs between them. She then gestured for Emily to remove her scarf. Doing so with a sigh.
Emily hesitated for only a short beat.
Before lowering the scarf gratefully.
Quite glad to be rid of the thing, frankly.
She wanted to tell the forbidding woman it was probably only just allergies, molds and whatnot, but held her tongue, sensing the less she said the better. When she felt that miserable old dust feather once again in the back of her throat, promising to invite that soft hellfire of a burn deep in her chest, she pinched at her wrist. Did so

subtly as to not be seen doing so, leaving a small flowering little red welt on her pale skin. Joining a parade of such little red welts.

She embraced its own soft little burn.

Not unlike a little hot flame licking at her.

Only to realize her eyes now closed.

Upon her eyes re-opening, she became certain the woman was staring at her pinching at her wrist after all. At that small flowering little hot flame of a welt turning darker against her pale skin.

She offered the woman a smile.

Though making sure not to show her teeth.

Teeth could be a show of aggression.

Her grandmother had once told her that while trying to instill in her the virtues of being a proper young lady. No teeth.

Among other such sincere aphorisms:

*Never groom yourself in public.*
*Keep covered your cleavage and posterior.*
*Always maintain good posture.*
*Be humble about your accomplishments.*
*Always speak in a quiet polite tone.*
*Always remember your please and thank yous.*
*Always be kind and courteous and decent.*
*Refrain from impure thoughts and behavior.*
*Watch your table manners and your cocktails.*
*Treat others as you would like to be treated.*
*Never show your teeth when you smile.*

The woman did not smile back at her. And Emily noticed she was fidgeting now. Pale hands restless in her lap. Those pursed lips trembling slightly. Her gray eyes twitching again. Both gray eyes. At the same time. A hard, involuntary series of heavy blinks.

As if suddenly exhausted by the pretense.

And as if not certain how to begin.

"I'm the caretaker," she said, then blinked hard again, as if not meaning that at all. Not like it sounded. "Of the child."

She paused here. Faltering.

The small fire crackled and hissed.

Emily found herself peeling off her coat without further invitation, being so close to the small fire. Most certainly an unforgivable breach of etiquette in her grandmother's handbook.

*I'm the caretaker*, the woman had said.

*Of the child,* she had explained.

# THE NIGHT SITTER

"You're not the child's mother, then?" Emily said.

Even as she heard her late grandmother gasp. Gasp at her impoliteness. Her boldness. Her complete lack of decorum.

This earned another hard, involuntary blink.

Then a glance at the decorative plaster ceiling and a large oval medallion housing the canopy of a hanging light fixture. A fanning candle-style tiered chandelier. Flickering softly. Or seeming to. Like the dark-globed table lamps in all the dancing firelight.

Though Emily doubted the woman was merely glancing at the ceiling or the fixture. But at what lay up there beyond it.

"Tell me about the child, Ms. Dancemore."

And once again, heard her grandmother's voice.

Disapproving. A *tsk tsk* as punctuation.

*Patience is always a virtue, young lady.*

"A girl," the woman hushed, as if it were a thing to be hushed, her gray eyes finally dropping from the ceiling. "Nine."

A girl. Nine. Perfect. No diapers, then. No potty-training. No squealing tantrums. OK. They were getting somewhere here.

Even if it suddenly felt as if she were pulling teeth.

As if she were the one conducting the interview.

"The young lady's name, if you please."

*Don't pry or be gossipy or judge harshly others.*

"Madelyn. Sometimes Maddy."

"Sometimes. I see. Precocious, is she?"

The first hint of a smile. Pride.

Or maybe it was a grimace.

There was no evidence of a child in the sitting room. Or anywhere else Emily had yet seen. No abandoned toys scattered about. No little doll-like shoes by the front door. Nothing at all.

And the house above them, so quiet.

So altogether much too-quiet. This house.

Houses with children, especially young children, from Emily's experience, had a most particular way of announcing themselves to people who worked closely with such young children. Like a crime scene might announce itself to a seasoned detective long before a layman might discern a crime had been committed there.

A spot of blood on a door panel. The absence of any cleaning products in the house. A missing bug screen on a window. A restless or overly-subdued dog. The harsh smell of bleach.

"Madelyn," Emily repeated. "Maddy."

The woman nodded thoughtfully.
Before another hard, involuntary blink.
"This is a live-in nanny position," she then said.
She then said with a bit more authority.
"Yes, I see," Emily acknowledged.
Darcey had been very specific about that particular stipulation if not at all specific about any of the other germane details.
"The previous nanny, our dearest Hannah, was with us here in this house for a very long time. Quite one of the family."
*A very long time. In this house. The previous nanny. Our dearest Hannah. Quite one of the family.*
Emily bit her tongue, resisting an urge to ask what might have happened to the former nanny, this dearest Hannah, most especially since any offer of explanation seemed unforthcoming.
"I have reviewed your resume," the woman revealed. "You've been doing this sort of work for many years now, it seems."
"Yes, ma'am," Emily agreed.
"Do you like this sort of work?"
"Yes, ma'am. I do, ma'am."
"And why would that be?"
Emily sat taller in her chair. It seemed a rather funny question. As if the answer might not be an obvious one in the end.
*Always maintain good posture.*
*Be humble about your accomplishments.*
*Always speak in a quiet polite tone.*
"I'm fond of children, Ms. Dancemore."
This earned a panoply of eye twitches.
Almost as if the woman didn't believe her.
"Your last charge was a sick child."
"Yes, ma'am. An immunodeficiency disorder."
"An inherited condition, yes?"
"Yes, ma'am. The disease is a terrible one. It compromises the immune system and left the child with a susceptibility to infections, especially respiratory infections. A particularly devastating possibility during a pandemic like the one we're facing, ma'am."
"The reason for your discharge, tragically."
"Yes, ma'am. I mean no, ma'am. No."
Emily assumed Darcey had discussed with her the specifics of the boy's situation. In fact, she was rather counting on it. And further assumed it was the reason she was here. Doubting this woman

had asked for her by name as Darcey may or may not have implied. It was getting rather difficult to remember clearly. Darcey working from home and being distracted as she was. Still, Emily was getting the intuitive sense this woman had been searching for someone, for the lack of a better description, who'd been tested by fire.

"There was no evidence of the virus."

"So, it was his condition, then. Only that."

"Yes, ma'am. Unfortunately, ma'am."

"This was a live-in position, I assume."

"Yes, ma'am. That is correct, ma'am."

"My condolences for your loss, dear."

"Yes, ma'am. Thank you, ma'am."

"And before he became seriously ill?"

"Ma'am?" she said, confused by the question.

"Your day-to-day responsibilities there."

"I worked in coordination with his nurse and his family. Strict protocols had to be followed to mitigate his condition."

"Such as, if you please."

"Diet. Meds management. So on and so forth. The nurse, she only visited the home twice a week, ma'am, for monitoring. Etc. It was a challenging assignment, but one I took most seriously."

"Because the consequences were grave."

"Grave. Indeed, ma'am. Precisely, ma'am."

"Of course. Hm. Anything else, then?"

"Anything else, ma'am?" she said.

Again, rather confused by the question.

"Any other peculiarities of the assignment?"

Emily thought about this for a moment. Then:

"He was not allowed to leave the house."

She had often sat with the boy in his bedroom window watching the world go by outside, his young parents more often than not gone at work, managing a failing dog grooming business. His older brother shooting hoops endlessly in the driveway and his older sister disappearing with older and older boys in a parade of cars pulling in and out of that same driveway. The leaves in the trees changing colors and falling, then budding again in the spring.

As one long year fell into the next.

And all the while the boy sitting there.

Gangly. Pale. His head too large. Hair thin.

Big blue eyes jaundiced. Lips purple.

The poor boy having to hide even then. Before.

Before the world had come so very undone by the virus.

Before the world knew what it was to be the boy.

Sometimes the neighborhood kids would wave at him as they passed by on their bicycles. Sometimes they would not. He always waved. The poor boy. He loved to read. To be read to. He didn't sleep much. He was always sick. Coughing and feverish. Headaches. There was discussion of a bone marrow transplant. But there were dire risks involved. The very direst of risks.

Emily explained this to Ms. Vivian Dancemore.

"He never left the house," she repeated. Before adding, shoulders shrugging: "Not unless there was a medical need."

Emily did not admit sometimes sneaking the boy out into the backyard when everyone else was gone from the home. She did not admit the pleasure it gave her to see his smile when the boy felt the warm spring rain on his cheeks or managed to coax over the lonely goldendoodle from next door through a gap in the fence.

And it was good that she did not--

For the woman seemed keen on this point.

Keen on this point for reasons of her own.

For reasons she would very soon reveal.

"You are able to follow rules, then," the woman said, glancing at one of the draped windows. The drapes long, thick, black.

It seemed less a question than directive.

"Yes, ma'am. Of course, ma'am."

She'd once taken the boy for ice cream. It had been a few days after his birthday and the rest of the family had been at the movies. He'd begged her to take him out for a banana split. She'd borrowed the boy's mother's car that day without telling the boy's mother, or anyone else in the family, and driven the boy the few blocks over to Dairy Queen where the other kids had always congregated.

He'd promised to stay in the car.

Only to disappear while she'd been inside.

*Poof.* Like magic. Just gone. The boy.

She'd found him a few frightful minutes later with the other kids around back. They were trying to teach him how to ride a bike. He had been wobbling around in circles, and laughing.

She'd never heard him laugh. Henry. The boy. Let alone laugh so joyfully like that. It was almost painful to listen to. That laughter. If she closed her eyes, it had almost sounded to her like tears.

# THE NIGHT SITTER

He did not eat his banana split and barely spoke for days after. Just sitting in that window again. But no longer waving. And all too soon there was no one to wave at any longer anyhow.

For suddenly the pandemic had flowered.

And she sensed the boy, that sickly boy, felt responsible. As if he had somehow *invited* the virus by his indiscretion. For suddenly, there were no more children going by on bicycles. Almost as if the entire world had contracted his terrible genetic mutation.

Almost as if *he'd infected the entire world.*

Leaving him more alone than ever before.

It was shortly after he'd had a terrible relapse.

Before his own condition had flowered malignantly.

Only this time there'd be no recovery.

Almost like he'd simply given up.

*And hadn't he? The poor boy? Henry? Given up?*

*Hadn't they whispered around it in so many words as the world outside had come to a skidding halt? When the sky had turned so gray?*

*The sky had still looked blue to her. But not to him.*

*To the poor boy, it had turned gray. Colorless.*

*Gray, colorless, as they had whispered around such things in his bedroom at the end of that long and dark hall far away from the others in the family. A bedroom that had always smelled of him. A moldering, decaying smell.*

*A sickly sweet smell of something slowly dying.*

*As he stared out at that world skidding to a halt.*

*Out at that blue sky turned gray. Colorless.*

*Perhaps she might have told him it was still blue even as it had begun to turn gray and colorless to her, too, as the life had faded from the boy.*

*That poor boy. Henry. After he'd given up.*

The woman was staring at Emily now with her own gray eyes. As if able to read her thoughts. Perhaps offering judgment.

Emily offered that smile again.

That smile without her teeth showing.

*Always be kind and courteous and decent.*

*Never show your teeth when you smile.*

"Rules, ma'am," she said, prompting her.

"Hm," the woman said. Then: "Perhaps I should more clearly describe the nature of this position, Miss Emily, before we start in on the house rules. Perhaps this would be the wisest course."

*Miss Emily. House rules. Nature of this position.*

"Of course," Emily agreed.

Ms. Vivian Dancemore then explained, the fire crackling softly beside her, throwing odd shadows over her pale face while dancing on the wood-paneled walls dressed with a dull gray wallpaper in the sitting room: "This position is for a night sitter only."

It was Emily's turn to flinch. *Night sitter only?*

"Night sitter?" she uttered softly. Trying the strange phrase in her own mouth. Wondering what it could possibly mean.

*For who'd be watching the child during the day? And why would anyone require a night sitter for a nine year old? Where would Ms. Vivian Dancemore be off to in the night? Most especially given the strict quarantine restrictions and imminent Martial Law requiring this to be a live-in nanny position in the first place? Night sitter? Had she actually heard the woman correctly?*

*Was this little Madelyn a freaking vampire?*

"You will have your days free, yes."

She had heard the woman correctly.

Emily felt herself flinch yet again.

"I understand this is an unusual assignment."

"It sounds interesting, I suppose."

Or so Emily heard herself say.

"I'm pleased you think so."

The woman's pale hands were fidgeting again, however. Fidgeting in her lap. Gray eyes twitching once more. As if she were uncomfortable with whatever explanation might soon be to come on this night. Might dare to explain such an unusual assignment.

"This peculiarity, Miss Emily, has to do with the nature of the child herself," Ms. Vivian Dancemore eventually continued.

"The nature of the child," Emily pushed.

*Perhaps little Madelyn, sometimes Maddy, not unlike a vampire, was allergic to sunlight. Perhaps this was no more sinister than that. What was that most bizarre disease called? Solar Urticaria or something or other?*

*Hadn't she seen a teenage-disease-flick on cable about such a disease? Involving a young sweet girl in love with a young sweet boy? The girl sneaking out only at night to be with the boy before tragically not beating the rising sun home one rather dreadful morning? Her skin swelling within moments of exposure to the dawn and reacting to all that invisible ultraviolet radiation?*

*Welts? Vomiting? A goddamn awful seizure?*

*The poor girl collapsing in the terrified boy's arms?*

*Her throat swelling terribly, reducing the passage of her airway to the size of a pinhole, then to nothing at all? The girl asphyxiating in his arms?*

*Her face turning red? Blue? Purple? As she died?*

## THE NIGHT SITTER

*As she died in the arms of the boy she loved so very much?*
*Did such a thing actually exist? Such a deadly malady?*
*A disease that turned the sun into a poison?*
    Emily wasn't sure it did. At least not in the hyperbolic manner it had been portrayed in that silly film on cable television.
    *It would be more damn likely this little Madelyn, sometimes Maddy, was a freaking immortal after all. That the little misfit dined on fresh blood. More damn likely, anyway, than such a deadly sun disease. At least in the hyperbolic manner it had been portrayed in that silly film on cable television.*
    *More damn freaking likely she was the undead.*
    *A soulless monster of a little misfit thing. This child.*
    *So then, if neither, why the need for a night sitter?*
    "Before we discuss further the reasoning behind this peculiarity--" Ms. Vivian Dancemore said. "Before we discuss the nature of the child herself, perhaps it would be prudent to discuss the house rules now. Assuming, Miss Emily, you're open to such an unusual arrangement, of course. Assuming you don't mind the night."
    Admittedly, at first blush, it seemed rather somewhat unnerving. The prospect of facing the night while others slept.
    Even poor sickly Henry had slept the night.
    *And is that what Ms. Vivian Dancemore herself would be doing? Sleeping while she fulfilled this rather unusual function as the night sitter? And were there others here in this much too-quiet house? Which re-begged the earlier question about who the girl's real mother might be. If not Ms. Vivian Dancemore. And perhaps, furthermore, who and where might be the girl's father.*
    *I'm the caretaker*, the woman had said.
    *Of the child*, she had explained. Only that.
    Regardless, given the night thing, setting aside these questions for now, Emily assumed such a position might very likely come at a premium, suggesting she might negotiate quite a pretty penny here. Something to get her on her feet for when this was done.
    *So why was she getting that feeling again?*
    *That spooked desire to turn around and just run?*
    *Even though she had nowhere else in this world to go?*
    "That would be just fine," she said agreeably even while she found herself fighting her shoulders to keep them straight. So tired again all of a sudden. With perhaps quite a very long night ahead of her. With perhaps so many more long nights to follow.
    "Wonderful, then," Ms. Vivian Dancemore said, seemingly relieved. Relieved Emily hadn't dismissed it at first blush.

*Had there already been others, then?* Emily wondered. *Other prospective nannies before her? Others who'd turned down the unusual idea? The most unusual idea of watching a little girl at night and only at night? And had these other prospective nannies experienced the same intuitive foreboding?*

"You'll find a copy of the house rules in your bedroom should you take the position, Miss Emily," the woman told her.

Ms. Vivian Dancemore had her own handwritten copy. Pulled from a side table along with reading glasses. The house rules rather elegantly handwritten on thick floral-scented cream paper with gold edges in gothic-calligraphy, imitating that wrought-iron sign outside on the front porch beside that obsidian black front door.

She perched those reading glasses on her nose so she could alternately read off the paper and still study Emily over them.

Emily adopted an impassive face. Trying her very best to mirror the woman's own bearing. The somber stoicism of it.

"The child, Madelyn, is to never leave her bedroom," Ms. Vivian Dancemore firstly stipulated. "Not without supervision."

*The child. Never to leave her bedroom.*
*Not without supervision. Madelyn.*
Emily catalogued this as Rule #1.
*Weird, sure. OK. Especially for a nine year old.*
She fought to maintain her impassivity.

Maybe the woman was just an eccentric, nothing more sinister than that. And the little girl a night owl. An insomniac.

*I mean, look at this museum of a house after all...* she thought. *Overstuffed with all these presumably valuable, if rather dusty antiques. Perhaps the woman just didn't want the girl fiddling about. Damaging things.*

"Questions?" the woman asked her. Staring over the perched reading glasses. Oval. Less like glasses really than spectacles.

It was only then Emily noticed these glasses didn't rest on the ears, too. Rather, Ms. Vivian Dancemore held them just below her gray eyes by a thin handle designed just for that purpose.

The handle silver. Etched with fleur-de-lis.

Emily shook her head. No questions.

Even though she had so very many questions.

"The child, Madelyn, is never to leave this house," Ms. Vivian Dancemore said. "Not under any circumstances. Never. No matter what she may tell you." More staring over those spectacles.

*Never to leave this house under any circumstances.*
*Never. No matter what she may tell you. The child.*

# THE NIGHT SITTER

Emily nodded. Rule #2, then.

"Neither you nor the child, Madelyn, are ever to enter my personal bedroom without my personal explicit permission."

*Never enter Ms. Dancemore's personal bedroom.*
*Not without her personal explicit permission.*

"Of course," Emily said. Rule #3. Feeling a need to say something here. Perhaps just to interrupt the woman's rhythm.

Earning an even sterner look for all that. A slight crinkling of the woman's cold pale skin between those cold gray eyes.

Maybe it was just best to nod. Stay quiet.

"The child, Madelyn, is not to drink. Alcohol."

This seemed a rather obvious rule.

A rather obvious rule begging more questions.

*Fine. No alcohol for the nine year old.* Rule #4.

"The same is to be asked of you, Miss Emily. No alcohol. At least between the working hours of midnight and sunrise."

Emily fought harder to maintain her impassivity.

She was just glad to hear there was booze hiding about somewhere in the house. Even if it required of her a day-drinker.

And speaking of hiding, Ms. Vivian Dancemore then admonished, offering to Emily quite a tasty little treat of a riddle:

"And there is to be no hide-and-seek."

The woman offered no explanation here.

No context for such an esoteric rule.

"No hide-and-seek," Emily eventually said even though she'd meant to stay quiet. It just sort of spilling out of her mouth.

"Is that a question, Miss Emily?"

"No, ma'am. Thank you, ma'am."

"Thank you, Miss Emily."

*No hide-and-seek, then.* Rule #5.

"Snacktime is midnight unless the child, Madelyn, is sleeping," Ms. Vivian Dancemore moved on. "Hands are to be washed before eating. No eating outside the kitchen. No exceptions."

*Snacktime. Midnight. Wash hands. Only in kitchen.*

That seemed simple enough. Rule #6.

"Bedtime is 5am. No exceptions."

Emily nodded again here. Silently. Dutifully.

"The child, Madelyn, is to brush her teeth. Comb her hair. Say her prayers. And be tucked in her bed at that time. No later."

*Bedtime. 5am. Teeth. Hair. Prayers.* Rule #7.

*Weirder still. Sure. Bedtime. 5am. But OK.*

Ms. Vivian Dancemore lingered for a moment here as if there might be an issue before moving down the list in her hand. "There are to be no cell phones in the house. No exceptions."

Emily stiffened at this directive.

Surprised. Already feeling amputated.

"Your cell phone is *only to be used* outside of this house. There are grounds out back. A nice walking path in the garden."

The woman was holding out her hand.

*Was she confiscating her phone? Now? Was this nutbag afraid of radiation waves? Did the phone offer the same danger as a poisonous sun?*

*Welts? Vomiting? Goddamn awful seizures?*

Emily removed her phone from her coat. The phone did seem a strange modern contraption in this house of antiques. Reluctantly, she handed the phone over to the woman. The woman tucked it neatly in the very back of the side table drawer from which the peculiar house rules and the reading spectacles had appeared.

At least it wouldn't be hard to find. The phone.

More of the honor system and Rule #8.

"There is a small TV in your bedroom, Miss Emily," Ms. Vivian Dancemore revealed. "It has been provided for your entertainment. The child, Madelyn, is not to watch the television."

*No TV for the munchkin.* Rule #9.

"No exceptions, Miss Emily."

"No exceptions," Emily agreed.

*Too bad. TVs could be great babysitters.*

Ms. Vivian Dancemore paused a beat again here, studying the list in her hand, suggesting she might be finished and taking a moment to make sure she'd not missed anything. At least that was the impression until her demeanor somehow became even more grave. The woman taking a deep breath. As if to regather herself.

Emily fought her tired sinking shoulders.

When Ms. Vivian Dancemore eventually continued, her voice was suddenly hushed again. Almost as if afraid of being overheard: "You are to please knock on all doors before entering."

Emily digested this. Blinking heavily.

*You are to please knock on all doors before entering.*

*And why would that be?* she wanted to know.

*To make a point of such a thing, anyway?*

*And why whisper it in such a hushed voice?*

## THE NIGHT SITTER

*And why did she get the feeling it had less to do with a simple politeness, and more to do with what might be waiting for her, waiting for her on the other side of such doors? Waiting for her if she presumed not to knock?*

Tired, she was. So very tired. A long journey.

A long and extensive and eccentric list.

*Perhaps she was still asleep...* she thought. *Asleep back in that terrible little motel apartment and all this just a crazy weird little dream.*

She felt herself pinching her wrist again.

Felt that soft little wonderful flame of a burn.

*OK. Knock. All doors. Before entering. Rule #10.*

*How many darn rules were there, anyway? Jeez.*

Ms. Vivian Dancemore blinked hard again.

Both those gray eyes at once. Before continuing:

"There are to be no guests. No exceptions."

*No guests. OK. No problem there. Rule #11.*

There was a quarantine on after all.

Still, Ms. Vivian Dancemore studied her. As if Emily might resist this directive. Before returning to the list. Moving on.

The next house rule offered bluntly:

"Tell the truth. No lying. No exceptions."

Hm. Interesting, Emily thought.

*No lying. Tell the truth. OK. Rule #12.*

Perhaps the child *was* precocious.

*If not an undead blood-sucking monster, anyway.*

At any rate, she had now accepted, as if there were any doubt, the rules were not just for the benefit of a precocious little girl, but for her own benefit, too. Evidenced by the next house rule:

A rule that rather had the ice pick stab deeper into the back of her neck, sending those tiny splinters back into her fingers:

"Don't hurt yourself or others," the woman said.

This woman in the long black dress. As she seemingly stared down at that small flowering little red welt on Emily's wrist. Joining a parade of such small little red welts on her pale skin.

The clock *tick-tocking. Tick-tocking.*

That large antique grandfather clock.

Standing proudly in the corner of the room.

Marquetry accented with fleur-de-lis.

Its brass pendulum swinging back and forth.

Sleepily back and forth like a metronome.

As if slowly trying to hypnotize her.

*Tick, tock, tick, tock. Tick, tock, tick.*
The house above them, meanwhile, so quiet.
Altogether so very quiet. Peculiarly quiet. Too-quiet.
"No exceptions," Ms. Vivian Dancemore added.
As if it needed to be said. Stressed. Rule #13.
Emily removed her precocious little pinching fingers from her wrist. Certain they'd come to an end with the rules. Somehow certain the rules would end on the *inauspicious* number thirteen.
A number that screamed its own forewarning.
Ms. Vivian Dancemore lowered the spectacles here.
And Emily had the sense a lecture might be coming.
But it was only to offer yet another house rule.
A rule the woman offered with a soft sigh.
"Furthermore, I would ask you to clean up after yourself."
Emily felt herself frown here. For a moment sure this rule hid its very only little riddle. Hid its very own little nefarious truth.
Assuming all the other rules did as well.
Little dark riddles to be solved over time.
If relieved to discover a rule number fourteen.
A seemingly less inauspicious number.
A seemingly less foreboding number at that.
"Including dishes," the woman added.
Emily almost laughed out loud when she gradually came to realize the woman was being literal. And quite serious at that.
God, she really was tired, So very tired.
*Dishes. Right. OK, then.* Rule #14.
She fought back a yawn. Easier than a cough.
"And the final house rule, Miss Emily."
*The final house rule. The rules coming to an end.*
Ms. Vivian Dancemore lifted her chin, staring down at Emily now. "Hold the child, Madelyn, accountable to all rules."
She offered this as if it were its own challenge.
As if it contained its very own stakes.
"Yes, ma'am. Certainly, ma'am. I will do that."
*An iron fist.* Rule #15. *Done and quite done.*
Emily expected Ms. Vivian Dancemore to again ask her at this point if she'd any questions now that the house rules had been fully unveiled. The woman did not, and Emily, biting down softly on her bottom lip, despite having many questions, frankly, restrained herself. Intuitively understanding she was expected to follow all of the

rules unconditionally and that *all else* regarding this unusual position would be revealed to her in the manner in which this strange woman of this peculiar house deemed fit, suggesting this strange woman of this peculiar house with its unusual charge *waiting for her somewhere upstairs in the darkness* might consider any such questions the equivalent, perhaps, of *entering doors without presuming to knock first.*
One question, however, that was answered now was compensation. The woman offered her terms. Very generous terms.
Emily agreed to them without hesitation.
The terms actually making her a little dizzy. Eccentricity offering a premium after all. A rather nice little premium at that.
She tried to ignore her grandmother.
Her grandmother's voice rising in the back of her head.
Warning her: *The covetous man is always in want.*
Whatever the heck that actually meant.
Instead, Emily dutifully followed her new employer, Ms. Vivian Dancemore, as the woman led her on a short tour of the house. Peeks and glimpses into rooms and nooks she'd eventually become intimately familiar with over time. The foyer staircase climbing to a dimly-lit narrow hall with faded plum-colored carpet and furnished with bronze sconces that not unlike the dark-globed table lamps in the sitting room now somewhere down far below them summoned for the imagination that long-ago-lost bygone era of oil and candlelight, insuring there was just enough flickering light to guide one's way, if little more, and inviting the resident shadows forward.
The second floor offering three bedrooms.
The master bedroom hidden behind a locked door.
Rule #3 after all. *Neither you nor the child, Madelyn, are ever to enter my personal bedroom without my personal explicit permission.*
The next bedroom full of a child's things.
But the bedroom missing the resident child.
As if the child were perhaps only a ghost.
Perhaps even sitting there on the bed, if unable to even crease the stiff clean bedsheets. Tiny little legs swinging silently in the air. Amused by her invisibility. Amused by her hide-and-seek.
*Where was this child?* Emily wondered again.
And heard Ms. Vivian Dancemore's hushed voice: Whispering in that sitting room now somewhere down far below them:
Rule #1. Spoken with such a firm resoluteness: *The child, Madelyn, is to never leave her bedroom. Not without supervision.*

*And yet, the bedroom sat empty. And not just empty, but feeling as if it had been empty for a very long time now maybe. Another intuitive feeling. As if everything in there was long-frozen in place.*
The third and final bedroom was on the opposite side of the hall from the other bedrooms. It faced the neighborhood street. Its large window set over the long and deep wraparound porch.
It featured a simple single bed. A tall wardrobe in the window corner. A small desk beside a radiator. And a small framed embroidered pattern on the wall above the radiator, featuring the following biblical reference in a now quite familiar gothic-calligraphy:
*Isaiah 32:18 My people will live in peaceful dwelling places,*
*In secure homes, In undisturbed places of rest.*
"This will be your room," Emily was told.
"Thank you, ma'am. Lovely, ma'am."
She'd lugged her suitcase up the staircase at the woman's behest and now placed it in the room at the foot of the bed.
It looked rather lonely sitting there. Like a child left behind at bordering school as she then followed Ms. Vivian Dancemore further up the hall. That long muted black dress now seeming to levitate the strange woman over the faded plum-colored carpet in that dimly-lit narrow hall furnished with its line-up of flickering bronze sconces mimicking oil and candlelit lamps from a long-ago-lost bygone era before the narrow hall turned a corner just past a tiny dark bathroom and revealed a small alcove and another staircase.
A much darker, narrower staircase.
Rising steeply to a thick black attic door.
Not unlike the front door below. Oak maybe.
With a rusted iron keyplate. Keyhole.
The keyhole dark and somehow forbidding.
As if *anything* could be locked beyond it.
Emily got that creepy feeling again. That cold stabbing sensation in the back of her neck. The awful splinters in her hands. Even before the woman said without an ounce of whimsy, her razor-thin chapped and waxen lips pursed more tightly than ever:
"The child. Madelyn."
*Excuse me, ma'am,* Emily nearly blurted out, biting down on her lip again, though more forcibly this time, and perhaps even tasting the iron-metallic nectar of her own blood. *I know you're not suggesting the child, Madelyn, is up there somewhere alone locked behind that thick scary-looking black oak door with that ugly rusted keyplate, miss. Like Rapunzel in*

*that grim fairy tale with the witch. Excuse me, ma'am, but I'm quite very certain that's not what you're trying to tell me here. I'm quite very certain, ma'am, that this must just be a most terrible misunderstanding on my part.*
*Please tell me this is a misunderstanding, miss.*
*Please tell me that child is not up there somewhere.*
*Not up there somewhere alone behind that black oak door.*
*Please tell me that's not what you're telling me.*
*Please tell me, miss. Ma'am, please.*
Those gray eyes fell on her. Blinking hard. Twitching once more. As before.

And Emily felt herself shivering. That ice pick stabbing again. And again. Her splintery hands falling numb. That terrible splintery numbness climbing, then spreading. As if her entire body might fall asleep. Might just fall asleep to all that splintery numbness.

In a paradox of pain and nothingness.

*I'm the caretaker*, the woman had said. *Of the child.*
*A girl. Nine. Madelyn. Sometimes Maddy.*

Those twitching gray eyes in the shadows of that dark narrow staircase leading up to that attic door suddenly looked forlorn. As if no longer able to conceal great pain. Round. Bloodshot. But nevertheless considering Emily with a cold severe judgement. As if quite able to divine every negligence and misdeed of her life and deciding in that moment if Emily was, indeed, worthy of this charge.

*Of whatever waited for her beyond that locked door.*
*Quietly. So altogether much too very quietly.*

Knowing there'd be no going back for Emily once Emily went through that door at the top of that dark narrow staircase.

Silently communicating this to Emily now.
Silently communicating it with those forlorn eyes.
Communicating it with that cold severe judgement.
*You are able to follow rules, then*, she'd said.
*This position is for a night sitter only*, she'd disclosed.
Before then explaining without explaining:
Offering another dark little morsel of a riddle:
*This peculiarity has to do with the nature of the child herself.*
*Assuming, Miss Emily*, she'd then said in the dancing firelight in that claustrophobic sitting room somewhere down far below them, her gray eyes twitching and her pale hands fidgeting about anxiously in her lap, *you're open to such an unusual arrangement, of course.*
*Assuming you don't mind the night.*

Ms. Vivian Dancemore seemed to come to a heavy conclusion now as she silently contemplated Emily in the shadows of that dark narrow staircase leading up steeply to the thick black oak door with that ugly rusted iron keyplate. For the woman's thin shoulders stiffened and her twitching gray eyes dimmed. Perhaps in relief at finally having come to reach such an urgent decision. She then offered Emily a thoughtful, if tired nod. But rather than motioning her up the dark narrow stairs to that waiting door, only motioned her back down that dimly-lit narrow hall with the faded plum-colored carpet and its flickering bronze sconces. Back down the foyer staircase and eventually right back to the small sitting room with its collection of spooky antiques and sleepy *tick, tock* of its grandfather clock.

A room the woman referred to as the parlor.

Where she offered Emily a glass of sherry.

And a most terrible, if peculiar explanation. Of a most terrible, most peculiar *peculiarity*. Of the like Emily had never heard.

Nor could have ever imagined.

# 3.

THE FIRE HAD BEGUN to die, reduced to a bed of softly glowing coals that, nevertheless, still managed some considerable heat. The heat radiating off the parlor's faded gray wallpaper as the parlor's own resident shadows grew. Stretching. As if awaking from a long dark nap. Unchastened by the dull flickering bulbs of the tiered chandelier or the dark-globed table lamps. Hovering about like invited guests. Conversing in hissing whispers. Like spirits of the past sharing space and time with the present.

Here and not here. There and not there.

Rather like the tattered vestiges of a dream.

A dream once remembered but almost forgotten.

Almost forgotten even as it still haunted.

Ms. Vivian Dancemore stood amongst these shadows, almost vanishing into them in her long black dress as if being embraced by the spirits, pouring the sherry from an exquisite crystal cut decanter into faceted sherry glasses before handing a glass to Emily.

The sherry seemed to sparkle. Like champagne.

Aided by the faceted edges of the sherry glasses.

Ms. Vivian Dancemore sat down. Back upon the chenille sofa. Emily, the fuzzy blue velvet armchair, with that low marble coffee table with the short gold-trim walnut legs between them.

The woman in black lifted her glass.

Emily mimicked her. Lifting her own glass.

The sherry seemed to sparkle all the more.

"To the only people who consistently tell the truth, no matter how difficult it might be to hear," Ms. Vivian Dancemore said, gray eyes twinkling now. As if offering yet another riddle. Before offering the answer: "Drunkards and children, Miss Emily."

With that, she issued a dry laugh.

Sounding very much like a hollow thing.

A hollow thing made of only dust.

Then drank her sherry in one swallow.

Emily followed her lead. The sherry tasted very dry and rather yeasty sliding down her parched throat, and she coughed.

Her eyes watering yet again.

Ms. Vivian Dancemore rose into the resident shadows and retrieved that crystal cut decanter and refilled their sherry glasses, but for the moment the glasses sat on the low marble coffee table with the gold-trim walnut legs between them. The sherry sparkling in the dimly-lit parlor. Twinkling on that faded gray wallpaper. The twinkling sparkles seemingly *fluttering* about the room. Reminding Emily of those fireflies. Down there on her grandparents' farm. A mason jar clutched in her tiny little hands. The tiny critters trapped inside it. Blinking. Flapping silently. Fluttering madly about as they desperately attempted to find any possible escape. Stymied by the thick glass and the tin lid. Unable to squeeze through the air holes.

Ms. Vivian Dancemore settled back down on the couch, those resident shadows seeming to join her. An interested audience.

"Drunkards and children," she said again.

*The only people who consistently told the truth apparently.*

The twinkle faded from her gray eyes. Forlorn again. Dimmed with that great pain. A pain that numbed even as it grieved.

Not unlike the splinters in Emily's hands. Stealing the feeling from her fingers. Even as it felt like a nest of yellowjackets.

Emily attempted to quiet them, these needle-like stings, as she impatiently waited for Ms. Vivian Dancemore, the woman in black, to unburden herself of whatever it might be she needed to *unburden*. Attempted to quiet them with another sly pinch of her wrist, relishing that soft little flame of a burn spreading across her skin.

She could make it grow and recede.

That soft little wonderful flame of a burn.

With only the squeeze of her fingers.

Of her fingers gone so splintery numb.

And imagined it slipping across her entire body.

That soft little wonderful flame of a burn.

Imagined such a burning flame consuming her.

She thought perhaps this strange woman sitting in front of her might understand. That perhaps fate had brought them together. A rather peculiar detour of her mind, perhaps -- *but wasn't fate just that, too? A detour from expected reality?* Emily had always found it to be so. Fate having other plans for her than she might otherwise have for herself. It was just then, as if in a response to Emily's metaphysical wanderings of the mind, Ms. Vivian Dancemore said:

"It happened some years ago."

Yes, this was how it began. Her testimony.

Her *unburdening*. The revelation of her dark truth.

A dark truth that would begin here tonight, but would not be fully unburdened from this strange woman in black for days yet to come. For as Emily would gradually learn in time, even as she intuitively felt it even now on this her very first night here behind these thick dark walls, this dark truth was not something that could just be spoken aloud all at once if it was to be properly digested.

Not without inviting a terrible skepticism.

Even as it also invited a most terrible fear.

This most very peculiar dark truth.

No, Emily would realize later. Rather, such a dark truth, in the end, could only reveal itself very slowly. Like a fever dream.

Only by taking her gently by the hand.

And leading her gradually into the darkness.

Until she could not find her way back out again.

"The girl's father, my husband, Alfred, held me responsible," the woman in black whispered as those shadows seemed to huddle even more tightly around her now, murmuring into her ears. "He held me responsible for the accident," she said, the twinkling sherry dancing about her pale countenance, turning those gray eyes white. "For what happened to the child. Madelyn. Our child."

*Girl's father. My husband. Alfred.*

*Accident. Held me responsible. For what happened.*

*To the child. Madelyn. Our child.*

Emily found her glass of sherry had somehow returned to her splintery hands and was pushing against her lips, that dry yeastiness sliding down her throat and making her eyes water again.

*What accident? What did she mean by accident?*

*What was up there in that attic? What was up there behind that thick scary-looking black oak door with that ugly rusted keyplate? Keyhole? What was this strange woman trying to tell her?*

*And where was her husband, anyway -- this Alfred? Was he somewhere in this dark house, too? Hiding somewhere in its deepest shadows?*

*Maybe not. The woman had used the past tense, hadn't she?*

*Held me responsible... she'd hushed quietly. Held.*

*Suggesting her husband was no longer here. Alfred.*

*Suggesting she was now alone in this large dark house, perhaps.*

*Alone with whatever was up there in that attic.*

"It was a most terrible accident," Ms. Vivian Dancemore said. "Of the kind the mind never quite completely comprehends."

Those gray eyes turned white -- blinked. A succession of those hard twitching blinks. Then turned deeply inward. Sinking.

"The child was lost only to be found," she then said.

*The child was lost only to be found? What in the hell might that freaking mean? What in the hell could it freaking mean? Lost only to be found?*

Those gray eyes turned white beneath that succession of hard twitching blinks swam forward again, finding Emily once more.

"I will require of you a final rule," she revealed.

*A final rule. How many rules did that make now?*

*And what did it have to do with an accident?*

*What did it have to do with a child lost only to be found?*

"You, Miss Emily, will be provided the key to the attic door," the woman in black with the gray eyes turned white said. "You will lock me inside the attic one half hour before midnight."

*You, Miss Emily, will be provided the key to the attic door.*

*You will lock me inside the attic one half hour before midnight.*

"You will then enter your own bedroom, Miss Emily. You will lock its door. You will only exit after the stroke of midnight."

*You will then enter your own bedroom, Miss Emily.*

*You will lock its door. You will only exit after the stroke of midnight.*

The grandfather clock continued to *tick, tock* in the corner as if providing a soundtrack to what the woman was telling her.

*Tick, tock, tick, tock. Tick, tock, tick.*

"You will find the girl in the attic after midnight."

*You will find the girl in the attic after midnight.*

"You are to be the night sitter, Miss Emily."

*You are to be the night sitter, Miss Emily.*

*Tick, tock, tick, tock. Tick, tock, tick.*

## THE NIGHT SITTER

"You will lock the child, Miss Emily, back inside the attic. Just as you found her. At no later than five in the morning."
*You will lock the child, Missy Emily, back inside the attic.*
*Just as you found her. At no later than five in the morning.*
"You will return to your own bedroom, Miss Emily. You will lock its door as before. You will not exit until after sunrise."
*You will return to your own bedroom, Miss Emily.*
*You will lock its door as before. You will not exit until after sunrise.*
"You will then come fetch me."
*You will then come fetch me.*
*Tick, tock, tick, tock. Tick, tock, tick.*
"No exceptions, Miss Emily."

Emily felt her head swimming. Trying to process, trying to digest, this peculiar nonsense. This most peculiar of *peculiarities*.

This charge unlike she'd ever had before.
*A most terrible accident. Some years ago.*
*Of the kind the mind never quite completely comprehends.*
*The child lost only to be found. Madelyn. Sometimes Maddy.*
*You are to be the night sitter, Miss Emily.*

"Ma'am," Emily heard herself say. Having questions. Needing answers. Despite any impoliteness they might dare imply.

Ms. Vivian Dancemore's eyes, meanwhile, slowly turned back from white to gray as the shadows seemed to recede a little.

She picked up her glass of sherry. Drank it. One swallow. A well-practiced swallow. Down into all that dusty hollowness.

She then shook her head. Dissuading Emily.

"*Tonight,* Miss Emily," she only said.

Suggesting it would provide answer enough. Suggesting only it would suffice. And any further words meaningless for now.

A final dark little morsel of a riddle.

A dark little morsel awaiting midnight.

# 4.

EMILY WAS GIVEN A BITE of supper in the kitchen. A leg quarter of roasted chicken with scalloped potatoes and a slice of frosted lemon cake retrieved from a wooden stand beneath a glass dome on an antique drop-leaf serving table.
    She was left alone to eat.
    And ate rather greedily at that.
    The roasted chicken and the potatoes moist and well-seasoned with fresh herbs from the garden. The lemon cake delicate and just perfectly sweet. But not too sweet. Not too sweet to turn the stomach. Just sweet enough to linger there for a moment on the tongue, then at the roof of the mouth before dissolving nicely and inviting the next bite. And the next. Until it was suddenly just gone.
    She wondered if the woman had cooked the supper.
    And if she'd baked the divine cake, eyeing the remaining cake sitting quietly on that wooden stand beneath the glass dome.
    *Of course the woman must've cooked the meal...* she scolded herself. *She'd implied the fresh herbs had come from the garden, hadn't she? And, after all, there seemed to be no one else in the house to cook it. Unless, of course, the child had done so. The child. The mysterious child in the attic.*
    Regardless, Emily hadn't eaten so well in weeks now. Certainly not since the restaurant doors had been padlocked. After she'd finished eating, she dared to peek into the kitchen pantry and found it to be quite deceptively large. And very well-stocked, indeed.

Emily imagined if there was a meat freezer somewhere on the premises, and she suspected as much, then she'd not have to worry about filling her stomach here. It was all rather startling, if reassuring given the current atmosphere of the world outside.
The world outside these thick dark walls.
The world outside that obsidian black front door.
The world outside the forbidding windows of this house with their long thick black drapes and these kitchen windows before her now hidden behind their own drawn dark wooden shutters.
Perhaps they all served a purpose. All of them.
The thick dark walls. Doors. Drapes and shutters. Concealing inside here a better life. A quiet, if better life than out there.
*Then again, if this was such a better life, then why was the child presumably locked up there in that attic?* she couldn't help wonder. *A mysterious child making not a whisper of noise. Madelyn. Sometimes Maddy.*
*What was waiting for her behind that attic door?*
Emily tried not to fixate on it. Just as she tried not to fixate on what it might mean to lock that strange woman in the attic and wait until the stroke of midnight. Just as she tried not to fixate on what she might then *find* on the other side of that attic door just after the stroke of midnight. Waiting for her. Waiting for her there.
She tried to embrace only patience.
The job paid exceedingly well after all, nearly double her normal rate. And her stomach was more than contently full.
Whatever it was on the other side of that attic door despite all the eccentricities of this woman in the long black dress--
*An accident. The child lost only to be found.*
It would be nothing more than she could handle. For she had seen much in her own life and it had prepared her for pretty much anything. God, that was most certainly true if nothing else.
Only to hear her grandmother's voice again:
*Cherish those who seek the truth, child.*
*But beware of those who find it.*
She washed her dishes. Rule #14. Placed them to dry in a dish rack. There apparently being no dishwasher in the kitchen.
She then stood in the middle of the room.
Uncertain whether she should leave it.
The kitchen was very Victorian like the rest of the house. Cast iron appliances. Dark wooden counters. Bronze cookware hanging from long iron hooks over an island with more dark wood.

There was exposed brick. Dark beams.

And those windows with the dark shutters.

She approached a window and slowly pulled a doodad to open one of the long shutter panels, peeking out at the garden.

A short flagstone patio pushed to that walking path Ms. Vivian Dancemore had mentioned. The walking path was composed of crushed white stone and meandered into a tall thick hedge row that would soon be flowering once the cold was truly gone. Beyond that tall thick hedge row remained a mystery. At least for now.

Emily closed the shutter panel. It made a whisper of a noise as it slid neatly back into place. A gentle sleepy sigh of a noise.

She stood there a few moments longer.

Then, sighing herself, wondering how long it might be before she no longer felt like a stranger in the house, summoned the nerve to finally exit the kitchen -- only to be further unnerved to find Ms. Vivian Dancemore standing in a short dimly-lit wood-paneled corridor between the kitchen and the foyer hall. Thin shoulders slightly slumped like she'd been standing there for some time.

Like an inert wind-up toy in need of a wind-up.

Like an inert wind-up toy that had gone to sleep.

But then those gray eyes flinched, belying the rather queer impression, and revealing the woman in black alert after all.

"Shall I show you back to your room," she wondered, though it seemed less a suggestion, frankly, than polite edict. "You must be tired after your journey and might want to rest a little."

*As if she'd come from mother-freaking Timbuktu.*

*And not from just the other side of town.*

"Yes, I think that would wise," Emily said.

She presumably had a long night ahead of her.

A rather long and most peculiar night.

# 5.

THERE WAS A LIGHT KNOCK on her bedroom door at precisely a half hour until midnight. Emily was lying on the bed. She'd tried to take a bit of a cat-nap, but found herself too-wired to sleep, wondering drearily if she'd have to seek out this strange woman in this dark gothic dollhouse of a Victorian.

The light knock on the door startled her.

Even as that light knock also relieved her.

Relieved her not to have to seek the woman out.

Emily rose from the bed, still dressed. She took a moment before a small vanity mirror to take stock of herself. Adjust her hair. Then crossed the room to the door only to find the bedroom door locked, having forgotten she'd locked it. Slightly embarrassed, she fished the room key from her pocket. A black antique iron key with a pleasant coat of patina Ms. Vivian Dancemore had provided her after the woman in black had shown her back to her bedroom only a few short hours ago. The woman had also provided her with the attic key. The pair of iron keys on a black antique iron ring.

The key jiggled noisily in the old lock.

The attendant bolt made a clacking noise.

The door creaking when it opened.

The noises obnoxious in the quiet house.

This much altogether too-quiet house.

Echoing in all that terrible quiet.

Ms. Vivian Dancemore stood in the hall shadows.

"Good evening, Miss Emily," the woman said.

"Good evening, ma'am," Emily said.

And with that, Ms. Vivian Dancemore, in her long black dress that more than ever appeared to levitate her over that plum-colored carpet, led Emily past all the flickering bronze sconces and the tiny dark bathroom and around the corner to that small alcove.

To that dark and very narrow staircase.

Rising steeply to that thick black attic door.

The thick black oak door prickly with age.

With its rusted iron keyplate. Keyhole.

The keyhole dark and somehow forbidding.

As if *anything* could be locked beyond it.

It was at this point Ms. Vivian Dancemore stepped back into a corner. Stepped back from the staircase threshold. Allowing Emily to go first. Emily hesitated before the dark narrow stairs.

Maybe it was just her imagination, but--

It felt *colder still* here in this part of the house.

And she imagined how cold the attic must be.

It was only the *tick-tock* of that grandfather clock somewhere down in the parlor far below her that got her feet moving again as if to the *tick-tock* of that clock, and she imagined its brass pendulum swinging back and forth, drawing the night ever closer to midnight, insisting she climb the dark and narrow steps up to the attic.

As before, Emily felt that ice pick stab at the back of her neck. And those numbing splinters like a nest of yellowjackets in her fingers. The numbing splinters making it somewhat difficult for her to retrieve the antique iron ring cleanly from her pocket. And the ring with its pair of black antique iron keys nearly slipped right from her splintery fingers and she found herself imagining with horror all of it falling to the dark wooden steps below her, bouncing all around, clanging in the shadows, escaping her desperately groping grasp to relocate them. Before then disappearing into the darkness.

Playing a game of hide-and-seek.

A forbidden thing. Rule #5.

*And what if she somehow lost the keys?*

*Somehow lost the keys, specifically the attic key, while this strange woman was locked inside the attic? What if she could not retrieve her at sunrise?*

*Or get to the child for that matter after midnight?*

*The child. The child lost only to be found.*

## THE NIGHT SITTER

*And what if she somehow became imprisoned inside her own bedroom, its key somehow wandering astray there? Slipping quietly away from her attention into the darkness in such a devious and mischievous manner? What if the silly keys had minds of their own?*
Emily took a deep slow breath and used both hands to handle the iron ring and its pair of antique iron keys. It all felt rather heavy in her hands. Quite large and cumbersome. As if it all could *never* be lost or misplaced. As if such a thing were an impossibility.

In the meantime, without any real memory of having ascended the dark and narrow staircase, she suddenly found herself on the second to last step. Rather eye-to-eye with the iron keyplate and its keyhole. The keyhole revealing only darkness beyond and a chilly, if musty draft of air. Emily felt herself shiver, gooseflesh popping out on her exposed pale skin, as she inserted the iron key into the lock, if partly only to discourage that chilly, if musty draft of air.

The iron key went in cleanly--
But the lock refused to disengage.

Emily fought with the key for a moment, imagining *a little girl on the other side of that door fighting the lock. Refusing to let its bolt slide free. As if a little girl would do such a thing, being locked in there as she presumably was. Playfully forestall her from opening this attic door.* Only to realize she was most likely using the wrong key. Her room key. After all, the keys looked practically identical, did they not? The only visible difference being the attic key had *three bits* and her room key only two. Rather almost impossible to distinguish in the dark. And upon further examination, she *could very well feel the three bits* on the black iron key still dangling from the ring. Sighing a ragged sigh, she withdrew the incorrect key, shuffled the two keys, then, with another ragged sigh, gently shoved the proper key into the waiting keyhole.

It slid in easily. And turned easily enough.

The bolt offering a familiar clacking noise not unlike her bedroom door. Though much louder here in this dark corridor.

She then listened for tiny footsteps.

No longer breathing. Her heart in her throat.

And though the door was not yet open--
*Noticed a small pale hand reaching out from the murk.*
Emily jumped, and perhaps even shrieked just a little, only to realize the hand only belonged to Ms. Vivian Dancemore.

The hand settling on the dark door knob.

Also iron. With curvilinear embellishments.

Very Victorian. Very old, old world.

The knob turned. The door pushed open.

The cold, musty air rushing out from the attic gloom.

The door's thick rusted hinges whining softly.

Emily could only see the vague outline of things in that darkness. Amorphous, shapeless things hiding in the deep inky shadows before a large dark multi-paned window set in the far wall.

The moon only that thumbnail-sliver. No stars.

Ms. Vivian Dancemore floated slowly up into the darkness, becoming her own amorphous silhouette before that large dark multi-paned window. *Floating*. Floating more so than ever now before the woman in black vanished completely into the inky shadows.

But for her suddenly *mesmeric whispering voice*:

"After midnight, Miss Emily," it said.

Emily blinked. Found herself closing the door. Found herself locking the woman inside. As she had been instructed to do.

The bolt clacking as it slid back into place.

Echoing loudly off the cramped staircase walls.

Leaving Emily alone on that dark and narrow staircase and the woman in black on the *other side of that thick black oak door*.

Emily blinked again, heavily, a twitching series of blinks really, then found herself descending the stairs. Backwards. As if afraid to put her back to the door until she was around the corner.

And then, she *was* around that corner, and moving past all the flickering bronze sconces, if still glancing back over her thin shoulder. Body moving sideways down the faded plum-colored-carpeted hall and eventually back to her own bedroom. As instructed.

She locked herself inside her bedroom.

And waited. Waited for the stroke of midnight.

*Tick, tock, tick, tock. Tick, tock, tick.*

Not making any sound. Just listening to the silence but for that *tick-tock* of the grandfather clock somewhere down in the parlor far below her. The silence heavy *about her. Above her.* Heavy like the key ring in her pocket. Thin cold metal bones against her thigh.

When that silence became too much to bear, she tried to make herself busy. It was better to be busy, she grimly decided, than to just stand there listening for that midnight strike of the grandfather clock somewhere down in that dark parlor far below her.

Busied herself with unpacking her suitcase.

Placing her things in the tall wardrobe.

# THE NIGHT SITTER

She found the television she'd been promised in the wardrobe and placed it on the empty desk. There was no cable hook-up anywhere in the bedroom and no cable plug on the TV itself, only thin rabbit ears. The television was small and of the plastic bubble variety and only received a UHF signal with three grainy channels. Local channels in black and white with long wavy jumping lines.

The sound was off, too. Fuzzy. Distorted.

Rather further unnerving her, to be honest.

She turned the set off. A plastic button.

There were small pastoral paintings on the bedroom walls, but the serene rural scenes did little to calm her frayed nerves and Emily found herself stopping before that framed embroidered pattern. The framed embroidered pattern hung above the radiator.

Gothic-calligraphy. Biblical reference.

*Isaiah 32:18 My people will live in peaceful dwelling places, In secure homes, In undisturbed places of rest.*

She did not feel at rest. Not in the slightest.

She discovered the house rules in the desk drawer.

Handwritten in still more gothic-calligraphy.

Thick floral-scented cream paper with gold edges.

She pushed to the only window and pulled back the long thick black drapes. The window was tall and dark, rectangular and multi-paned. Just like the windows she'd seen from the street.

Just like the large window *up there* in the attic.

There was still no evidence *of any tinting* even at this close angle despite the fact each individual pane was thick and quite black. The thick black panes, meanwhile, making the night appear even darker outside and drearily promising to turn daylight into night.

Suddenly she needed some fresh air. She reached for the lever that opened the window only to find it wouldn't budge. It was only then she saw a small rusted keyhole lock set in the frame. And realized the window frame, including each of the individual pane cross-sections, *were constructed of solid black steel.* Not unlike jail bars.

She fished the key ring from her pocket.

Attempted to use her room key. The attic key.

Both were far too large for the window lock.

There was no way to open the window and this brought back an absent, if almost dismissed memory of the front door.

The front door somewhere down far below her.

Obsidian black. Thick. Probably oak, too.

*Hadn't she seen a similar, if larger keyhole lock on the inside of that door as she'd entered the house before setting her suitcase down beside that newel post and that staircase rising into the shadows? A similar keyhole lock on the inside of that obsidian black front door maybe rather than just on the outside?*

*And as she'd done just that, set her suitcase down on that foyer floor next to that newel post and that staircase rising into the shadows--Hadn't she just maybe heard the jiggle of a key behind her?*

*Ms. Vivian Dancemore securing that front door? Locking it from the inside, perhaps? Absently heard such a thing even as she'd dismissed it?*

*Even as she'd been distracted by the odd house itself?*

*The house colder than outside seemingly. The air stale-tasting.*

*And if so, if there was actually such a dreadful lock on the inside of that obsidian black front door somewhere down far below her, did it not suggest there might be similar dreadful locks on all the windows and all the doors?*

*What in god's name was she trying to keep out, this strange Ms. Vivian Dancemore? Or, pray tell, what was the woman trying to keep in?*

Emily felt herself pinching her wrist.

Once again embracing that soft little burn.

That soft little wonderful flame of a burn.

Embracing that burning flame licking at her skin.

Only to then suddenly imagine a *conflagration*.

A *conflagration* of such flames *setting ablaze the old Victorian house*. This house: Roasting and sizzling. Bubbling and crackling and popping. The large black multi-paned windows melting even as all that solid black steel held fast. But the melted windowpane openings far too small for her to squeeze through. *Trapping her* in the angry roaring flames. Allowing the flames to feed hungrily upon her. Her own flesh melting. Her eyes bubbling and crackling and popping. Small bones roasting and sizzling. As that large grandfather clock gonged midnight somewhere down in that parlor far below her.

*Gong, gong, gong, gong, gong, gong...*

Emily blinked hard now and realized it wasn't just her imagination. The grandfather clock was actually striking midnight.

*How long had she been standing there at the window?*

*It had felt to her only just a few short minutes.*

The venerable house walls, despite their thickness, seemed to tremble, or *shiver*, with each impressive gong. And still felt as if they were trembling, *shivering*, long after the grandfather clock far below had fallen quiet. Maybe it was just the echo of that clock. The echo of that clock reverberating inside the very skin of the house.

# THE NIGHT SITTER

Emily could feel herself trembling.

And could hear the rush of her breath now.

She had a tendency, at times, to become overexcited. Not that these very peculiar circumstances didn't warrant such an overexcited reaction, of course. Still, it did no good to lose her senses.

And so she focused on her *mantra*.

Something her grandmother had taught her. Taught her when she was still a little girl. For when she became overexcited.

*I have control over my emotions. And I choose to feel at peace.*

She closed her eyes and repeated this to herself. Repeated this to herself over and over again. Breathing in. Breathing out.

She felt herself beginning to calm. Her heart in her chest slowing. Apparently it had been pounding like a freaking drum in there. Cranking-up her freaking lungs. Turning dizzy her head.

She felt better now. More solid now.

Like she could maybe walk now.

And found herself confronting the door.

The bedroom door across the short room.

A door she actually had a key for.

*You will lock me inside the attic one half hour before midnight. You will then enter your own bedroom, Miss Emily. You will lock its door.*

*You will only exit after the stroke of midnight.*

*You will find the girl in the attic after midnight.*

*You are to be the night sitter, Miss Emily.*

Emily swallowed a deep controlled breath, if having to suck it raggedly down, and found her hand still trembling as she lifted the room key to the bedroom door lock. Fighting to slide it in. Cranking it hard to the left. The bolt making that clacking noise.

The door opening to the dimly-lit hall.

To those flickering bronze sconces.

To all those waiting shadows.

She fought a most desperate terrible urge to turn to the right and head, instead, for the descending staircase to the foyer.

To try her keys in that front door.

Her room key. The freaking attic key.

Even as she intuited the foolishness of such an errand. Knowing there would be no liberation. Accepting she was, at least for the time-being, anyway, locked inside this old venerable house.

*The child, Madelyn, is never to leave this house.*

*Never. No matter what she may tell you.*

Emily thought of her cell phone tucked away in that side table and briefly thought of retrieving it. Maybe calling for help. Assuming she could get a signal. Assuming someone would actually come for her. Given the deteriorating state of the world *out there.*

She felt her heart become rabbity again. The blood filling her ears noisily. Her breath again rushing. Turning dizzy her head.

*I have control over my emotions. And I choose to feel at peace.*

She eventually stepped out into the hall. And managed to turn to the left. Pushing deeper into this strange old dark house.

*You will find the girl in the attic after midnight.*

Deeper into its watchful resident shadows.

*You are to be the night sitter, Miss Emily.*

Moving up that long plum-colored carpet. Almost as if *she were floating now.* As if being *pulled along* by a dark current. Pulled around the tight corner just past the tiny dark bathroom to the small alcove where she now noticed a small bookcase hidden in the dark.

A bookcase filled with children's books.

And below it a small food dish. A water bowl.

The food dish said FRISKY on the side in big cartoonish letters. There were crumbs inside of it. Purplish little morsels.

And she again found herself thinking of all those multi-paned windows with their solid steel frames and cross-sections. The individual panes far too small for her to squeeze through *unless she were a cat. And once again she imagined those flames engulfing the house as such a mangy beast managed to slip right through a solid steel-framed cross-section and out of the house as the house burned. As the house turned to black ash.*

*The flames dark and angry and screaming loudly.*

Then suddenly she was *ascending.*

As if being lifted by a tall black wave.

*Floating up* the dark narrow attic staircase.

The thick black oak door growing larger and larger before her. That ugly rusted keyplate growing larger, too. With its dark forbidding-looking keyhole. Only the keyhole was no longer dark.

A *soft golden light* now spilled out from it.

This *soft golden light* spilling out from the keyhole momentarily blinding her as Emily found herself kneeling before the keyhole. As Emily found herself peering through the keyhole into the attic beyond it. Needing to know what was beyond the attic door.

Needing to know was *waiting for her* in the attic.

*You are to please knock on all doors before entering.*

## THE NIGHT SITTER

Fortunately for Emily, Ms. Vivian Dancemore hadn't said anything about peering through keyholes And Emily's efforts revealed to her a small cot beneath a softly glowing carriage light.
A child was asleep on the small cot.
A rather angelic-looking child for all that.
The softly glowing carriage light painting the child in a golden relief. The aura warm and fuzzy -- as if creating around the sleeping angelic-looking child a warm and fuzzy protective cocoon.
The rest of the attic still left in shadows.
The shadows unable to invade that cocoon.
Emily watched the slow and steady rise and fall of her back as she slept. The child. Listened to the whisper of her breath.
She appeared to be deep in sleep.
The child. Madelyn. Sometimes Maddy.
Sleeping so very peacefully, indeed, in that golden light behind this heavy locked door as the shadows surrounded her. Waiting for the carriage light to fail, perhaps. To eventually *extinguish* like a candle. Waiting to rush forward to take her. To take her into their cold embrace. Startling her from her safe slumber, Emily imagined, even as she tried to dissuade herself of such nonsense. To take her into their cold embrace as if drowning her in a cold black water.
*Should she knock?* Emily wondered.
*Should she wake this peacefully sleeping child?*
*Should she rouse her from her pleasant little dreams?*
*If only to maybe keep those dark shadows at bay?*
*Or should she allow the child to sleep? Madelyn. Allow the child to sleep without knocking? The shadows nothing more than that? Just shadows?*
*But what then? Return from whence she'd come? Careful not to make a sound? Return to her own room? Endeavor to get some rest herself?*
*They had not discussed a sleeping child.*
*Ms. Vivian Dancemore and she.*
And with that persnickety thought, as she peered more closely through the keyhole, the child coming into an even sharper focus despite the warm and fuzzy golden light, Emily came to understand a most profound and a rather most disquieting revelation.
Belied by the child's little white cotton nightie.
Belied by the child's gently braided hair.
Gently braided hair tied in long white ribbons.
Belied by a large doll collection gathered on long dark shelves. Watching from the shadows. China dolls. Pale porcelain faces.

Their dark eyes wide open in the dark.
Fully alert. Watching over the sleeping child.
But also seemingly watching *her*. Emily.
As if quietly anticipating her intrusion.
Belied by a pogo stick in the near corner just beyond the small cot. Belied by a child's doodles on the wall above the bed.
Belied by a wooden rocking horse peeking from the darkness. Belied by a wooden toy chest filled with mysterious things. Things hidden in the darkness below that dark multi-paned window.
Belied by a sucking thumb in the child's mouth.
The child. This peacefully sleeping child.
Belied. For the child was not that at all.
Belied. For the child was *not a child*.
For upon closer scrutiny, her eyes blinking hard, twitching and flinching quite madly, that child, Madelyn, was revealed to Emily to be none other than *good old Ms. Vivian Dancemore herself.*
Disguised as a child, certainly.
Impersonating a child, undoubtedly.
But *not a child* all the same.
Despite being curled-up on the small bed like a child in a position rather most unnatural to an adult. Her thin back arched like a cat toward the dark ceiling rafters. Her knees tucked tightly into her chest beneath her. Her thin arms wrapped around her legs.
Her head pushed down at a severe angle.
Her right cheek buried into a small pillow.
A small pillow with faded red roses.
But breathing so slow and steady for all that. In a whisper. As if deeply asleep. Comfortably so. As if she might never wake.
Or desire to ever be awoken.

# 6.

EMILY RETURNED TO her bedroom, pulling the door closed tightly behind her and locking it. Unfortunately, the clacking sound of the bolt offered her little comfort for she assumed the strange woman sleeping in the attic presuming to be a child to possess keys for all the doors in this place. For all the windows for that matter. In this lockbox maze of a dollhouse.

Emily sat on the bed. Shoved her fingers into her temples and closed tightly her eyes. Trying to think clearly. Rationally.

*The strange woman was obviously insane. Could there be any other logical explanation? Other than the woman being a complete crackpot?*

*Other than her being completely batshit fucking crazy?*

Emily frowned with the thought and shoved her naughty-little fingers harder into her temples. Her eyes pushing even more tightly shut. Her head dipping down toward her lap. Her mind desperately trying to unravel this most definite peculiar of *peculiarities*.

Of course, the strange woman sleeping in the attic presuming to be a child had mentioned an accident, now hadn't she?

An accident from some years ago.

*The girl's father, my husband, Alfred, held me responsible...* she'd said to her, hushed to her, surrounded by all those dark hovering shadows. *For what happened to the child. Madelyn. Our child. It was a most terrible accident. Of the kind the mind never quite completely comprehends.*

Her gray eyes turned white in that parlor.

*The child was lost only to be found...* she'd also said.
This strange woman. Her queer employer.
*You, Miss Emily, will be provided the key to the attic door.*
*You will lock me inside the attic one half hour before midnight. You will then enter your own bedroom. You will lock its door. You will only exit after the stroke of midnight. You will find the girl in the attic after midnight.*
*You are to be the night sitter, Miss Emily.*
Emily's naughty-little fingers dug even harder still into her soft temples. As if able to somehow turn the cogs of her brain.
*An accident. Some years ago. Of the kind the mind never quite completely comprehends. A most terrible accident. The child lost only to be found.*
Only to suddenly have the answer. For it made perfect sense, she realized now as those naughty-little fingers dug deeply into her soft temples. A perfect, if a rather terribly horrible sense.
Another dark morsel of a riddle undone.
If a rather most *un-tasty* one at that in the end.
Yes, now that she was thinking more clearly, it made a perfect, if a rather terribly horrible sense. The woman was *grieving*. Grieving terribly for the child she had lost. For an accident for which she felt responsible. An overwhelming guilt that had not only remained for years, but had, indeed, festered for all that time, burrowing deeper and deeper in her fragile mind like a caterpillar. Cocooning there in the cold lonely darkness. Before *blooming* into a dreadful butterfly of sorts. A dreadful butterfly of sorts with ravenous teeth. Born of her overwhelming guilt *so that it might then feed on all of that unbearable despair and hopelessness.* If only to ease her mind of its burden.
Easing it by *splitting her mind in two.*
And again Emily thought of those fireflies.
Down there on her grandparents' farm.
A mason jar clutched in her tiny little hands as she ran about, chasing those little flying critters, the long grass pleasantly cool beneath her bare feet. The already-captured soft-bellied beetles blinking desperately inside that jar. Flapping and fluttering madly about. Attempting to find any possible escape. Stymied by the thick glass and the tin lid. Unable to squeeze through the air holes. And again, Emily thought of those moths, too. The black and white moths on the porch somewhere down far below her. Buzzing about that suspended lantern outside this lockbox maze of a dollhouse.
Mistaking the light for deliverance.
For a way out of the falling darkness.

# THE NIGHT SITTER

Emily slowly opened her eyes.

Taking solace in her intuitive intelligence.

The tension draining from her body only to have that tension *suddenly* ratchet back up again. For just as she opened her eyes, *something slunk against her leg* in the bedroom dimness. She heard herself shriek. Recoiling *at its touch along her shin*, retracting her legs into her chest, only to discover a *black cat* stretching on the carpet beside the bed, presumably having just *slunk out* from underneath it. The black cat then sat there a moment in the bedroom dimness. Licking at its paws. Staring up at her with dark green almond-shaped eyes.

*Who might you be?* those eyes seemed to say.

*And what might you be doing in this house?*

*And perhaps you might think about opening the door.*

Or so it seemed to cajole her, rising, stretching a final time, its front legs straight out, its chest pushing to that carpet, back arching toward the low ceiling, black hair springing upright like tiny needles before it began circling slowly at the locked bedroom door.

Emily fished the key ring from her pocket.

Unlocked the bedroom door. Pulled it open.

The cat, however, loitered in the doorway. Circling again. Staring at her again with those dark green almond-shaped eyes.

She gave it a small push with her foot. It made a hissing noise, then disappeared up the hallway toward the attic staircase.

Emily pushed shut the bedroom door.

Locking it. The bolt clacking obnoxiously.

She would have to keep her door shut all the time. Even when she was absent from the room, she decided. Not unless she wished to invite strange unwelcome critters like that *slinking* black cat.

She shivered at the memory of its *slinking* touch.

The way it had *slunk against her leg* in the dimness.

The brush of all those tiny needle-like hairs.

Shivering again, her mind gradually returned back to her odd employer. To what she'd discovered in that attic up there.

*Was Ms. Vivian Dancemore aware of her condition?*

*She was certainly aware of the little girl's existence after all.*

*But was the woman aware the little girl was only just a manifestation? A manifestation of such a condition and not a real little girl at all?*

*Maybe. It might explain the draconian house rules.*

*Or were such rules born of her deep subconscious where the actual truth of the matter remained buried? Where it remained hidden even from her?*

*It seemed unlikely. Unlikely the woman did not know.*
*Given the draconian house rules. Given the fact the woman willingly came and went from the attic. Willingly allowed herself to be locked inside.*
*Of course this strange woman knew of her mind's duality, then. It wasn't just the draconian house rules or her willingness to be locked inside the attic one half hour before midnight -- but in her somber confession of a most terrible accident. Of the kind the mind never quite completely comprehends.*
*A child lost only to be found after all.*
*Yes, it seemed certain the woman knew the truth.*
*Not unlike Dr. Jekyll with his terrible Mr. Hyde.*
*Even as she was helpless to prevent the manifestation.*
*Somehow needing the tragic child to live. To exist.*
*For her own sake of mind. Her own sanity.*
*Sanity in the unlikely form of insanity.*
*Perhaps the better question was this question:*
*Was the little girl aware of Ms. Vivian Dancemore?*
*Was the little girl aware she was not a little girl at all?*
Emily found herself shaking her head.
Shaking her head in the bedroom dimness.
*It seemed unlikely the little girl knew the truth.*
*For only this explained the need for a night sitter maybe.*
    Emily felt that ice pick stabbing once more at the back of her neck, sending those awful tiny splinters back into her fingers before moving down into her legs this time and numbing her feet.
    She took a heavy step forward just to make certain she could still walk only to find herself unlocking the bedroom door and exiting. Pushing up the dimly-lit hall. Shuffling past that tiny dark bathroom. And around the corner to the small alcove. Before ascending the dark narrow staircase. Approaching the black oak door.
    And its keyhole spilling that soft golden light.
    Peering through the keyhole once more as if she were moving in a dream. No longer in control of herself. As if she'd assumed an *alter ego*. Achieved her own dual nature. Her trespassing eye blinking as it located the child. *Madelyn. Ms. Vivian Dancemore.* In rather quite the same position as she had left her. Still deeply asleep.
    Only to feel something *brush against her shin.*
    That black cat. Purring softly. Its back arching.
    Those tiny black needle-like hairs stiffening.
    Staring up at her with those dark green almond-shaped eyes.
    *Are you going to let me in?* those eyes seemed to say.

## THE NIGHT SITTER

*You only need open the door an inch, or two, and I can slink inside. Perhaps you should just forsake the knocking so we needn't wake her.*
*I won't tell, miss,* those eyes seemed to say.
*It can be our little secret. Our first of many, dear girl.*
Emily whispered an apology and left the cat outside the door. It settled there, its eyes narrowing with discontent as it licked at its paws once again, dismally studying Emily over them as she retreated, that black cat eventually vanishing in the murky darkness at the foot of the attic door below that narrow spill of soft golden light as Emily pushed around the corner, moving back down the hall.

She found herself *shirking* her bedroom, however.

The bedroom suddenly too small. Confining.

Found herself drearily pushing further down the long narrow hall past the dimly-flickering bronze sconces and eventually down the foyer staircase before cautiously *wading out* into the heavy darkness below as if she were wading out into a sea of black water.

The house having been put to bed for the night.

She wandered the nocturnal house, feeling less conspicuous in the darkness somehow. Like a spirit. Unseen. And unheard. A draft passing *here and there.* An intangible thing, she imagined. Capable of passing through all keyholes. Rusted keyholes, both large and small, she found *wherever* she looked. On all the house doors. All the large dark rectangular steel-framed windows. In the foyer and the great room. Parlor and kitchen. The formal dining room. The downstairs bathroom and study. Everywhere she looked. Everywhere.

Keyhole locks on the outside *and the inside.*

Her room key and the attic key entirely useless.

She returned upstairs after a spell to find the same disquieting arrangement. The windows on the second floor similarly *secure.* Including in the small bedroom next to the master. The bedroom full of a child's things. The bedroom missing its resident child.

As if the child were only a ghost, too.

*And perhaps she was only just that after all...* Emily accepted in the shadowy dimness. *Perhaps she was only just that after all in the end.*

Of course, Emily considered, it was always possible the master bedroom *didn't have any keyhole locks on the inside of its windows.*

Perhaps if she could only get past its door.

A door she found to be locked. Not surprisingly.

*So you're already plotting your escape,* she thought as she attempted to open the master bedroom door with her pair of keys.

Ignoring Ms. Vivian Dancemore's hushed voice admonishing her inside in her numb head: *Neither you nor the child, Madelyn, are ever to enter my personal bedroom without my personal explicit permission.*
But finding neither key adequate for the job.
And felt that cold stab of an ice pick again. This time it shivered down her spine. Shivered down it like a frozen snake.
*Was there something to fear here, then?* she wondered. *Something that must eventually be escaped from? Was she in danger? Should she be afraid?*
She stood in the dimly-lit hall, contemplating these questions. Fascinated by them really. The idea she *might be in danger*. Fascinated by the morbid idea this prison of a house might not just be for the benefit of that child that was not a child -- *but actually for her, too. To prevent her from leaving her charge. This most strange and peculiar of charges. As if it might all be something that must eventually be escaped from.*
Afraid. Maybe. A little. At least overexcited.
It seemed an honest reaction *even* as it tended to fascinate her. She wasn't often afraid even if she sometimes became overexcited. It took her by surprise to find herself actually feeling fear.
She blinked at the thought. Twitched really.
Before eventually slipping back into her room.
Locking the bedroom door behind her.
She took a moment to search the bedroom.
In case that *slinking* black cat had made its return.
Searched for it despite the fact she'd remembered to close the door in her absence. As if it could sneak past closed doors.
But she found no evidence of the varmint.
Assuming it could be found if it didn't want to be.
She knew she'd be unable to sleep and decided to turn on the small television if for no other reason than to displace all the heavy silence around her before her mind really got the better of her.
*I have control over my emotions. And I choose to feel at peace.*
There, then. Breathe in. Breathe out.
Breathe in. Breathe out. In. Out. In. Out.
She flipped quickly through the three local channels. The only channels received by those thin archaic UHF rabbit ears. The small plastic bubble TV's black and white channels more grainy than ever tonight and corrupted all the more by those long and wavy jumping lines. The sound fuzzier and more distorted than ever, too.
She found only local news and finally just settled on the clearest image of the bunch. A Presidential briefing from earlier in the

day according to the bottom scroll. The President looking especially dour and dispirited. So very unlike his usual arrogant and narcissistic self. Surrounded by expressionless military figures rather than his usual coterie of medical experts. Announcing the entire country would be under Martial Law starting at midnight tomorrow night. No exceptions. And would be until further notice. A military general then took over the briefing. The chairman of the joint chiefs. A tall bald man from the Army with a no-nonsense demeanor, delineating the draconian particulars of such an order. The order broadly including, at that stroke of midnight tomorrow night, the immediate suspension of all civil law, civil rights, and *habeas corpus,* whatever the heck *habeas corpus* might mean, and the extension of military law onto everyday American civilians, including the imposition of military tribunals for violators of the Martial Law mandates.

As for the Martial Law mandates themselves:

There was only one that really stood out. All the others simply encouraging compliance of this one stern inviolable edict:

A mandatory shelter-in-place directive.

In other words, no one would be allowed to leave their homes any longer without receiving written legal time-stamped permission from a local military magistrate. No exceptions. Allowances would still be made for essential workers, but the definition of an essential worker would be revised forthwith. Not surprisingly given the fact the military would now finally be assuming, among other vital and more mundane activities, all food and medical distributions.

Emily found herself flipping the channel.

Turning the plastic TV knob rather frantically.

There was a hopeful, if pollyannaish news story about a Manhattan-type Project involving the nation's top pharmaceutical companies. An endeavor to create a vaccine with the additional promise of immediate emergency-use authorization from the FDA.

The FDA was already signing-up volunteers.

Human volunteers. Appealing to one's patriotism.

As if any solution were only just days away.

Emily jerked the plastic knob again.

Earning a burst of static before learning:

Protestors had been shot in Michigan. Elsewhere. Shot by an advancing wall of those menacing soldier automatons in their inky-black combat gear and their Darth Vader-like masks.

Shot protesting the Martial Law decision.

Emily flipped off the television. Abhorred.
Silently watched the grainy image fade away.
Fade into a tiny white dot. Blink off.

She climbed into bed, slipping beneath the cool bedsheets, not bothering to undress, suddenly feeling so very exhausted. Her eyes fluttering, then slipping shut to the distant *tick-tock* of that grandfather clock somewhere down in the parlor far below her.

At some point she finally fell asleep.

Fell into a deep and dark sleep.

Deep and dark but for the rhythmical *tick-tock* of that grandfather clock somewhere down in that parlor far below her, offering a dull cadence to the strangest and most peculiar of dreams.

She found herself outside on the front porch just beyond that obsidian black front door, standing beneath that flurry of black and white moths, staring out from this deep cul-de-sac at those rows of quiet houses stretching off into the distance with their string of dull street lamps. The houses and street lamps turning hazy in the night before disappearing into the darkness beyond, abandoning her here on the very edge of the world. On the very edge of existence.

Beside her was that large cast iron bell.

Hung on the house wall beside the black door.

Its mounting shaped like a sleek black dragon from a haunted fairy tale, featuring detailed wings and dark oily-looking scales.

She found herself peeking inside that bell.

Peeking inside that giant cast iron dragon bell.

Mesmerized by its large cast iron clapper.

Imagining what a racket the bell might make in this deafeningly quiet neighborhood here on the very edge of the world.

And before she could stop herself, yanked a black chain hanging from the clapper and shook the dragon bell. Cringing with anticipation of its certain alarm. *But hearing nothing. Nothing at all.*

Despite feeling that large clapper moving inside.

Striking the interior of the dragon bell.

And found herself yanking at that black chain harder still and feeling that cast iron clapper striking that bell interior with an even greater force. And yet, seemingly, magically, still emitting no sound. No sound at all. Certainly none she could discern, anyway.

The dully-lit houses with their drawn curtains and their locked doors and their overgrown lawns undisturbed. Unprovoked.

Their sleepy inhabitants warm and cozy inside.

## THE NIGHT SITTER

    And yet, seemingly, magically, for all that, as she now violently shook that seemingly, magically, soundless dragon bell, there manifested in the dark night sky far above the rows of dimly lit houses with all their drawn curtains and their locked doors and their overgrown lawns and their string of dull street lamps at the very edge of the world -- *a congregating flurry of dark monstrous-looking shapes.*

    Dark monstrous-looking shapes that were rendered only black silhouettes against that vast dark night sky far above this very edge of the world, but revealed as pale-white against that dull thumbnail-sliver of moon. A pale-white as they seemingly gathered about that thumbnail-sliver of moon much as the moths below gathered about the porch lantern. Dancing in and out of its cold pale light.

    Winged-beasts. Howling. Shrieking.

    Before *descending* toward the dark house.

    This dark house on the very edge of the world.

    To the bell that made no sound.

# 7.

EMILY AWOKE TO THE dull light of a Victorian ceiling lamp above her bed. A stained glass, yellow, white and red, finished in vintage bronze with a flush mount. She was still dressed. Albeit tucked snugly in the bedsheets. The dimness of the room beyond the dull light of the ceiling lamp suggesting to her she still had a few hours left before sunrise. Only to notice a *little intruding sliver of light* peeking through the long drawn black drapes.

*Oh, for heaven sakes*, her mind screamed.

She glanced at a watch on her wrist.

A watch once belonging to her mother.

It was a quarter after seven in the morning.

*Oh, for freaking heaven sakes, Emily...*

She'd been tasked to *fetch* Ms. Vivian Dancemore from the attic just after sunrise with the unspoken implication that it should be done in a posthaste manner. Just after the sun had peeked over the horizon given the fact *the woman had been in the attic all night.*

Emily rose from the bed, her head swimming woozily for the moment from the sudden change in elevation, and yanked open the black drapes, the bedroom shadows shrinking to the bedroom corners, to find a hazy sunlight imbuing the sky with a yellowish-orange hue above the neighborhood. Over all those Victorians and Tudors and Colonials. The dawn nearly a half hour old, perhaps.

*Oh, for freaking heaven sakes, indeed, Emily.*

She briefly fought with the bedroom key in the bedroom door as if the key might have other ideas before escaping the room and hurrying up the dimly-lit hall with the plum-colored carpet, pushing past the tiny dark bathroom to the small alcove around the corner, hiking the dark narrow staircase to the thick black oak door.

The attic key ready in her hand. Poised.

Only to find herself pausing at the top step.

*For there were voices on the other side of that door. Whispering. Conversing. Arguing, perhaps. An adult voice, surely. A child's voice, maybe. Only for the voices to fall abruptly quiet as if aware they could be overheard.*

Emily made a soft coughing sound to announce her presence and was just about to slip the attic key into the lock when she suddenly had the presence of mind to step back. Knock first.

*You will please knock on all doors before entering.*

A light polite knock on the thick black oak door, then waiting for an affirmative response. But there was none forthcoming.

*Maybe just a final strident whisper, perhaps.*

*Followed quickly by a low shushing noise, maybe.*

With another soft cough, her heart beating a little too quickly in her chest, her breath coming in desperate little pants, she inserted the iron key into the iron lock. The key making its noisy jangling sound. The bolt then offering its customary clacking sound. Before she found her trembling hand employing the iron knob, cool to the touch. The thick black oak door swinging open before her.

Ms. Vivian Dancemore, adorned once more in that long black dress, stood in quiet silhouette facing the large multi-paned window on the far side of the attic, gray shadows lurking about her.

The dawn a gray dullness in the sky beyond her.

Only a gray dullness on *this* side of the house.

The woman didn't at first acknowledge Emily's presence. She appeared lost in her own thoughts, staring at a thick woods beyond a long wrought iron fence guarding the back of the property.

The woods slowly filling with the dawn's hazy light.

Despite the gray dullness on *this* side of the house.

The gray dullness in the sky over those woods.

The hazy light pushing back the darkest of the shadows, pushing those darkest of the shadows deeper into the trees. Where they consorted in the thickest foliage and waited impatiently, seemingly, at least in Emily's dizzy mind, for the return of the night.

Emily waited meekly in the attic doorway.

Not certain if she should announce herself. Certainly Ms. Vivian Dancemore must have heard the attic door opening.

Slowly, Ms. Vivian Dancemore turned toward her, turned toward Emily. And once again seemed to float, especially in the midst of the gray shadows. *Float slowly past* the long dark shelves with that collection of china dolls staring from those gray shadows.

Only those dolls were no longer staring.

Rather, their dark eyes were now *tightly closed*.

As if the dolls were now quite *fast-asleep*.

Emily thought it strange their eyes should be closed. Generally speaking, the glass eyes of such dolls only closed as they were laid down *as if to sleep* and only opened again when they were lifted back into an upright position. The mechanical movement of their dark lifeless eyes aided by tiny hidden weights attached to them.

And yet the dolls were in the same position.

The exact same position as the previous night.

The dolls sitting quietly in their neat little rows, their eyes now closed, in their frilly cotton dresses and dull stockings, along with a scattering of masculine dolls in black button-down timeworn velvet suits. The dolls appearing much larger than they'd initially appeared the previous night. Each doll nearly thirty inches in height.

Their porcelain faces rather too human-like.

Their skin tinted in order to resemble flesh.

If still a ghostly pale for all that nonsense.

With deftly painted cheeks, lips, and eyebrows.

And what appeared to be real human hair.

A thought that made Emily's tummy do flip-flops.

And push hot sticky bile into her dry throat.

Though maybe on second glance it was only mohair.

Maybe it was only mohair at that in the end.

Her imagination getting the better of her here.

She hadn't imagined those voices, however.

*Whispering. Conversing. Arguing, perhaps.*

*An adult voice, surely. A child's voice, maybe.*

*A final strident whisper. Before a low shushing noise.*

Ms. Vivian Dancemore, meanwhile, passed (*floated*) before the giant slumbering creepy dolls like a specter in the gray shadows and out the attic door and down the dark narrow staircase and around the corner into the hallway without so much as a word.

Emily followed her down into the hall.

# THE NIGHT SITTER

If only after locking the attic door behind her.
If only after locking in those giant creepy dolls.
Those giant creepy *sleeping* human-like dolls.
And followed the strange woman down the hall, past the narrow avenue of dimly-flickering bronze sconces, if for no other reason than Emily knew not what else to do but to follow her.
The woman produced her own iron key.
Produced it neatly from a hidden hip pocket.
She let herself into the master bedroom, slipping like morning mist through the cracked bedroom door. Emily unable to see anything beyond it even as her employer turned toward her.
Her face pale like one of those creepy dolls.
Her features seemingly frozen (*painted*) in place.
As if she were still lost in a terrible trance.
Or at least still trying to *awake* from one.
"Good morning, Miss Emily," she hushed.
The strange woman then vanished, without another word, behind the bedroom door, the bolt clacking loudly into place, leaving Emily standing in the dimly-lit hall. Standing there alone.
"Good morning, ma'am," Emily said quietly.
Said quietly to the locked bedroom door.
And with that, her first night was complete.
Her first night as the night sitter.

# 8.

EMILY FOUND A PLATE of breakfast waiting for her in the kitchen. French toast spiced with cinnamon and ginger, and apparently cloves, along with four slabs of crispy bacon on a ceramic plate kept warm by a ceramic plate cover beside a tiny pitcher of dark and thick maple syrup. There was also a side serving of fresh fruit in a small glass bowl. And, most importantly, coffee. Kept hot in a ceramic coffee pot. The pot decorated with a stenciling of black roses amid a furious tangle of sharp thorns.

Emily stared at the breakfast with wonder.

She stared at it with wonder because the lady of the house had not reappeared from her bedroom since disappearing behind her bedroom door and Emily, therefore, had no earthly idea who might have made it. This breakfast before her. It suggested strongly to her there was at least one other here in this large dark house.

She'd not asked about staff after all.

Perhaps she was not alone here in this place.

Not alone behind rusted iron lock and key.

Not alone with this strange woman.

It buoyed her spirits. This idea there might be another. Someone with whom she might share confidence. Someone with whom she might eventually spend her days and maybe evenings.

Of course, this assumed she was staying.

*But why not?* she wondered to herself.

# THE NIGHT SITTER

Wondered to herself as she sat down to eat.
There being no question the breakfast was for her.
It being accompanied with a handwritten note with her name. The note offering more elegant, if austere gothic-calligraphy, politely suggesting she might explore the garden after she'd eaten.
An iron key residing in the back door.
The back door leading from the kitchen and out into that very garden. *So much for her being a prisoner, then*, she also thought.
And the salary was very generous, indeed.
Rather more than she'd been expecting.
Rather more than she deserved, perhaps.
And the woman (*child*) *had* slept through the night.
Or at the very least had seemed to do so.
Emily hadn't heard a single peep from the attic.
If the previous evening was any indication of things to come, then this gig might very well be a rather easy one at that. Especially given what was happening out there in the larger world.
*Yes, perhaps she would be staying on after all.*
She certainly wasn't going to let the breakfast go to waste, her tummy rumbling hungrily and her mouth already watering.
She dug in into the food and sighed happily. The French toast moist and sweet and custardy. Sprinkled with a delightful powdered sugar. Practically not even needing the maple syrup. The fruit in the small glass bowl a bright medley of tart berries. And the coffee residing in the ceramic pot rich with cream and sugar and indeed hot. And yet, despite her newfound enthusiasm, Emily felt a slight chill move through her as she ate the food, waking the sharp splinters in her hands. This breakfast rather just too perfect seemingly. Just the sort of thing she might have ordered for herself in a roadside diner, quite frankly. Right down to the preparation of the coffee.
As if someone knew her all too very well.
Of course, perhaps such a thing had been inquired of her previous employer. Perhaps it was no more nefarious than that. After all, Darcey had intimated she'd been requested. A referral. Or so it would seem. Though offering only scant details beyond that.
And she ought to at least explore the garden.
And perhaps have a walk through those woods.
She could hear songbirds out there.
With everything happening in the larger world, it seemed a rather peaceful and invigorating thing to do. A rare treat.

Emily finished her breakfast.

Washed her dishes. Rule #14. Then placed them to dry in the dish rack, noticing that her washed dinner dishes from the previous evening were now absent. Someone having put them away.

*Someone moving about in the shadows unseen.*

*Someone moving about in the shadows unheard.*

Emily bit down on her bottom lip.

A little mystery to be solved, perhaps, among so many riddles inside this odd house. The riddle of the cooked food. Of the rusted iron locks on all the doors and windows. Rusted iron locks on the outside *and the inside*. The riddle of *what happened to that poor little girl*. Madelyn. Sometimes Maddy. *A terrible accident. Of the kind of the mind never quite completely comprehends. A child lost only to be found.*

Unsolvable for the moment, these nagging riddles, if best contemplated, perhaps, with a bit of fresh air and a leisurely walk in the brisk morning sunshine. Assuming such riddles should be contemplated at all necessarily on such a beautiful morning as this with her belly so contently full -- and not revealed in their own time.

As had been intimated by her peculiar employer.

Her peculiar employer who paid so very handsomely.

*The covetous man is always in want...* her grandmother whispered once again in the dark of her mind. Hissing it at her really.

Emily sighed. Her grandmother so suspicious.

*The unwanting soul sees what's hidden...* her late grandmother then exhorted her. *And the ever-wanting soul sees only what it wants.*

Emily could still readily see her grandmother's large toady eyes staring at her. Staring at her over her dark knitting glasses.

Those eyes unblinking. Full of reprimand.

The very same eyes that would demand Emily go outside and pick herself a switch from a sapling in the yard when she'd misbehaved. Emily had learned not to pick a thin switch. The thin switch would bend, snap, but not break. Making an awful cracking sound. She'd learned to pick a thicker branch. One that would enflame her grandmother's rheumatism. The rheumatism in her grandmother's swollen wrists. And more likely play short the punishment.

Her grandmother had her maxims.

And little Emily, her little clever tricks.

Tricks that had helped her survive.

Assuming she stayed, she would learn the tricks of this house, too. She would learn how best to survive here. To thrive.

# THE NIGHT SITTER

Just as she'd always done. Clever as she was. *Tempt not the devil to whisper into your ear...* she heard her grandmother remind her now. *You're much too pretty to be this clever.* Emily had secretly embraced this one. The idea of being too pretty to be so clever. Better to be pretty and clever than ugly and stupid. Something she'd said to her grandmother once. Earning those large toady eyes. And another errand out into the yard to pick a switch. Though she thought she maybe saw the hint of a smile appear, if ever so briefly, on her grandmother's face as she'd pushed out the door.

As for this morning, before pushing out the back door and into the waiting garden, Emily slipped into the parlor. The fire having long gone cold from the previous night, the ashes a dull gray. Warily glancing over her shoulder, as if somehow fearful of being overseen, she hurried to that side table beyond the chenille sofa. Pulling open the drawer, half-expecting it to have *vanished* during the night, Emily found her phone right where it should be next to those reading spectacles and that fancy stationary with the house rules.

Handwritten in that gothic-calligraphy.

In that elegant, if austere gothic-calligraphy.

Emily shoved the phone into a pocket and found herself hurrying back to the kitchen and toward the back door before that key *might suddenly disappear, itself.* As if it could be made to do so.

As if the house had a mind of its own.

Its own set of rules. Little clever tricks.

But the key was still right where it should be.

Waiting for her there quite very patiently.

Emily used it to unlock the back door.

The key turning easily enough *as if turning itself.*

And with a final glance over her shoulder, irrationally sensing to the very end that someone or *something* might still try to stop her, slipped out, darted really, into the brisk morning sunshine.

That early morning grayness was long gone now, but she still found a cold chill hovering in the air. Dewy and pausing her briefly on the back patio flagstone. Almost forcing *back* inside to retrieve a coat. But the house looked dark and judgmental and again she had that insane thought that if she went back for her coat *the key might vanish, the back door locking again.* That she ought to accept this invitation while it was offered. To embrace the morning chill, too.

To allow that chill to invigorate her.

To remind her how fortunate she was to be strolling in such a beautiful garden in such cool fresh morning air behind such a stately grand house. How so very fortunate enough, indeed.

And the garden was beautiful. Mesmerizing.

And quite a bit larger than it had appeared from the other side of that kitchen door. The crushed stone path pushing deep into the garden before then spoking off into the tall thick hedges in all sorts of mysterious directions. The tall thick hedges acting like walls that served to separate venues of the garden, creating a maze not unlike that Victorian dollhouse itself. In addition to the hedges, there were colorful plants of all kind. Roses, lavender, delphinium, citrus-hued daylilies, and purple alliums, among more wild-looking things. Some plants ordered in neat little rows and others crowded lushly together as if springing organically from an untamed meadow. There were trained vines and climbers climbing walls and trees and trellises and small arbors and draping wisteria blooms heavily perfuming the air. Wooden benches sitting just inside or just outside collisions of light and shadow. Marble birdbaths with bubbling fountains. And a fish pond in the southwest corner with dark water that offered blinding flashes of large, pale, and rather carnivorous-looking fish.

The meandering paths sometimes wound back on what Emily took to be the main path and at other times hit dead-ends.

There were moments when she tried to negotiate herself back to the main path only to find herself quite turned around and right back at the very dead-end from which she'd just escaped.

A soft breeze tickling in the trees seemed to laugh at her. Only a whimsical laughter that she accepted to be friendly while imitating a gentle applause in those very same trees about her when she finally managed to find her way out of any particular impasse.

She eventually stumbled onto a gazebo.

She sat down inside the gazebo, relishing a warm slant of sunlight. A thick fragrant rose bush hugging the gazebo and that warm slant of sunlight made her feel suddenly rather sleepy like she could just lay down her head and maybe sleep a hundred years.

With that breeze still laughing softly. Applauding.

And to the distant echo of those songbirds.

She yawned and pulled the phone from her pocket. Shifting it from that warm slant of sunlight into the shadows in order to read the screen. Only to find the battery was dangerously low.

Still, she found herself calling *him*.

Found herself calling Adam.

Frankly, she'd intended to ring Darcey, or so she told herself. To bring her up to speed. To fill her in on the most peculiar details of this most peculiar assignment. If for no other reason than needing Darcey to be aware *of what was going on* inside this strange house. To be aware of what was going on here inside its dark and rather forbidding Victorian walls in this world gone so very mad.

Just in case. Only that. Just in case.

Instead, Emily found herself ringing him.

After all these many months. Adam.

The phone rang and rang and she almost hung-up rather than bother with a message, not really sure why she'd called him. Somehow almost believing the garden itself had made her do it, that soft breeze whispering gently in her ear maybe coaxing her.

But just before she might've hit END--

Suddenly there was a click on the other end.

And then his voice. Adam. Her Adam.

Thick-sounding like he'd been asleep.

"Em-?" he said hoarsely before attempting to clear his throat. "Em, that you?" he then said, though not sounding very convinced. Perhaps believing he was still asleep and this but a dream.

"I woke you," she eventually said.

Like they'd only spoken just yesterday. Not those long months ago now and that horrible shit that had been said between them the last time they'd spoken to each other had never been said.

"Hey, no, wait, Em," he said. "Don't go."

As if she might change her number again and disappear once more out into the dark ether. Perhaps for years this time.

It had happened before. Years passing like days.

Even as days sometimes passed like years.

Time turning on itself. Shrinking. Stretching.

Distorting. Warping. Unpredictable.

Which made her think of that grandfather clock.

Back in the parlor. Inside that dark house.

*Tick, tock, tick, tock. Tick, tock, tick.*

Only to hear herself sighing at such fanciful wanderings of her silly and overtired mind. At the idea of time shrinking and stretching. Distorting and warping. Becoming unpredictable.

*As if time could actually do such a thing, anyway.*
*Shrink. Stretch. Distort. Warp. Become unpredictable.*

She heard him standing. Clearing his throat.
She heard him whispering to someone.
Then clearing his throat again and moving. Moving away from that someone -- and imagined *she'd* been in the bed beside him. The curtains drawn. Keeping out the morning light. *Her.* Still half-asleep as she'd turned over to mumble to him *who you talking to, hon?* Him giving her a non-committal answer. More of a grunt and that clearing of the throat as he moved away from her. Exiting the bedroom now. And pulling closed the bedroom door between them.
Emily wondered if the girls would be awake.
*How old were they now? His girls? Nine and eleven?*
"Em, are you OK?" he wanted to know.
Like he could read her mind even over the phone.
Something he'd been able to do, read her mind, from the very first moment they'd met as children who'd seen a little too much of the world and knew how mad it could become long before anyone knew anything about a *Reaper Virus.* Yes, even as a young silly boy, he'd been able to read her mind from the very beginning, staring at her silently with his large intelligent pale blue eyes. Anticipating her thoughts. Her actions. Even her freaking moods. And more.
She was surprised, frankly, she'd caught him asleep. Surprised he hadn't somehow clairvoyantly *anticipated* her phone call.
His clairvoyance could be downright creepy.
Yet also somehow downright comforting.
As if two sides of the very same coin.
Of course, it had occurred to her he was not clairvoyant at all, that perhaps *she* was the clairvoyant one. Able to silently communicate with him her needs and wants without speaking. As if he were a trained puppy simply reacting to the stiff pull of a leash.
The fact he'd been asleep, it discomfited her.
The idea their *connection* might be fading.
She felt that familiar ice pick stabbing at the back of her neck again, radiating that terrible pain down that highway of nerves into hands, making like tiny splinters in her fingers. Her splintery fingers soon falling numb. And then that splintery numbness climbing into all the rest of her. As if her entire body might fall asleep to all that splintery numbness. In a paradox of pain and nothingness.
She imagined embracing it. That sleepiness.
Allowing it to embrace her back. Slipping into as if slipping into a warm bath. *As if slipping down beneath the warm water itself.*

*Drowning* in it. In that sleepiness.

In that paradox of pain and nothingness.

"Em," he tried again. "Said, you OK, Em?"

She heard a dog barking. He'd gotten a dog. Probably the girls begging him for one. Or maybe it was just the neighbor's dog. Better it was just the neighbor's dog, she thought. Hoped.

A fucking dog. Walks. Vet bills. Responsibility.

A dog was for a family. A dog was a commitment.

As if children, two young girls, were not.

*Had he always had a freaking dog?* she wondered.

She stabbed END. And he was just gone. Again.

She stared down at the phone thinking he might call her back. But the phone remained silent, the display pitch-black. As if Adam had fallen down a dark terrible tunnel. Down a dark terrible rabbit hole, perhaps. Or, perhaps, it was she who'd done so. Again.

Sighing a ragged sigh, she finally phoned Darcey.

Only to receive Darcey's outgoing message.

Emily considered leaving a voice message, but didn't. Instead, she fired off a quick text as the morning chill produced tiny goosebumps on her skin in the shadows of the garden gazebo.

*I'm here...* she simply wrote. Only that.

Her stupid phone was about to die, anyway.

She stuffed the phone back into her pocket and exited the gazebo. Got moving again on the path. Intending to head back to the house, but getting lost again and finding herself at the wrought iron fence guarding the back of the property. The garden grounds being at the bottom of a gentle slope, she discovered the fence to be significantly taller than she had expected. At least eight feet in height. With sharp-looking spikes on the top. And thick iron bars through which only that strange black cat slinking around back in the house behind her might be able to successfully squeeze through.

The path eventually found a back gate.

A section of the path passed under the gate before disappearing up into those woods, turning from crushed stone to dirt.

Emily was unable to follow that path.

The back gate being secured by its own lock.

She tried the kitchen back door key just for giggles, but it was woefully small for the lock. Her room key was also a no-go. As was the attic key. She stood there a moment feeling queer.

As if someone were watching her.

She turned to find the house staring down at her. Those black windows. Including the attic window and Ms. Vivian Dancemore's bedroom window in which she thought, for an unsettling moment, the strange woman might be standing in the dark shadows.

Standing there. Watching her. Maybe.

But the more Emily squinted her eyes, staring up at it, the less certain she became it was anything but more dark curtains.

Still, she felt as if she were being watched.

Felt it as she slowly followed the crushed stone path along the border of the wrought iron fence, the ivy and wisteria and creepers and climbers hiding those thick iron bars here and there before the fence took a hard right toward the looming house where it revealed to her a narrow side gate to a carport and a gravel driveway. An old Buick LeSabre slumbered under the carport. A dull sheen of brown patina over what had once been white paint. Ropey cobwebs growing out from beneath its sagging frame and about its thin flattened tires seemingly fettering the automobile to the gravel driveway, and suggesting the car hadn't been driven for a very long time.

Meanwhile, the side gate, not surprisingly, had a lock. It resisted her efforts to open it, too. Undeterred by her iron keys.

Meanwhile, the eight foot tall fence with all those sharp spikes on the top continued until it was flush against the house, effectively imprisoning her there in the garden, providing her no exit.

*Perhaps she really was a prisoner after all...* she decided. *Perhaps she shouldn't be staying on. Then again, perhaps she ought to simply demand a key for the front door, if not the windows and the garden gates, and whatnot. Just politely ask for one rather than create such excitable fiction in her head. Rather than become overexcited. Something she was sometimes wont to do.*

It was only then she noticed the black cat.

The same black beast from the previous evening.

The one that had *slunk* against her leg.

It was curled in the sun at the kitchen back door, its long and fluffy black tail flicking lazily in the cool morning air. Its dark green almond-shaped eyes staring at her with wry amusement.

And suddenly she felt like Alice.

Like Alice in her strange Wonderland.

And the cat a version of the Cheshire cat.

And as that black cat stared at her now, lazily flicking its long and fluffy black tail, Emily thought maybe she might've said:

*Would you tell me, please, which way I ought to go from here.*

And thought maybe the cat might've said:
*That depends a good deal on where you want to get to.*
*I don't much care where...* she might've then said, perhaps, silently conversing with the black cat without actually speaking.
*Then it doesn't matter which way you go...* it might've said.
It might've said if they were actually conversing.
Which they were not. It only being her imagination.
Playing Alice to the black cat's Cheshire cat.
And yet, it seemed that *that* was exactly what the black cat lazily flicking its tail *might've said* if she'd said what Alice had said.
For Emily felt just about as lost and turned around in this upside down world with nowhere else in this world to go as Alice had felt in her very own strange upside down Wonderland world.
"How did you get out here, anyway?" she only then said in the end, thinking maybe it had slipped out the kitchen back door in her shadow. Perhaps not such a good thing. Perhaps this slinking black cat only being a housecat and, quite by her gross negligence, in peril out here in this big upside down world gone so mad.
Disquieted by the thought, she tried to coax the black cat back inside the kitchen after pushing open the kitchen back door, nudging at it gently with her foot, and then a bit more roughly.
But it wouldn't budge. Not this morning.
Content to lie out there in the morning sun.
She then jumped at it with a little scream only to have the cat stare at her a beat like she might be a little soft in the head before it slowly rose, stretching. And with a long hiss voicing its disapproval, turning its back to her and sauntering off into the garden.
Disappearing amongst the many blooms.
Pulling its dark slinky shadow with it.
Pulling that dark slinky shadow past a congregation of tiny ceramic leprechauns hiding amongst a furious tangle of foliage, peeking out. She'd not noticed them before. The tiny leprechauns, peeking out as they were. *Watching her* as they appeared to be. With their large yellow eyes, sneering little grins, mouths full of teeth.
Unnerving, they were. Hiding there.
Hiding there in plain sight as they were.
Emily returned inside the house and thought to leave the iron key in the kitchen back door just as she'd found it earlier.
It seemed the rather polite thing to do.
The antique grandfather clock was gonging.

She listened, counting the gongs.
Counting the gongs as they rang out.
Heavy distinct penetrating bellowing gongs.
One...two...three...four...five...six...
Seven...eight...nine...ten...eleven...twelve.
It gave her more than a small start.
*Noon, already? It couldn't be. Where'd the time gone? How long had she been out there in that garden? It had seemed more or less only half an hour.*
*After all, she had seemingly woken Adam. Her Adam.*
*He'd seemingly still been in bed. Just moments ago.*
*In his home. With her. His young girls. A barking dog.*

The house seemed to tremble with each of the gongs. And to continue trembling long after they were done as it was wont to do. And she found herself stumbling up the foyer staircase, then up the narrow dimly-lit hall past Ms. Vivian Dancemore's locked bedroom door to her own bedroom, locking her own bedroom door behind her and taking a deep breath with her back against the door. Trying not to become overexcited. Trying to settle back down again.

*I have control over my emotions. And I choose to feel at peace.*

She realized her eyes were closed and when she opened them again stared at the bedroom before her. Blinking. Twitching.

*For the bed had been neatly made in her absence.*

*And the thick black drapes drawn again. Pulled shut.*

She felt that ice pick stab at the back of her neck.

Those numbing splinters in her hands and feet. Even as it also shivered (*slithered*) down her spine like that awful frozen snake.

*I have control over my emotions. And I choose to feel at peace.*

Well, there, then. This confirmed it. Assuming it had not been the lady of the house, and Emily somehow felt quite strongly, intuitively, it had not been -- there was obviously staff here hiding in the walls of the house. Maybe even *more* than one person given the size of the house. Staff obeying their own *set of rules* as they went about their business silently. The most obvious rule being to stay out of sight. Perhaps it'd be amusing to try and catch them at it.

*Not unlike catching those leprechauns in the garden.*

*Hiding there in plain sight. Peeking out as they were.*

*Watching her as they had appeared to be.*

OK, maybe it was weird, sure. But, dovetailing nicely with the *peculiarities* of the house, it was more than likely just how the strange lady of the house wanted it. And probably paid damn well.

At least she wasn't truly alone here, then.
Wasn't truly all alone with this strange woman.
*This strange woman who believed herself a child.*
That ought to give her some comfort.
Or so she thought to herself as she dug her phone charger out of the wardrobe. Having buried it in a drawer with her underthings as if it were a vulgar contraband that needed to be hidden.

She plugged the charger into an electrical outlet, then plugged the charger into her phone, having not returned her silly phone to that side table somewhere down in the parlor far below her.

But her dying phone refused to charge.
*There are to be no cell phones in the house. No exceptions.*
She changed electrical outlets with the same result.
*Your cell phone is only to be used outside of this house.*
*There are grounds out back. A nice walking path in the garden.*

Emily unplugged the small black and white TV, then tried its outlet. But the stupid phone continued to fade. As if mindful of the house rule. Just before it faded into oblivion, however, *a text flashed on its tiny screen.* From Darcey *out there*. Out there in this world gone so very mad. Flashing before it faded away into obscurity.

*Here where?* it said. That flashing fading text.

As if she knew not where Emily had gone. As if she knew not of this house or its charge. As if she'd not sent Emily here herself. As if Darcey knew *nothing* of this most peculiar assignment.

That ice pick in Emily's neck stabbed harder still.

Turning her entire body cold. Numb. Even as it swirled with a tornado of splinters. In a paradox of pain and nothingness.

The phone screen then went horribly dark.

Offering to her briefly one of those *charge me* animations. The one that was a blue outline of a battery. A battery with an exclamation point. Before dissolving into all that awful blackness.

The phone falling very still. And very quiet.

Dying there in her splintery numb hands.

# 9.

EMILY RETURNED DOWNSTAIRS after a spell, moving in a daze, rather a bit shaken really, if trying to convince herself that Darcey was just having a bit of uncharacteristic fun with her; or, more disquietingly, had somehow displaced in her own mind the fact she'd sent Emily here on this assignment in the first place. Working from home these days. Distracted by her children. A barking dog. Her husband. Her crazy stupid life.

Then again, an even darker thought--

Perhaps she *knew*. Darcey. *Perhaps she knew.*

Knew exactly *where* Emily was and understood exactly the *peculiarities* of this assignment. Either *intuiting* them or having *heard something* or other. Or having *gotten it*, perhaps, straight from the horse's mouth herself. Unfiltered. From Ms. Vivian Dancemore.

It wouldn't have been the first time after all. The first time she had gotten Emily such a job with such peculiar arrangements.

Henry, the poor soul. Others before him.

As if Emily were perfectly suited for such oddness.

And she could imagine Darcey enjoying the scandalous idea of sending her to such a place as this. To such a certifiable woman. To such a home under lock and key. They had never really quite gotten on after all, she and Darcey. Not that Emily blamed her.

Emily had always found it difficult to get on.

To get on with people in general, frankly.

Relationships, whether romantic or platonic, always seemed to start well enough, only to get weird. Uncomfortable. As if whatever people saw on the outside of her was nice and pretty and seemingly familiar enough only to have that nice prettiness become transparent. *Allowing people to see through it as if it were only a clever façade.* As if it were only just that in the end. If maybe not so very clever.

Emily and Darcey had once gone out for drinks on a Tuesday night with some of Darcey's friends. Laughs and giggles. But Emily had seemed to laugh and giggle at all the inappropriate times. During awkward lulls in the conversation that she'd unfortunately initiated more often than not. Awkward lulls initiated by simply opening her mouth and saying the wrong things at the wrong time. Misinterpreting the conversation. Their moronic expressions.

By simply offering to them her smile.

*Never show your teeth when you smile.*

She'd not been asked out for drinks again.

Yes, perhaps Darcey thought this perfect for her.

This responsibility. This odd assignment.

These *peculiarities*. Given her own peculiarities.

She'd always gotten on better with children, especially the peculiar ones. Children were more curious. More open. Innocent and less guarded. Less prejudicial. *The peculiar ones most especially.*

*The odd. The misunderstood. The unusual.*

At any rate, Emily found her lunch waiting in the kitchen. She wasn't very hungry, but sat at the table anyway. And now that she thought about it, she thought just perhaps her lunch *had been waiting for her* when she'd returned inside the house earlier to the bellowing gongs of noon from that grandfather clock in the parlor.

Bread. Cold cuts. Mixed greens.

And for dessert, a big giant red apple.

She made a face at the apple with its bright red glistening skin, wondering where the delicious lemon cake had gone. That delicate and just perfectly sweet, but not too sweet divine cake.

The wooden stand under the glass dome on the antique drop-leaf serving table was now rather depressingly empty.

She ate the bread. Cold cuts. Mixed greens.

But left the apple right where it was.

Thinking of Snow White. The poison apple.

And what her grandmother would quote to her from the film when they were picking apples from that small apple grove.

That small apple grove on her grandparents' farm.

Her grandmother would invariably select one apple from the dozen in their wicker basket and hold it out to Emily in the palm of her hand. And hush softly to her it was a *magic wishing apple*.

*One bite* and all her dreams would come true.

But they hadn't in the end, had they?

Emily didn't think so. Not at all.

None of her dreams had ever come true.

Not ever. Only her worst nightmares.

Emily tried to push aside these nightmares, these most terrible of nightmares, clearing her dishes, washing them, and placing them neatly to dry in the dish rack. *Rule #14. Clean up after yourself.*

Only to find herself staring at the back door.

The iron key from that morning was gone.

Quite disappeared now as if into thin air.

The back door once again steadfastly locked.

Steadfastly locked and impassable.

# 10.

THESE MOST TERRIBLE of nightmares.
Yes, *these most terrible of nightmares*, hissing and chortling darkly, snuffling and scratching and biting, smelling of dead and rotten fetid things, had gathered her, as a quite very young girl, into their tenebrous clutches not long after her ninth birthday.

Nightmares beginning with her father.

Beginning with her father, more or less.

He'd left Emily's mother after learning he was not Emily's biological father. Emily had no earthly idea who her biological father might *actually* be only that bloodwork ordered by her pediatrician to monitor a persistent ear infection ultimately revealed an incompatible blood type with the only father Emily had ever known.

Emily could still remember the sound of her mother begging him desperately to stay and her father not saying much of anything at all as he'd packed a single suitcase before vanishing out the front door on a cold and blustery winter day. Then only silence. But for her mother's tears that lasted for months. Only finally ending with her mother's overdose. Pills. A motel room. Dying alone.

Her father had never returned.

Not even for her mother's funeral.

Little nine year old Emily was sent off to live with her paternal grandparents on their farm. Her mother's own parents having died in a car accident when Emily's mother was at university.

Her *nonbiological* paternal grandparents.
That bloodwork demanding no actual relation.
Down to that farm with all those fireflies.
Blinking and glowing in the darkness.
Those silent swarms of little flying critters.

And she imagined the ruptured brain aneurysm that eventually took her grandmother from her late one winter night on the evening of her eleventh birthday to resemble the sudden twinkling flash of such a firefly as that blood vessel in her brain exploded.

Her grandmother had appeared asleep.

Asleep the following morning. Despite it being almost eight in the morning and well after the rise of the sun even in early January. Her grandfather sitting there at the kitchen table in the gray morning shadows, waiting impatiently for his breakfast like a child. Sending Emily up to fetch her grandmother. Something Emily had never had to do before. Feeling a flutter of panic even then.

The farmhouse so very quiet. Too-quiet.

Her grandmother had looked so very horribly peaceful. Lying there alone in the bed in the darkness behind those still-pulled curtains. Still in her flimsy night things. Her hair in curlers.

It had been her grandmother's large toady eyes that had finally told the truth. The truth of the fatal bleeding in her head.

Those large toady eyes were wide open. Almost as if her very eyes were screaming. The whites filled with a gelid blood.

Her wrinkly skin cold as snow to the touch.

Her grandfather had been in no position to raise a young girl by himself. He drank too much. Maybe he had always done so, but Emily suspected even as a child it had gotten much worse after she had arrived. After his son had done his vanishing act. Knowing her blood wasn't of his blood. Knowing she was not his family.

At least not in the traditional sense of the word.

Furthermore, adding a bit of punctuation to the matter, Emily didn't appreciate how her grandfather would sometimes look at her when he was deep inside the bottle. Eyes angry, drunkenly whispering devil-tongued things at her beneath his foul-stinking breath. As if *she were to blame*. For all of it. His son's vanishing act. Her mother. That motel room. The pills. Overdose. Her grandmother.

As if she were some kind of terrible curse.

And so she was quickly sent off to the state. Disappearing into the foster care system. Like being flushed down the drain.

# THE NIGHT SITTER

But she found a hardass little shiny diamond down in that terrible sewer. That was how she'd always imagined their relationship, anyway. A hardass little shiny diamond discovered in the filth. As if cavalierly discarded by someone who knew not its worth.

Or altruistically discarded for only *her* to find.

Full of sharp hard edges, but so sparkly in the light.

And hiding inside of it a tiny separate universe.

A tiny separate universe where anything was possible.

A tiny separate universe promising happiness.

A young boy about her age. Adam. A boy who would become her family. Her forever. Not by blood, but by circumstance. Inseparable by neither time nor distance nor any cold and heartless earthly convention, either. A tiny separate little universe born *of each other*. Lost as they otherwise were in that terrible sewer of filth.

Or so she'd always imagined it. Him. Her.

Fate conspiring against the terrible nightmares.

Fate. Like a warm kiss in the cold darkness.

It had been Emily's third placement.

Her third house. Her third family.

Adam had arrived about a month before her and had the bedroom across the hall. Emily had just turned twelve. The placement had lasted almost nine and half months. Including Christmas.

Perhaps it was because of Christmas.

The hollowness of it in the pit of her stomach.

That scrawny little *Charlie Brown* Christmas tree slowly dying in that tiny claustrophobic living room of that bunker-like brick house on the east edge of town, the scrawny little tree shedding a circle of ugly brown needles as it stared sullenly out a dingy front window at that overgrown city park teeming with the crazy indigent.

Or the gifts beneath that scrawny little tree.

Stuff donated by the county. Socks, underwear.

Stupid things other kids took for granted.

Adam never really spoke specifically about why he was in the system, but Emily deduced from this and that conversation, usually whispered privately between them late at night when the rest of the house was asleep, that his old man (that was how Adam referred to his father) was no longer in the picture, possibly incarcerated, and that his mother was a hopeless drug-addict and alcoholic.

Implying he'd suffered neglect. Abuse.

Possibly worse. Whatever that might mean.

Conversations had in the middle of the night.
After Emily had snuck across the hall between them.
Lying there face-to-face. Nose-to-nose.
In the quiet darkness beneath his bedsheets.

He always smelled faintly like chicken soup and she would often fall asleep staring at him, that young boy becoming a man, as he stared at her, a young girl becoming a woman. Their eyes becoming heavy-lidded. Fluttering reluctantly. Before slipping shut.

It wasn't long after they began *experimenting*.

Awkward fumblings that soon became less awkward and less fumbling and tended to flush the skin and steal the breath from the lungs and eventually finally caught the awareness of the foster family. A mother and an unemployed father with twin little girls still in diapers. Requiring of the system an immediate separation.

There would be thirteen such placements.

Thirteen such placements for Emily.

None lasting longer than five months after the placement with her Adam across the hall in that bunker-like brick house.

With no overtures of adoption. None.

Not that she'd have invited any such overtures.

God, she certainly wouldn't have at that.

The good placements only meaning more food. And being ignored, more or less. Being ignored usually preferable to the alternative. Especially as Emily had gotten older. Prettier. Feistier.

She spent her final years in a group home before finally being *emancipated* from that awful sewer of a system. But if she were being truly honest with herself, however, the nanny gigs were not all that different from foster care. Moving from one odd house to the next. Trading one temporary home for another. Adopting one temporary odd family for another, too, but never quite feeling at home.

Never quite feeling like she truly belonged.

Never quite feeling like she'd been truly *accepted*.

She sighed raggedly with the ill-thought.

Sighed raggedly as she now found herself standing quietly outside of Ms. Vivian Dancemore's locked bedroom door.

Of course none of the other nanny gigs had come with locked doors and windows. Not with locks on the outside *and the inside* and keys that appeared and disappeared from back doors. Kitchen back doors that led out to large gardens imprisoned by tall wrought iron fences with more locks securing impassable gates. Until now.

# THE NIGHT SITTER

Until this dark and forbidding Victorian home.
Until this lockbox maze of a dollhouse.
With its dim lights and dark shadowy corners.
Dark shadowy corners and darker crevices.
She deserved a key to the front door.
She deserved at least that much. At least the courtesy of being able to come and go as she pleased, the looming Martial Law order beginning at midnight that night notwithstanding, anyway.
Assuming she decided to stay, of course.
Assuming she didn't just pack-up and leave.
Assuming she could leave. *A funny thought.*
*A funny thought that Ms. V might not let her do that.*
*Might not let her leave even if she desired it.*
She had now begun thinking of Ms. Vivian Dancemore simply as Ms. V. Perhaps it was because she'd seen the woman at age nine in that golden light through the attic keyhole. In a silly white nightie with her long dark hair braided childishly and decorated with those silly long white ribbons. And sucking on her thumb besides.
It allowed her to demystify the woman.
Reduce her to something less than--
*Something less than what?* she asked herself as she stood outside Ms. V's bedroom door in that long narrow dimly-lit hall. Hesitating before that door. *Something less than what?* she asked herself again. *Is the possible answer to that question what's keeping you from knocking on this door and causing the terrible dryness in the very back of your throat and a cold sweat to rise to your forehead? Is the possible answer to that question the reason your heart is maybe palpitating so very uncomfortably in your chest and, indeed, now causing your breath to come in those small little catching gasps?*
*Go on, knock. Confront this mysterious riddle.*
*Demystify this mysterious Ms. V, why don't you?*
*Go on, my dear, reduce her to something less than what?*
*What're you so afraid of, anyway, Miss Emily?*
Emily grimaced. Shook her head.
And lifted her hand to knock. Rule #10.
*You are to please knock on all doors before entering.*
Only to find that black cat slinking out of the shadows. Blinking at her with those clever dark green almond-shaped eyes.
As if warning her against such a thing.
Or rather, perhaps, encouraging her possibly.
Or maybe both. The sinister little shit.

Licking at its paws. Lazily flicking its tail.
Doing so as it sat there before her.
Grinning. Or at least appearing to do so.
Not unlike that fat insufferable Cheshire cat.
The one from Alice's Wonderland.
*In that direction lives the Hatter...* it might've said.
*And in that direction lives a March Hare...*

Nodding first at Ms. V's locked bedroom door. And then over its scrawny little shoulder at the very end of the long narrow dimly-lit hall. The alcove. Attic. *Visit either you like; they're both mad.*

*But I don't want to go among mad people...* she might've said to the silly black cat. Assuming she might've said anything at all.

Its Cheshire grin seemed to expand, dark green eyes twinkling. *Oh, you can't help that, we're all mad here. I'm mad. You're mad.*

*How do you know I'm mad?* she might've said.

*You must be, or you wouldn't have come here.*

And with that, the black cat was gone again. Slinking back into the shadows. Slinking back to wherever it had come from.

Vanishing into the shadows like a magic trick.

*Poof.* Here one moment, then just gone.

Which begged a more obvious headscratcher.

How it had come to be *here* from *there* at all.

Wherever it had *just come from* just now.

For she might've asked it how it had *gotten back inside* this grim fortress of rusted locks. Seeing how she'd left it outside in the garden earlier that day. And quite *on the other side* of that locked kitchen back door. Only to rather drearily suppose the mysterious black cat might've simply remarked to her *the same way I got out, my dear.*

Trading one silly riddle for another.

If a rather unnecessary silly riddle, frankly.

*For obviously someone had let it out and then back inside.*

Someone moving about in these same shadows.

Unseen staff hiding inside these dark walls.

Meanwhile, she noticed her hand was still in mid-air, poised to knock on Ms. V's bedroom door, her shoulder cramping, her forearm stiff, her fingers drained of blood, turning pale, tingling with all those tiny splinters, splinters now moving into her poor arm.

She dropped the hand. Stretched her fingers.

Felt the blood returning. Making her hand heavy.

Too heavy to lift again. Much less knock.

Only to hear Ms. V's voice in her head:

Hissing: Scolding her: *Neither you nor the child, Madelyn, are ever to enter my personal bedroom without my personal explicit permission.*

As if she'd meant to trespass just now.

As if she'd meant to enter without knocking.

Without seeking her explicit permission.

Emily found herself trudging to her bedroom, promising herself she'd address the subject of the front door key later that evening. Assuming Ms. V *ever* exited her own room, of course, and feeling a sharp sting at the idea that *Ms. V might never do so again.*

That she might be truly trapped here.

Truly trapped inside this fortress of a house.

She'd looked for a landline earlier and found none. If only she could get to that dragon bell on the front porch. That big cast iron bell, thinking once more of the terrible racket it might make in this deafeningly quiet neighborhood. Certain to raise the dead.

Only to then remember her strange dream.

Those winged-beasts. Howling. Shrieking.

Black silhouettes against the dark night sky.

Pale-white against that dull thumbnail-sliver of moon.

Before *descending* toward the dark house.

This dark house on the very edge of the world.

To that bell that actually made no sound.

Made no sound at all in her silly dream.

In her silly dream. Only just that. A dream.

Of course, thinking more logically, should she have an opportunity to ring the bell, then she would already be outside. Out. And in no need of the bell at all in the end. Soundless or not.

Unless, of course, the house *came after her*. Whatever that might mean. She imagined a large scaly black hand reaching out from the house shadows. That large scaly black hand adorned with long ugly claws. Snatching at her as she tried to run into the night.

As she tried to *escape* from this place.

More moronic silliness, she told herself.

As she found herself *drifting past* her bedroom.

Drifting past her bedroom down the long narrow dimly-lit hall as if her feet knew *where to take her* even before her mind had such a notion itself. Pulling her past the tiny dark bathroom, then around the corner to the small alcove at the base of the attic stairs.

To the bookcase filled with children's books.

Stepping around the small food dish with FRISKY in big cartoonish letters on the side, and its sidekick water bowl, she studied the bookcase and discovered many familiar titles in its collection of dusty old books. Books she had adored as a child along with books she'd never heard of. She supposed the books she'd never heard of in their dusty old coats given the fact they quietly shared the bookcase in this dark little attic alcove with such well-loved titles might advocate to her these dusty old books she had never heard of came quite well-recommended and selected one at random now.

She then finally returned to her bedroom.

Hugging the book closely to her chest just below her nose, savoring its sweet musky smell with just a mild hint of vanilla.

She'd once heard that *lignin*, which was present in wood-based paper, was closely related to vanilla and offered that strange vanilla-like scent as it slowly broke down over the years. Decades.

The smell of secret things long-forgotten.

After locking her bedroom door behind her, she sat upon the windowsill. The ledge was fairly large and accommodated her comfortably, especially when she situated a pillow behind her back. She subsequently found herself sitting in that window before that empty neighborhood street lost in the book's dusty pages for hours as if such hours could be magically turned into minutes only to be gradually woken from her deep trance by the sudden gong of the grandfather clock somewhere down in the parlor far below her.

Echoing in the old walls of the house.

*One...two...three...four...five...six.*

Six o'clock. Six o'clock in the evening.

Only about an hour left of daylight. If that.

Emily blinked. Rubbed her weary eyes.

Watched the sun slowly slip from the sky. Fading toward the unseen horizon somewhere on the other side of the house.

The sky beginning to turn from blue to black.

Promising the cold night. Darkness.

# 11.

AS THE DARKNESS DESCENDED on this day turned to cold night, Emily found her dinner waiting in the kitchen below. A bowl of spicy gumbo with a wedge of crunchy bread. Another personal favorite. And yet, most queerly, something she might have perhaps noticed before, this being her *fourth* meal in this strange house, there was no evidence the mouth-watering meal, or any of the previous meals for that matter, had actually *been cooked in this kitchen*. No pots or pans or cooking utensils silently drying in the dish rack beside the sink. Neither was there any obvious lingering aroma of simmering andouille sausage, beef bouillon, succulent shrimp, or sweet onion. Nor any celery, garlic, or Creole spices perfuming the cold stale kitchen air. Other than what came from the bowl in front of her. It was as if the meal had *simply and spontaneously appeared from nowhere*. And Emily, in spite of the eager rumblings of her tummy, found herself debating, her eyes beginning to twitch, if she should even dip a spoon into the gumbo concoction. As if it all might just be a clever magic trick hiding something sinister.

Hiding something most sinister, indeed.

Again thinking of Snow White. That poison apple.

There was also dessert. Not an apple, but a big slice of chocolate torte. The remaining torte on that wooden stand. That wooden stand beneath that glass dome over there on that antique drop-leaf serving table. Where the lemon cake had once resided.

Sweet but not too sweet. That lemon cake.

Emily stared at the gumbo. Bread. Torte slice.

Hesitating. Fighting her awful creepy-crawly feeling.

Alone in the growing shadows of the kitchen as that darkness descended out there on this day turned to cold night.

In the end, however, her stomach won out.

And Emily found herself devouring the meal, washing it down with a glass of iced tea. The iced tea cold and heavenly sweet.

(A cold and heavenly sweet glass of iced tea had accompanied her lunch that day and supper the previous evening as well.)

Afterward, feeling pleasantly full, if somehow unpleasantly defeated, she washed her dishes, placing them neatly once again in the dish rack to dry. Washed her dinner dishes -- but for one.

She left behind her cake plate and fork. Left them sitting there conspicuously at the bottom of that kitchen sink. Unwashed. Dirtied with the chocolate and a dusting of powdered sugar.

*There, then...* she thought to herself, nodding her head. *Let's see what they make of that.* Whoever *they* might turn out to be.

A rule broken. And rather defiantly so.

# 12.

AT PRECISELY EIGHT O'CLOCK, just as the grandfather clock began to gong somewhere down in the parlor far below her, there came a light knock on her bedroom door. Emily rose from the windowsill where she'd been sitting ever since supper, absorbed in that dusty old book she'd quietly pilfered from the small bookcase in the dark little alcove below the attic staircase, if occasionally staring out past the long thick black drapes and dark multi-paned window at that dark empty street. At those houses and street lamps turning hazy in the night, becoming fuzzier and fuzzier still before just disappearing into all that darkness beyond.

Emily used her room key to unlock her bedroom door to find Ms. V standing in the long narrow dimly-lit hall. The strange woman, who'd not made a single appearance or even a whisper of sound the entire day after vanishing into her bedroom after being released from the attic early that morning, appeared to be wearing the same long black dress she'd been wearing ever since Emily had first met her (the white nightie of the sleeping child notwithstanding).

"Good evening, Miss Emily," she said.

"Good evening, ma'am," Emily said.

"I was wondering, Miss Emily, if you might care to join me in the parlor for a glass of sherry," Ms. V hushed to her.

Hushed to her as those gongs bellowed.

"Yes, ma'am. Thank you, ma'am."

Emily followed the strange woman in her floating black dress down to the parlor just as she had the previous evening. There was a fire crackling softly in the fireplace. Its nictitating light dancing in the parlor shadows on the faded gray wallpaper. And leaving Emily to wonder who might have made the fire. Stacked the kindling and the wood. Lit the match. Stoked the first tongues of flame.

And again thought of those leprechauns.

Hiding in that furious tangle of garden foliage.

Peeking out. Seemingly watching her.

Large yellow eyes. Sneering little grins.

Mouths full of teeth. Sharp little teeth.

*Hiding there in plain sight as they were.*

Ms. V stood once more amongst the shadows just beyond the dancing firelight, almost vanishing once again in that black dress as if being embraced by the shadows themselves, pouring sherry from that fancy crystal cut decanter into those fancy faceted sherry glasses. The faceted glasses that managed to catch that dancing firelight, inducing the sherry to sparkle wildly. Like champagne.

She politely handed a glass to Emily.

Then settled on that chenille sofa while Emily perched as before on the fuzzy blue velvet armchair. The low marble coffee table with the short gold-trim walnut legs again between them.

The strange woman lifted her glass. A silent toast this evening. Only just that. Emily copied her like a mirror reflection.

The sherry sparkling all the more.

And tasting somehow sweeter tonight, bubbling in her nose. Making her giggle softly. Her giggles surprised the woman. And her gray eyes seemed to twinkle. As if trying to share the joke.

"You're making yourself at home, then," she said.

'Yes, ma'am," Emily said. "It's a fine home, ma'am."

"So, you've decided to stay on with us."

This did not particularly seem a question.

As if Emily might not have a choice.

Behind all these locked doors and windows.

"I suppose I have at that, ma'am."

It *was* only four hours until Martial Law after all.

And she really had nowhere else in this world to go.

Ms. V nodded at this. Satisfied. Though yet again seemed a bit surprised. Revealed, perhaps. As that twinkle faded from those gray eyes. Causing Emily's tummy to turn in a slow somersault.

Ms. V rose. Refilled their faceted glasses.
But the sherry only twinkling dully now.
As if only a mimicry of its former cheeriness.
As if that cheeriness had been but a façade.

It was then Emily thought she might broach the subject about a key to the front door. But found herself hesitating as before. That terrible dryness again in the very back of her throat. Heart palpitating uncomfortably in her chest. A cold sweat rising to her forehead. For the terrible truth was this: *If she never asked for the front door key, it could never be denied to her and she'd, therefore, never have to contemplate any terrible meaning of its denial. Contemplate she truly was a prisoner.*

They sat in silence for a moment. Just the sleepy crackle of the fire and the occasional creak and moan of the old house.

Before Ms. V seemed to find the courage to say:

"You've met the child, then. Madelyn."

Emily set aside her glass of sherry.

Twinkling dully. Those odd dizzy bubbles.

She thought back to the strange child.

The child that was not really a child at all.

Peeking at it through the attic keyhole.

Deeply asleep the child had been on that small cot. Painted in golden relief in that softly glowing attic carriage light. A little white cotton nightie. Dark braided hair with long white ribbons.

And it occurred to Emily to wonder:

*Why only midnight to dawn? Why did this strange mysterious child only manifest then? This mysterious child that was not really a child at all.*

Another little riddle, perhaps. Or not so little.

*Perhaps it had something to do with the time and manner of death. Maybe the child, Madelyn, had gone missing during a long dark night.*

*Her body only to be found just before dawn.*

*Or something dreadful to that effect.*

She desperately wanted to ask this strange woman, Ms. V, this question, among so many other nettling little questions.

Instead, clearing her throat, she only said:

"No, ma'am. She was asleep, ma'am."

Ms. V had risen to pour herself a third glass. Her back now to Emily. Stiffening. Or maybe it was just a play of the shadows. She stood there longer than a moment as if she just might actually vanish into those shadows, causing Emily to become more uncomfortable still. More uncomfortable enough to eventually say:

"There was a cat. There is a cat, ma'am."

Ms. V turned around. Those gray eyes white.

Turned white as before. White as bone.

If perhaps only a play of the parlor shadows.

"Here in the house. The garden, ma'am."

This earned Emily another nod. And just maybe even a wistful one at that. Before the strange woman in black then said:

"Marbles. It hides from me, you see."

Apparently FRISKY was just a brand name.

A silly brand name on a silly food bowl.

"Hm. It hides from you, ma'am."

"It's the child's cat, my dear. Madelyn."

Ms. V did not return to the sofa. She drifted.

Drifted through the interplay of nictitating firelight and the intervening shadows, then past the flickering light of the dark-globed table lamps. Before disappearing from the room altogether.

As if finally vanishing into thin air.

Vanishing into thin air without a sound.

Neither a muted footstep in the foyer nor a single one climbing the foyer staircase. Almost as if she'd never been there at all. As if she were as much a ghost as her mysterious daughter. Her daughter presumably lost to this world. Even as the young girl presumed to still exist. Or so Emily thought to herself now. Alone.

Only to hear the soft sound of laughter.

Interrupting all that strange awful silence.

A darkly amused laughter at that.

# 13.

THERE WAS ANOTHER LIGHT KNOCK on her bedroom door at precisely a half hour before midnight. Emily unlocked the door, the bolt making that obnoxious clacking noise in the quiet house, to find Ms. V in the hall shadows.

"Good evening, Miss Emily," she said.

"Good evening, ma'am," Emily said.

As if they hadn't exchanged pleasantries earlier.

And with that, Ms. Vivian Dancemore, in her long black dress, floated up the plum-colored carpet. Past that long avenue of dimly-flickering bronze sconces and around the corner to the waiting alcove and that dark narrow staircase leading up to the attic.

She stepped back just as she'd done the previous night only to stumble for a moment, suggesting she was a bit tipsy this evening. That third glass of sherry in the parlor perhaps having a bit of sport of her. A pale hand reaching for a dark wall to steady herself.

Allowing Emily, as before to ascend the stairs first.

Allowing Emily, as before, to unlock the thick black oak door with the unceasing *tick-tock* of that grandfather clock echoing in the house somewhere down in that parlor far below them. Emily imagining, as before, its brass pendulum swinging slowly back and forth, drawing the deepening night ever closer still to midnight as she felt that ice pick stab at the back of her neck, those tiny numbing splinters in her fingers as she turned the dark attic door knob.

Iron with curvilinear embellishments.
The thick black oak door slowly swinging open.
Its thick rusted hinges whining softly.
And releasing a cold, if musty rush of air from the attic darkness waiting beyond. Waiting so very patiently. Silently.
Emily stepped aside from the threshold.
Careful not to stare at all those dolls in there.
Gathered as they were on those long dark shelves.
With their pale porcelain faces and dark eyes.
Their dark eyes *wide open again. Awake.* No longer closed. Staring at her again. Staring at her from within the attic darkness.
Yes, she stepped aside from the threshold.
Stepped aside from the threshold. As before.
And Ms. Vivian Dancemore floated up the stairs.
Floated up that dark narrow staircase. In that long black dress. Before being *swallowed* by the attic darkness. But for her hauntingly mesmeric whispering voice somewhere in that darkness:
"After midnight, Miss Emily," it said.
Only it sounded less like instruction tonight.
And more like an invitation, frankly.
And as Emily pulled shut that thick black oak door and locked it, she thought maybe she heard more of that darkly amused laughter on the other side of that door. From the attic darkness.
Ms. Vivian Dancemore, certainly.
But not only her. But a chorus of laughter.
A chorus of darkly amused laughter.
Giggling and snickering and such.

# 14.

EMILY RETURNED QUICKLY TO her bedroom, locking the door behind her. Her palpitating heart now making like a soft sledgehammer in her chest. Her breath coming in those small little catching gasps. Standing with her back against the locked door, she slammed closed her eyes and counted slowly from zero to a hundred, then backward from a hundred down to zero. A relaxation exercise Adam had taught her in that other life behind its own variation of locked doors and windows. That other life in that hellish labyrinth of a government system without any escape. Each long narrow corridor leading only to just another dead-end without any exit. For that dark terrible maze was only an illusion of a puzzle to be solved because it hadn't actually been a puzzle at all.

Rather a dark terrible prison in the end.

A dark terrible prison she'd never truly escaped.

*Breath. Just breath. Twenty, nineteen, eighteen…*

Not even when she'd aged out at eighteen. And been unceremoniously thrown into the streets. The world offering her nothing more than a larger unsolvable dark terrible prison of a maze.

*Breathe. Twelve, eleven, ten, nine, eight, seven, six…*

Full of its own long narrow corridors.

Its own shadowy inescapable dead-ends.

Its own illusion of a puzzle to be solved.

*Just breathe. Three, two, one… Zero.*

She opened her eyes. Slowly.

And took a deep, cleansing breath.

Scolding herself for becoming overexcited.

For letting her mind get away from her.

For there was power inside this maze, she reminded herself. It might not be a puzzle that could be escaped, but a clever mind *could* make quite a home for itself in these long narrow corridors.

In the recesses of these shadowy dead-ends.

If it kept itself from becoming overexcited.

For there were treasures in the maze. If one only knew how to properly negotiate it. If one only knew where to find them.

And she did. For she was a survivor.

She had always been a survivor.

She wasn't her mother. God forbid.

*She wasn't her fucking batshit crazy mother.*

*God forbid she ever become that fucking crazy loon.*

And with that uneasy thought she heard the grandfather clock begin to gong in the parlor below. Announcing midnight.

The house walls trembling yet again.

Even the floor seeming to move beneath her.

*Jesus, it felt like she'd just gotten back into her room.*

*Where had the time gone?...* she wondered.

Time, as she'd contemplated before, and, despite herself, feeling a little batshit fucking crazy with the thought, a little like a fucking crazy loon, it was either crawling forward like a freaking snail or being gobbled up by the mouthfuls in this peculiar house. Distorted. Beyond reason. As if it *could* be stretched and diminished.

*Eight, nine, ten, eleven...twelve gongs.* Midnight.

She found herself once again staring over at that small framed embroidered pattern hung on the wall above the radiator, featuring in that gothic-calligraphy its rather insistent biblical reference:

Isaiah 32:18 My people will live in peaceful dwelling places,

In secure homes, In undisturbed places of rest.

It should have calmed her nerves.

To know that the strange woman who believed herself a child had hung it there. Assuming it had been she who'd hung it.

*So why, then, wasn't it calming her nerves?*

*Why did it only seem to be straining her nerves?*

*Why did it only seem to be making her more overexcited? Her palpitating heart making like that soft sledgehammer in her chest beating even faster?*

Emily shook her head. Hard. Felt that ice pick.
That ice pick stab at the back of her neck.
*I have control over my emotions. And I choose to feel at peace.*
*Isaiah 32:18 My people will live in peaceful dwelling places,*
*In secure homes, In undisturbed places of rest.*
*I have control over my emotions.* One, two, three, four…
*And I choose to feel at peace.* Five, six, seven, eight, nine…

Her mind possessed with mantras and numbers, she let herself out of the bedroom into the hall. She moved quickly up the hallway tonight with a purpose. Settling into that dark invisible current. As before. That odd sense of *floating* up the hall. Past the tiny dark bathroom. Around the corner to that dark alcove with all the children's books. The small food dish and the water bowl. The food dish with FRISKY in those big cartoonish letters. Freshly filled tonight with purplish little morsels. The water dish also freshly tended.

The house leprechauns. Probably. Certainly.

Which did beg another absent thought:

*Why had the house leprechauns not been charged with the task of locking Ms. V into the attic at night? Why had the house leprechauns not been charged with the task of night sitter over the child that was not a child at all? And of releasing Ms. V from the attic after the break of dawn? Why not them? The little unseen ones that apparently cooked, cleaned, kept the strange house otherwise sorted. Scurrying about without any sound in the house shadows.*

*Why not, indeed, these secretive leprechauns?*

*Why, indeed, her, instead? A stranger of a girl?*

*Or had she been requested after all as Darcey had implied?*

*Was she not as much a stranger as she believed?*

More strange riddles, she contemplated to herself in the heavy midnight quiet as she ascended the dark narrow staircase.

Ascended it as if being lifted by a tall black wave.

The thick black oak door growing larger before her.

The ugly rusted keyplate growing larger, too.

Its keyhole spilling that soft golden light.

Momentarily blinding Emily as it had the previous night as she kneeled down before it yet again, peering into the attic, and revealing the small cot beneath the softly glowing carriage light.

Only tonight she found the bed *empty*.

The bedsheets flung off against the wall.

The child that was not a child at all off *somewhere* in those surrounding shadows. Hidden in that surrounding darkness.

Beyond the spooky doll collection.

With their pale porcelain faces and dark eyes.

Some staring off into that darkness beyond while others seemingly stared at *her*. Stared at her peeking through the keyhole.

Stared at her seemingly with bated breath.

And for a rather silly terrible moment Emily thought, perhaps, Ms. V had *turned into a child after all. Into one of those spooky dolls and was hiding amongst them, possibly staring at her with her own dark eyes. Watchful. Waiting with bated breath. Swallowing back a mouthful of snickers.*

*Knowing what was in the darkness beyond.*

*Knowing what waited for her. Emily.*

Emily knocked softly on the attic door.

*You are to please knock on all doors before entering.*

Only to hear that loud clacking noise as she unlocked the attic door with its iron key. The attic door swung open, its hinges making that creaking protest of a whine. Perhaps a final warning, Emily thought, before she dared step across its deep threshold.

But step across that deep threshold she found herself doing as if *her body was no longer her own*. The old floorboards beneath her also whining. But less in warning, maybe, than simple greeting.

She blinked in order to peer past the soft golden light and into the surrounding gloom where a dark silhouette took shape.

Sitting in the corner past the window.

Wearing that ghostly little white nightie.

Sitting Indian-style. A small pillow beneath her.

That small pillow with the faded red roses.

Small little feet pale-white and bare upon it.

Dark hair braided with those long white ribbons.

That black cat on her lap. Purring. Marbles.

*How had it gotten in here?* Emily wondered dully.

*Had it stolen in with her shadow earlier that evening? Just as it might've done out the back door into the garden? Or was this just yet another silly little riddle of a game? And what might the answer to such a riddle offer?*

Emily blinked again. Twitched really. Her eyes adjusting as she dared to put the softly glowing carriage light behind her now, pushing into that heavy dimness just past the dark multi-paned window overlooking the garden and the woods. The spooky dolls providing her a quiet audience. Some staring at the child that was not really a child at all in the corner past the window while others continued to stare at her *as if their host of dark little eyes were, perhaps, moving with her, tracking her as she moved across the room,* while others still stared silently back at the open doorway as if danger now lurked there.

As if *something* might be coming behind her.

Coming up those dark narrow stairs.

And for a most silly terrible instant Emily wondered if her key would work *on this side* of the attic door. As if by some dark magic it would not. If she might become *incarcerated* in here should that door suddenly slam closed and that lock bolt *reengage itself,* trapping her in here *with her.* The child that was not really a child at all.

*Breathe. . .* she commanded herself, shaking her head, even her thoughts coming in short little gasps. *One, two, three, four, five...*

*Just breathe. Six, seven, eight, nine, ten, eleven, twelve...*

Emily kept counting in her head, counting up to one hundred, then right back down again. And would drearily wonder later *if she'd ever stopped counting once she'd entered the attic on that night* or if the numbers had risen and fallen, risen and fallen, for an eternity from this moment. From this moment that could never be undone.

Even as time itself lost any real meaning.

*Breathe. Just breathe you batshit fucking crazy loon.*

*Sixty nine, sixty eight, sixty seven, sixty six...*

It was in this moment, as the shadows slowly slipped from the child that was not really a child at all, Emily had the most profound revelation. She realized Ms. V, whom she would from this moment forward begin to think of only as Madelyn between the dark hours of midnight to dawn, was far smaller in stature than she'd given her credit for. At only one hundred pounds or so, and surely not more than five foot in height, dimensions masked by the long black dress, yet somehow made more plain by that simple white nightie, Madelyn was revealed to her to be a rather small and wispy thing.

A rather very *childlike-thing* in the end, really.

And from this moment forward it would become a rather easy thing for Emily to think of her as just that. Only a child.

Only a child between midnight and dawn.

And not an adult at all, remarkably.

An eerie, if complete transformation only further enhanced by how the child moved. Rising effortlessly with a small bubbling giggle from her sitting position without the use of her hands (the cat, Marbles, slinking off under the long dark shelves of spooky dolls). Only to then move about the attic room on her tippy-toes.

Lacking any self-consciousness.

Dancing. Skipping. Pirouetting. Her head thrown back, braids hung toward the floor, white ribbons dangling. Thin pale arms outstretched from her willowy little body, her small pale hands turning slow circles in the air as she, in turn, turned in slow circles.

Eyes catching that softly glowing carriage light.

Managing to turn those gray eyes to gold.

Those gold eyes held on Emily as the girl slowly twirled about, studying Emily without any forced politeness, only curiosity.

As if Emily were but a curious thing herself.

"Dance with me," she eventually said.

Spinning. Her shadow rising on the wall. Falling.

Not unlike all the numbers in Emily's head.

"It's easy," the girl promised her.

Only her words came out more like:

*Dan-th with me... It-th eethee...*

At first Emily thought it was the sherry.

That the child was tipsy. Still. From earlier.

From the parlor somewhere down far below them.

But that wasn't it. The wasn't it at all, frankly.

And it almost felt a sacrilege to think it.

At least under these most peculiar of *peculiarities*.

The butchered "s" sound, along with the muffled rush of air it produced, revealing another explanation. Something rather familiar to people like Emily. People who often worked with small children. Revealing the child suffered from a lisp. The obviousness of which only added to the child's complete lack of self-consciousness. That and the way she spun to a stop. A quite sudden stop with one hand still in the air suspended far above her braided head while the other swiped at a runny nose before cleaning itself on the nightie.

"What's your name, then?" she said. Now standing, balancing, on one foot. The other foot pushed against her opposite calf.

*What-th your name, then...* Sniffling. Staring. Impertinent.

"Emily," Emily heard herself answering the girl.

The girl smiled. Those gold eyes sparkling.

As if she'd expected Emily to perhaps lie to her.

*Tell the truth. No lying. No exceptions. Rule #12.*

Yet her gold eyes somehow reminding Emily of the sherry in the parlor somewhere down far below them before it turned dull in those faceted glasses. As if only a mimicry of its former cheeriness. Suggesting to Emily its cheeriness had been but a façade.

"And you must be Maddy, dear," she said.
The girl's smile grew crooked on her little face.
Like it *might somehow just slip right off* that little face.
"Snacktime, Emily," the girl then said merrily. *Th-nack.*
Before skipping gracefully right from the attic.
And nimbly right down the dark narrow staircase.
Disappearing around the corner into the hall.
Forcing Emily to run to keep up with her, or, if not the girl, at least her nymph-like shadow bouncing on the dimly-lit walls.
It was rather like chasing after tinker bell.
And Emily only finally caught her in the kitchen.
Emily found Madelyn standing before the table where she ate her meals, staring at an empty silver tray where Emily usually found her food waiting for her. Staring rather curiously at her reflection in the silver tray as her reflection deemed to stare back at her.
It was clear the child was accustomed to finding her snack (*th-nack*) on the silver tray and was flummoxed by its absence.
"Oh, pooh," she said. The child. Madelyn.
Staring down at herself in that empty silver tray.
Emily noticed the pantry door was now outfitted with a rusty padlock as well as the fridge. The fridge being of the old-fashioned kind with a thick metal latch and metal locking pin. The metal locking pin secured firmly in place with its own rusty padlock.
Emily didn't bother with her room key or the attic key on the antique iron key ring deep in her pocket. The rusty padlocks on the pantry door and the fridge much too small, certain to foil any effort to pry them open. The contents beyond them irretrievable.
"Oh, pooh," Madelyn said yet again.
And wrinkling her tiny little nose this time.
The antique drop-leaf serving table was gone, too. Along with that mouth-watering chocolate torte beneath the glass dome.
Which caused Emily to turn to the sink.
Her clean dishes were gone from the dish rack.
The dishes she'd bothered to wash.
The cake plate and the fork, however, she found, with a cold stab at the back of the neck, those tingling splinters pushing down into her fingers, still resided *in the bottom of the kitchen sink.*
Just where she'd left them. Defiantly so.
Unwashed. Dirtied with the chocolate.
Dusted with the powdered sugar.

*There, then...* she'd thought to herself when she'd so very cavalierly left them lying there. *Let's see what they make of that.*

Whoever *they* might turn out to be.

Well, while it remained a mystery as to who *they* might be, one mystery had seemingly been solved -- at least as to the consequence of such a disobedient act. Made plain by that silver tray sitting there *empty* on the kitchen table where the child's snack usually, apparently, resided. Made plain by the small ugly rusty padlocks.

Emily pondered what *might happen* if she bent over the kitchen sink and *washed* the cake plate and the fork now. If the child's snack would *suddenly appear*. And if those small ugly rusty padlocks would simultaneously *suddenly disappear* while her back was turned.

But Emily found herself unable to do it.

Quite unable to turn her back to the room.

Quite unable to wash that cake plate and fork.

Out of fear of what *might happen* if she did.

*For if such a snack were to suddenly appear just like that and if those small ugly rusty padlocks were to suddenly disappear just like that at just that very freaking moment,* Emily wasn't sure she could handle that.

Not without becoming very overexcited.

Even as she understood it could not happen.

Not such impossibly magical things.

*For if such impossibly magical things like that could happen right here in only but an instant*, then just maybe there was no coming back from that. Better to believe in those silly little leprechauns moving about mischievously. Her whimsical term for the unseen staff. Yes, better to accept that than let her mind interpret a more deleterious explanation and end up like her poor mother in some awful motel room somewhere all alone with only a freaking bottle of pills, too.

*Maybe even that tiny shit-hole motel apartment.*

*That veritable rat's nest with stained threadbare carpet and tattered curtains and the mini-fridge with a noisy compressor screeching to life every hour of the freaking night and day beneath that filthy window staring-out toward that desolate drive-in theater next door with all that trash blowing around in endless circles. The trash grimly unable to escape the wretched theater's rusty chain-link fence in a rather miserable waltz of the discarded and the forgotten.*

*What had her poor mother seen at the very end? All alone with her bottle of freaking pills in her very own freaking grim little motel room?*

*And before that? Before that grim little motel room?*

*Before she'd gone there with those awful pills?*

# THE NIGHT SITTER

*What had she been screaming at like a crazy woman in the middle of the night for weeks on end when she'd thought her daughter asleep?*

And had the only father Emily had ever known *really left because he'd found out she was not his biological daughter or had there been other reasons? Reasons to do with her mother's odd behavior? Because hadn't her mother been a batshit fucking crazy loon long before he had gone? Long before the only father she'd ever known found out she was not his biological daughter?*

*Had her freaking mother always been so overexcited?*
*So unpredictable and maniacal and selfish and insane?*
*Where had the only father she'd ever known gone?*
*And why had he left her behind like that? Why? Why had he left her all alone with such a batshit fucking crazy loon for a mother for god sakes?*
*Hadn't he loved her, the only father she'd ever known?*
*And why hadn't he come back for his own mother's funeral?*
*Let alone for the funeral of Emily's mother. His wife.*
*And who in god's freaking name was her real father?*
*And why had her mother refused to tell her?*

Emily closed her eyes. Shook her head hard.

Scattering these terrible nightmarish thoughts.

Scattering them off into the dark places.

The dark places of her mind where she, admittedly, sometimes found herself stumbling. Surrounded by those most terrible nightmares that inhabited those cold ominous shadows, *preying on her from the ghastly darkness, hissing and chortling, snuffling and scratching and biting, smelling of dead and rotten fetid things as they gathered her into their tenebrous clutches, having done so ever since she'd been a quite very young girl.*

She opened her eyes to find Madelyn staring at her. Staring at her with her silly little lopsided grin *as if knowing something of this ghastly darkness and of those most terrible nightmares that inhabited it.*

"Shall we play a game?" she said. *Th-all.*

Asking this with another small bubbling giggle.

Her gold eyes twinkling mischievously.

Twinkling as she again pirouetted about.

Pirouetted about on those tippy-toes.

Those long braids hanging in space.

"A game," Emily said to her. The child.

"A game," the child acknowledged, smiling.

"What kind of game?" Emily said.

The house shadows seeming somehow longer tonight. Darker. If more playful. Jaunty. As if anticipating just such a game.

"You say Marco," the girl said. *Th-ay.*
Pirouetting about on those tippy-toes.
"And I'll say Polo," she explained. *Th-ay.*
Before coming to a sudden stop and instructing with that silly little lopsided grin: "Close your eyes, Emily." *Clo-the eye-th.*
Emily shook her head again. Even as she offered a wry smile. Even as she could not help herself but offer such a wry smile.
*Never show your teeth when you smile.*
A wry and a rather knowing smile.
Remembering that most queer house rule.
*There is to be no hide-and-seek. Rule #5.*
For this sounded suspiciously just like that.
*A rose by any other name smelling just as sweet.*
Something her grandmother had also often said.
Quoting Shakespeare. Romeo and Juliet.
Most often in reference to Emily's questions about her real father. Her absentee nonbiological father. Her mother. Questions her grandmother had never truly answered. Only made riddles of.
As if Emily might be *untouched* by all of it.
By all of that nonsense. Abandonment. Discord.
Of whatever had happened and might still.
Emily kept shaking her head now as her smile faded. Wondering why this should occur to her here. What any of *that* might have to do with any of *this*. With this silly game by any other name.
Madelyn giggled madly, her gold eyes flashing *as she pirouetted a final time, then vanished into the long dark shadows beyond the kitchen. As if becoming only a shadow herself, and nothing more, with only the sound of her echoing bubbling laughter giving her away before it faded off, too.*
Faded off into the large dark dimly-lit house.
For a moment Emily just stood there, wondering if she should give chase or if that might only encourage the child -- the child that wasn't really a child at all, but for whom Emily could offer no other description in her own mind, the transformation so very seemingly, hauntingly, seamless. In the end, she felt her feet moving. Felt herself giving chase. Passing in and out of all those shadows.
Chasing that fading bubbling laughter.
Or at least the faint lingering echo of it.
At least until she finally thought to say: *"Marco."*
If saying it rather much too softly at first.
Rather much too softly at first at that.

Only to say it louder and louder to find her own voice drearily echoing back at her, nearly concealing the child's response. Distant. The child's response. As if coming from inside the walls.

Inside the walls of the dark dimly-lit house.

Still, Emily did her very best to follow it.

To track it down. That distant voice.

It seemed to originate from the parlor. Then the foyer. Before moving upstairs. Seemingly from behind Ms. Vivian Dancemore's locked bedroom door. The bubbling laughter rising obnoxiously on the other side of that door. Only to fade off again when Emily put her ear to it. Somehow returning back downstairs to the main level. Perhaps from the study. Only to seemingly move *outside*.

Outside the doors. Steel-framed windows.

With their host of insidious locks.

She imagined Madelyn pirouetting in the garden in the moonlight before dancing down the crushed stone path, becoming lost in that maze of tall hedges, her pale hand trailing behind her, brushing along those tangles of roses, lavender, delphinium, citrus-hued daylilies, and purple alliums, among more wild-looking things.

Some plants ordered in neat little rows. Others crowded lushly together as if springing organically from a quiet meadow.

She imagined her eventually pausing in that moonlit darkness beneath a draping wisteria bloom, its perfume thickly-sweet in the night air, a soft breeze *pulling* her bubbling laughter back toward the giant black house. Imagined Madelyn stifling that bubbling laughter with those pale hands, gold eyes alight in the moonlight.

So certain was she the child was *outside* she hurried back to the kitchen to yank on the kitchen back door *only to find it locked.*

*Only to suddenly find the sound of that obnoxious bubbling laughter coming from the house above her once again. Yet to then suddenly have it come from somewhere below her upon rushing back up the foyer staircase, feet pounding on the stairs. Forcing her to return back to the foyer. Quite breathless now. Where she just stood in place. Just stood in place without moving any longer.*

"Marco," *she said softly to it. That laughter.*

*Her ears straining terribly to hear the response.*

*A beat. Two beats. Before, finally, hearing:* "Polo."

*And the sound of that playful, if whispering voice suddenly much too close to her, frankly. Startling her. Causing her skin to crawl as if with bugs.*

*As if the child were only in the corner shadows.*

"Marco," *she finally said again to it.*

*"Polo," it said. Only to be distant once more.*
*The corner empty but for its deep recess of shadows.*
*So very impossibly distant seemingly. The child's voice.*
*And with each call-out a more confusing rejoinder.*
*The child's voice somehow bouncing all about the house again at a dizzying speed. High and low. Left and right. Up and down. Close and afar. As if the child were somehow everywhere and nowhere at the same time.*

This game of cat-and-mouse went on for hours. The passing time either crawling drearily forward like that freaking snail, and yet at other times being gobbled up as if by those mouthfuls.

The grandfather clock gonging in the dimness.

Emily chasing her own tail before finally giving-up and finding herself returned back to the foyer. As the clock gonged four in the morning. Quite rather surprising her. The night almost gone.

The final hour sure to be gobbled up.

And what then if she'd not found the child?

*Bedtime is 5am. No exceptions. Rule #7*
*Brush teeth. Comb hair. Say prayers.*

Emily went silent. Took a deep breath.

Knowing there had to be an explanation.

*For the child seemingly being everywhere at once.*
*And yet seemingly being nowhere at all in particular.*

And found herself discovering a dark air vent hidden behind a decorative cast iron grate at the base of the foyer wall. A secret tiny air passageway constructed not for any modern central air or complex heating system, but rather to *ventilate* the old house back in the old days, or so she remembered learning about old homes like this. A secret tiny air passageway designed to remove the moisture from between the walls to prevent any mold from gathering about there in the darkness and making sick the occupants of the house.

*But perhaps making a fool of her, too.*
*Such a secret tiny air passageway in the dark.*
*Ferrying the child's voice, mostly likely. Madelyn.*
*Taking it from here to there and right back again.*
*Turning a silly nanny about in dizzy circles.*

Emily sighed with the thought.

With this rather elegant explanation.

*One little riddle solved, perhaps, among so many.*

She sat on the floor at the cast iron grate, blocking it with her back and just listened after repeating once again: *"Marco."*

*"Polo,"* the child's floating voice said.
*Floating down from above now. Unquestionably.*
Emily floated up the staircase in the dimly-lit shadows and followed the *"Polo"* of that little impish voice to her own *"Marco"* up the long narrow hall past her own bedroom and around the corner to the dark narrow staircase climbing back up to the attic.
*From whence the voice surely came.*
*It being so very obvious to her now.*
*From whence the child was surely hiding.*
*Hiding somewhere up there in the gloom.*
Emily slowly entered the small attic.
The old floorboards creaking beneath her.
She closed the attic door behind her this time.
Placed her back to it. Leaning against it.
Staring into that softly glowing carriage light at that small cot. Empty. Before turning her stare to those dark shadows beyond the radius of that softly glowing carriage light as the spooky doll collection stared both at *her* with their dark little eyes set deeply into their pale porcelain faces and into those very same dark shadows.
She pushed toward that darkness. As before.
Expecting to find Madelyn sitting there. As before.
Sitting in the corner past the dark multi-paned window.
In her little white nightie and long white ribbons.
Her small little feet pale-white and bare.
The black cat on her lap. Purring. Marbles.
But encountered only the wooden rocking horse peeking from the darkness. Rocking slowly back and forth, back and forth. Ferrying an invisible rider from here to *nowhere* and back again. And that wooden toy chest filled with its host of most mysterious things. An antique toy sewing machine. A wooden yo-yo. An enamelware tea set for the tiniest of hands. And more toys and games hidden in the darkness beneath them. She also found in the room's far corner an antique music box with a dull glass-topped lid that mimicked a red and white circus big-top tent. She imagined how the antique music box might sing should the dull glass-topped lid be opened.
The music box sat on an old steamer trunk.
One with thick leather straps and heavy buckles.
And Emily, if she dared, could almost imagine Ms. V's body lying in there in metaphorical repose in order to allow her alter ego to exist. This nymph of a lost girl turned quite invisible.

This nymph of a lost girl not to be found.

Perhaps, Emily reflected, sighing deeply with the thought, the child's voice had *not come from here*. Perhaps she'd only been tricked yet once again. Tricked by the machinations of this house.

Emily backed away from the darkness and felt her back eventually come to a stop against the closed attic door. And once again she imagined the thick black oak door *locking itself*. And her attic key not working. Of becoming trapped here. Inside this attic.

Only to then hear a *small little whisper*.

A *small little whisper* so very close to her now.

A *small little whisper* that hushed: *"Close your eyes."*

*Clo-the eye-th*. Of course. The rules of the game.

Always rules in a house of so many rules.

Emily closed her eyes. *"Marco,"* she said.

Before she heard very softly: *"Polo."*

Her eyes gradually slid open to find Madelyn, the child, in the bed. Curled comfortably beneath the sheets. Sleeping soundly. Tiny back rising and falling. A sucking thumb in her mouth.

Perhaps she had been there all along.

Of course she had been there all along.

Hiding in plain sight beneath the bedsheets.

Emily thought to kneel beside the bed and to perhaps give the child a gentle shove. A gentle encouragement to perhaps brush her teeth, comb her hair, say her prayers, but instead found herself exiting the attic, the thick black oak door *opening for her* after all.

She pulled tightly shut the thick black oak door, then used its iron key to secure its rusted lock before returning back to her own room and tightly shutting and locking her own door.

She tried to sleep but found her sleep interrupted. Interrupted by a soft sibilating voice in the darkness of her bedroom.

A small teasing echo of a thing.

Hissing: *Dan-th with me… It-th eethee…*

Emily covered her head with her pillow.

Until she could hear no more on this night.

Until sleep finally overtook her.

# 15.

EMILY AWOKE BEFORE dawn, the small bedroom still dark. She'd slept in her clothes again beneath the bedsheets as if she might just change her mind at any moment. Rouse herself from her slumber to play *Polo* to her exhaustion's *Marco*. As if sleep might offer to her a danger. A terrible vulnerability.
    She blinked in the morning darkness.
    A heavy blink not unlike a twitch.
    Then sat up in the bed and waited for the very first glimpse of dawn's pale light to peek through those heavy black drapes.
    As she waited silently, her dreadful exhaustion hanging heavily over her, turning wooden her each and every extremity, she had the terrible sense she was not alone. She blinked again. Twitched really. And found snoozing quite soundly at the end of the bed, snuggled there against her feet, that incorrigible black cat. Marbles.
    The phantasm of a cat that was seemingly able to slip through locks and under doors and through the very walls themselves.
    *It hides from me, you see...*
    *It's the child's cat, my dear. Madelyn.*
    Its dark green eyes slowly slid open.
    Staring up at Emily sleepily in the darkness.
    Long and fluffy black tail flicking lazily.
    *We're all mad here,* it reminded her, speaking without speaking, as the sly beast was wont to do. *I'm mad. You're mad, honey.*

It seemed to grin at her now. Rising.

Purring. Arching its long back. Stretching.

Producing those tiny black needle-like hairs.

And a monstrous shadow on the bedroom wall.

A monstrous shadow revealing the very first glimpse of dawn peeking over the horizon through those heavy black drapes.

Emily rose. Stretching her wooden limbs.

Wooden limbs full of their own tiny needles.

Or at the very least tiny little splinters.

She let herself out of her bedroom with her key. The black cat followed, but it slinked off into the shadows toward the descending foyer staircase while Emily moved up the hall to fulfill her morning charge. She rounded the corner and climbed the dark narrow stairs, before pausing, as before, before that thick black oak door.

Listening. Listening for voices.

There were no voices this morning.

Only a dark and heavy silence.

She took a deep breath, then knocked.

A light and polite, if firm knock. *Rule #10*.

There was no answer. Only that silence.

She slipped the attic key into the lock. The key making its jangling sound. And the bolt its customary clacking sound.

She then slowly pushed open the attic door.

As the previous morning, adorned in her long black dress, Ms. Vivian Dancemore stood in quiet silhouette before that large multi-paned window. Sable shadows lurking about her. The sun only but a gray dullness in the sky on this side of the house as she stared out at the woods beyond the garden and beyond that tall wrought iron fence. But a woods gradually filling with dawn's hazy light.

Despite the gray dullness on *this* side of the house.

The gray dullness in the sky over those woods.

The hazy light pushing back the darkest of the shadows, pushing those darkest of the shadows deeper into the trees. Where they consorted in the thickest foliage and waited impatiently for the return of the night like the tattered remnants of a nightmare.

A nightmare not to be fully forgotten.

Not even in this hazy light of a new day.

Emily waited silently, if somewhat impatiently, as before, and eventually the woman in black turned toward her, floating through the dimness before those dark shelves of creepy-ass dolls.

Their eyes closed. Sleeping. Silently.
Those creepy-ass dolls on those dark shelves.
*But for one doll.* A red-headed little thing.
Staring out with *dirty blue eyes.*
Emily found herself staring at that doll even as the woman in black floated past her out the attic door and down the dark narrow staircase and about the corner into the narrow dimly-lit hall with its ever-present flickering avenue of antique bronze sconces.
It was then a rather odd thing happened.
That red-headed doll *seemed to grin.*
It actually *seemed to grin* at her. Animate.
Reminding her of that cat. Its Cheshire grin.
But maybe not. Maybe not a Cheshire grin.
No, that was altogether wrong somehow.
But a sad grin. A forlorn grin. Maybe.
But, of course, it was only a trick of the light.
Or, indeed, the lack of it in the dimness.
The idea this thing was *grinning* at her at all.
Cheshire grin. Sad. Forlorn. Or otherwise.
Emily pulled shut the attic door and locked it and hurried after her employer, arriving at the end of the narrow hall just in time to witness her slipping into the master bedroom, though not before turning in the dimly-flickering light and hushing in her trance:
Hushing most softly: "Good morning, Emily."
"Yes, good morning, ma'am," Emily said.
Before the strange woman vanished without another word into the bedroom, the door locking behind her, leaving Emily standing there in the hall. Standing there all alone. As before.
And with that, her second night complete.
Her second night as the night sitter.

# 16.

EMILY ATTEMPTED TO return to bed, but found sleep elusive. And so, she began her day, slipping inside the small bathroom at the end of the hall and performing her morning routine, including what she hoped to be a long and hot shower, only to find the water pressure weak and the water lukewarm, causing her to shiver as she fought the shampoo from her long wet hair and the soap lather from her naked goose-pimpled body, cursing all the while beneath her breath, her poor teeth chattering. The water pipes themselves clinking and clanking long after she'd turn off the shower. Rather quite obnoxious noises inside the old walls.

Assuming it wasn't the *leprechauns*, of course.

Moving about inside the walls unseen.

She was still thinking about those leprechauns as she made her way downstairs into the kitchen to discover an empty ceramic plate hidden below a cold ceramic warming cover where she'd found her breakfast only just the day before. It all sat in front of the ceramic coffee pot. Also cold and empty. The ceramic coffee pot from the previous morning. The ceramic coffee pot decorated with a stenciling of black roses amid that furious tangle of sharp thorns.

The cake plate and fork were still in the sink.

Unwashed. Dirtied with the chocolate.

Dusted with the powdered sugar.

Just as she'd left them the previous evening.

Untouched by any invisible hands.

The antique drop-leaf serving table was still missing, too.
Along with that wooden stand and its glass dome.
Meanwhile, those rusty padlocks that had appeared out of thin air the previous evening still secured the pantry door and the thick metal latch with its accompanying locking pin on the fridge.

Ms. Vivian Dancemore's voice played in her head. *Furthermore, I would ask you to clean up after yourself. Including dishes. Rule #14.*

Emily felt that cold stab of an ice pick again.
Felt its coldness shivering down her spine.
Imitating once more that frozen snake.
She pushed to the kitchen sink and washed the cake plate and the fork before placing them neatly to dry in the dish rack.

She felt that terrible frozen snake still *wiggling* against her spine as she turned back to the kitchen table. Somehow morbidly certain she would find *her breakfast now waiting for her there*. Magically so. Appearing as if out of thin air, too. Piping hot and nourishing.

But she found no breakfast there.
Only the cold ceramic breakfast dishes.
Still empty. Rather solemnly so.

She just stood there staring at them in the silence of the house and found herself contemplating with a sense of dread the potential consequences awaiting her for the other house rules she'd summarily disregarded, either quite willfully or by matter of course.

The child had not brushed her teeth. She had not combed her hair. Said her prayers. Transgressions of the previous night.

*Brush teeth. Comb hair. Say prayers. Rule #7.*

The game of *Marco Polo* had been dubious. Yet, she had entertained it, more or less. If only in an attempt to conclude it. Not that this would necessarily earn her any consideration, perhaps.

The rule was clear. *No hide-and-seek. Rule #5.*
And then there was the final house rule. *Rule #15.*
*Hold the child, Madelyn, accountable to all rules.*
So, three rules broken. At the very least.
No, four. Given the neglected dishes.

And there were probably more she couldn't remember or had not specifically catalogued at the time. She searched her brain now, but found herself so very tired after so very little sleep.

So very tired, indeed. Her mind fuzzy.
Wait, shoot, her cell phone. Now in her bedroom.
Removed from the side table in the parlor.

A clear violation of the house rules. *Rule #8.*
*There are to be no cell phones in the house. No exceptions.*
*Your cell phone is only to be used outside of this house.*
*There are grounds out back. A nice walking path in the garden.*

It was only then she thought to notice the glaring absence of a handwritten note on the kitchen table. Like the note with her name that had been waiting for her only just the previous morning in that elegant, if austere gothic-calligraphy. The note cordially inviting her to explore the garden after she had finished her breakfast.

An iron key waiting in the back door.

There was no iron key this morning.

Just like there was no handwritten note.

Just like there was no breakfast.

That frozen snake slithered from Emily's spine into her empty belly now. Coiling there. Hissing. Turning cold her insides.

Her insides turned *even colder still* when she heard the *distant dull ring of her phone.* She was halfway up the foyer staircase before realizing the sound was *somehow coming from below. From the parlor.*

She hurried from the foyer into the parlor.

The fire long gone. The ashes cold.

The ringing *originating, seemingly, from inside the side table beyond the short chenille sofa. The leprechauns apparently having returned it there.*

Emily absently wondered to herself as she fought to open the side table drawer how the phone might be ringing at all given she'd been unable to charge the damn thing the previous night.

Absently wondered such a thing as--

She found the drawer unwilling to budge.

As she found the drawer tightly locked.

Resisting her efforts to open it.

She imagined the phone bouncing up and down next to those odd reading spectacles and the fancy stationary with its house rules, rattling about with impatience inside the dark locked drawer.

Emily pulled at the drawer more firmly as if that might somehow disengage the lock. The nasty little leering grin of a lock.

Only to hear the phone fall still. Silent.

She briefly entertained the thought of locating, perhaps, a letter opener. One with a long sharp silvery blade. Jamming it into the crevice of the stupid drawer and disabling the lock clasp.

Yet somehow knew it would foil her.

The drawer with its leering grin of a lock.

Perhaps even breaking such a blade.
And leaving obvious her insurrection.
She shoved her fingers to her temples, closing tightly her eyes, trying to think clearly, rationally, as if her fingers might slowly turn the cogs of her over-exhausted brain. Turn them in the *opposite direction* and thereby relieve her of her overexcited thoughts.
For the giant house was just too-quiet.
And yet also much too alive. Too watchful.
The dark windows like too many eyes.
Staring simultaneously outward and *inward*.
The dimly-lit walls like a rough-patched skin.
Yet a terrible leviathan seen from the *inside-out*.
As if she had been consumed by such a leviathan.
Consumed to now be slowly digested by it.
She needed fresh air. She needed sleep.
She returned to her bedroom upstairs and pulled tightly closed the long thick black drapes, turning her bedroom pitch-black. Then climbed into the bed and buried herself in a tight fetal ball beneath the bedsheets still dressed as she was wont to do. And falling into a deep and dark *dreamless slumber*. As if her poor weary mind suddenly could no longer be trusted with itself. So very weary, indeed.
She woke to the grousing of her stomach.
The grandfather clock gonging below her.
The gongs echoing drearily in her numb head.
She tried to count them only to lose count.
But thought she heard it gong twelve times maybe.
Twelve gongs. Revealing it was already noon.
For a most terrible moment, however, given the pitch-black of the bedroom with its drawn drapes, Emily had the grim apprehension *it wasn't midday at all, but already midnight*. That she'd managed to somehow *sleep through the entire day*. And imagined Ms. V in her black dress pacing downstairs in the parlor, *floating* back and forth before that short chenille sofa and that wicked little side table, flummoxed by Emily's contumacious absence while that dancing firelight made her shadow shimmer and sway on the gray-wallpapered walls in the flickering light of those dark-globed Victorian table lamps.
But a quick pull of the long thick black drapes revealed to her, instead, a pale sun sitting high in a dull blue afternoon sky.
Her stomach groused again. Loudly.
She checked her face in the vanity mirror.

The small vanity mirror on the bedroom wall.

Then, reasonably satisfied, despite the presence of little purple sacks beneath her increasingly bloodshot eyes, exited the bedroom and headed for the falling staircase only to find herself pausing outside the locked bedroom door of her strange employer.

Just as she'd done the previous afternoon when she'd wanted to ask for that key to the front door. Before her nerves had gotten the better of her as her nerves were also often wont to do.

The courtesy of being able to come and go from the house as she pleased even if it were only for a small bit of fresh air. A small bit of fresh air *unencumbered* by a tall wrought iron fence with sharp-looking spikes and thick iron bars not unlike thick jail bars.

The courtesy of being able to come and go from this house as she pleased regardless of the *peculiarity* of this strange charge.

Regardless of the *peculiarity* of this strange woman.

The strange woman hidden behind this door.

This locked bedroom door before her.

*Neither you nor the child, Madelyn, are ever to enter my personal bedroom without my personal explicit permission...* the woman had scolded.

For unlike the *peculiarity* of Madelyn, *the child that was not a child even as she presumed to be*, Emily was *not a prisoner* and should not have to behave like one. There being no rules specific to her leaving. No house rules specific to her leaving this most strange house.

If only for a small bit of fresh air maybe.

If only for that. And nothing more than that.

She watched her hand lift to knock only to fall once again. To fall down beside her hip. Defeated. But telling herself she'd address the subject that evening at sherry. A nightly ritual seemingly.

*Yes, she would finally address it then. Regardless of any fear of being told she could not have it. Of being told she would not be given such a key.*

*For what had Ms. V toasted to on that first night?*

*To the only people who consistently tell the truth. No matter how difficult it might be to hear. Drunkards and children, Miss Emily,* she'd said.

*So what of the truth of this matter, then?* Emily wondered.

*What of the truth of this matter, then, Ms. Dancemore?*

*After all, there were locks, large and small, indeed, on the inside of all the doors and windows in this strange house. And for a reason, surely.*

*Just as Madelyn wasn't let outside for this reason, surely.*

*The child, Madelyn, is never to leave this house. Not under any circumstances. Never. No matter what she may tell you. Rule #2.*

So perhaps she would not be granted a key. Perhaps she'd not be trusted with it given what might be at stake in this house.

Whatever that might very well be in the end.

*Perhaps this truth would be most difficult to hear. Difficult to hear in all its strange peculiarity. Perhaps she was truly trapped inside here, indeed. But at least she ought to be told as much, then. And perhaps given a proper explanation for this sacrifice. Perhaps she deserved that much consideration.*

*Drunkards and children after all.*

Which caused her again to consider what lay beyond this bedroom door. Whether or not the dark forbidding multi-paned windows beyond this door were similarly outfitted with such stubborn rusted locks only to realize with a sudden pang in her chest that any such windows most likely would overlook the large garden.

The garden guarded by the wrought iron fence.

The one with those sharp-looking spikes.

*Still, perhaps,* she thought, blinking hard with the thought, *if she could access a window, she might be able to make it onto the roof, and then from there move to the front of the house, and by some means access the street below. Climbing about the assorted gables, utilizing the decorative trimming, brackets, and moldings. Or maybe just descending a simple drainage pipe, if careful not to slip on the scale-like shingled house siding. Careful not to break her freaking neck in the process. But, in the end, escaping this dark strange house.*

*If need be, of course. Only if need be in the end.*

*Assuming the locks were just to keep things inside and not outside things from coming in. Assuming this place was only a prison for a child that was not a child at all, and not a fortress. Assuming the true danger didn't actually lurk out there somewhere in the night. Out there in the darkness of the night.*

*Something more than just a simple terrible virus.*

*Whatever the hell that could possibly mean...* Emily thought, having not the foggiest idea *what it could possibly mean* or *where such a peculiar thought might've come from in the first place, frankly.* She was hungry. She was tired. Her mind failing her, perhaps. Not her own.

And yet, she found herself stepping closer and pushing her ear to the door. As if answers might be discovered beyond it. Pushing her ear to the door and holding her breath. And listening.

The wood of the door cool against her skin.

And for the strangest of moments had the most *peculiar* feeling the strange woman was standing *just on the other side of that door* doing the exact same thing in the dark. Listening. Listening to *her.*

Listening to her and *holding her own breath.*

Her stomach suddenly grousing louder in the quiet stillness of the house, and fearing it would give her away, exposing her treachery, or at the very least her unforgivable impoliteness, Emily gasped softly and got herself moving again, descending the falling staircase and maneuvering her way to the kitchen. Half-expecting to find the table still quite horribly bare. Her transgression unforgiven.

Instead, she found lunch waiting for her.

More bread. Cold cuts. Mixed greens.

And for a dessert: A big giant red apple.

Perhaps even *the* big giant red apple. The very same fruit she'd neglected the previous day at lunchtime. Or so she intuited.

Not that she was complaining. Not that.

She sat down gratefully and began to eat before *it all might vanish again* only to find the bread a bit stale and the greens a bit wilted. The apple rather just a bit mushy on the inside maybe.

She also noticed, blinking curiously, the padlocks remained on the pantry door. The fridge. And that the antique drop-leaf serving table was still absent from its place against the wall. A slight discoloration against the wall where it had once resided quietly.

However, buoying her spirits--

The iron key was back in the back door.

Inviting her back into the garden.

She finished her lunch, every single bite despite the stale bread and wilted lettuce -- if not the apple after only just one curious bite. She took the apple out with her into the garden, intending to enjoy it in the warm sunshine, whether the apple was mushy or not. But only did so after diligently washing clean her lunch dishes and placing them neatly in the dish rack next to the kitchen sink where her cake plate and fork had since magically disappeared. Only then did she disappear herself into the garden. Amongst the tall hedges and various blooms. The hazy dappling sunshine and resident shadows. Eventually finding a thin wooden bench beneath a fig tree next to a small croquet lawn with wooden wickets staggered neatly about the lawn and ready for a game, if slightly warped with age and weather. The balls and their corresponding mallets stored in a wooden stand beneath another fig tree. The mallets hung from wooden pegs, the balls tucked in a narrow wooden sleeve between them, the old mallets and the balls dimpled and chipped here and there, rather pleasantly so, and nearly faded of their original colorful stripes.

Red, orange, green, yellow, and blue.

# THE NIGHT SITTER

Strangely, however, one mallet was missing.

An empty slot with a faded black stripe.

Its black ball, dimpled and chipped, was tucked in the narrow wooden sleeve with the other balls. Red, orange, green, yellow, and blue. Its black stripe faded to a faint gray. The old mallets and the balls sleepy and rather dull in the hazy afternoon sunshine.

The apple in her hand rather dull in that hazy afternoon sunshine, too. As if fading of its very own original bright color.

Still, she took it in her mouth. Biting into it.

She chewed the pulp slowly between her teeth.

Definitely mushy. The juice dripping down her chin.

A bit sour-tasting, too. And maybe a little mealy. A little mealy on the back of the tongue, but otherwise satisfying enough.

Or so she felt a need to convince herself.

As she heard her late grandmother hushing softly beneath her breath in the back of her mind from that small apple grove back on her grandparents' farm, she had for her a *magic wishing apple*.

*One bite* and all her dreams would come true.

It was only then, as she swallowed the mushy apple flesh, wiping the juice away from her chin, and trying not to fixate on where that *missing black mallet might've gotten off to, as if it were a thing demanding a most immediate explanation*, she noticed the west edge of the croquet field was bordered by that tall wrought iron fence with all its sharp iron spikes. Beyond it were those encroaching woods, shimmering in the hazy dappling sunlight nearest the fence, but the very darkest of its shadows hiding amongst the thickest foliage in the deep heart of those dark watchful trees, consorting and waiting impatiently, at least still in Emily's fertile mind, for the return of the night.

She thought she might be able to see the walking path there in the shadows. The path composed of crushed white rock here in the beautiful garden, but turned to dirt as it passed beneath that gate of the wrought iron fence. The path was difficult to judge in the forest underbrush of dense saplings and shrubs and tangled vines, but she believed *she could just make it out,* meandering mischievously.

And something else besides. Something lying in ruin beside it. Beside that hint of mischievously meandering path in the shadows. Something *lying there* on its side, choked by the forest foliage. Nearly lost in the jungle undergrowth of suffocating ferns and moss and mushroom fungi beneath the thick dark wooded canopy.

*Silver. Catching just a wink of light.*

*The silver badly faded like a decaying skin.*
*And a sticker. A badly blanched sticker.*
*Tattered and peeling like an old scab.*
*But still just legible. Reading: HUFFY.*
*Exposing a rusted gear shifter and more silver.*
*An old bike frame with faded piping. The faded piping, rather hauntingly, seemingly mimicking the very same faded colors of the croquet set.*
*Red, orange, green, yellow, and blue.*
*With one long black stripe down the crossbar.*

Emily rose and crossed the croquet field, leaving small damp footprints in the grass like footprints in the snow. She approached the fence, pushing close to its thick wrought iron bars, studying the object, but that old bike, certainly having once belonged to a small child, now lost in the undergrowth beneath the thick dark wooded canopy, *somehow seemed even more difficult to see.* As if it were somehow sinking. *Sinking even at that very moment deeper into the forest floor.*

As if it were playfully hiding from her.

*There is to be no hide-and-seek. Rule #5.*

Playfully hiding even as it attempted to reveal itself.

And her mind flashed back. Rather dizzily.

To that day she'd snuck Henry out of his house a few days after his birthday while the rest of his family had been at the movies. Snuck him out of that house despite his unfortunate condition. The poor little boy who'd otherwise *never been allowed* to leave that house only to watch the world pass by outside his bedroom window. Including the neighborhood kids on their bicycles. The neighborhood kids who would sometimes wave at him as they passed by his lonely bedroom window. And sometimes not. Snuck him out, she had done. Snuck him out into a hazy afternoon sunshine rather like this very afternoon, in fact. In spite of his pale skin and blue jaundiced eyes and purple lips. Snuck him out for a banana split. Borrowing the boy's mother's car without telling her, taking the boy just a few blocks over to the local Dairy Queen where all the other neighborhood kids tended to congregate, arriving on their bikes.

He'd promised to stay in the car.

Only to disappear while she'd been inside.

*Poof.* Like magic. Just gone. The boy.

She'd found him a few frightful minutes later with the other kids around back. They were trying to teach him how to ride a bike. He had been wobbling around in circles, and laughing.

She'd never heard him laugh. Henry. The boy. Let alone laugh so joyfully like that. It was almost painful to listen to. That laughter. If she closed her eyes, it had almost sounded to her like tears.

Circling around, he'd been. Henry. Laughing.

Maybe even crying, too, in retrospect.

A bike one of the large kids had loaned him.

Silver. A gear shifter. Colorful piping.

One long black stripe down its crossbar maybe.

A sticker. Cartoonish lettering. HUFFY.

HUFFY, she believed it had said.

That sticker with the cartoonish lettering.

She pushed into the fence now with the memory, but the bike had somehow been *swallowed* into the forest undergrowth.

*Poof.* Like magic. Just gone.

Assuming it had ever been there at all.

Assuming she wasn't just seeing things.

Assuming she wasn't going crazy.

Then again, *maybe she was only going crazy if she couldn't convince herself she was just seeing things.* And so convince herself Emily did. And blinking hard, twitching really, put her back to those woods.

Put her back to those woods for now.

And any secrets they might very well contain.

For a mind as admittedly fertile as her own.

And returned from the beautiful garden into the giant beast of a house looming darkly over her and the garden behind it.

The giant beast of a house greeted her silently.

Its resident shadows welcoming her home.

# 17.

WHEN AN AFTERNOON NAP shrugged off her invitation, despite her exhaustion, Emily found herself sitting again upon that windowsill with the dusty old book she'd quietly pilfered from that almost hidden small bookcase in the dark little alcove below the steep attic staircase. Yearning the warm sunshine that had now moved off to the other side of the house, Emily considered taking the book out into the garden, but fretted the iron key would almost surely be missing from the back door despite the fact Ms. Vivian Dancemore had yet to leave her bedroom.

Instead, she grabbed a throw blanket from the end of the bed. And snuggled agreeably beneath it in the bedroom window.

The book was a story about mythical things.

Princes and princesses and knights. Elves, dwarves, and other creatures that fell into league with man. It involved a great quest. A grueling odyssey made more dangerous by shadowy creatures. Goblins, ogres, trolls, and serpents. And a clan of sister-witches.

Though she had always enjoyed such books, Emily had always felt a certain kinship, and thus an empathy, with such less desirable creatures forced to live in the shadows. To hunt and to scavenge in order to survive while their nemeses lived in castles and pretty little villages next to pretty little clear bubbling streams. She knew what it was like to feel unwanted. To be an outcast. A less than desirable. To be a thing without a proper home to call her very own.

An impediment to another's happiness.
To be misunderstood and ridiculed.
She secretly rooted for such undesirables.
For goblins, ogres, trolls, serpents, and witches.

To lay bare the obvious treacheries and the greed and the self-entitlement of the castle-dwellers and those from pretty little villages next to those pretty little clear bubbling streams.

Not that her wishes were ever granted.

For undesirables were undesirable for a reason. And that reason was to be *overcome* by those castle-dwellers and their sanctimonious lot. Undesirables were to be tricked, deceived, defeated. And, in far too many heinous cases, slayed. To be left rotting in the cold hard ground from which would only grow vile weeds with poisonous black flowers. An unsightly reminder of what they'd once been before they'd been tricked and deceived. Defeated. Slayed.

Still, she read such fanciful little books, relishing in their ability to steal her away from the here and now, the everyday, even as she secretly pined for a different ending. A happier ending.

A darker happier *ever after* ending.
For once, please. Just for once, thank you.
In the name of simple fairness. Justice.
Rather than this endless perversion.
This endless perversion called fairy tales.
These so-called allegorical tales of morality.

And yet, it was just too bad, Emily thought, and perhaps horribly ironic, the real world only too often *resembled such fiction.*

Such silly dreadful terribly-bigoted fiction.

It was just too bad, and perhaps horribly ironic, the real world only too often made heroes of the villains just like in the fairy tales. And only too often villains of those lost in the shadows.

Of those *forced* into the shadows.

Perhaps she would only read half the book, leave the story at the midpoint when the so-called villains, the undesirables, had their moment of glory. Leave it just before the castle-dwellers and those from pretty little villages next to pretty little clear bubbling streams regathered themselves and engaged in their malfeasance.

Perhaps she would just do that this time.
And perhaps she would probably not.
Unable to help herself even as she cringed.
As she wished for a different ending.

She read until the daylight faded and she could no longer read the words on the page without dipping her nose into the book and squinting, the worn pages of the dusty old book offering, as before, that sweet musky scent with just that mild hint of vanilla.

She relished that strange sweet smell.

Breathing it in as darkness fell on the world.

Eventually, her reverie was interrupted by the grousing of her stomach once more as the grandfather clock gonged below.

Six loud distinct bellowing gongs. Dinner.

*Gong, gong, gong, gong, gong...gong.*

She sighed and exited her bedroom.

She made certain to lock her bedroom door behind her before making her way past Ms. V's own locked bedroom door, if giving it hardly a glance tonight, not giving it the satisfaction, pushing down the foyer staircase in the dimness. Meaning to head for the kitchen only to find herself detouring into that parlor, instead. *Suddenly needing that phone. Needing to feel it in her hands again. Needing to hear his voice. Adam. Suddenly needing that more than anything else. Inside these black walls in this mad world gone so dark.* Thinking there might just be enough of a charge to offer that. If only for the briefest of moments. It would be enough. If she could just *hear* his lovely calming voice telling her everything would be okay. Telling her he'd forgiven her for the last time they'd really spoken. If he could just *whisper* into her ear as he'd always done lying in the dark as children while the rest of the foster house had been asleep. His long warm body pushed tightly against her own cold skin, causing him to shiver slightly in her arms.

As if she were carved from a block of ice.

"I'm summer, you're winter," he would tell her.

Shivering in the dark. Lying tightly against her. *Whispering* softly into her ear. As she'd have him do now. So very softly.

The outside world *fading away* as he held her.

The world becoming only just the two of them.

*I have control over my emotions. And I choose to feel at peace.*

Yes, she found herself detouring into the parlor.

Intending to find that letter opener *or any object* that might defeat that side table lock. To pick it open. Or to tear it open. Only to arrive at the side table and find its little drawer slightly ajar.

She pulled open the drawer to find those spectacles. The ones with the thin silver handle. Etched with that fleur-de-lis.

The house rules on their fancy stationary.

But her phone *absent*. Missing. Gone.
She blinked. Twitched. Annoyed.
She found its absence rude. Unacceptable.
*How dare the leprechauns vanish her phone like this.*
*It was one thing for them to slyly remove it from her bedroom per the silly house rules, but it was quite another to simply make it disappear.*
Now she was angry. Quite angry really.
This would have to be immediately rectified. This would have to be addressed promptly. *Tonight.* After dinner. During sherry. Period. She would address the absence of the phone and the need for a key to the front door. These were now non-negotiables.
Feeling better, stronger, more in control, she exited the parlor for the kitchen to find her supper waiting for her there.
A large plate of smothered pork chops.
Served with dirty rice and a cob of corn.
Things her grandmother used to make.
Usually with hot banana pudding.
Emily noticed, however, with chagrin, and a tiny nervous flutter in her belly, the antique drop-leaf serving table with its wooden stand and glass dome *were still missing* from the wall. Leaving behind that slight discoloration. Only that. And nothing more.
Sighing, still able to taste that lemon cake and chocolate torte, she, nevertheless, dove into her dinner only to find the pork slightly dry and the entire meal somewhat rather lukewarm.
She thought again of that apple. Mushy.
Those wilted greens. That stale lunch bread.
Thought again of that cake plate. Fork.
She would have to be more careful.
After all, now that she cared to peek, those impish little rusty padlocks were still on the pantry door and the fridge, too.
Suggesting they might not ever leave.
And so, despite the relative dryness of the pork chops and the lukewarm temperature of the entire meal itself, Emily still ate every last bite, not only because she was hungry, but because she did not wish to dare tempt the ire of *whomever* had made it for her.
She washed it all down with another glass of iced tea. The iced tea that was usually cold and heavenly sweet. But an iced tea Emily found to be tepid on this evening, the ice nearly melted away in the glass, and leaving the tea itself rather weak and bland.
Afterward, she washed every last dish.

Obediently washed her glass and utensils, too.

Placing them all to dry in the dish rack.

As always, straining belief at this point, there was no evidence of any pots or pans to suggest any cooking had actually been done in the kitchen. Nor any lingering aroma of such a thing. It was as if the food had just magically appeared right out of thin air.

Or, more likely, prepared elsewhere.

Emily was still pondering this (as she noticed the iron key was once again missing from that back door leading out into that deepening evening darkness, the night cold already leeching through the thick house walls around her) when she thought she perhaps heard the *distant ringtone of her phone*. Somewhere above her. Perhaps in her bedroom, she considered, already heading for the staircase.

The ringing seemed to grow slightly louder.

Slightly louder as she ascended the stairs.

As she ascended the stairs faster and faster.

Hurrying up the long narrow dimly-lit hallway.

Past the flickering parade of bronze sconces.

Out of breath, she unlocked her bedroom door, after fumbling with the key, to discern that ringing (which suddenly sounded altogether too faint now to be so very close) to be originating *from inside the wardrobe*. She pushed through the bedroom shadows and yanked open the wardrobe doors only to have the awful teasing ring cease. Suddenly and completely. Suggesting it had never been there at all. Perhaps. Maybe. Suggesting she'd only been hearing things.

She stood there. Quite flummoxed.

Later, as she waited for her nightly sherry invite, fighting every urge to knock on Ms. V's own bedroom door and demand that this *peculiar* silliness end, Emily drearily thought she could perhaps hear her phone again. Maybe. Ringing somewhere in the distance.

Somewhere inside this dark giant house.

Below her. Beside her. Above her. Elsewhere.

Faintly calling out to her. From inside the walls.

From inside the very skin of the house.

# 18.

EMILY REALIZED AS SHE AWOKE to a terrible shudder that she must have fallen asleep not long after returning to her bedroom after dinner. She awoke to hear that grandfather clock down in the parlor gonging eight in the evening and to a light knock on her bedroom door. *Ms. Vivian Dancemore.*

As she slowly rose to a sitting position on the bed, shaking off this terrible shudder, rubbing wearily at her weary eyes, she gradually became aware of a rather painful throbbing behind her right eye. The painful throbbing, as she rose to a sitting position, subsequently radiated across her entire skull and was accompanied by the uncomfortable sensation of feeling rather just a bit too warm all over. A feeling she was not altogether familiar with. Not at all.

*"I'm summer, you're winter," he would tell her. Adam. Whispering softly into her ear. Holding her in the night against his long warm body.*

This headache and the terrible warm feeling dove-tailed with a rather worrisome scratchiness deep in the back of her dry throat. A rather worrisome scratchiness that made it hard to swallow.

She sat there for a moment on the bed.

Sat there as that grandfather clock gonged.

As that one light knock faded to echo.

Wondering if she felt a little nauseous, too. Feeling her head swim as she finally stood. Her thin knees weak beneath her.

The terrible shudder grabbing at her again.

Shaking her. Shaking her from head to foot.

Perhaps it was just simple overtiredness, she thought drearily, trying to convince herself, swaying a little. *But perhaps it was something more, too. Something more, perhaps, than she wished to contemplate.*

Sighing, she pushed to the door, unlocking it with her key, the bolt once again making that loud clacking noise. Opening the door to find Ms. V standing in the long hall in that black dress.

"Good evening, Miss Emily," she said.

"Good evening, ma'am," Emily managed.

"I was wondering, Miss Emily, if you might care to join me in the parlor for a glass of sherry," Ms. V hushed to her.

Just as she'd done the previous evening.

As if this were a reenactment of that evening.

Offering Emily a prickly rush of *déjà vu*.

Something, déjà vu, she realized now, *that had been with her, more or less,* upon first entering this strange house days ago. As if *whatever was happening here* had somehow *already happened* just maybe.

Or, at the very least, was *simply fated to do so.*

"I'm sorry, miss," she said to the strange woman in the dimly-lit hall, finding herself hiding behind her half-open bedroom door. "But I don't feel well this evening. My regrets, ma'am."

Her tongue felt thick, too. Fuzzy.

She wondered if she was standing back the obligatory six feet. If she should be wearing her scarf. A mask. If it even freaking mattered without a window to be opened in this strange house.

*Stop-the-spread. Do-the-right-thing. Wear-a-mask.*
*Stay-at-home. Shelter-in-place. Alone-together.*

"Poppycock, Miss Emily," Ms. V said.

Emily almost smiled at that. Almost did.

The word, *poppycock*, a funny thing on Ms. V's tongue. Spoken with such vigor and with such sincerity. In this world undone by an invisible virus. A tiny microscopic invading alien race.

"Poppycock?" Emily heard herself repeat.

"Poppycock," this strange woman in the black dress said again as if Emily had just agreed with her. "You're out-of-sorts."

"I'm out-of-sorts, ma'am?"

"Quite, indeed, Miss Emily. Your body clock-- It's still adjusting to working the night. Throwing off your biorhythms."

"Is that so, ma'am? Biorhythms?"

Another quite funny word. *Biorhythms.*

"Fatigue, dear. Mental indexterity. Malaise."

The strange woman in the black dress standing in the dimly-lit hall delineated these conditions as if she were very familiar with all of them. As if she were forever haunted by all of them.

Her gray lifeless eyes turning white. Blinking.

A succession of hard twitching blinks.

Before finding Emily once again. Settling.

And slowly turning back to gray.

Emily followed the strange woman in her floating black dress down to the parlor. Just as she'd done the previous evening. There was a fire crackling softly in the small fireplace. As before. Its hazy shimmering light dancing about on those gray parlor walls.

Ms. V poured the glasses of sherry.

The faceted glasses catching the firelight, causing the sherry to twinkle. If still only dully. Still only a mimicry of its former cheeriness. As if that cheeriness had really only been but a façade.

Emily perched on the fuzzy blue armchair.

Ms. V settling on the chenille sofa.

Moreover, the sherry was no longer as sweet-tasting or bubbly in her nose. Nor dry and yeasty sliding down her throat as it she'd found it to be on her very first evening. *Rather, Emily found she could now barely taste it. The sherry flat and without any flavor on this night.*

The terrible shudder returned. A mini-earthquake.

Perhaps she really was *coming down with it* after all.

The thick walls of this strange house no protection. The virus having followed her in from the outside, making itself at home. She could feel that tickle in her throat again. A tickle now turning rather peppery, rising from all that terrible scratchiness in the very back of her throat as if the very back of her throat had been scrubbed hard with sandpaper and left raw and blistering sore. Her eyes instantly beginning to water as she fought back the urge to cough.

To cough and spill droplets into the air.

To spill out that tiny microscopic alien race.

That malignant invisible virus. *The Reaper Virus.*

She imagined Ms. V becoming terribly sick. The child. Curled into a small fetal ball. Curled into a small fetal ball up there in that dark attic above them. Coughing and sneezing and moaning. Overcome by a most dreadful fever. Body aches. And vomiting.

*Neither woman nor child able to leave the attic.*

*From midnight to dawn to midnight. Ad infinitum.*

*What would become of this strange woman and her even stranger alter ego should she become so sick? Invalid? And for that matter, what would become of herself,* Emily wondered, *if she were unable to attend to this strange woman and her even stranger alter ego? If she were trapped in her own bedroom coughing and sneezing and moaning with fever, body aches, and vomiting?*

*And what if matters turned truly dire? Deathly?*

*Respiratory distress? Pneumonia? For herself in this black house and for this strange woman and that child? --What would become of their peculiarity in such a circumstance? Would the spell be summarily broken, then?*

*Or would their peculiarity become even more peculiar?*

*More peculiar in sickness than in health?*

*And what could that possibly mean?*

The fire, near her, it suddenly felt unbearably too warm, crackling and spitting softly. She'd always felt *too cold.* A barren cold.

Had genuinely felt so her entire miserable life.

*"I'm summer, you're winter," he would tell her. Adam. Whispering softly into her ear. Holding her in the night against his long warm body.*

But now, with that painful throbbing behind her right eye, radiating across her entire skull, she felt as if a single thrown ember from that fire *might somehow ignite her* and that *she'd burst into flame like a wicker man. Burn, burn, burn.* Eventually crumbling to ash. Becoming *neither hot nor cold* like the ash in the morning fireplace.

*Ashes to ashes, dust to dust. Ashes, dust.*

Emily shuddered again. *As if her body might somehow just shake off this discomfiting heat. As if it were only a playful thing groping at her.*

Only to hear herself say: "I will need a key."

Her voice sounding fuzzy, too. Faraway.

Her tongue feeling thicker than ever.

"A key," Ms. V said, her gray eyes paling again.

Blinking. Twitching. Even as she grinned.

That grin, it looked rather unnatural and forced on her countenance as if it were being manipulated there. As if invisible puppet strings were forcing her to grin. Turning that grin morbid. As if she were on the precipice of more darkly amused laughter.

A darkly amused laughter painful to her.

As painful as that morbid-looking grin.

"To the front door, yes," Emily explained.

The grin *seemed to grow.* Stretch. Stretch most unnaturally across the woman's mouth. Looking more painful than ever, perhaps.

*Never show your teeth when you smile.*

Reminding Emily of Madelyn's lopsided grin.
*Clo-the eye-th. Dan-th with me. It-th eethee.*
"Anything else, Miss Emily?" the woman said.
As if anything could be granted. Or nothing at all.
"Yes, ma'am. Please. My phone, ma'am."
That painful grin stretched further. Falling.
Falling now. As if under its own terrible weight.
Resembling something more akin to a frown.
"Your phone, Miss Emily," she said.
The parlor shadows pushing in on them.
"It's missing. It's been misplaced, I'm afraid."
As if a maid had done such a thing.
Done such a thing only absent-mindedly.
And not out of any maliciousness.

"I can hear it ringing. In the walls," she explained rather lamely. Head really beginning to pound now, especially behind that right eye. Her skin feeling on fire as she shuddered even harder.

"In the walls. Ringing, Miss Emily."

"Misplaced," Emily said again, the peppery tickle in her throat suddenly filling her sinuses, causing her to gag, then finally cough. Only just managing to cough into the bent crook of her arm as she had been taught on TV. Her eyes bleeding water. Salty tears spilling down her round pale cheeks as the coughing grew worse.

A blistering hellfire in her lungs now.
The coughing fit seeming to last forever.
Her eyes blinking shut. Gushing more water.
The salt in the corners of her mouth.
Stinging the chapped skin there.

She was stunned to find the woman's pale hand resting on her knee when the coughing fit finally subsided. Long bony fingers.

Her head slowly lifted from the woman's hand.
Slowly lifted to find those pale-white eyes.
And that terrible painful morbid-looking grin.
The woman's hushed voice falling even lower now.
As if quite truly afraid of being overheard.

"As for your phone, Miss Emily," the woman said, barely audible. As if Emily were now only reading her lips. "I fear the house has it now. As it has you. As it has you now, Miss Emily."

*I fear the house has it now. As it has you.*
*As it has you now, Miss Emily.*

Despite the lack of volume in her whispering voice, Ms. Vivian Dancemore, Emily's most peculiar employer, appeared to offer this strange sentiment with very much the same vigor and with the same sincerity in which she'd pronounced *poppycock* earlier.

*Poppycock* to the idea of the virus trespassing.

The virus trespassing inside these dark strange walls.

The dark strange walls of this most peculiar house.

*That apparently now had her phone. And her as well.*

*As it has you. As it has you now, Miss Emily.*

*Whatever the hell that could possibly mean.*

Or, perhaps, Emily thought to herself, she really *did* have a fever and this rather strange ending to their conversation over sherry only just the dark whimsy of a *fever dream* and nothing more.

*But, if so, where had such a fever dream actually begun?*

*And, pray tell, where would such a fever dream finally end?*

# 19.

EMILY TUCKED HERSELF into a tight little ball on the bed, knees folded into her chest, shivering despite a warm sweat bubbling-up to the surface of her burning skin even as a rash of tiny hard gooseflesh broke out across her entire body. As if her poor shivering body simply knew not if it was hot or cold. A rash of tiny hard gooseflesh which somehow resembled to Emily scales maybe. Which made her think of this black house.

*This giant looming monster of a beast of a house.*

*Its dark scalloped shingles that only too closely resembled scales, too, amid its host of tall dark rectangular multi-paned windows that tended to stare silently out and inward like a congregation of many watchful black eyes.*

She had no memory of finishing her glass of sherry in the parlor. Just a vague memory of stumbling back upstairs, and the foyer staircase leaving her more than a touch out of breath, thinking she might need a wink of sleep before her midnight duties, and perhaps maybe an aspirin or two as she'd collapsed onto the bed.

The bedroom spinning. *Spinning. Spinning.*

She sat up gingerly now only to feel that throbbing return behind her right eye. Keeping slow rhythm with her discordant heartbeat. She sat there a long spell. Breathing. Just breathing.

Or at least trying to breathe normally.

Her lungs feeling heavy. Reluctant. That blistering hellfire of a peppery coughing fit from earlier scalding them, encouraging them to ooze with a dark fluid. And imagined such a dark fluid collecting in the bottom of her lungs and slowly rising. Filling them.

Filling them like black water balloons.

She found it was now difficult to even cough. The effort producing a *disquieting rattling sound*. Her body ached, too. Tender to the touch. As if somehow riddled with many invisible bruises.

*Maybe it was just allergies*, she thought desperately.

As she'd considered back on that bus to here. To this peculiar place seemingly at the very edge of the world. Of existence.

She'd always suffered from sinus pressure.

Associated migraines. General unwell feelings.

From winter molds. Early spring blooms.

Or so she tried to convince herself even though neither over-the-counter nor prescription allergy meds had ever seemed to *alleviate* such symptoms. Not even in the slightest, in retrospect.

Rather, they'd only seemed to *accentuate* them.

Somehow place them into even sharper focus maybe.

Which made her think of what Ms. V had said.

Her strange employer. The woman in black.

*Fatigue, dear...* she'd said. *Mental indexterity. Malaise.*

*Working the night. Throwing off her biorhythms.*

*Pulling her out-of-sorts. Any other explanation poppycock.*

*Suggesting this to her as her gray lifeless eyes had turned white.*

*Blinking. A succession of hard twitching blinks.*

*As if this woman had somehow known better than that, too. Had somehow known Emily had always preferred the night. Had done so ever since she'd been a small child and it, therefore, offered no explanation for any fatigue, mental indexterity, or malaise, either. That she'd always felt such things.*

*That such things had always been a part of her.*

*Fatigue. Mental indexterity. Malaise.*

*Rather like a black shroud over her difficult life.*

*And allergies be damned. If not poppycock.*

Yet this *was different*, wasn't it? Her burning skin. The scale-like gooseflesh. The painful throbbing behind her right eye. The black fluid filling her peppery lungs. These terrible body aches.

The scratchiness in the back of her dry throat.

The touch of nausea souring her stomach.

*So maybe the Grim Reaper had touched her, then. Reached out his dark hand and blithely tapped her on the shoulder when she wasn't looking.*

*The death rate at thirty percent and climbing.*

*But then again, it would be just like her to get overexcited. To overreact. To feel his hand. The Reaper. Blithely tapping her on the shoulder.*
*Just like her to think the worst had finally come.*
She closed her eyes. Sighed. Lungs rattling softly.
Even as she tried to ignore that soft rattling.
*I have control over my emotions. And I choose to feel at peace.*
*I have control over my emotions. And I choose to feel at peace.*
She embraced the simple mantra. Sighing again.
The simple mantra her grandmother had taught her.
Had taught her for when she became overexcited.
And for a moment believed she could smell the woman. Lilac and chicken soup. And feel her standing right there beside her.
Her late grandmother. So far gone from this earth.
Yet the feathery touch of her hand touching her own.
She sighed a final time. Coming back into herself.
Feeling more solid again. More grounded.
Still, she made a startled mewling noise when the door rattled. As if death were just on the other side of that door. As if the Grim Reaper himself were standing out in that narrow dimly-lit hall with the plum-colored carpet *requesting her company for all of eternity.*
Grimacing at her foolishness, she pushed off the bed. Pushed unsteadily to her feet. Only to then find herself holding her head in her hands. That throbbing behind her right eye intensifying terribly again as her heart fluttered wildly in her chest. Spasming.
She felt somewhat like a bobble-head. As if her neck muscles had grown tired like old rubber bands and rendered useless.
Not so very different from her legs beneath her.
Offering their own imitation of wet noodles.
*Perhaps death would be a mercy...* she then considered. *A kindness. Perhaps, rather than suffer any longer, she'd just take the Reaper's black hand. Perhaps he'd even dance with her. Dance with her as she no longer felt a thing. As she floated down the narrow dimly-lit hall like Ms. V herself.*
*Which made her think of the girl, of course.*
*"Dance with me," she'd said in the dark attic.*
*"It's easy," the odd girl had promised her.*
*Spinning. Her shadow rising on the wall. Falling.*
*Dan-th with me, she'd said. It-th eethee.*
And for just a moment, for just the fleeting briefest of passing moments, Emily thought she could hear a distant music. Like that of an approaching carnival or circus. And found herself imagining a

long train of cars slowly slipping along the rails into a small town in the middle of the country in the middle of a dark night.

Ferrying clowns and freaks and wild beasts.

Big-top tents and kettle corn and funnel cakes.

Fried pickles and strange foreign meats on sticks.

Booths featuring games of chance and skill.

Balloons, banners, and clouds of confetti.

Calliope music, it was, this music she heard for just a moment, for just the fleeting briefest of passing moments. But this music in the walls of the house, rather than played at a bright lively tempo as was the tradition of such music, carnival or circus music, seemed to be playing at the wrong speed. Warped and distorted. Stretched like cold taffy. As if she were hearing it from beneath dark water.

As if her ears were also filling with dark fluid.

Its tune unnaturally slowed down. Perverted.

Into something macabre and unnatural.

Something dark and rather sinister.

And for some reason, perhaps because of the corrupted music itself, perhaps because of her morbidity, she found herself remembering that strange antique music box in the attic darkness.

Almost hidden in the shadows it had been.

Almost hidden there on the other side of the room.

Almost hidden despite its inherent garishness.

Beneath where the attic roof slanted low.

The antique music box with *a dull glass-topped lid mimicking a red and white circus big-top tent*. And how in the darkness of the attic she'd imagined, almost forlornly, how that antique music box might sing should that dull glass-topped lid finally be lifted opened.

Perhaps it was finally singing now.

Or perhaps she was only imagining it.

The distant music she thought she was hearing for just a moment now in the night, for just the fleeting briefest of passing moments, only just a ragged, if fading edge of that *fever dream*.

Regardless, it had been preceded by one light knock, she realized now. *One light knock causing her locked bedroom door to rattle.*

And suddenly, without any memory of *unlocking* the door, lost in this fleeting briefest of passing moments that seemed to pull and stretch unnaturally now like cold taffy, found herself following Ms. V in her long black dress up the narrow dimly-lit hall.

Ms. V seemed to *float higher* than usual.

Feet not touching the plum-colored carpet.
Revealing the bare soles of her pale feet tonight.
As if her feet were clawing through the air.
And never quite touching the ground.

Then suddenly, in yet another terrible feverish-jerk forward in time (without any memory of locking Ms. V inside the attic, as was her charge), Emily found herself *back in her bedroom* again, lying fully clothed beneath the bedsheets as she was wont to do, the bedroom door locked, and the grandfather clock gonging below her.

Twelve long and sustained gongs.

Midnight. Further evidenced by her watch.

Her late mother's watch. Parisienne. Art Deco.

The blue-lacquered hour and minute hands pointing at twelve o'clock. The watch hands and small Art Deco numbers housed in a 14K white gold case with a unique red tone enamel pattern.

An antique her mother had never removed.

Only to have it removed *from her* postmortem.

Leaving behind a pale ring of skin about her wrist.

A ghostly impression in that casket with her.

Emily blinked, twitched really, as those twelve long and sustained gongs faded to echo in the bones of the dark house.

The thick house walls still trembling long after.

*You will find the girl in the attic after midnight.*
*You are to be the night sitter, Miss Emily.*

But rather than heading directly to the attic after releasing herself from her bedroom with her key, Emily found herself descending the staircase to the foyer, then hurrying down the narrow corridor past the parlor to the kitchen, almost taking the corner too fast in the shadows, nearly banging her throbbing bobble-head into the dark wooden door frame, her feet, *despite feeling somewhat like they were floating themselves, along with the rest of her,* slapping noisily on the stone floor as she desperately tried not to dwell on the disconcerting fact that confusion and disorientation were hallmarks of the virus.

Instead, she focused on the kitchen table.

The kitchen table before her in the dimness.

Relieved to find the silver tray, the very one from the previous evening, was no longer empty. Rather, it showcased a glass pitcher of milk, two china cups on saucers, and a large white serving platter replete with neatly arranged bite-sized finger sandwiches.

Delicate finger-sandwiches filled with jam.

There was also an array of freshly-baked frosted ginger cookies *if no perfume of any such thing in the air, the oven cold and dark.*

And lastly, a silver vase with white flowers.

Large white whorled flowers with pink pistils.

She leaned over and sniffed the flowers.

Thought perhaps they smelled faintly of apricot.

Lush and sweet, calming slightly her nerves.

With a deep sigh, she picked-up the silver tray at the side handles, careful not to disturb its neatly arranged contents, and carried it from the kitchen, up the stairs, through the narrow dimly-lit hall past her bedroom and the tiny dark bathroom to the attic staircase. She paused with it at the bottom of the staircase, listening.

If she strained her ears, she thought, perhaps, she could hear, if only very faintly, that strange macabre calliope music again. Rising and falling beyond the thick black oak door. Looping over and over again. And, perhaps, the faint shuffle of many feet.

Of many tiny cavorting drunken little feet.

Well, maybe not cavorting. Maybe *dragging*.

*Shuffling* and *jerking* and *scraping* and *straggling*.

Which made her think of all those dolls.

*All those dolls with their own watchful dark eyes.*

*Dark eyes but for that peculiar red-headed little thing.*

*That red-headed little thing with dirty blue eyes.*

*Staring at her in the morning dimness as the other dolls had silently slept. Actually seeming to grin at her. Animate. Reminding her of that strange black cat. Marbles. Its Cheshire grin. Only that red-headed's grin being sad. Forlorn. Maybe. As if perhaps warning her of something. That sad forlorn grin.*

*And for a moment found herself rather dissuaded.*

*Rather dissuaded, and maybe more than a bit overexcited, by what might be waiting for her on just the other side of that thick black oak door.*

*Dragging. Shuffling. Jerking. Scraping. Straggling.*

*Dan-th with me,* the child had said. *It-th eethee.*

And she nearly turned around despite her charge.

Only to suddenly hear *nothing at all*. The silence deafening once more. As it certainly had always been. Her overexcited imagination getting the better of her, especially given her un-wellness.

*Un-wellness. Her mother had been unwell, hadn't she?*

*Of course her poor silly mother hadn't any virus to blame.*

As if moving in a dream, a *fever dream*, and at the mercy of the dream itself, Emily found herself taking the final steps in the darkness two at a time as if her feet were no longer her own, but being guided by another, the silver tray jostling about, the pitcher of milk nearly sliding off of it, the china cups and saucers clattering against the silver vase with those apricot-smelling flowers, the neat presentation of all those bite-sized jam finger-sandwiches and frosted ginger cookies ruined. Balancing the tray on a hip with one hand, Emily saw herself then unlock the attic door with the other hand, shove it open, only to realize she'd *not remembered to knock first* as that door, rusted hinges welcoming her once again with their familiar protesting whine, swung open, revealing the soft golden glow of that carriage light and the resident attic shadows. The resident attic shadows turning darker and darker still like a *black undertow* the further they slipped away from that softly glowing carriage light.

She stepped into the attic with the tray.

The many things sliding and clattering again.

Yes, she stepped into the attic with the silver tray only to accept, her trepidation flowering, she was inadvertently defying *another* house rule. The rule about *eating outside the house kitchen.*

Defying it out of no maliciousness, of course.

Defying it because she feared the child being outside the attic for another night with her antics. Disappearing as she had into the walls of the house *only to reappear* as she had in this very room.

But what if she *had not reappeared*, the child?

What if this giant beast of a house *had taken her, too?*

Then again, *perhaps the house had already done so.*

*As it has you. As it has you, Miss Emily.*

Emily pushed aside the thought. Such a slippery thought even as those creepy-ass dolls stared at her with their dark eyes.

Stared at her from their long dark shelves.

*But for that red-headed doll with those dirty blue eyes.*

*Dirty blue eyes and that sad forlorn-looking grin.*

For the red-headed little thing was *absent* tonight.

Absent on this evening. Just after midnight.

Gone. Missing from its own place on the shelf.

A dark hole amongst the other creepy-ass dolls.

*As if the red-headed doll had just gotten up and left.*

And it wasn't the only thing rather most terribly absent on this particular evening, Emily discovered, at just after midnight.

Madelyn, the child, was *also missing.*

Inexplicably and disquietingly missing.

Emily carefully set down the silver tray on the small cot in the soft golden glow of the carriage light, then pushed closed the heavy attic door, those rusted hinges whining even more loudly now, as if screaming softly. She then used her attic key to lock the attic door *from the inside*. Thinking Madelyn's *absence* might very well be another incorrigible little game of this incorrigible little girl. *An incorrigible little girl who might cleverly use the resident shadows of the attic to just perhaps slip like a shadow herself right out the otherwise open attic door* when Emily had her back turned or her attention otherwise distracted.

The lock made a deep echoing noise as the bolt slid noisily into place. The room suddenly feeling very small with the door shut. The resident shadows now moving about seemingly. Restless.

That *black undertow* wishing to *grab at her maybe*.

To grab at her this time *and perhaps never let her go*.

But instead, like a receding black tide, the shadows revealed to her a *short narrow door* set into the far wall across the small room.

*A short narrow door. For a small person. A child maybe.*
*A short narrow door she had never noticed before.*
*A short narrow door that had never been there before.*
*Of course it hadn't. Because this was maybe only still a dream.*
*Maybe only still a most overexcited fever of a dream after all.*
*And she, perhaps, back in bed waiting for midnight.*

The short narrow door was set into the wall beside the antique music box with the dull glass-topped lid mimicking a red and white circus big-top tent and the old streamer trunk with the thick leather straps and heavy buckles upon which the music box sat. The door's outline *nearly invisible* in the darkness on the far side of the attic, but yet also so very obvious now that she had finally noticed it.

And suddenly she felt herself *floating* again.

*Floating* toward the short narrow door.

Arriving before it, feet once again settling on the floor, Emily found the very odd door to be *nearly a foot shorter than herself*. A door she'd have to probably *turn sideways to maybe squeeze through*.

The door was fashioned with *a silver knob and a silver keyplate that appeared to be oversized -- if only because of the truncated size of the door itself*. The silver knob and the silver keyplate were embellished with more of that *flowery fleur-de-lis*. Not unlike the antique grandfather clock in the parlor with its own accented marquetry or the thin silver handle of Ms. Vivian Dancemore's kooky antique reading spectacles.

But as she peered closer at the design--

Emily became less and less certain it depicted stylized black lilies as was the tradition of such *fleur-de-lis* ornamentation. Rather, as she peered closer in the dimness, her eyes blinking, twitching really, she gradually came to realize what she'd initially mistaken for black petals were actually, perhaps, the *flared black hoods of dragons.*
*Flared black hoods framing gold spheroid eyes. Fangs.*
And *further realized*, in retrospect, the antique grandfather clock in the parlor, and Ms. V's antique reading spectacles with their thin silver handle, shared the very same *motif*. And that, *furthermore,* maybe, that intricate stenciling of black roses amid the furious tangle of sharp thorns on that ceramic coffee pot in the kitchen was actually *the black profile of a flying winged-beast -- the furious tangle of sharp thorns a spiny coiled tail. Not unlike the flying winged-beasts of her recent nightmare (a nightmare now finding refuge inside this fever dream). A nightmare precipitated by that peculiar dragon bell and this strange house. A strange house that probably had such peculiar motifs hidden all about it if one cared to notice or if the house cared for one to notice them. Not unlike this odd little door.*
*This odd little door with its silver door knob.*
*And its equally odd accompanying silver keyplate.*
Emily saw herself reaching down for the silver knob, thinking, if in an absent dreamlike way, this odd little door perhaps explained Madelyn's otherwise inexplicable absence from the attic.
That perhaps the little girl was *beyond it.*
Most naughtily snickering in a small dark closet.
In yet another illicit game of hide-and-seek.
*There is to be no hide-and-seek. Rule #5.*
Well, then, she could put an end to this, Emily thought to herself as her hand settled on that silver knob only to find the knob as cold as ice. Her hand quite nearly slipping from its slick surface *as if the thing were actually made of ice.* As if the silver knob might desire to keep undisturbed *whatever* hid behind the short narrow door.
*A whatever that might be in there with the little girl.*
*Having coaxed her into its dark lair beyond the door.*
*Holding her very close to it. Whispering into her ear.*
*And causing her, perhaps, to naughtily snicker.*
*The child. Madelyn. Sometimes Maddy.*
And for a moment, Emily paused her hand on the silver knob, maybe *not wishing to disturb* this *whatever* hiding beyond the short narrow door in this darkest corner of the room. A *whatever* that might wish to remain undisturbed even as it might also seek to suggest its

existence to her, but then saw *her hand turning as if of its own accord* the slick silver knob that had quite nearly slipped from her grasp.

The knob turning easily enough in the end.

But the short narrow door itself *refusing* to budge.

*Of course*, she thought. *Of course this odd little door was locked.*

*And without any key to satisfy her most terrible curiosity.*

*The accompanying silver keyplate most terribly empty.*

Still, she thought to perhaps try knocking.

This being only a *fever dream* with its own rules.

*You are to please knock on all doors before entering.*

She saw her hand then lift and knock and heard those knocks echoing deeply inside the wall *beyond this odd little door* as if the space beyond it might be an impossibly large and cavernous place.

And not just a simple small dark closet.

She put her ear to the door to listen.

To listen to her knocks echo into that void.

And thought she maybe *heard* a naughty snicker.

*Madelyn or something only pretending to be a child.*

Only to then hear herself say to it: *Marco.*

*There is to be no hide-and-seek. Rule #5.*

Before hearing it reply as clear as a bell: *Polo.*

Causing her to jump. To quite startle.

Not because she'd not expected a response--

This being a strange *fever dream* after all.

*But only because this response had not come from beyond the short narrow door. Rather, because this response had come from directly behind her.*

Emily found herself turning about dizzily. Turning about dizzily to discover *Madelyn seated on the small cot back across the room.* Her thin legs outstretched. Her back pushed against the wall below her collection of doodles. A big lopsided smile. Tiny mouth covered in thick red jam. Her lips, chin, even the tip of her tiny nose.

Smeared with the thick red sticky stuff.

As if she'd been sitting there for a while now.

Sitting there quite happily stuffing her little pie hole.

Stuffing it with those jam finger-sandwiches.

Marbles, the cat, meanwhile, sat contently on her lap, greedily licking at Madelyn's jammy little fingers, eyes half-closed in ecstasy, as Madelyn, her large gold eyes twinkling rather merrily in the soft golden glow of that carriage light just above her, whispered:

"You locked the door. This you daren't do."

# THE NIGHT SITTER

*You locked the door. Thi-th you daren't do. Thi-th.*
She, of course, meant the attic door.
And not this mysterious short narrow door.
Emily felt her head swim dizzily again.
"And why is that?" Emily heard herself say rather than telling Madelyn, the child, the truth. That she'd done it to keep her inside the room. To keep her from disappearing into the house.
Disappearing once more into its very walls.
*But who was to say she wouldn't just do so, anyway?*
*Who was to say this odd little door that was never here before even as it somehow existed now wouldn't open just for the child? Wouldn't provide for her its missing key? Allowing her to disappear into the house walls again?*
Madelyn's spectral gold eyes sparkled even brighter.
As if she could read Emily's thoughts and was amused.
As if she had a secret. This little girl. *Thi-th.*
A most terrible awful secret, precipitating bubbling laughter to rise now in her small narrow chest and causing the girl's shadow on the wall to shimmy about as if trying to quite tear itself *from the little girl.* As if her shadow were trying to free itself and escape.
As if her shadow could do such a thing.
And somehow maybe take the little girl with it.
*That part of her that was still just that little girl.*
Perhaps Emily asked her out loud about such shadows and little girls and odd doors in walls that *appeared out of nowhere after having never been there before* Or at least about secrets. That throbbing behind her right eye making it very difficult to think clearly now. Or perhaps this queer little girl sitting before her *could* just simply read her mind after all. A rather most unsettling thought in itself.
For Madelyn, the child, said to her:
Singing it in a playful, if teasing melody:
"The-crets, the-crets are no fun..."
"The-crets, the-crets can hurt thumb-one..."
The lopsided grin growing ever more lopsided.
Painted by the sticky red blood-like jam.
"Secrets," Emily repeated, slowly nodding.
As if the word were a clue to a *larger riddle.* Perhaps to the very *largest riddle of all.* The largest riddle that *explained all the riddles.*
Wanting to feel the word in her mouth.
Even as all this felt more and more like a *fever dream.*
Just a most crazy and befuddling *fever dream.*

She closed her eyes for an extended beat.

Trying to feel the pillow on the back of her head.

A warm blanket pulled over her still-sleeping body maybe.

Listening for that clock below her to gong midnight.

Only to hear *Madelyn's shadow moving on the wall*. Yes, if she were being completely honest with herself, Emily thought she could hear just that. She really was ill. Quite out of her head. Delirious.

Her eyes slid open to find the cot empty.

But for the silver tray and its assorted items.

Including the remnants of those jam sandwiches.

A bubbling laughter jerked her head left, then right.

A shadow moved along the wall. A shadow seemingly dispossessed of any body. Only to reveal Madelyn at the toy chest.

That cat wrapping itself around her legs. Purring.

Madelyn's thin legs pale-white below her white nightie.

The white nightie billowing like a large white bell.

Billowing even more as she subsequently spun about.

Pirouetting. Head back. White ribbons spinning.

Sending the black cat scurrying off into the darkness.

Marbles. That infernal little devil of a beast.

Until Emily could only see its dark green almond-shaped eyes. Blinking languidly as those eyes stared out at her from the darkness with disinterest. As if already knowing what was to come. The answers to all the riddles. Large and small. And bored by the simple inevitably of it all. Even as the black cat could not quite bring itself to look away. Just in case there might be a surprise in store.

A dark and rather quite delicious surprise.

At any rate, Madelyn, the child, had now stopped madly spinning, though her right knee remained at a clean ninety degree angle, her bare right foot hanging in the air, perfectly balanced--

As she then delved down into the toy chest.

Digging through its shadowy contents. The old wooden yo-yo spilling out from the chest and rolling around in a big circle on the floor, dragging out its long string like a frayed intestine as that child dug past a tin kaleidoscope with a cracked lens, a rubber-band paddle boat with NEATO! painted on its stern, a cowboy cap gun with a decayed leather holster (that smelled faintly of mold), a pile of old wooden blocks, and a collection of antique board games in severely faded cardboard boxes, their once colorful illustrations turned *nearly invisible* by the unrelenting passage of time. Familiar board games like Backgammon and Parcheesi. And terribly unfamiliar ones with funny-sounding names like Tiddlywinks, Husker Do?, Fun At The Circus, Wa Hoo, and How Silas Popped The Question.

And then she was *half-hidden* in the toy chest.

Her little tummy on its edge. Madelyn. The child.

Her white-ribboned head vanished from view.

Small pale bare feet high-up in the air.

And for a moment Emily was certain the toy chest would *swallow the little girl whole* and that she'd dig desperately for that little girl through the toy chest's deep shadowy contents *only to find its freaking bottom fell right through this attic floor and into a dark void not unlike the one hidden behind that odd short narrow door maybe* from which Emily herself would only just manage not to topple as her own feet lifted briefly, dangerously, off these floorboards, and gravity in all its dark humor tempted her toward that black abyss. Yes, she'd discover as she just managed to secure her own feet back to the floor that she'd recovered nothing more of the little girl than a stray white ribbon.

Fluttering in her hand, it'd be, this stray ribbon.

As the girl *tumbled down* into that darkness beyond.

*Tumbled down* into that most terrible dark void.

Calling out her name. Or *Polo* to her *Marco*.

Perhaps with that same awful bubbling laughter.

Full of a dark mischief, perhaps. Attempting to trick her down into that darkness even as the child knew she'd not follow. Promising to *come back for her*, perhaps, when her back was turned to it.

When Emily was weaker. Her guard down.

The void always there. Always waiting for her.

But Madelyn, the child, eventually reappeared, having secured in her pale right hand whatever it was she'd been searching for.

She slipped down from the chest to the floor. Sitting Indian-style. Placing the thing before her. The thing she'd been desperately searching for. Her narrow back leaning against the toy chest.

"Sit," she said to Emily. "Please." *Thit. Plea-th.*

Emily sighed. Found herself doing just that.

Mimicking the child. Sitting Indian-style.

So very tired. Not feeling herself. Skin too warm.

Meanwhile, the black cat had circled back to the small cot and was now helping itself to milk from the pitcher. Slurping indelicately at it as the soft golden carriage light slowly revealed to Emily the thing the child had pulled from the bottom of the toy chest.

Revealing it to be a *small dark burlap sack*.

The small dark burlap sack looked rough to the touch. With a flourish of more gothic-calligraphy hand-painted in a sallow yellow. Barely legible as if done a very, very long time ago, indeed.

It read: *Bag of Frights and Delights.*

Then, most cryptically: *Truth-sayer.*

Before finally: *Test Your Family, Friends, and Neighbors.*

A novelty item. A most macabre thing.

"Truth-sayer. Clever, isn't it?" the child said.

*Truth-thayer. Clever. Ith-nt it. Thit. Plea-th. The-crets.*

"Truth-sayer. Quite clever, I suppose," Emily agreed with the little girl even as she felt a slight chill touch her feverish skin.

"It reads your mind," Madelyn then said, little voice falling to a dramatic whisper. Not unlike her peculiar mother over sherry.

*Thit. Plea-th. Ith-nt it. Truth-thayer. The-crets. Read-th.*

"And how do you suppose it does that?" Emily said.

Madelyn's lopsided smile grew. "Show you." *Thow you.*

She slid a tiny pale hand into the small dark burlap sack.

Those gold eyes sparkling wildly now like fireflies.

"Ask me anything. Anything at t'all, Emily." *A-thk.*

"Anything at *t'all?* OK, then. Let me think."

"Don't think. Just ask, Emily," she said. *Just a-thk.*

Emily glanced at that short narrow door in the shadows. Only to hear herself ask, instead: "Would you like a ginger cookie?"

The ginger cookies untouched on the silver tray.

The silver tray across the small room on that small cot.

Madelyn groaned. Rolled her firefly gold eyes.

"Boring," she said. "Too easy. Dumb." *Ee-thee.*

"You want me to ask you another question."

"Don't think. Just ask, Emily. Just ask." *A-thk.*

"OK. Do you miss the sunlight, Madelyn?"

The rather insensitive question just kind of popped out of her mouth as if she had a plastic ring in the middle of her back and the old house had yanked on that ring, pulling on an attached cord, and thereby commanding her to ask such a terribly insensitive question as if she were a doll preprogrammed to ask just such a thing.

A stupid Chatty-Cathy doll or something.

Inanimate and brainless and stupid.

*Still, didn't those gold eyes seem to sparkle brighter still? As if this peculiar child had been waiting for perhaps just that very question, indeed?*

The black cat had stopped slurping.
It was lazily flicking its tail now. But watching.
Watching incuriously. But watching all the same.
As if that dark and rather delicious surprise it sought might be in the offing after all if it were just patient enough. For Marbles had to know better than anyone that the poor little girl had not seen the sunlight for some time now. For how long Emily simply could not know, of course, not without knowing what had happened.

What had *happened* to this poor little girl.
What had imprisoned her in this small attic.
At the top of this giant beast of a house.
What had imprisoned here to *only the night*.
Perhaps there would finally be answers here.
Perhaps the little girl would *confess them*.
Untie the riddles like so many tight knots.
Perhaps Emily had only needed to ask. Make a game of it with this child's game. This macabre child's game offered to her.
In the form of this small dark burlap sack.
The one in which Madelyn, the child, still had her hand tucked deeply inside. Almost to her elbow. Her small pale hand *well-hidden* beyond an intervening curtain of black felt. The intervening curtain of black felt concealing *whatever the peculiar bag might contain*.
Whatever it was inside that might *divine truth*.
The thought of which produced another slight chill.
A nasty little chill that now *wiggled* under Emily's feverish skin. A nasty little wiggling of a chill she did her best to ignore.

*Frights and Delights...* the bag said. *Truth-thayer.*
*Test your Family, Friends, and Neighbors.*
"Sunlight," Madelyn said softly. *Thun-light.*
"Yes, sunlight, child," Emily repeated.
Madelyn leaned toward Emily over the small dark burlap sack, her little voice falling again to that dramatic whisper, if singing now in a haunting droll of a melody: *"The sun was shining on the sea. Shining with all his might. He did his very best to make the billows smooth and bright. And this was odd because it was the middle of the night."*

The words sounded rather quite unreasonably familiar to Emily despite the fact they presented yet just another riddle. Unable to immediately identify them, she said: "I don't understand."

*Thun. Thy-ning. All hith might. Odd. Middle of the night.*
That lopsided smile grew more lopsided still.

Her small pale hand slipping even further down into the small dark burlap sack, she went on: "*The moon was shining sulkily because she thought the sun had got no business to be there after the day was done. It's very rude of him,*" she lamented, singing, "*to come and spoil the fun.*"

*Moon. Thy-ning. Thulkily. Thun. No bith-neth.*
*After the day wha-th done. Rude of him. Th-poil fun.*

"Is that so?" Emily said, leaning back now.

Sensing that perhaps she *ought to lean back*. Suddenly not knowing *what might come out* of that dark burlap sack before her. And just then, the child's small pale hand quite suddenly *flew out* of the small dark burlap sack. Clutching *something* very tightly in its palm.

Emily instinctively cringed with anticipation.

Only to watch that small pale hand open.

And reveal *nothing*. Reveal nothing at *t'all* there.

Nothing at *t'all* anyway but a slant of moonlight.

Or maybe it was just that trespassing sun.

Caught now in the palm of her hand.

And with that, her childish voice still that dramatic little whisper of thing, Madelyn, the child, continued with that eerie little lopsided grin on her round pale face: "*The sea was wet as wet could be. The sands were dry as dry. You could not see a cloud, because no cloud was in the sky. No birds were flying overhead. There were no birds to fly. In a wonderland they lie. Dreaming as the days go by. Dreaming as the summer die.*"

*Thee. Wet a-th wet could be. Thand-th dry a-th dry.*
*No cloud wha-th in tha-kie. No bir-th flying overhead.*
*No bird-th to fligh. In a wonderland they lie.*
*Dreaming a-th day-th go by. A-th thummer die.*

And it was then Emily finally had it. Finally placed the unreasonably familiar words. Realizing where they'd been made *known* to her. It being so very apparent once she had it. It was Alice. Alice in her Wonderland, of course. A book Emily's mother had read to her over and over again, among other such classics. But *Alice in Wonderland* being her most absolute favorite. Alice in her strange Wonderland. Almost as if this child had known it. *As if she could.*

Which caused Emily to glance at that silly cat.

That silly black cat watching her so incuriously.

As if it might have an explanation for her.

*We're all mad here. I'm mad. You're mad…* the silly cat seemed to remind her haughtily. Its dark green almond-shaped eyes twinkling rather madly in the soft golden glow of that carriage light.

"We're certainly that, I suppose," Emily agreed.
As if the silly black cat had actually spoken out loud.
Only to hear herself then quietly ask the child:
"What's behind that odd door over there?"
Apropos enough given Alice in her Wonderland.
Given Alice's *own odd door at the bottom of that rabbit hole*. A door which had been *impassable*, but not *impossibly impassable*. Not if Alice read the directions and was *directly directed in the right direction*.
Or so the door knob had advised young Alice.
That strange magical talking door knob.
Something or another to that effect, anyway, in that classic of a book Emily's mother had read to her over and over again.
Emily glanced at the door again, *almost invisible* in the shadows, just to be sure it *was* still there. That it had not disappeared.
As if a door could do that. Could just vanish.
*But why not, if it could somehow suddenly just appear?*
*Could suddenly just appear in the attic wall out of nowhere.*
*Suddenly just appear with its silver knob and keyplate.*
"You're turn," Madelyn only said. Just that.
And held open the small dark burlap sack for Emily *to stick her hand deeply into*. Emily hesitated not only because she was miffed the child had not answered her question about the door, but as if Emily somehow intuitively understood she was not cagey enough *to fool whatever it was that might lie in wait deep inside that bag*. That she, unlike the child, possessed not the acumen to confuse it with a clever riddle. Assuming that was what the peculiar child had done.
"Curiosity often leads to trouble," she heard herself say.
And thought herself rather clever for saying it.
The child winked at the quote from Alice in her Wonderland, but only extended the small dark burlap sack ever closer to Emily. Quietly prompting her now with: "Curioser and curioser."
*Curi-a-ther and curi-a-ther.* Indeed, Emily thought.
And found her rather treacherous right hand, as if she never quite really had a choice in the end, *slipping into* the small dark burlap sack. Pushing past that intervening curtain of soft black felt. Then down into a warm and fuzzy-feeling darkness beyond it.
Hm. Just a warm and fuzzy-feeling darkness.
Perhaps this was only just a game after all.
A silly child's game requiring only imagination.
Perhaps she ought to just play along.

"Ask me anything. Anything at t'all, child," she said, imitating Madelyn from only a moment ago, including her enthusiasm.

"Anything at t'all? OK, then, Emily. Let me think."

Imitating Emily from only just a moment ago.

Madelyn scrunched her little pale forehead in deep concentration as if she were truly trying to come up with a question.

"Would you like a ginger cookie?" she tried, teasing.

"Boring," Emily teased back. "Too easy. Dumb."

"You want me to ask you another question." *A-thk.*

"Don't think. Just ask, Madelyn. Just ask."

*Boring. Too ee-thee. Dumb. Just a-thk. A-thk.*

The child's pale forehead scrunched once more.

"OK," she said. "But remember it reads your mind."

"I remember, child. It reads my mind." *Read-th.*

"And you daren't not tell the truth, Emily."

"I suppose I haven't a choice, do I?" she said, offering a shrug of foreboding as her treacherous hand *pushed even deeper into the small dark burlap sack through that intervening curtain of black felt.*

Meanwhile, she could feel all those dolls on those dark shelves watching her *even more closely*, but for that dirty blue-eyed red-headed doll that was most mysteriously absent. The dolls having seemingly *turned* ever so slightly in her direction, their dark eyes peering at her in the gloom with the same incuriousness as that black cat.

*But yet sensing something out of the ordinary.*
*Something that might spell them of their boredom.*
*Or was there something else behind those dark eyes?*
*Something that spoke to the opposite of boredom, perhaps?*
*As if they could not look away even if they wanted to?*

Emily sighed. Shaking the thought from her head.

And said again: "Ask me anything. Anything at t'all."

It was a silly child's game. That. Nothing more.

Madelyn, the child, nodding, the lopsided grin frozen there on her face, the red jam still sticky on her fingers and stuck in the corners of her mouth, finally asked her question. It was a question that suggested the entire purpose of this obnoxious game was a ruse to simply ask this question. *A-thk.* This guileful little question.

"Is your name *really Emily*, Emily?" she said. *I-th.*

Emily froze in the shadowy attic dimness.

Wondering if she'd heard the question correctly.

*I-th your name really Emily, Emily?...* she'd said.

"What a silly question that is," Emily responded.
*But already beginning to slide her hand from the dark sack.*
*Sliding it toward the surface perhaps just a little too quickly.*
*Sensing she should perhaps do so before it was too late.*
While adding in a whisper, again thinking herself rather clever, yet another riddle of an *Alice in Wonderland* quote: "It's no use going back to yesterday because I was a different person then."
*But as her hand slid back toward the bag opening, toward that intervening curtain of black felt, she felt a rush of something moving, slithering terribly, deep inside the small dark burlap sack. Her hand moved faster still, but moved not nearly fast enough in the end. As this terrible slithering something suddenly struck at her. From deep inside that dark bag. Snatching at her.*
*A mouthful of sharp little spiny needles.*
*The spiny needles sinking deeply into her flesh, reminding her of a moray eel. The thick slick monsters from the ocean deep. Creatures that lived in dark coral reefs and snatched at unsuspecting divers with razor-sharp teeth. And not just one set of teeth, but a second set deeper inside the jaw like an alien.*
Emily cried out in pain, jerking her hand.
*But those little spiny needles only sunk deeper into her hand.*
*Yanking her hand deeper into the burlap sack. Into its darkness. Pulling her down almost to the elbow now. Perhaps meaning to take her arm.*
Madelyn giggled that dark bubbling laughter.
Giggled at Emily's horrible plight. Her painful cry.
Those gold eyes suddenly quite very large and seeming to spin about like gold saucers in her round white-ribboned head.
*Or maybe it was she that was spinning*, Emily decided.
Thinking maybe the dolls were giggling, too.
If not choking on their own dark bubbling laughter.
*I-th your name really Emily, Emily?...* she'd said.
*Madelyn, the child. Laughing so darkly at her now.*
*You daren't not tell the truth...* she'd warned.
*Warned in a rather whispering hiss of a voice really.*
*Rather like a long slithery thick snake-like moray eel might speak with a terrible mouthful of sharp little spiny needle-like bloodthirsty teeth.*
*The small dark burlap sack somehow nearly to her bicep now.*
*Those horrible spiny teeth sinking down even deeper still.*
*Their serrated edges scraping noisily against bone.*
*Producing liquid warmth. Blood. Frothing seemingly.*
Emily cried out again. Tugging harder on her hand.
*Only to see her arm disappear up to her shoulder.*

*And she thought of Alice and her rabbit hole. Plunging. Tumbling down and down and down, head over foot, into that deep, dark, winding corridor. As if she, herself, like frightened young Alice, could somehow be tumbled down into the small dark burlap sack. But instead of tumbling past cupboards and bookshelves and pictures into a magnificent Wonderland promising grand adventure, tumbling down into a nightmarish world full of shadowy ugly things where sunlight was absent other than a mimicry of it reflecting off a sulky moon. A terrible underworld without tea parties and mad hatters and white rabbits in waistcoats with pocket watches. Only awful jabberwockies. Lonely predators of such dark and lonely dungeons impatiently waiting for a misstep from above. A long and deadly fall begun, perhaps, with only the bloody snatch of a hand.*

Madelyn, the child, was still laughing. Darkly.

Along with that chorus of doll laughter maybe.

And perhaps singing again, too. The child.

For Emily thought she heard against her ear:

In that child's whispering hiss of a voice:

*"The-crets, the-crets are no fun…"*

*"The-crets, the-crets can hurt thumb-one…"*

"Madelyn, please," Emily moaned. "*Hurts.*"

Emily realized her eyes were closed. The throbbing behind her right eye suddenly originating behind her neck. As if that *stabbing ice pick* were stabbing through her spine right into her very brain.

*Just tell the truth, Emily. You daren't not to.*

Or so the child might've said again. Singing it.

In that whispering hiss of a voice against her ear.

*I-th your name really Emily, Emily?… Tell the truth.*

*As Emily felt the tiny bones in her hand snapping.*

*Snapping like little twigs. Like kindling in the fireplace.*

*I-th your name really Emily, Emily?… Tell the truth.*

*Just tell the truth. Tell the truth. You daren't not to.*

"*No!*" Emily finally gasped out, desperately.

And immediately felt herself *flying backward, her aggrieved hand released from those jaws*. She landed heavily on the hard attic floor. Right on her back. The stale air *whoofing* from her lungs. As she struggled to breathe, *that dark fluid rising heavily in her heaving lungs like a dark wet cement, threatening to turn her lungs from black balloons into black stones,* her eyes flitted open to discover Madelyn kneeling beside her. Her gold firefly eyes no longer spinning. No longer sparkling brilliantly.

Rather, they now mimicked dying embers.

Still plenty hot, but their light fading.

Fading to a simmering charcoal of a gray.

And for just the fleeting briefest of passing moments, thought maybe she saw Ms. Vivian Dancemore kneeling over her.

And an expression of chagrin on her pale face.

An expression devoid of any amusement.

But then the woman was gone again. *Absent.*

And Madelyn, the child, returned there. The soft golden glow of the carriage light gradually filling those gray eyes once again with that golden color. Chagrin fading away. *Poof.* Like magic.

Replaced by that incurious curiosity.

As if she'd known before she asked the question what the answer to that question would be and was both fascinated and unsurprised by the answer. Possessed by it and yet undaunted.

Emily, lungs hacking terribly, breaking apart *black chunks of that dark fluid only to feel it resettle heavily again,* found her feet, the black cat nearby, still staring at her with its own incurious curiosity.

Not unlike those rows of creepy-ass dolls.

Emily stumbled forward, grabbing into her pocket for the key ring with the iron keys, including the attic key, *intending to free herself* from this horrible attic and this strange little girl with the incurious curious gold eyes. Only to find her pocket hollow. *Empty.*

She grabbed frantically at her other pocket.

Doing so even as she half-expected *something to be waiting for her deep in that pocket. A nightmarish something with more spiny needles for teeth.* Only to find this other pocket also quite hollow. *Empty.*

She spun around wildly to find she was *no longer on her feet,* but scrambling about on her knees now, her small pale hands grasping about, searching in the murky shadows for the lost key ring.

But finding nothing but more darkness.

Handfuls of it. Clutches of it. This darkness.

Noticing absently as well *there were no bite marks on her right hand.* No lacerations or cuts or bruises or any frothing blood. Not a thing seemingly having touched her flesh. Not a single scratch.

*If this wasn't a fever dream, then she was going batshit crazy.*

*Batshit crazy not unlike her batshit crazy mother.*

And came to realize she was *screaming.* An *I'm in a strait-jacket in a padded room* kind of scream. A completely mad scream.

It was then another thought occurred to her.

That thought about *what might happen* if she was, indeed, *trapped* on this side of the thick black oak door *with her.* The child.

*With the child that wasn't really a child at all. At t'all.*
*For maybe something more insidious was going on here than just the idea that Ms. Vivian Dancemore herself was freaking batshit crazy, too.*
*For what if this poor aggrieved woman was not simply conjuring this most peculiar possession herself from some terrible grief of her own mind?*
*What if there was a darker, more fantastical possibility?*
*Might it suggest the dead child was actually to blame?*
*Might it suggest the dead child somehow still lived on?*
*A ghost of her former self, but present? Here? Inside the thick dark walls of this house? From midnight until dawn, anyway? This dead child?*
*And what might this dead child want of her?*
*And what of that odd little door over there?*
*What of that odd little door over there against that far wall appearing out of freaking nowhere where no door had seemingly ever been before?*
*What might it portend? That odd little door?*
*What might be waiting beyond that odd little door?*
With such ghoulish thoughts in her head--
--even as she reminded herself *this just had to only be but a terrible fever dream* as she scrambled insanely about on the attic floor desperately searching for the lost key ring in the darkness--
*I have control over my emotions. And I choose to feel at peace.*
--Emily noticed *a shadow moving on the wall of dead-eyed dolls.*
*Growing, this shadow, as it moved slowly before the dolls.*
*At first she believed it was the child, coming for her after all, tearing itself free of Ms. Vivian Dancemore, as somehow she knew it could, only to realize it wasn't any such dreadful miscreation -- only the thick black oak door. Moving. Creaking. Opening to that dark narrow falling staircase. Promising that plum-colored carpet and beyond. Moving hauntingly of its very own accord without the need of an iron key or, perhaps, even the turn of its rusted iron knob.*
Still, Emily found herself not hesitating, *simply wanting out. Now.* Running. Tripping. Lifting herself. Running again mindlessly.
Scrambling down the attic staircase. Tripping again.
Landing heavily on the plum-colored carpet.
Falling flat on her face. Lungs heaving.
Scrambling back to her feet. *Gagging. Choking.*
Stumbling past her bedroom without any memory of doing so for suddenly she was on the staircase descending to the foyer with gravity *grabbing at her.* Trying to tumble her head over foot.
Part of her desperately convincing herself *the front door would also be moving. Creaking. Opening. Offering her escape from this house.*

*Obsidian black. Thick. Probably oak, too. The front door.*
But she arrived in the foyer to find the front door still locked. As if it would be *anything else* even in this her *fever dream*. Still locked from the inside. Remaining rather quite *impossibly impassible.*
Its own most terrible riddle yet to be solved.
*Without any directions to directly direct her in the right direction.*
*But wait, couldn't she maybe feel a draft of fresh air?*
*A delicious and unexpected draft of fresh air?*
Emily thought maybe she just could and followed it upstream away from that *impossibly impassible* front door and through the narrow corridor past the parlor into the kitchen where she then found *the key in the kitchen back door and that door standing wide open.*
*An invitation seemingly.* Into the garden. At night.
She might've paused here, she would think later. Might've hesitated *at such an unusual invitation at such an unusual hour.* She might've been, indeed, suspicious, but, instead, found herself *darting* through the open door and out into the cool night air of the garden.
Gulping frantically at that cool night air.
Swallowing it down frantically by the mouthfuls.
As if the cool night air were cold water and she dying of thirst. And she could feel that dark fluid in her lungs *pulling apart into those black chunks* and a coughing fit *disgorging that invisible black muculent out into the darkness*, allowing the cool night air to fill her lungs.
And she gulped at it even more frantically.
More frantically as she found herself running into the maze of a garden and further away from *the giant looming beast of a house.*
*As if the giant looming beast of a house were coming after her.*
*A large scaly black hand reaching out from its dark girth.*
*A large scaly black hand adorned with long ugly claws.*
*Snatching at her as she tried to run out into the dark night.*
*Meaning to drag her back inside its thick dark walls.*
*Dark walls with large spiny needle-like teeth.*
The tall thick hedges seemed to offer little protection, but still she pushed forward as if *escape* might be possible, stumbling on her wet noodle-like legs down the crushed stone path, the air thick with the aroma of roses, lavender, delphinium, citrus-hued daylilies, and purple alliums, among the more wild-looking things. Some plants in neat little rows. With others crowded lushly together as if springing organically from an untamed meadow. Only to eventually find herself in the southwest corner. At that fish pond. With its dark water

and its large, pale, and carnivorous-looking fish that now appeared and disappeared in brief blinding flashes in the pale moonlight as if nothing more than twinklings of that pale moonlight playing on the pond's black surface, and reminding her as she arrived at a sudden halt at the pond's edge, bruised lungs heaving in her chest from her efforts, of that *thing* deep in the small dark burlap sack with its own terrible mouthful of sharp little spiny needles and just maybe fangs, too. *Yes, now that she thought about it, she thought that just maybe that thing had fangs, too. The unscathed state of her hand notwithstanding.*

*That thing deep in that small dark burlap sack.*
*Sharp little spiny needles. And just maybe fangs, too.*
*And maybe small gold spheroid eyes. A flared black hood.*
*A flared black hood not unlike a dragon, perhaps.*
*As opposed to a little silly brainless moray eel.*
*A flared black hood not unlike a freaking dragon.*

She stood there a moment in the darkness catching her breath and finally thought to ask herself *where* exactly she was running given the fact this garden, not unlike the front door back in that giant beast of a house looming behind her, was similarly *impossibly impassible with its wrought iron fence and locked gate.* And so, there she stood in the darkness before that dark fish pond in the southwest corner of the nocturnal garden, contemplating such a predicament *only to have her thoughts suddenly intruded upon by a dark bubbling giggle that sounded like it was coming from directly behind her, causing her to spin wildly back in the direction she'd just come from only to hear yet another dark bubbling giggle. Yet another dark bubbling giggle somehow coming from directly behind her yet again, from the fish pond, and spinning back toward the pond to find Madelyn sitting there at the pond's edge, thin legs dangling from the stone lip of the pond. The little girl imbued with pale moonlight, reminding her of those winged-beasts of her other dream. Black silhouettes against the dark night sky, but pale-white against that once dull thumbnail-sliver of moon that had now slowly grown fat. A fattened moon that stared down at them now like a giant pale-white eye. A giant unblinking pale-white eye. As if belonging to god Himself. Or at least a god maybe. A god with an incurious curiosity for such events below.*

Madelyn, the child, in her white nightie, had dipped one of her tiny pale hands into the black pond water and was slowly stirring it, causing actual pale moonlight twinkles to *twinkle*. Emily, made even dizzier by all those blinding *twinkles* of pale moonlight, watched the child's hand spin in this whirlpool of *twinkling flashes*, cringing at the rather frightening idea of one of those large, pale, and carnivorous-looking fish *suddenly grabbing at her hand. Grabbing at it with a mouthful of sharp little spiny needles, and perhaps fangs, and ripping Madelyn, the child, from her stone perch at the pond's edge down into all that black water which for some reason, most likely, Emily realized, because this was only a silly, if rather disturbing fever dream, Emily imagined to be impossibly deep.*

Madelyn seemed to smile at that thought.

As if she could truly read Emily's thoughts after all.

And was again amused by what she found there.

Her hand continuing to stir. If undisturbed.

And that was when Emily noticed the large, pale, and carnivorous-looking fish were huddling *at the opposite side of the pond* not unlike a herd of frightened animals with a predator in their presence. And that wasn't all. It occurred to her the garden was quite unnaturally quiet. The familiar tweets and twitters and whistles of the garden birds absent. Perhaps it was only because dawn was still a couple long hours away; *but then again, perhaps not unlike the huddling school of spooked fish, maybe it had something to do with the child. Another silly, if rather disturbing fever dream of a thought, but there it was all the same. There it was all the same with that giant pale eyeball staring down at them.*

*Staring down at them with its incurious curiosity.*

*Unblinking. Sensing something out of the ordinary.*

*Something that might spell it of its boredom.*

And with that, Madelyn's eyes twinkled themselves, a flash of that gold even in the absence of the attic carriage light, and she was off in a twinkling flash, skipping down the crushed stone path, following it through the tall thick hedge maze with Emily *pursuing* her without any memory of moving, suddenly just in motion.

The cool night air suddenly heavy and still.

*As if god Himself were holding His breath. Or a god.*

Emily followed the skipping child through the tall thick hedge maze and eventually across the small croquet lawn with its assortment of wooden wickets staggered neatly about the lawn and ready for a game, if slightly warped with age and weather. The balls and their corresponding mallets stored in a wooden stand beneath that small fig tree. The mallets hung from wooden pegs (*but for that still-missing mallet quite absent from its slot with the faded black stripe*), the balls tucked in that narrow wooden sleeve between them, the old mallets and the balls dimpled and chipped here and there, rather pleasantly so, and nearly faded of their original colorful stripes as the child left in her skipping wake *not a single discernable mark in that short dewy grass* even as Emily left small, damp, but heavy footprints on that small croquet lawn like a trail of footprints in the snow. Her passing obvious and cumbersome even here in this her *fever dream.*

The crushed stone path also crunched noisily beneath her feet as she tried desperately to keep up with Madelyn as the child disappeared around the meandering bends in the tall thick hedges, offering *only brief blinding flashes* of herself in the pale watchful moonlight, the child appearing more like an *apparition* than ever before.

Before vanishing completely in the night.

As if simply *winking* from existence.

Leaving the night somehow all the darker and more menacing for her absence. For her absence of twinkling pale light. The fattening moon now ducking behind a dark cloud. Hiding, perhaps.

The air becoming even heavier. More still.

The surrounding quiet heavier and even more quiet.

"Madelyn," Emily hushed as she hurried on.

"Madelyn, you mustn't," she scolded.

*The child, Madelyn, is to never her leave her bedroom.*

*Not without supervision. Rule #1.*

*The child, Madelyn, is never to leave this house. Not under any circumstances. Never. No matter what she may tell you. Rule #2.*

*There is to be no hide-and-seek. Rule #5.*

*Hold the child, Madelyn, accountable to all rules. Rule #15*

Emily rounded a bend in the tall thick hedges, slipping past a thick spider-web of ivy, wisteria, creepers, and climbers to discover Madelyn standing stoically before the back gate of that tall wrought iron fence with its high row of medieval sharp-looking iron spikes, eyeing that section of the path passing under the gate, disappearing up into the thick woods, turning from crushed stone to dirt.

The lock still secured the gate, of course.

Making entry to those woods *impossibly impassable.*

Those dark encroaching woods rising in the night.

Madelyn turned to Emily and smiled at her.

Smiled at her with that lopsided smile.

A lopsided smile that turned even more crooked *as she somehow slipped through the far-too-narrow gate's wrought iron bars as if she were only a cat. That magician of a cat. Marbles. Or as if she were simply made of air. She then peered through the iron bars at Emily with that lopsided grin.*

*Staring at her for a moment as if she meant to leave her behind.*

*As if she meant to leave Emily behind in the garden.*

*Before sliding a hand back through the bars.*
*A pale hand. Reaching back for Emily. Beckoning her.*
*As if Emily could ever hope to perform such a necromancy.*
*Or quite rather have it somehow performed upon her.*
*Still, Emily found her hand reaching for Madelyn's hand. Felt the coldness of the child's touch as Madelyn's hand took very her own. Felt an electrical current run through her entire body -- a cold burning electricity -- only to rather suddenly find herself on the other side of those far-too-narrow iron bars.*
*Magically on the other side of that gate lock.*
*Magically on the other side of that prison-like wrought iron fence.*
*As if she were but a cat or simply made of air herself.*
*Her feet on the path turning from crushed stone to dirt.*
*A path rising up into those dark now-waiting woods.*
*Freed from that giant looming beast of a house.*

Emily heard herself emit a rather loud squeal. A loud squeal of complete bewilderment but also elation *only to see the oddest expression appear on Madelyn's round pale face*, her gold eyes turned white.

Turned white but for brief flashes of gold.

Brief flashes even in the absence of the carriage light.

And for a moment Emily was reminded of Henry.

To that day she'd snuck him out his house a few days after his birthday while the rest of his family had been at the movies.

Snuck him out despite his unfortunate condition.

The tragic little boy with the pale skin and blue jaundiced eyes and purple lips who'd otherwise *never been allowed* to leave that house only to watch the world pass by outside his bedroom window. Including the neighborhood kids on their bicycles who'd sometimes wave at him as they passed by his lonely bedroom window.

She'd snuck him out for a banana split.

Borrowing his mother's car without telling her.

Taking him a few blocks over to Dairy Queen where all those neighborhood kids tended to congregate on their bikes.

He'd promised to stay in the car. Little Henry.

He'd crossed his heart and hoped to die.

Yes, she could now remember him saying that.

And she could still remember the expression *on his face* as he'd sat in his mother's borrowed car waiting for his sundae. Part of her had known he would not stay there while she was inside the restaurant purchasing his treat. That he might just disappear.

*Poof.* Like magic. Just vanish.

She'd found him a few frightful minutes later with those other kids around back. They were trying to teach him how to ride a bike. He had been wobbling around in circles, and laughing.

She'd never heard him laugh. Henry. The boy. Let alone laugh so joyfully like that. It was almost painful to listen to. That laughter. If she closed her eyes, it had almost sounded to her like tears.

Circling around he'd been. Henry. Laughing.

Maybe even crying, too, in retrospect.

A bike one of the larger kids had loaned him.

Silver. A gear shifter. Colorful piping.

One long black stripe down its crossbar maybe.

A sticker. Cartoonish lettering. HUFFY.

Laughing. Crying. A sad joyful relief.

A sad joyful relief. The very same expression that had been on his face when she'd left him in the car to go inside the restaurant to get his treat. Plain as day if she'd cared to notice. Belying his promise to stay in the car. Cross his heart and hope to die and all.

A sad joyful relief. Despite the dangers.

The dangers of his illness outside the house.

Yes, she was reminded of *Henry* as she stared at Madelyn here *on the other side* of the wrought iron gate facing that dark rising now-waiting woods. Madelyn wore an expression that, even in the night darkness, plain as the night on her tiny face, also spoke to the relief of being beyond the harsh restrictions of her existence. Beyond the rules. Only her expression did not mimic Henry's simple sad joyful relief. Not that in the end. Rather there inhabited in her expression a wantonness. Rather than anything Emily might've otherwise mistaken for joy, there inhabited an unsettling primal lustfulness.

A *hunger.* In those white eyes flashing gold.

And in a flash, Madelyn was off again.

A little wild dervish of a thing in the night.

Skipping up the dirt path into the dark woods.

Emily slipped once, maybe even twice, her head spinning dizzily again, before securing her own footing and giving pursuit. Giving pursuit *and trying not to notice a flash of silver in the dark trees.*

*An old bike frame with faded piping. The faded piping, rather hauntingly, mimicking the very same colors of that croquet set seemingly. The croquet set back in the garden behind that formidably locked wrought iron gate.*

*Red, orange, green, yellow, and blue.*

*With one long black stripe down the crossbar.*

*Tried not to notice a badly blanched sticker.*
*Tattered and peeling like an old scab.*
*But still just legible even in the darkness.*
*The tattered, peeling sticker reading: HUFFY.*
*Exposing a rusted gear shifter and more silver.*
*Silver. Not unlike that silver door knob and keyplate on that short narrow door back up in that attic. An odd little door appearing out of nowhere. Where no door had seemingly ever been before.*
*A silver knob and keyplate with more of that rather most strange flowery fleur-de-lis ornamentation that was not fleur-de-lis at all. At t'all.*
*Flared black hoods of dragons for black lily petals.*
*Flared black hoods framing gold spheroid eyes. Fangs.*
*I-th your name really Emily, Emily?...* she'd said.
*Just tell the truth. Tell the truth. You daren't not to.*
*The-crets, the-crets are no fun...* she'd warned.
*The-crets, the-crets can hurt thumb-one...*

Emily shook her heavy feverish head and *turned away* from that flash of silver in the dark trees. From that something lying there on its side. Choked by tangled vines and *nearly lost* in that jungle undergrowth of suffocating ferns, moss, and mushroom fungi.

But not before thinking *she maybe saw him, too.*
*The boy. Henry. Standing there in the darkness.*
*Little gaunt Henry. Shouting at her without speaking.*
*Dan-th with me... It-th eethee...* he seemed to say to her.
*Seemed to shout at her without making a sound.*
*Laughing that laugh that would sound like tears.*
*Tiny jaw rotten, hanging from long frayed tendons.*
*Eyeballs turned white. No longer jaundiced or blue.*
*Seeing without seeing. Shouting without making a sound.*
*Laughing soundless tears that would sound like joy.*

She thought she might've let out another squeal as she pushed up the steep dirt path *away from him* with Madelyn nearly lost in the darkness ahead of her. The path becoming rather difficult to judge in the darkness and the dense forest underbrush, and suggesting to Emily she might easily stray from it and become lost in these dark bewitching wood *with him*. Only to find herself suddenly at the crest of the wooded hill and the path descending somnolently down into a brief clearing. A brief clearing from which *jagged teeth* rose from a wild intertwisted patch of pigweed and bull thistle. *Jagged teeth which quickly revealed themselves to be stone grave markers in the darkness.*

Headstones. Three of them. Side by side.

A short wrought iron fence surrounding them.

Its gate stuck halfway open, choked by the weeds.

Madelyn had already *slipped* past the choked gate and the three headstones, her shadow once again disappearing somewhere down into the darkness *beyond* the cemetery's back fence as if she'd somehow simply *passed right through* the fence into the dark trees.

But Emily found herself hesitating. Here.

As if understanding the path had brought her here.

To this hallowed place in these dark woods.

That it was the main reason for the path's existence.

This narrow dirt path in these dark woods.

She was forced to kneel down (the ground damp beneath her, the cold wet seeping through her pants) and brush aside the snarls of pigweed and bull thistle and other less identifiable prickly weeds and their dull flowers to read the headstones in the murk.

The first headstone read:

ALFRED MILTON DANCEMORE
BORN 1948 DIED 1995

Accompanied by the epitaph:

REMEMBER ME AS YOU PASS BY;
AS YOU ARE NOW, SO ONCE WAS I;
AS I AM NOW, SO YOU MUST BE;
PREPARE FOR DEATH AND FOLLOW ME.

Emily once again felt somehow much too warm and yet a chill as these prophetic words penetrated her feverish brain. And yet the words on the headstone seemed to her feverish brain less prophetic than a warning somehow. A warning against *resisting* death.

As if a person *could* deny the Grim Reaper.

Could somehow escape his or her final fate.

Could somehow escape Death itself in the end.

But that only held her attention for just a moment.

Her head shaking with a deeper puzzlement.

She wasn't a math savant, but she could certainly add and subtract well enough and therefore was able to quickly deduce that Mr. Alfred Milton Dancemore, according to the date of death inscribed there on his headstone, *had been dead for twenty seven long years.*

*That he'd been forty seven years old when he'd died.*

*Which would have made him seventy four years old today.*

*Given he'd left this world way back in 1995.*

She stood there trying to process *this* with her feverish brain, a cold rising wind whispering in the dark trees about her, prompting her to acknowledge a related, if equally mysterious riddle.

For the math just didn't make any sense.

Ms. Vivian Dancemore, her strange employer, couldn't be any older *than her late-thirties*, if that, and yet the headstone before Emily in this hidden weedy clearing in these dark woods dared to suggest this very same Ms. Vivian Dancemore, therefore, *could not have been any older than a young preteen when her poor husband had died.*

It was as this riddle toyed with her feverish brain, Emily found herself slowly turning her attention to the middle headstone.

A much smaller headstone. A child's marker.

This eerily smaller headstone read:

MADELYN MARIE DANCEMORE
BORN 1984 DIED 1993

Accompanied by the epitaph:

NOW I LAY YOU DOWN TO SLEEP;
I PRAY THE LORD YOUR SOUL TO KEEP;
SLEEP, MY LITTLE ONE, SLEEP.

Emily felt a hard tug on her heart strings at the epitaph's sentiment and imagined Ms. Vivian Dancemore offering such a prayer over her dead child. That her dead child might find sleep.

That her dead child might find restful peace.

And yet, the math made even less sense.

*For this headstone dared to suggest this nine year old child had been dead for twenty nine long years. Furthermore, given the child's date of birth inscribed on the eerily small headstone, and given Ms. Vivian Dancemore's presumed age at around her late-thirties, then this headstone also dared to suggest that Madelyn's mother, Ms. Vivian Dancemore, could not have been any older than that young preteen when her daughter, Madelyn Marie Dancemore, had died; and therefore, not any older than a mere toddler when she had been born.*

Impossible. Simply *impossibly impassable.*

*Unless, of course, she was not the child's mother after all.*

*What had the woman said during their initial interview after Emily had arrived at the house? At that giant looming beast of a house back below?*

*I'm the caretaker...* she'd said. *Of the child.*

Of course, she'd also said that same evening:

*The girl's father, my husband, Alfred, held me responsible.*

*For the accident. For what happened to the child.*

*Madelyn. Our child...* she'd said to her.

*A most terrible accident. Some years ago.*
*Of the kind the mind never quite completely comprehends.*
*The child lost only to be found. Madelyn. Sometimes Maddy.*
*You are to be the night sitter, Miss Emily.*
And that was when Emily observed the stone grave marker itself was rather *askew*. As if it had been disturbed, perhaps. And that the ground before the marker was rather *noticeably sunken as well*.
*As if the child buried there had been disturbed maybe.*
*As if the child had not been allowed to find that restful peace.*
If she let her feverish brain suggest such a thing.
Blinking, twitching really, she moved over to the final marker. The final headstone. Bookending the child's headstone.
The final headstone read in the night:
VIVIAN CYNTHIA DANCEMORE
BORN 1960 DIED ----
Accompanied by the epitaph:
NEVER WILL I LEAVE YOU;
NEVER WILL I FORSAKE YOU.
There was yet no date of death, of course, because Ms. Vivian Dancemore was *still* alive. Had out-lived her husband and daughter by *almost three long decades* according to the headstones in this hidden family plot in these dark woods. Yet, the profound mystery continued given the math still just didn't make any freaking sense.
*For the final headstone dared to suggest that Ms. Vivian Dancemore had been born sixty two years ago. Of course, this would have made her a far more believable twenty four years old when her daughter had been born.*
*Assuming Madelyn was her own child, of course.*
*But there was no way that woman was now sixty two.*
*That* seemed utterly *impossibly impassible*.
Emily rose to her feet and took solace in the fact she was lost in a *fever dream*. She really had no idea what her *fever dream* was trying to tell her, having always believed dreams were harbingers of something or another, *assuming this dream wasn't simply a scrambled mess given it was a fever dream*. Nevertheless, she found herself moving forward again, pursuing the child lost down into those dark woods.
She managed to negotiate the short wrought iron fence on the opposite side of the small graveyard where the child had vanished moments ago, careful to avoid any mishap on its own sharp-looking decorative spikes, and finding the ground falling even more steeply beyond the fence, and the dirt path much narrower still.

She nearly lost her footing once or twice.

The ground slick here. Inviting a misstep.

Eventually, however, the path began to level off and the forest of trees began to thin, giving way to a long wet grass that slapped at her shins and ankles. Through these final remaining trees and their sleepy shadows, she spied a playground in black and white.

A small, if rather familiar-looking playground.

One she'd seen on her journey here to her new charge.

Surrounded by fluttering yellow caution tape.

Appearing like an abandoned crime scene.

A swing set, jungle gym, and slide frozen in the darkness over a bed of dirty sand as if trying to blend into the shadows.

A brief parking lot blocked off by sawhorses.

All behind a large PARK CLOSED sign.

The small playground backed by the dark woods was set back from the residential street where street lamps glowed along Washington Irving Way before those massive Victorians and Tudors and Colonials still predictably dark given the early morning hour.

One could almost imagine the world hollow.

All the people gone. Erased from existence.

But for Madelyn. The peculiar child.

Madelyn, barefoot, her feet half-buried in the cold playground sand, was standing in the middle of the playground in the darkness. As Emily approached, she spoke without turning around:

"Swing," she hushed with glee. *Th-wing.*

She then did a quick pirouette in the sand and skipped over to the swing set, leaping backward into the saddle of a swing.

"Push me, Emily," she said. *Pu-th me.*

Emily acquiesced to her demand, but only after making Madelyn promise they would stay only a few minutes before returning to the path, the woods, and the giant looming beast of a house.

*The child, Madelyn, is never to leave this house. Not under any circumstances. Never. No matter what she may tell you. Rule #2.*

*Hold the child, Madelyn, accountable to all rules. Rule #15*

*And what would the consequences be for this and all the rules broken on this night for it seemed just about every rule had been fractured, if not broken. Almost as if the house rules had been created only to be broken.*

*A rather most peculiar and strange idea.*

*And yet, then again, what did it all really matter?*

*What did it all really matter in the end?*

*If this were truly all just a silly fever dream, then there could be no consequences. And if it were not, then she could just walk past the fluttering yellow caution tape, the parade of sad sawhorses, and vanish down Washington Irving Way and maybe even catch that bus again. Catch it right out of here.*

*But, of course, there would be no buses.*
*Not with Martial Law. Just roadblocks. Guns.*
*Still, she was clever. And she was finally out of that house.*
*Out of that giant looming beast of a peculiar house.*
*With all its locked doors and all its locked windows.*
*She could just disappear. Never to return to it.*
*And, in the end, leave this creepy little kid right here.*
*This kid that wasn't at kid at all. At t'all.*

Madelyn scooped her pale legs in on the descent and shot her pale legs out on the rise as Emily pushed her on the swing with the rusty swing chain rattling loudly in that cold rising wind as the child rose higher and higher up into the night darkness. And for an eerie moment Emily imagined the child *suddenly just disappearing* into that darkness, the returning swing saddle *suddenly quite empty.*

*Imagined her rising up into all that darkness above.*
*A winged-beast of a howling, shrieking thing in the night.*
*A thing with scales, claws, needle-like teeth, and terrible fangs.*
*A monstrous thing that would chase her down in the night if she attempted to run. If she attempted to escape from it. If she attempted to hide.*

And that was when Emily heard a *shriek*.
Followed quickly by a guttural *howl*.

Only the swing saddle returned to her with Madelyn, the child, still in it, her little white-ribboned head turned toward a dark copse of shade trees and park benches where dark shadows moved.

Her white eyes flashing with that jaunty gold.

And that was when things got truly peculiar. Truly strange on this, Emily's third night as the night sitter. As if things could get any more peculiar or stranger than they'd already been during her short, if mystifying stint as the night sitter. Yes, things got truly peculiar at this point. Truly strange. Moving as if in a *fever dream*. Remembered later in only *brief terrible snatches* of black and white and red.

The dark shadows stepping forward.
Forward from those shade trees. Benches.
Revealing themselves to be soldiers in their inky-black combat gear. But no longer automatons. Their Darth Vader-like masks lifted from their heads. Almost as if they had been beheaded.

Revealing young rosy-cheeked faces.
Their faces rosy-cheeked from too much drink.
Tall bottles. Hard liquor. Dark and clear.
Two young men and a woman. These shadows.
Appearing from these shade trees. Benches.
Stumbling from the drink. From their merriment.
Merriment enjoyed secretly in the darkness.
Merriment producing *shrieks* and *howls*.
Rifles slung sleepily over their shoulders.
Reminding her that she might've heard *gunshots* the other night while she'd been sleeping. Gunshots out in the dark night.

Somewhere out in this world come so undone.

Emily would also remember the woman-soldier perhaps being rather miffed by the intrusion. By the attention the two men subsequently placed upon Emily and the whimsical, nearly naked woman in the sheer white nightie, her black hair in white ribbons.

As for her impression of the soldier-men:
One was heavy. A dark beard and dark eyebrows.
The other thin. A sharp nose and beady eyes.

She would remember the inebriated men scolding them about ignoring the Martial Law dictates, requesting their absentee paperwork while offering to them the bottles. Dark and clear.

She would also remember scolding Madelyn.
For imbibing too much of the stuff. The hard liquor.
*The child, Madelyn, is not to drink. Alcohol. Rule #4.*
These were only *glimpses of memory*, of course.

*Fuzzy* and *faded*. Revealed only in those *brief terrible snatches* and out of order. A weird kaleidoscope of sheer escalating horror.

Black and white and red. Eventually red.

She would remember Madelyn's shadow on the ground as one of the men, the one with a dark beard and dark eyebrows, reached for her somewhat gruffly in the darkness to place her on his lap on a park bench in the shadows of those shade trees, laughing drunkenly, his large hands dark with thick copses of wiry hair.

A swarthy man, he was. Badly intoxicated.
She would remember the thin one, too.
Fighting the bigger one over the girl. Madelyn.
Or, perhaps, maybe just trying to share her.
This child-like angel in the white nightie. Ribbons.
And she'd remember those white eyes flashing gold.

Revealing what was *residing* in those eyes.
Revealing once again that wantonness.
That primal lustfulness. That terrible *hunger*.
Revealing in the playground darkness--
The cold dead expression of a *predator*. Of a *thing* that hunts in the night. In the darkness. In the shadows absent of light.
And she would remember turning away from it.
From what the child, Madelyn, was *becoming*.
*Staring, instead, at its shadow on the ground in the pale moonlight in the cold rising wind as that shadow began to flinch. Twist. Morbidly dance.*
*Monstrous. Child-like and yet not a child at all. At t'all.*
*That flinching and twisting and morbidly dancing shadow.*
*As if something seemingly in deep struggle with itself.*
*Tearing at its hair. Flesh. With sharp claws.*
*Head throwing back in a soundless dark and painful laughter. Revealing an elongated jaw, a mouthful of large spiny needle-like teeth, and fangs.*
*Its white-ribboned braids suddenly curved horns.*
*And suddenly, appearing from its thin torso, giant dark coriaceous wings. Splaying wide and lifting it up into the night sky as it finally howled. Shrieked. Flicking a long spiny coiled tail. Its fearsome shadow darting here. There.*
*The inebriated men screaming now. The larger swarthy one. The thin one. The woman-soldier, too, who'd been ignored for the angelic child.*
*The angelic child with who'd become this terrible devil.*
*This predator of the night. This flying winged-beast.*
*And then there was the horrible silhouette of body parts being ripped and torn and the sound of feeding. In a black and white world turned red.*
*But, of course, it was only a frightful fever dream.*
*For what else could it be but only a thing of the mind?*
*Only a thing created by an overexcited imagination?*
Or so Emily desperately tried to convince herself *as she dropped to her knees and closed her eyes from it all and shoved her hands over her ears. Screaming herself. Screaming herself only to feel herself lifting. Only to feel herself slowly lifting up into the night. Into that cold pale moonlight. Into that cold rising wind. Only to feel herself floating. Floating like never before.*
*And tasting ambrosia on her screaming tongue.*
*The food of gods. The sweetest and most divine of nectars.*
*And yet screaming. Screaming. Screaming.*

# 20.

SCREAMING. SCREAMING. Screaming in the dark night. Her ears ringing with the terrible shrieks of her own screams until eventually she found herself contemplating, in an admittedly absent out-of-body kind of way, whether she was still actually screaming or just listening to their ghastly ghostly echoes.

It was in the midst of these terrible screams, or in the midst of their ghastly ghostly echoes, Emily heard a hushed voice:

A soft hushed warm whisper of a voice:

*Sleep, little one, sleep...* this soft hushed warm whisper of a voice said from the darkness. A darkness now embracing her like a black blanket. *Dream yourself awake, and all of your dreams will come true.*

The screams faded with the hushed voice.

And then there was only the heavy darkness.

Gradually, a dull gray light penetrated that darkness and Emily *awoke* to find herself back in her bed in the giant looming beast of a house with black clouds gathering heavily in a gray morning sky, the gathering black clouds already quite thick, implying they would only grow thicker still, pressing down on this world below them, preparing to smother this world as a cold whipping wind churned beneath their dark gathering embrace, the cold whipping wind already snapping at tree branches and howling in the house eaves.

Promising a terrible storm. A black storm.

The gray light already paling. Fading.

Fading beyond the bedroom window.
The thick black drapes *pulled open* this morning.
As if done so by those mischievous leprechauns.
Inviting her to witness what was to come.
The world coming even further undone.

Still, Emily felt invigorated. Felt like she'd slept for a year. Her headache, that horrid throbbing behind her right eye, departed. Her lungs clear. Her skin no longer too warm. Burning. Shivering. Tiny hard gooseflesh breaking out across her entire body. As if her body knew not if it was hot or cold. Resembling to her scales.

Which made her think of her fever dream.
That most awful tormenting fever of a dream.
That most horrible of feverish nightmares.
*Madelyn, the child. The thing she'd become in her fever dream.*
*The terrible screams in the park. In the darkness. Played out in shadows on the ground. Body parks being ripped and torn. The sound of feeding.*
*The taste of ambrosia on her own screaming tongue.*
*The food of gods. The sweetest and most divine of nectars.*
*As if she were feeding along with Madelyn, the child.*
*Feeding along with that terrible thing Madelyn had become.*
*That thing the child had become in her fever dream.*

Still, she felt better. Better than she'd felt in a very long while. And she lifted herself from the bed, stretching, staring out at those gathering black clouds and the cold whipping wind snapping at tree branches and howling in the eaves in the fading gray morning light with the promise of a terrible black storm only to suddenly realize with a shudder, given the events of the previous evening had been only but a terrible fever dream, *she'd slept through the entire night, apparently, her third night as the night sitter*. Moreover, Emily could now hear the grandfather clock somewhere down in the parlor far below her begin to gong. Punctuating her laxness. Indeed, tardiness.

The clock issuing *nine loud punctuating gongs*.
For it was somehow already *nine* in the morning.
Her mother's watch confirming the late hour.
Not only had she failed to heed her nightly charge--
Leaving the poor child all alone inside the attic--
*You will find the girl in the attic after midnight.*
*You are to be the night sitter, Miss Emily.*
She'd failed to fetch her strange employer at dawn once again. Had left her behind that locked attic door. *Waiting. Waiting.*

# THE NIGHT SITTER

And that was when she noticed the black antique iron key ring was missing from the small desk. Her room key. The attic key. She always left the iron key ring on the desk. Always. Without fail. And for a most horribly paralyzing moment she thought she'd be unable to *escape* this very bedroom let alone free Ms. V from the attic. That they'd both be trapped behind their own locked doors and barred windows in this giant looming beast of a house with whatever voices they might hear whispering softly to them from the walls.

Ms. V already spoke to such whispering voices.

And now Emily had heard *her own such voice.* Again.

*Sleep, little one, sleep...* it had said. That soft hushed warm whisper of a voice in the darkness as she'd gradually *awoken* to this late gray morning thick with black clouds gathering beyond her window bars. *Dream yourself awake, and all your dreams will come true.*

*How long would it be before she spoke to it as well?*

*And what would such a voice ask of her, whispering from the dark walls of this giant looming beast of a house sitting on the very edge of the world?*

Then again, perhaps such answers would become known fairly quickly to her, she decided, as she turned in bed to find--

Her bedroom door cracked open. Invitingly.

The dark narrow hall waiting for her. *Waiting, waiting.*

She warily slipped out of the bed. Stood. *Only to find herself nude from head to foot.* This surprised her. This rather alarmed her.

The morning cold brushing at her pale skin.

Flummoxed, she realized she must've stripped off her clothing during the night in a fever rage. In her sleep. *Burning, burning.*

Perhaps it also explained the open door and her missing keys. The previous night lost to a most terrible feverish delirium.

She dressed quickly. So very late. Hoping perhaps Ms. V had a spare attic key tucked away somewhere in the dark house.

Just in case she could not locate her own keys.

Trying not to dwell on that rush of blind panic from her fever dream when she'd lost the black iron key ring in the attic.

Scrambling about in the darkness. Screaming.

*An I'm in a strait-jacket in a padded room kind of scream. A completely mad scream. A batshit crazy not unlike her mother kind of scream.*

*As she found nothing but more darkness in that attic.*

*Handfuls of it. Clutches of it. Rather than those naughty keys.*

Yes, she tried not to dwell on such things.

Such things of the overexcited imagination.

Even as the reality of this morning's odd riddles and the unreality of her fever dream settled their claws deeply into her.

Blinking, twitching really, Emily found herself *floating* up the plum-colored carpet in that dimly-lit hall with its flickering rows of bronze sconces, then *floating* around the corner into the dark alcove only to find the *attic door ajar, too,* above the dark staircase.

*Ajar. As if waiting so very patiently for her. Silently.*

The gray late morning light spilling down upon her. Providing a gray tunnel of light to *float* through. And suddenly she was *floating* into the attic itself. The fading echo of the grandfather clock gongs moving the musty air about her *as if the house were floating, too.*

Emily sighed and felt her feet slowly settle on the floorboards. The old warped splintery long black floorboards of the attic. Felt as much as heard their gentle creak. A creak that maybe sounded a bit too much like a whisper. A soft hushed warm whisper.

*As if something to be translated. Understood.*

*Attempting to tell herself something most direly important.*

She shook her head with the absurd thought amongst so many absurd thoughts only to feel her heart seize in her chest as if a cold black hand were suddenly grabbing at her very heart when she noticed the long dark attic shelves were now strangely empty.

The creepy-ass doll collection just *gone.*

With their porcelain faces rather too human-like.

Their skin tinted in order to resemble flesh.

If still a ghostly pale for all that nonsense.

With deftly painted cheeks, lips, and eyebrows.

And what appeared to be real human hair.

And dark little glassy moribund staring eyes.

*Gone.* The entire little army. Simply absent.

As if they'd just gotten up and walked away.

As for Emily's most peculiar employer--

Ms. Vivian Dancemore was also *absent.*

*So who or what had liberated her from the attic?*

*Had it somehow been that creepy-ass little army of dolls?*

*Did their absence somehow answer the riddle to her absence?*

*Or maybe those mischievous little leprechauns, then?*

Fortunately, to her momentary relief, she noticed there was no short narrow door in the wall on the opposite side of the attic. Just a plain dark wall beside the old steamer trunk and the antique music box. The antique music box looking dull and sleepy in the gray

late morning light. A disused, forgotten thing of the past. Left here to gather dust. Amongst so many disused, forgotten things.
*But no short narrow door. None of that nonsense.*
Emily took a deep breath. Thinking.
Perhaps in a feverish disorientation she'd let her most peculiar employer out of the attic this morning per the usual schedule.
Perhaps that was not so far-fetched to imagine.
She rather liked this rather inelegant explanation.
The idea, in such a feverish disorientation, that she'd let Ms. V out of the attic before her terrible fever had finally broken.
It was as Emily silently congratulated herself on this admittedly rather inelegant explanation in the absence of any other--
*In the absence of those dolls and Ms. V herself--*
Her right heel bumped into something.
Bumped into something beneath the small cot.
Bumped into something that *clattered*.
Emily lowered herself to a knee to peek under the bed, feeling her skin crawl with tiny prickly heebie-jeebies. Lowered herself to a knee to find *that silver tray with its remnants of sticky jam finger-sandwiches and frosted ginger cookies beneath the small cot. Its pitcher of now curdled milk and vase of large white whorled flowers with pink pistils. Large white whorled flowers that smelled just faintly of apricot. Lush and sweet, if failing to calm her horribly strained nerves on this late gray black-clouded morning.*
Emily retrieved the small silver tray and placed it on the small cot. She stared at it, her forehead wrinkling. Trying to process what its existence here might mean in terms of her fever dream.
*Did it suggest there had been no such fever dream?*
*Did it suggest her dark adventures were actually real?*
*The small dark burlap sack and the toothy thing inside of it?*
*The silver HUFFY bike buried in the woods? Henry?*
*The stone grave makers in those very same woods?*
*The most terrible events at the playground?*
*Or did the silver tray beneath the bed only suggest that some of the previous evening was real? That some of it was true? That some of it had happened? And that the rest of it, the fantastical terribleness of all the rest of it, had not? Her illness simply getting the better of her and sending her back to her bedroom early and all the rest of it simply having been imagined in her sleep?*
*Of course. Of course that was the answer.*
*What other explanation could there possibly be?*
*What other explanation for such fantastical terribleness?*

*Furthermore, it was not inconceivable to think, perhaps because of her delirious feverish state, Madelyn, the child, had managed to get a hold of the iron key ring and had liberated herself from the attic. Stolen off into the shadows of this giant looming beast of a house unsupervised. Perhaps better explaining her hollow absence from the attic on this late gray black-clouded morning.*

*Or, more correctly, Ms. V's absence, anyway.*
*Given the late hour of the morning itself after all.*
Emily took solace with this less silly thought.
The idea her fever had made a sport of her.
A sport of her for a child that was not a child at all.
Only that. And nothing more fantastical.
*The child, Madelyn, is to never her leave her bedroom.*
*Not without supervision. Rule #1.*
Yes, Emily took solace with this less silly thought even as she began fretting about *where* Ms. Vivian Dancemore, her most peculiar employer, might have *found herself* this morning at dawn.

*Might have found herself when the naughty child slipped away from her in the predawn darkness after liberating herself from the attic last night.*
*After spending the night unsupervised. Wandering.*
*Wandering about this giant looming beast of a house.*
*Perhaps with that little creepy-ass army of freaking dolls.*
With a tremulous breath, she gathered the silver tray from the small cot and removed it from the attic, balancing it against her hip with one hand and using her free hand to pull closed the attic door behind her, if being unable to lock it on this late gray black-clouded morning. Only to notice as the attic door slid closed with a muffled sigh, a small framed embroidered pattern on the wall just inside the shutting attic door. Gothic-calligraphy. A biblical reference. A thing she'd never noticed until just now. A thing that almost seemed to shimmer in the cool gray late morning light as that gray late morning light began to pale, fade, as those black clouds gathered.

*Proverbs 3:33 The Lord's curse is on the house of the*
*wicked, But he blesses the home of the righteous.*
She stared at the quote hanging there on the wall in the paling, fading gray late morning light and began to wonder if just perhaps the quote sounded just a bit strident. Just a bit overexcited.

A cry-out in the darkness. A hollow thing.
A thing of only superstition. Otherwise powerless.
Especially here in this giant looming beast of a house.
Here on the very edge of the world. Of existence.

More silly thoughts, she scolded herself. Scolded herself as she then descended the dark narrow staircase with the silver tray before pushing down the plum-colored carpeted hall, pausing momentarily outside Ms. Vivian Dancemore's locked bedroom door, wondering if, given the events of last night, she should perhaps knock--

*You are to please knock on all doors before entering.*

--and confirm the woman wasn't -- *what?*

*What word she was looking for here?* she asked herself rather suspiciously, standing there awkwardly in the plum-colored carpeted hall outside her employer's bedroom door. *What state of mind precisely did she wish to dismiss with such a confirmation? With such an inquiry?*

*What did she fear to find behind this bedroom door?*

*What did she need to dismiss her mind of this odd morning?*

*It had only been a fever dream after all. Nothing more.*

*Nothing more darkly fantastical. Monstrous.*

Balancing the silver tray against her hip, she knocked on the door. Short hard raps. If nothing more than to ask for the woman's confidence back in her maybe as well as to politely request back her iron key ring. Keys. And that was when Emily heard it.

*Pitter patter. Pitter patter. Scritch scratch scritch.*

The sound of little feet. But not from the bedroom.

Rather, coming from the foyer staircase, perhaps.

Scowling, she got moving down the long narrow hall.

Past the last of the dimly-flickering bronze sconces.

Only to find no one on the foyer staircase.

Just those lingering resident shadows.

*Perhaps it was only the storm...* she thought to herself grimly. The gathering of those black clouds producing that cold whipping wind. The dark house trembling, creaking in the coming storm.

And that was when she heard it once more.

This time coming from the foyer shadows below.

*Pitter patter. Pitter patter. Scritch scratch scritch.*

Only to rather too quickly descend the foyer staircase and find no one in the foyer, either. Just more dark shadows.

And yet, Emily suddenly felt as if there was little eyes everywhere. *Dark little glassy eyes, perhaps.* Staring at her from around every dark corner. From the short dark hall ahead. Its own shadows.

Little hands over little mouths stifling little snickering laughter at her expense. And that was when she heard it yet again.

*Pitter patter. Pitter patter. Scritch scratch scritch.*

The kitchen maybe. Coming from the kitchen.

She hurried through the short dark hall and into the kitchen to find no breakfast waiting for her on the table this morning.

*Just an apple. Sitting there dully in the fading gray morning light.*
*Big nasty squishy black spots on its listless red skin.*
*Listless red skin collapsing inward like a rotting pumpkin.*

And again heard her late grandmother hushing softly beneath her breath in the back of her mind from that small apple grove back on her grandparents' farm, she had for her a *magic wishing apple*.

*One bite* and all her dreams would come true.

Emily began to feel a bit woozy.

Began to feel like she might just faint.

No longer invigorated or like she'd slept a year.

Rather, she felt as if she might still be dreaming.

Might still be asleep. None of this real.

Blinking hard, twitching really, she found herself crossing the kitchen, dumping the silver tray leftovers into the bin, including the remnants of those sticky jam finger-sandwiches. The jam now congealed here and there. Dark red. More blood-like than ever. Moreover, there rose from them a rather most peculiar smell.

Rather than smelling fruity sweet--

*They suddenly smelled sweetly sour. Of rotting things.*
*Of roadkill, perhaps. Buzzing flies. Maggots.*

She imagined it, as it had been, *all over the child's pale little face*. In the corners of her little mouth. On the tip of her nose. Chin.

Dirtying her little fingers. Under her nails.

Emily attempted to convince herself she could smell none of this, of course, and busied herself with dutifully washing the silver tray and its platters and the milk pitcher in the kitchen sink.

She set them all neatly to dry in the dish rack.

Placing the vase of apricot-smelling flowers on the table.

She briefly glanced at the kitchen back door. But there was no key waiting for her. No polite invitation out into the garden.

And that was when she heard it yet again. That--

*Pitter patter. Pitter patter. Scritch scratch scritch.*

The sound of little feet sounded like they were directly behind her now and she spun around wildly, expecting to finally find that army of *dark little glassy eyes* staring at her from the shadows.

A little army of those missing creepy-ass dolls.

But spun around to find no one there, of course.

# THE NIGHT SITTER

But still, she found herself following the *pitter patter, pitter patter, scritch scratch scritch* back up the foyer staircase, then up that long narrow hall with those dimly-flickering bronze sconces--
Only to find Ms. V's *bedroom door now ajar.*
Amid all those dimly-flickering bronze sconces.
A soft warm sunshine spilling out from the bedroom.
*Pitter patter. Pitter patter. Scritch scratch scritch.*
A soft warm sunshine that simply could not exist.
*Pitter patter. Pitter patter. Scritch scratch scritch.*
Not on this late gray black-clouded morning.
*Pitter patter. Pitter patter. Scritch scratch scritch.*
A soft warm sunshine that seemed to offer her an *invitation* into the bedroom *hidden* in all that soft warm spilling sunshine.
*Pitter patter. Pitter patter. Scritch scratch scritch.*
"Ma'am," she heard herself inquire.
Only to hear nothing but sudden silence as that *pitter patter, pitter patter, scritch scratch scritch* fell quiet. It was in this heavy silence she eventually heard faintly, oh, so very faintly, a *small little voice.*
A *small little desperate voice.* Or so she imagined.
Calling her name maybe. Asking for help.
Madelyn. The child. Sometimes Maddy. Maybe.
Then again, maybe *it wasn't just one voice at all. At t'all.*
*But rather a chorus of voices pretending to be just one voice.*
*A chorus of voices pretending to be a desperate child.*
A *chorus of mischievous voices* belonging, just perhaps, to that *pitter patter, pitter patter, scritch scratch scritch* that had led her back here.
Led her back here to this bedroom threshold.
A bedroom now *spilling soft warm sunshine. Door ajar.*
Emily found herself *stepping into that sunshine.*
*Stepping into it* as if her feet had a mind of their own.
Crossing over the threshold into the bedroom.
Only to hear Ms. V's voice in her head:
Hissing: Scolding her: *Neither you nor the child, Madelyn, are ever to enter my personal bedroom without my personal explicit permission.*
Followed by, that voice suddenly paling, fading:
*You are to please knock on all doors before entering.*
Too late, Emily thought, rather somewhat dreamily, having to use her hand to shield her eyes from the sunlight as she found herself, instead of a bedroom, *inexplicably standing in the middle of a marshy meadow. The ground soggy beneath her feet, smelling of most rotten things, forc-*

*ing her to plug her nose with her other hand. With her free hand. The hand not presently shielding her eyes from all this most inexplicable sunlight.*

The sunshine altogether warm on her face.

Perhaps too warm and softly burning her skin.

As if her fever had returned. *Burning, burning.*

The marshy meadow featuring dense green bulrushes with tall yellowish-brown cattails that appeared to sway lazily in a breeze she could not feel. There was thick pondweed and overlapping patches of waterlilies floating above a dark stagnant swampy water. And the raucous din of frogs, birds, and other critters along with the sudden crash of a larger, startled animal splashing in the reeds.

*And a woman. A woman in front of her.*

A *woman* Emily instantly recognized. The bottom of her house dress stained with mud as she plodded forward in the marsh.

Emily instantly recognized the woman *because it was herself.* Not that she had any idea what she might be doing in a swamp. Muttering to herself, she appeared to be. Hair a mess. Hanging in her face. Her round face flushed from the humidity. Or feverish.

Her eyes wide and searching frantically before settling upon a small tree in the middle of that vast marsh. A rather magical thing. This tree. Standing there in the middle of the marshy meadow. Rising from all that dark and fetid stagnant swampy water.

She *followed herself* plodding toward that tree.

Mud-stained house dress lifted above her knees now.

Pale legs pushing through the dark stagnant water.

This small magical tree -- it was *blooming.*

Blooming with large white whorled flowers.

Large white whorled flowers with pink pistils.

And as she got closer to this tree with its bloom of large white whorled flowers with pink pistils, *following herself* in her mud-stained house dress, her hair hanging messily about her round face flushed from the humidity, or feverish, the perfume of sweet-smelling apricot filling the thick warm air, compliments of the tree's large white whorled flowers with pink pistils blooming *here* in the middle of the vast marsh amid its otherwise most terrible rotten smell, it was only then, as she observed *herself* picking these flowers and stuffing them into an apron, Emily realized with a start *that the woman was not herself at all. At t'all.* Though it was an understandable mistake.

But rather, that the *woman* was *her mother.*

Much younger and prettier than she remembered.

And it was at that moment Emily actually saw *her real self* in the murky muddy reflection of the dark stagnant water below her.

*Saw herself at only nine years old.* Pigtails. Ribbons.

In her own mud-stained dress. Lifted nearly to her waist. The warm muddy water rising well above her little knobby knees as she was, at only nine years old, much shorter than her mother.

Saw herself as a child. A pale little girl.

Saw herself turn toward her mother before her.

As her mother turned toward her in the sunlight.

Her eyes round and bright blue and crazy.

*Ask my anything, baby. Anything at t'all.*

Or so they seemed to say, *those eyes*, without her mother uttering a single word out loud as she feverishly stuffed the large white whorled flowers with the pink pistils deep into her apron.

*Why are we here, mother?* Emily asked her mother standing there beneath the small magical tree in the middle of that vast marsh in a too-warm sunshine that began to pale, fade. Lose its color. Turn to gray with the sudden fall of an evening dusk. *Why do you look so sad, mother? What are you going to do with those strange flowers, mother?*

*I seem to remember being here with you, mother.*

*I remember the terrible rotten egg smell of the mud and the sharp smell of booze on your lips when you drove us back to town, you fighting the car to keep it on the road, the road with no street lights, the darkness jumping out at us at every bend, threatening to swallow us whole. That darkness, mother.*

*I remember the fireflies, too, mother. A world of fireflies.*

*Not unlike the stars in the sky, mother. Only earthbound.*

*I remember them outside the car in silent swarms.*

*Dying on the windshield. Paling. Fading to dark.*

*Why were we in this marsh, mother? Why?*

Her mother only offered her daughter a lopsided smile. A sad and forlorn smile. Her bright blue eyes gone muddy, then fading to nothing at all. *At t'all.* As her mother then vanished into the gathering night, leaving behind only that sad forlorn-looking smile.

Frozen there. Illuminated. A string of fireflies.

A fuzzy golden afterimage. An apparition.

Before scattering apart. Paling. Fading to dark.

Emily subsequently found herself in a cold darkness, the only light behind her in the shape of that open bedroom door.

Leading back to the plum-colored carpet.

The dimly-flickering line-up of bronze sconces.

Instead, she stepped deeper into the cold darkness of the bedroom that wasn't a bedroom at all. *At t'all.* And in the distance saw a faint light -- a faint light she found herself now *floating* toward like one of those black or white moths on that dark porch somewhere down far below her. One of those black and white moths fluttering desperately about that porch lantern, certain to get burned.

*Only to suddenly find herself in a small gymnasium.*

If a rather familiar small gymnasium.

The small gymnasium of her long-ago elementary school days with large colorful murals of *Alice in Wonderland* and *Snow White* and *Fantasia* decorating the otherwise ugly yellow concrete walls.

She was sitting -- *at all of nine years old* -- in a small hard wooden chair before a gray backdrop, facing a short balding man in a cheap blue suit, his big apathetic eyes magnified almost comically by thick eyeglasses. The funny-looking man gripped a hand-held trigger to a huge Nikon camera with an even more enormous flash set upon a black tripod under a reflective white umbrella light-modifier.

"Say, cheese, honey," the funny-looking man sighed as if he'd said the same stupid thing a hundred times to a hundred other kids already that day. The Nikon camera flashed. Blinding her.

*And suddenly she found herself in her childhood home.*

Sitting at the kitchen table. With her mother. And the only father she had ever known. The same father who would leave in only a few weeks with a single suitcase on a cold and blustery winter day. Never to return. Never. Not for Emily's mother's funeral. His wife. Not even his own mother's funeral only a couple years later.

She stared at him now. Her father.

The only father she had ever known.

Stared at his large soft brown eyes over chicken and rice. The warmth of his smile. The hollow dimple in his right cheek. The way his beard mimicked an evening shadow by the very end of the day and how tickly it would be when he tucked her into bed.

There was a stiff white envelope on the table.

Sitting there so rather innocently between them.

Stamped: WILSON PHOTOGRAPY.

The only father she had ever known was reaching for it over his chicken and rice and Emily felt herself *inside her little nine year old body wanting to scream at him. To scream at him not to open it.*

*Not to open the envelope with her $4^{th}$ grade portraits.*

Despite having almost no memory of this moment.

This moment somehow *erased from her mind* despite a desperate desire now to scream at the only father she had ever known.

Somehow knowing what was contained inside.

Somehow knowing without remembering. Not just yet.

The memory just too painful. Too awful to bear.

*But finding herself unable to muster that scream as she helplessly watched him open that envelope.* His warm smile slipping right off his face with that tickly evening shadow. His soft brown eyes turning hard.

Her mother, leaning over to the view the portraits for herself, immediately frowning deeply. Face turning pale. Only to shake her head, quickly dismissing *whatever was revealed in those portraits.*

"Well, we'll just have to have them redone," she only said, only just that, and began to clear the table of the dinner dishes.

The only father Emily had ever known said nothing. Nothing *at t'all.* He just sat there. Staring at the portraits. Then at little Emily. His face twitching at the only daughter he had ever known.

Like an animal sensing danger in the woods.

And trying to decide if it was real. If it should run.

*And just like that she was back in that gymnasium.*

The funny-looking man muttering, "Say, cheese, honey," again with even less enthusiasm. Followed by that blinding flash.

*Before yet another jarring and disorienting transition.*

*Throwing her right back into her childhood home. Weeks later.*

In her bed. In the dark. A cold rain hitting the roof above her. Listening to her mother screaming at the only father she had ever known down the hall. Her father not saying a thing. Just slamming bureau drawers. A closet door. Or maybe it was just simply Emily's poor mother doing all that dreadful slamming of things.

Her poor and distraught mother.

Frantic, she was. Inconsolable. Afraid.

The school portrait retakes had come in the mail that evening. And though Emily had forgotten this memory, too, *the horrid memory came rushing back to her now as she lay in bed in her little nine year old body with a cold rain hitting the roof above her and drawers and a closet door slamming down the hall.* For Emily could suddenly remember--

The expression on her father's face upon opening the second stiff white envelope stamped: WILSON PHOTOGRAPHY.

The horror. Disbelief. Twitching. His skin turning as white as that stiff white envelope beneath his evening beard shadow.

The evening shadow that so often tickled her.

Before shoving the portraits back inside that stiff white envelope *so that Emily might not see them. Her little nine year old self.*
She'd snuck out of bed that night amid all that noise down the hall from her bedroom. Snuck to the dark kitchen and peeled open that stiff white envelope. Pulled out those school portraits.
The retakes as well as the original copies.
The two sets were remarkably *indistinguishable.*
Both showing a rather disturbing image of Emily.
Though at first both appeared to only suggest a *double exposure.* Nothing more sinister. But upon closer examination, and given the fact the two sets *were taken weeks apart,* what at first appeared to be a double exposure *suddenly appeared to be something else entirely.*
*It was almost as if -- she could no longer be photographed. Belying all the other school portraits taken over the years residing in their dusty little frames on the fireplace mantel. The photographic image of her little nine year old self most horribly hazy. Vague. Almost ghostly. In these most recent portraits.*
But it was even more than that. Unfortunately.
For both sets of school portraits revealed *a horribly hazy, vague, almost ghostly, double-exposure-like terrible lopsided grin. This terrible lopsided grin showcasing a little mouthful of tiny sharp-looking teeth in several repeating rows along with a frightening pair of impossibly-long fang-like eyeteeth.*
Both portrait sets. Taken weeks apart.
Her father, the only father she had ever known, spooked, and unconvinced by Emily's mother's desperate explanations, meant to leave that very night. The very night the second set of photographs had arrived on their doorstep. Of this Emily had no doubt.
A suitcase half-packed on her parent's bed.
But Emily's mother somehow, tearfully, talked him out of it. Whispering to him in their bedroom shadows. Guilting him. Still, at his insistence, they'd taken her for bloodwork the very next morning. Ordered under the guise of a persistent ear infection.
*And suddenly she was in her pediatrician's office.*
Sitting in that small cold windowless examination room on the stainless steel exam table with the harsh crinkly tissue. Her pediatrician drawing vials of her blood. A dark, almost black blood.
A dark, almost black *thick molasses-like blood.*
Emily, in her little nine year old body, blinked, twitched really, *and suddenly they were back in that pediatrician office a few days later.*
After hours. The place dark and quiet.
Long dark shadows everywhere she looked.

Emily sitting in that small cold windowless examination room with the stainless steel exam table and the harsh crinkly tissue while her parents vanished with the doctor into his private office.

A private office off down a dark narrow hall.

Emily wasn't meant to overhear, but it was after hours and the place was so very quiet with no one else there, and found she could hear small snippets of what the doctor was telling her parents:

If, admittedly, terribly confusing snippets:

*Getting to the age when we might expect to see changes...*
*Bio-chemical and bio-physiological signifiers...*
*Metamorphosis. A perverted or corrupted puberty...*
*Haven't had any experience in my practice...*
*There is no treatment. No reversal of symptoms...*
*This a chronic condition. Monstrous...*

Emily's mother sobbed on the way home.

With more cold rain hitting the car windshield.

And the only father Emily had ever known not saying a thing. Just staring. Staring at Emily, the only daughter he had ever known, with his soft brown eyes turned hard in the rearview mirror.

Staring at her like that animal sensing danger.

Only now that animal knew the danger was real.

And she thought maybe her pediatrician had worn a very similar expression when he'd shown them out the door of that medical building. After hours. Dark and quiet. And she thought, yanking on this ghastly memory like a rotten tooth, maybe the pediatrician had also said in all that dark and quiet, "I'll have to report this."

Her mother begging him not to. Pleading.

Pleading later that night, too. A night of turmoil.

With more slamming of drawers. That closet door.

Her mother begging her father. Sobbing again.

The only father Emily had ever known.

Her father, his voice shaking terribly, muttering to her mother the strangest and most peculiar of questions amid the tumult:

*Who or what is the father...?* he'd wanted to know.

The only father Emily had ever known.

Her mother not having an answer for him. None that satisfied him, anyway, despite her tears. Ending with the only father she had ever known walking out of their house the next morning with only that single suitcase. Never to return. Never. Not for Emily's mother's funeral. His wife. Not even for his own mother's funeral.

*And suddenly there were more memories. Dizzy ones.*
*Dizzy little memories almost nearly erased from her mind.*
*She and her mother packing their own suitcases. Stuffing things into boxes. Photo albums and keepsakes they couldn't live without. Toys. Food. Water. Throwing all of it into the back of her mother's old red hatchback.*
*Then just driving. Driving off into the falling night.*
*A long string of motels off desolate backroads.*
*She and her mother. On the run. In that old red hatchback.*
*Her mother finding that obituary in a rundown diner.*
*A newspaper another customer had left behind.*
*An obit for Emily's pediatrician. Apparently, he'd had an accident.*
*Stepping in front of a bus. Right in front of his office.*
*Her mother trying to make sense of it. Trying to figure out what it might mean. Wanting to be hopeful. But hopeful not being in her nature.*
*Wanting to go home. But finding herself too uncertain.*
*Her mother always crying herself to sleep. And suffering the most godawful dreadful terrible nightmares when she could actually find any sleep.*
*The days passing into nights. Moving in the nights.*
*While the rest of the world was asleep in their warm beds.*
*The money running out. The desolate backroads running out.*
*The world gradually shrinking before them seemingly.*
*Nowhere left to go. Nowhere left to hide, her mother said.*
*Then suddenly they were in that large marshy meadow.*
*With that small magical apricot-smelling white-flowered tree.*
*Before a final little motel in a small farming town.*

The shades tightly drawn over the window. A single bed and a little kitchenette with a two-burner stove and a tiny oven.

Her mother in that mud-stained house dress.

Humming to herself. A dark melancholy hymn.

And baking. Baking a tray of ginger cookies in the tiny oven in that final little motel in that small farming town. Baking as expressionless tears stained her pale cheeks. Humming a dark melancholy hymn as she then frosted those still-warm ginger cookies.

And Emily feeling *her little nine year old self* yawning with terrible exhaustion after all their running on all those dark nights with suddenly *nowhere left in this big shrinking world to go.* A softly-buzzing digital clock beside the single bed reading midnight. And little nine year old Emily, despite yawning with her terrible exhaustion, being unable to sleep, sensing this final little motel in this small farming town was finally, finally, the end of the shrinking road for them.

Evidenced by her mother's manic baking.
Her mother's manic baking at midnight, no less.
A tray of ginger cookies, no less. Frosted.
Her mother's favorite. Emily's, too, perhaps.
*How could she have forgotten about those ginger cookies?*
Her mother had baked them every Christmas.

Her mother turned to her now even as she scraped the cookies off the cooking tray and placed them neatly on a platter.

On a platter with a vase of white flowers.
Despite it being months now after Christmas.
Large white whorled flowers with pink pistils.
The flowers smelling faintly of apricot.
As the cookies smelled so strongly of ginger.

Her mother speaking without speaking. Wearing that lopsided smile, bright blue eyes gone muddy. And yet still Emily could hear her: A wistful serene voice despite her expressionless tears:

Heard her even as her lips refused to move:

*I thought you might not eat the cookies...* she said without speaking a word. Without her lips moving. Just staring at her with her bright blue eyes gone muddy. *I thought you might resist what had to be done. But I didn't even have to ask you. I'm not sure I could've asked you, in the end, if I'm being honest with myself. The poison, it works very quickly. Depressing the nervous system. Slowing body functions. Causing first the loss of consciousness. And then respiratory failure. Before eventually, mercifully, death.*

It was as her mother spoke to her without speaking Emily noticed on the counter beside that tiny oven a blender. Into which her mother had stuffed some of those white flowers, stems and all.

Reducing them to a very fine white powder.

*It's a powerful poison. Potent in small doses. Potent.*
*Nature's own little most terrible awful miracle.*

Adding them, presumably, to the cookie batter.

*I thought to myself how peaceful you looked slipping into that sleep from which I thought you would never wake. I thought how peaceful I would feel once I joined you. And while you slept, I ate a cookie. And then another.*
*Just as you had done before you'd fallen into that sleep.*
*And I let that peaceful sleep fall over me, too.*
*Not pills, baby. Not an overdose. Just poison, baby.*
*Not what you were later told to spare you the ugly truth.*
*A truth your grandmother thought would devastate you.*
*That I meant to take both of us. Together, baby.*

And that was when Emily noticed in the bathroom mirror: the single bed against the opposite wall. Her mother lying there on top of the bedsheets. Little nine year old Emily lying beside her.

*Emily now separate from her little nine year old self.*

*Her little nine year old self now lying there beside her mother.*

Their eyes closed. Sleeping that peaceful sleep.

Frosting still on their fingers. Waxen lips.

Emily noticed, as well, that same bathroom mirror offered her no reflection of herself. *For she was not really there, was she?*

She was invisible. Just a ghost fly on the wall.

Only a visitor to a past she was only now remembering.

A disquieting past somehow *forgotten* to her until now. Perhaps because of that poison. A past that had been kept from her.

And in the ether of this *forgotten* memory, she heard her mother's voice again: A soft hushed warm whisper of a voice:

*Sleep, little one, sleep…* this soft hushed warm whisper of a voice said. *Dream yourself awake, and all of your dreams will come true.*

Something she'd hushed to her. As Emily had *fallen asleep* after eating the frosted ginger cookies. Falling into a deep sleep.

But then she blinked. Twitched. Heavily.

*And found herself waking on that single bed. Found herself back inside her little nine year old body. Her little nine year old mind muddled by the poison. And in this rather most delirious, confused, hallucinatory state--*

*Noticing a tall man sitting in a chair in a corner of the room of that final little motel in that small farming town. Just sitting there in its deepest shadows. One long thin leg folded neatly over the other. As if he were merely waiting for a bus or train. Dapper in a long black suit. His long angular face an ashen gray. His chin razor-sharp beneath a black fedora tipped very low over his brow. His hair a long bone-white underneath the hat. His eyes gleaming. Gold.*

*And for some reason reminding her of a very old book, this tall man sitting there in that chair in the deepest shadows. Musty worn pages with just the hint of vanilla. A very old book in which the bad guys maybe weren't so bad in the end. A very old book in which the bad guys just maybe thrived.*

*She didn't know why she thought such a thing. Maybe it was the way the tall man in the long black suit winked at her sadly. And then beckoned her to follow him as he seemed to float through the motel room to the door.*

*Seemingly whispering in a soft hiss: Dance with me.*

*Offering back his left hand. Ashen with excessively long fingers.*

*His right hand resting on the handle of a black walnut cane. The handle itself carved from alabaster and shaped rather like a long sharp claw.*

## THE NIGHT SITTER

*She found herself rising, floating, from the bed and her mother and taking the tall man's hand, the tall man in the long black suit, and then following him right through the motel room door as if the door were not even there.*
*As if the silly motel room door were only made of air.*
*Exiting that final little motel room in a small farming town.*
*A final little motel she'd later learn was only a few short miles down the road from her grandparents -- the parents of the only father she'd ever known, now disappeared. Only a few short miles from their cozy little farm.*
*That cozy little farm with all those magnificent fireflies.*
*Her mother's own parents having died in a car accident.*
*A car accident when her mother was at university.*
And then she blinked again. Twitched. Heavily.
*As her nine year old self floated through that motel room door.*
*The aroma of ginger and faintly of apricot still about her.*
*Only to find herself still inside that little nine year old girl, if now standing in an old church staring down at her dead mother lying in a casket.*
Her grandmother tightly squeezing her tiny hand.
Telling her *not to fidget*. Toady eyes emphasizing the point.
Dull sunlight spilling through stained glass windows.
Stained glass windows featuring biblical stories.
Genesis. Revelations. And other stuff in-between.
Life. Death. Suffering. Sacrifice. Martyrdom.
Red, orange, green, yellow, blue. Black and gray.
Little nine year old Emily desperately trying not to fidget in an itchy new black dress *as she stared down at her dead mother in that casket.* Her grandmother in her own long black dress and a frilly black veil. And her grandfather sitting alone in a front pew, grimacing angrily, drunkenly, eyes rheumy. A dark gray suit and thin black tie.
There was a priest. A few other mourners.
Pale faces nine year old Emily didn't recognize.
Not that she offered them much attention.
Rather, she found herself becoming fixated on that *watch*. Her mother's most treasured possession. The only thing she still had of her poor dear late mother in this world come so very undone.
She had a fuzzy memory of it hanging loosely about her wrist, this *watch*, as she stood over her dead mother in that casket.
Yet that fuzzy memory became *even fuzzier* now.
*The memory of her mother's watch hanging loosely about her wrist.*
Parisienne. Art Deco. Much too large for her.
*Much too large* for her little thin nine year old wrist.

An antique her mother had never removed.
Only to have it removed *from her* postmortem.
Leaving behind a pale ring of skin about her wrist.
A ghostly impression in that casket with her.

For yet there was no pale ring of skin. No ghostly impression.
*For the beautiful watch, her mother's most treasured possession, an antique her mother had never removed, was still there on her wrist in the casket.*

*A casket that was suddenly disappearing down into an open grave.*
*Disappearing down into the cold hard earth of a cemetery.*
*As the priest, head bowed, began over the open grave:*
*"Though I walk through the valley of the shadow of death--"*
*The old church left behind. Just beyond a short stone wall below.*
*The cemetery sitting on a hill overlooking the farming town.*

*Emily found herself standing over the open grave in her little nine year old body, fidgeting in her itchy new black dress, her mother's most treasured possession inexplicably absent from her little thin wrist. Watching that casket vanish down into the shadows of that open grave with her mother inside it still wearing that watch. Her most treasured possession. The casket disappearing down into an everlasting darkness. A large pile of earth waiting sheepishly nearby beneath a tarp beside a small backhoe with a small muddy excavation bucket. Waiting to fill that deep hole. To bury her mother in that everlasting darkness.*

*To bury her mother still wearing that watch.*

Her grandmother tightly squeezing her tiny hand.

Glaring down at her with those toady eyes.

Glaring down at her as the casket lowered, the gentle whine of a crank sounding like someone whistling into a cold wind.

Her grandmother then *leaning down to her.*

And whispering into her little nine year old ear:

A strident little whine of a scolding whisper:

*Never show your teeth when you smile…* she said.

As if there were anything to smile about.

Before demanding another most peculiar thing:

*From now on, child, we shall call you Emily after my dear late mother…* her grandmother said in that strident little whine of a whisper, staring down at her with those toady eyes to emphasize the point. *After your great-grandmother. A pious, god-fearing woman, my mother.*

*And that was when Emily noticed the tall man from the motel room.*
*The motel room somewhere a few odd miles down the road.*

*The tall man in the long black suit. Standing between the old church and that short stone wall in the deepest shadows of a cypress tree. Long angular face an ashen gray. His chin razor-sharp below a black fedora tipped very low over his brow. His hair a long pale bone-white. His eyes gleaming. Gold.*

*Gleaming gold in the shadows of that cypress tree.*

*Not unlike a pair of silently hovering fireflies.*

*His right hand resting on the handle of a black walnut cane. The handle itself carved from alabaster and shaped rather like a long sharp claw.*

And then Emily blinked. Twitched. Heavily.

*And he was gone. This tall man in his long black suit.*

*But that wasn't quite true, was it? Like a daydream, she'd often see him again over the passing years. In crowds and around street corners. Sitting in the back of courtrooms. Standing in the rain one night outside her bedroom window during an especially poor foster placement. One where they fed her only hotdogs while they fed their own fat little nasty children steak and potatoes.*

*Always there without her consciously noticing it.*

*Always hovering at the periphery of her dark little life.*

*As if he were just a part of her very own shadow.*

*Walking right there beside her in the sinking cold when she didn't own a proper coat. Humming into her ear and numbing her exhausted mind when she went to bed hungry and missed most terribly her dead grandmother.*

*When she missed most terribly her dead mother.*

*And the only father she had ever known, still long gone.*

*And later when she was missing him. Her Adam.*

She blinked a final time. Twitched. Heavily.

And found herself suddenly back in that narrow plum-colored carpeted hall corridor with the dimly-flickering bronze sconces. Ms. Vivian Dancemore's bedroom door *slipping shut behind her.*

Its bolt making a punctuating clacking noise.

It was only then Emily noticed Marbles, the black cat, slinking along the wall shadows, staring back at her haughtily, its own shadow rising on the wall and appearing to her *almost human-like.*

*A tall man, perhaps. Black suit. Fedora. Cane.*

*If she allowed herself to believe such a thing.*

Staring back at her haughtily. That black cat.

Marbles. With its dark green almond-shaped eyes.

Beneath its *almost human-like* wall alter ego.

Dark green almond-shaped eyes that vanished with it into the deeper hall shadows. Before reappearing, levitating in the darkness, and seemingly *glinting with gold* before vanishing once again. Vanishing with the beast into the darkness. Vanishing completely this time with that shadow. A most strange and peculiar of shadows.

Emily found herself slowly returning to her bedroom, slipping under her waiting bedsheets, shivering despite feeling too-warm all over. Fearing, perhaps, that her terrible fever had returned.

Or, perhaps, had never actually left her.

Perhaps only this explaining her continuing delirium.

*Assuming she was not falling in and out of consciousness. Slipping from an ever-increasingly slippery reality into fever dream and back again.*

*Then again, perhaps it was aspects of both conditions.*

*Delirium and fever dream a difference without a distinction.*

She fell into a deep and troubled sleep as that fever caused her skin to burn and she felt as if she were burning in her sleep. In her sleep as she dreamt of this giant looming beast of a house.

As she dreamt of it being *consumed in flames.*

*The old Victorian house beset with a conflagration of flames. Here at the very edge of the world. Roasting and sizzling. Bubbling and crackling and popping. The large black multi-paned windows melting even as all that solid black steel held fast. The melted windowpane openings far too small for her to squeeze through. Trapping her in all the angry roaring flames. Allowing those flames to feed hungrily upon her. Her own flesh melting. Her eyes bubbling and crackling and popping. Her small bones roasting and sizzling. As that large grandfather clock gonged midnight somewhere down in that parlor far below her.*

# 21.

THE GRANDFATHER CLOCK was bellowing midnight somewhere down in the parlor far below her as she awoke. Her skin feeling as if it were still on fire. Blistering. *As if that conflagration had rather somehow followed her out of another fever dream.* Her brain roasting and sizzling, bubbling and crackling and popping, in her sweat-soaked head. That terrible ice pick once again stabbing at the back of her neck into her febrile brain behind her right eye, but suddenly feeling less like an ice pick than a fiery-hot poker.

And as that grandfather clock bellowed its bellicose midnight tune somewhere down in the parlor far below her, the gongs echoing through the old bones of the dark house, reverberating through the floorboards, shaking the walls, and causing her teeth to chatter, Emily thought she could discern the *fuzzy distorted echo of voices*. The *fuzzy distorted echo of voices* within those heavy bellicose gongs.

She fought to cock open her right eye. An almost painful gesture. To discover the small black and white television with the thin rabbit ears on that otherwise empty desk beside the black-curtained window was on without any memory of having turned it on.

*Perhaps it had been the leprechauns…* she thought drearily. *Perhaps the little gremlins had done so while she'd been sleeping so very fitfully.*

*Sleeping so very fitfully through the rest of the day until midnight, no less. If those heavy bellicose gongs were to be believed. Reverberating. Echoing.*

She found herself fighting to sit up in the bed.

The President was back on TV. In the Oval Office. Surrounded as before by his cadre of expressionless military figures.

Only it wasn't midnight after all. A silly mistake.

Rather, the live TV broadcast revealed it was only *noon* on this most terrible black-clouded day turned to a mimicry of night.

The TV image was as grainy as ever, forcing her to squint past the attendant long and wavy lines jumping up and down, a shifting picture creating two Presidents. Doubling his military cadre.

The sound *fuzzier* and *more distorted* than ever, too. The President sounding like a silly cartoon character. His voice stretched and echoing in stereo as the man read off a prepared statement:

"...*heavy heart I tell you the virus was created*..."

*(tell you the virus was created)*

"...*and released into the general public with*..."

*(released into the general public with)*

"...*the very best of intentions.*"

*(very best of intentions)*

"*This terribly difficult decision was not taken lightly and was only put into motion when all other avenues of less invasive extermination were*..."

*(all other avenues of less invasive extermination were)*

"...*eliminated as possibilities.*"

*(eliminated as possibilities)*

"*Furthermore, I can assure you there was absolutely no indication to any of us, either during the creation of this virus or its testing, there was any danger to the general public from this virus prior to its subsequent release.*"

*(this virus prior to its subsequent release)*

"*Unfortunately, however, as we have now come to know and lament, this virus was fraught with unintended consequences...mutations...*"

*(fraught with unintended consequences...mutations)*

"*This virus meant to liberate us from them. A virus elegantly designed to be transmitted from you, the carrier, my fellow Americans...*"

*(from you, the carrier, my fellow Americans)*

"...*to its intended target, this–*"

*(intended target, this–)*

It was at that very moment those long and wavy lines jumping up and down on the television screen abruptly burst into a cloud of horribly snowy static, completely corrupting the image and sound, but not before Emily believed she heard the President expound, his large beefy fists maybe pounding on the Oval Office desk.:

"...*undead scourge...these parasitic bloodsuckers...*"

But of course he hadn't said any such thing.
*But of course he hadn't said anything such thing at t'all.*
*All of it being only her imagination. The corrupted TV signal.*
*A terrible fiction of her fever returned. The virus. Delirium.*

With no memory of leaving her bedroom, Emily found herself at Ms. Vivian Dancemore's bedroom door. Stumbling there.

Knocking on her door. Short hard raps.

*You are to please knock on all doors before entering. Rule #10.*

"Ma'am," she said. Her voice weak. Hoarse.

"Ma'am, I'm unwell," she managed.

And not unwell in a simple *body clock adjusting to working the night throwing off her biorhythms* sort-of-way. No. Uh uh. And not unwell in a related *fatigue, mental indexterity, malaise* sort-of-way, either.

Rather, she felt as if she were dying.

Her every last joint tender. Enflamed.

Her eyes blurry. With terrible black spots.

And she was once again having trouble breathing. Her rattling wheezing breath coming in awful sucking grabs *as if that oozing dark fluid* were again filling her lungs like black water balloons.

*Rising heavily. Thickly. Like a dark wet cement.*

*Threatening to turn her lungs into those black stones.*

"Ma'am, please" she choked out. "Ms. Dancemore."

Emily found a pale hand testing the door knob.

Only to find it steadfastly locked, of course. No invitation. No soft warm sunshine. No marshy meadow. None of that.

These figments of her delirium. Fever dream.

Just this plum-colored carpeted hallway.

And its line-up of dimly-flickering bronze sconces.

And that was when Emily heard yet again--

Heard it yet again as she had in her fever dream--

*Pitter patter. Pitter patter. Scritch scratch scritch.*

*As well as little hands over little mouths stifling little snickering laughter at her expense. Coming from up the dimly-lit hall on this occasion.*

Coming from the attic alcove. The attic staircase.

The dark attic above this giant beast of a house.

*Pitter patter. Pitter patter. Scritch scratch scritch.*

And Emily found herself suddenly moving -- *floating* -- up the narrow dimly-lit hall and around the corner, rising up that dark narrow staircase into the soft golden glow of the carriage light.

The carriage light *having been turned back on.*

*Probably by those mischievous little leprechauns on this black-clouded day turned to night. The carriage light usually being turned off after dawn.*

The rest of the attic in dark shadows, she found herself standing before the small cot. Her back to those dark shadows.

The carriage light drawing her attention to:

*The collection of doodles on the attic wall above the small cot.*

*The collection of doodles drawn in the hand of a child.*

She'd never really looked at them before. A funny thing given the riddles of the house, she reflected now, leaning forward.

The doodle at the center of the collection featured a small girl in a white nightie with white ribbons in her braided hair. The small girl offering a lopsided smile. A lopsided smile that was slowly slipping off her round pale face, *revealing a pair of missing front teeth.*

*The-crets, the-crets are no fun...* it seemed to say.

That lopsided smile slipping off her face.

*The-crets, the-crets can hurt thumb-one...*

And on her lap, that black cat. Marbles.

Its black tail curled like a snake beneath its chin.

And beside the small girl, a young woman. Blonde hair. Brown eyes. Rather plain-looking. Nervous-looking. Cheeks gaunt, hollow. Skin sallow. As if she'd maybe not eaten for days. The poor woman peering back over her shoulder while her small pale hands clutched at something dangling from a necklace around her neck.

A *large silver crucifix*. Clutching at it desperately.

Hard enough to reveal thin bones in her fingers.

Peering back over her shoulder fretfully into the shadows behind the small girl with the lopsided smile. Peering back at shadows *that appeared, upon closer scrutiny, to perhaps not be shadows at t'all.*

*Shadows that appeared to be hovering over the small girl.*

*Shadows that appeared to have long ashen gray faces.*

*Including a rather feminine shadow with long red hair.*

*Evidenced by a slight smudge of faded maroon.*

*A rather feminine shadow that was somehow familiar.*

*Somehow familiar to Emily as she stared at it. Maternal.*

But it was the largest shadow in the middle of all these haunting shadows that truly held the eye. *A shadow looming just behind the small girl.*

*A razor-sharp chin. A black fedora dipped very low over its brow maybe. An ashen gray hand with excessively long fingers clutching at the dark swath of a cane. The cane little more than a dash of black charcoal, but its handle, perhaps, carved from alabaster and shaped rather like a long sharp claw.*

# THE NIGHT SITTER

*If Emily allowed herself to believe such a thing.*
*Its hair a bone-white maybe. Eyes gleaming. Gold.*
*In fact, all the hovering shadows seemed to have such eyes. Such gleaming gold eyes. Assuming it wasn't just a trick of the golden carriage light.*
And standing just off to the side of these shadows in this center doodle, Ms. Vivian Dancemore herself. As if she were a part of this shadowy ensemble -- *and yet also somehow separate.* Her gray eyes turned white. Large white holes. *Large white whorled holes.*

*Large white whorled holes* staring blankly at the small girl with the lopsided smile slowly slipping off her round pale face.

The small girl with those *missing front teeth.*

As for the young woman clutching that silver crucifix dangling from a necklace around her neck in the midst of all these foreboding ashen-gray-faced shadows hovering over the small girl--

Emily somehow instinctively understood her to be her *predecessor. The former nanny.* Instinctively understood her to be Hannah.

And suddenly she could hear Ms. V's voice:

Back down in that parlor: The night of her arrival:

*The previous nanny, our dearest Hannah, was with us here in this house for a very long time. Quite one of the family...* she'd explained.

*A very long time. In this house. Our dearest Hannah.*

Emily had bit her tongue that first night in the parlor, resisting the urge to ask *what might have happened* to this former nanny. To this dearest Hannah. Her predecessor. *Quite one of the family.*

And that was when she noticed the other doodles to offer variations of this centermost doodle. The small girl in the white nightie, white ribbons in her braided hair, always at the forefront of the ashen-gray-faced hovering shadows. Ms. Vivian Dancemore always standing off to the side, staring with *large white whorled holes.*

The only difference being Nanny Hannah.

Her *deterioration* for the lack of a better word.

Initially, she appeared a portly, pink-cheeked young woman in the earliest doodle renditions before *shrinking in her own skin.*

*Those rosy cheeks turning sallow. Gaunt. Hollow.*

*As if the life itself were being sucked from her.*

*Meanwhile, despite the fact neither the small girl at the center of these peculiar doodles nor Ms. Vivian Dancemore nor that infernal black cat Marbles ever seemed to grow even a single day older, the poor young woman, their dearest Hannah, began to only too quickly age in these peculiar doodles. As if decades were passing only for her as time somehow remained stagnant for them.*

*Only too quickly becoming gray-haired. Stooped.*
*Her hands arthritic. Her fingers twisted and gnarled.*
*Her veins turning varicose. A dull smattering of broken blue.*
*Her eyes filling with cataracts. Staring out almost blindly.*

An unnatural aging. Perhaps only because it was in juxtaposition to the small child and Ms. Vivian Dancemore and that infernal black cat's refusal to seemingly age even a single day in the very same peculiar doodle collection.

But perhaps it was something more dreadful than that as the young woman, their dearest Hannah, appeared to be aging well beyond her years.

*As if time were being gobbled up for only just her.*

And suddenly Emily found herself contemplating those grave markers in her fever dream. The grave markers found along the dirt path at the crest of the hill in the woods behind the house.

Headstones. Three of them. Side by side.

Like jagged teeth in all that pigweed and bull thistle.

A short wrought iron fence surrounding them.

The inscribed dates on the initial headstone indicating that Alfred Milton Dancemore *had been dead for twenty seven long years.*

*That he'd been forty seven years old when he'd passed.*

*Which would've made him seventy four years young today.*

The inscribed dates on the eerily small middle headstone indicating Madelyn Marie Dancemore *had been only nine years old when she had died. And that she'd been dead for some twenty nine long years.*

The inscribed birth date on the last headstone, a marker without yet a date of death, indicating that Ms. Vivian Dancemore herself *had apparently been born sixty two very long years ago.* A woman who, even to the most causal eye, *appeared to only be in her late thirties, not a year older. And yet, defying the natural laws of physics, at least according to her birth date on that last headstone in those woods, could not have been any older than a preteen when her husband and daughter had left this earth.*

*Which meant, of course, impossibly impassable, the woman couldn't have been any older than a mere toddler when her daughter had been born.*

*And now, appearing not to age, not even a single day, just like her ghostly daughter and that infernal black cat Marbles, in these peculiar doodles as she silently stared at her daughter with large white whorled holes for eyes.*

*As if time had somehow remained stagnant for them.*

Unlike poor dearest Hannah. The previous nanny. Quite one of the family. Only too quickly becoming gray-haired and stooped in comparison. Hands arthritic. Fingers twisted and gnarled. Veins turning varicose. A dull smattering of broken blue. Eyes filling with cataracts. Staring out almost blindly.

*Appearing to age well beyond her years.*
*As if the life itself were being sucked from her.*
*As if time were being gobbled up for only just her.*
And that was when Emily heard the antique music box behind her. As if it might provide her an answer to these riddles.

As if *something* in this house might do just that.

Finally. On this black-clouded day turned to night.

Calliope music. Like that of an approaching carnival or circus. And again found herself imagining a long train of cars slowly slipping along the rails into a small town in the middle of the country in the middle of a dark night. *Or a black-clouded day turned to night.*

Ferrying clowns and freaks and wild beasts.

Big-top tents and kettle corn and funnel cakes.

Fried pickles and strange foreign meats on sticks.

Booths featuring games of chance and skill.

Balloons, banners, and clouds of confetti.

But rather than played at a bright lively tempo as was the tradition of such music, carnival or circus music, playing at the wrong speed. As it had done before. Warped and distorted. Stretched like cold taffy. As if she were hearing it from beneath dark water.

Its tune unnaturally slowed down. Perverted.

Into something macabre and unnatural.

Something dark and rather sinister.

She turned to find *its dull glass-topped lid mimicking a red and white circus big-top tent open, revealing a spinning carousel inside. A spinning carousel of circus animals. Lions, tigers, elephants, monkeys, and zebras.*

*Only the circus animals had adopted human faces.*

*Human faces wretched with terrible expressions of agony.*

Spinning on top of that old steamer trunk.

The old steamer trunk in the far corner shadows.

With its thick leather straps and heavy buckles.

The *ghoulish spinning carousel* offering spinning speckles of twinkling golden light about the entire attic. *Spinning, spinning.*

Like a maelstrom of golden fireflies.

And that was when she noticed the door.

Its outline nearly invisible in the darkness.

*A short narrow door. For a small person. A child maybe.*

*A short narrow door that had disappeared. Poof. Like magic.*

*Only to suddenly reappear in that back wall now.*

*On this black-clouded day turned to night.*

*A black-clouded day turned to night foreshadowing a most terrible storm. The cold wind howling even louder in the house eaves now. Moaning.*

She found herself approaching the door, those black spots still spinning in front of her eyes as if shadows of those spinning speckles of twinkling golden light coming from that music box.

The attic suddenly feeling like an oven against her *feverish* skin. The fiery-hot poker slicing through her brain behind her right eye. Making it difficult to think clearly. To maintain coherent thought as she felt as if she were now suddenly *floating* toward the door.

This most mysterious short narrow door.

A most mysterious door fashioned with *a silver knob and a silver keyplate that appeared to be oversized -- if only because of the truncated size of the door itself.* The silver knob and keyplate embellished with more of that *flowery fleur-de-lis that was actually not flowery at all. At t'all. For it was not stylized black lilies as was the tradition of such fleur-de-lis ornamentation; but rather, the flared black hoods of dragons. Wild winged-beasts.*

*Flared black hoods framing gold spheroid eyes. Fangs.*

Emily reached down for the silver knob. *Knowing it might playfully slip from her grasp. Gripping at it tightly so it would not do so, turning it.* Thinking perhaps the short narrow door might finally open.

Might finally open *despite* the absence of a key.

Only to find it *refuse to budge.* As before.

This most mysterious short narrow door.

Appearing. And disappearing. And *reappearing* now.

Her shoulders sinking, she just stood there.

Just stood there as if it might change its mind.

Not wanting to take her eyes off the door.

Not wanting it to just *disappear* again.

And that was when she noticed a *flashing silver glint* amongst all those spinning speckles of twinkling musical golden light.

*A flashing silver glint resembling a giant silver key.*

*Like tinker bell glittering on the short narrow door before her.*

*A ghostly reflection. A mirage of a glittering thing.*

*And with it, a voice. A voice in the shadows quite near her.*

*As if the voice were somehow a part of the darkness itself.*

*A familiar soft warm hushed whisper of a voice.*

*Sleep, little one, sleep,* this soft warm hushed whisper of a voice whispered to her. *Dream yourself awake, and all of your dreams will come true.*

*Whispered to her from the shadows quite near her.*

*As if the voice were somehow a part of the darkness itself.*

Emily turned, her feverish head now spinning even more dizzily as all those shadowy black spots spinning before her eyes tried to keep pace with all those spinning speckles of twinkling musical golden light, to find it sitting there. Sitting there silently. It.
In the window corner shadows. Darkness.
As if *materializing* from that very darkness itself.
Sitting there in a chair so very silently.
An elegant chair speaking of French aristocracy. Richly upholstered with chocolate paisley fabric and a crème brulee wood finish and baroque hand-carved details. *Hand-carved details resembling the wild winged-beasts on that short narrow door's silver knob and keyplate.*
*Fleur-de-lis that was not fleur-de-lis at all. At t'all.*
The doll. Red-headed. Dirty blue eyes.
The doll that had been missing from this attic.
Missing from its place on its long dark shelf.
A dark hole amongst the other creepy-ass dolls.
*The other creepy-ass dolls that were now missing themselves.*
It *seemed to grin* at her. As before. Animate.
Not a Cheshire grin. Not like that black cat.
But rather, a sad forlorn-looking grin.
A grin that was *probably* only a trick of the light. Or the lack of it certainly in this terrible dimness. Or so Emily desperately tried to convince herself as she noticed its small hands. *Its small pale porcelain hands were outstretched from its little body, offering to her something.*
*Something glinting like a silver wink in the darkness.*
*A key. A silver key with a decorative fleur-de-lis bow.*
*A decorative fleur-de-lis bow that was not fleur-de-lis at t'all.*
*But a black dragon. In full flight. The winged-beast screaming. Its clawed feet clawing at the air. Its black forked tongue spitting black fire.*
*Flared black hood framing gold spheroid eyes. Fangs.*
*Its black nostrils expelling black smoke.*
With the heavy black clouds pressing down hard on the world, preparing to smother it in their dark gathering embrace as that cold whipping wind somehow blew ever-harder still, howling, *moaning*, in the house eaves, snapping at tree branches beyond the multi-paned attic window, foreshadowing a most terrible black storm--
Emily found herself *floating* toward the doll.
A doll smelling faintly of apricot. Ginger maybe.
Red-headed. Dirty blue eyes. Unblinking.
Found herself, hand shaking, *reaching for that key.*

*That silver key with that screaming winged-beast.*

For a moment she thought the red-headed doll might be tricking her. That the silver key was only a diversion. *That something might suddenly jump out from the darkness while she was preoccupied with it.*

*Something with sharp little spiny needles for teeth.*

*And maybe fangs, too. Long sharp fangs.*

*Something that would grab at her and not let go.*

*Maybe even the ugly red-headed doll itself. Flashing a terrible grin of such sharp little spiny needles, and perhaps fangs, too. Before lunging. Biting.*

But suddenly the silver key was in her hand.

Resting on her palm. Heavier than she expected.

As if *weighted* with a certain authority. The silver key.

The queer doll seeming to grin harder at her.

But rather than appearing only sad and forlorn--

That grin now seemed to possess a *sad joyfulness*, too.

*An expression not altogether unfamiliar to Emily.*

Blinking, twitching really, she then found herself turning back to that short narrow door in the wall. Part of her was surprised the door had not *disappeared* while her back had been turned to it.

Surprised to find the door still waiting for her.

Part of her was also afraid. Not just overexcited, but genuinely terrified. Tiny hard gooseflesh again rising like scales.

That cold black hand squeezing her heart even tighter.

Her lungs heavy with that dark wet cement.

*I have control over my emotions. And I choose to feel at peace.*

*I have control over my emotions. And I choose to feel at peace.*

Or so she told herself *as she slipped the silver key into the short narrow door's silver keyplate*, having to stoop down a bit to do so, her thin legs more than ever feeling like wet noodles beneath her.

The dark air wheezing in and out of her stone-hardening lungs as if through a straw. Her heart seemingly seizing in her chest.

It slid in rather easily in the end. The key.

And with all those black spots spinning even more dizzily still before her eyes as if shadows of those speckles of twinkling golden light coming from that antique music box, the shrill circus or carnival calliope music coming from that antique music box rising to a maddening crescendo, louder and louder still, she *turned the key.*

It turned rather easily in the end, too. The key.

Only to have the bolt refuse to disengage.

Only to have the mysterious door *refuse to open.*

# THE NIGHT SITTER

Emily stood there dumbfounded for a moment, wheezing terribly, her free hand against her sternum, *watching herself as if out of her own body desperately rotating the key back and forth. Back and forth.*

Only to have the stubborn grim lock hold fast.

Still hunched over, she took a small step backward, that loud shrill calliope music now threatening to make her head burst.

To make her throbbing head burst with gray goo.

Only for the antique music box to fall *suddenly quiet.*

Its speckles of golden light still spinning deliriously.

If silently like a maelstrom of golden fireflies.

Spinning silently about her as she came up with the answer to this riddle as she stood there before this mysterious little door hoping it would *not simply disappear before her very eyes* this time.

She closed her eyes and knocked softly on the mysterious little door while hushing beneath her wheezing breath: "*Marco.*"

*You are to please knock on all doors before entering.*

Her knocks echoed as if reverberating in a dark chasm beyond the door before she eventually thought she heard from somewhere deep in that dark chasm a dark echoing response: "*Polo.*"

Not necessarily the tiny voice of a child.

Something much more ancient. Wiser. Maybe.

A deep dark voice possessing its own *sad joyfulness.*

A *sad joyfulness* echoing in the old bones of the house.

Echoing now through her very own bones, too.

Without opening her eyes, *she turned the key again* and heard the distinct sound of the bolt *disengaging* with a loud clacking noise. She then turned the silver knob -- and the door swung open.

Toward her. Its rusted hinges squeaking.

Inviting a rush of cold darkness into her face.

She opened her eyes to find herself staring at a *dark narrow corridor* leading into an even heavier darkness. Heavier coldness.

*A dark narrow corridor proceeding into the very walls of the house.*

She would need a flashlight, Emily decided.

But was afraid to abandon the door now that it was open, certain it and the dark narrow corridor would *disappear* in her absence. Only to notice a small shelf just beyond the door. A small shelf *with a long thin white candlestick and a candlestick holder. The candlestick holder a rusted iron and bedecked with more of that black dragon fleur-de-lis.*

As if left there by the house leprechauns.

And beside it a *sleeve of long dark matches.*

Emily pulled a match. Lit it against the door frame.

A pale flame *burst to life* in the shadows. *Sizzling*.

Pushing back the heavy darkness before her, seemingly reducing the heavy darkness to but a harmless congregation of retreating black ghosts groveling now before this god of white light.

*It was in this white light she then heard her grandmother:*

*Her grandmother's voice whispering as if from this white light:*

*Cherish those who seek the truth, child...* the old woman reminded her. Before quickly admonishing: *But beware of those who find it.*

And yet, despite her grandmother's warning--

Emily pushed forward into the dark narrow corridor.

She had to duck her head, of course, to pass through the short narrow doorway as well as turn sideways despite the fact she possessed narrow shoulders. Once inside the dark narrow corridor, she found she had to keep those shoulders uncomfortably hunched to avoid hitting her throbbing head on the low corridor ceiling.

She found it all unnervingly claustrophobic.

Wheezing and gasping. Heart *paralytic* in her chest.

And for a moment considered *turning around*.

Only to be reminded of the very same feeling upon first arriving outside this black house. Such a desire to *turn around*.

But having nowhere else in this world to go.

*But it had been more than that, hadn't it? It was almost as if she could not turn around even if she'd wanted to. It was almost as if her whole miserable freaking life had led her here to this giant looming beast of a house.*

*Almost as if this black house had been waiting for her.*

*Waiting for her so very patiently. So very patiently, indeed.*

*And not just this house, but whatever it was inside its black walls.*

*Whatever it was at the end of this dark narrow corridor.*

*Whatever it was that had yet to fully reveal itself to her.*

*Waiting. Waiting. So very patiently, indeed.*

*Dark and ancient and wise. This thing that waited.*

The pale candlelight guttering before her with its own *sizzling* noise, she proceeded down the dark narrow corridor into the thick walls of the black house only to have that dark narrow corner turn sharply to the right before heading steeply downward. Meanwhile, in the darkness back behind her, she thought she just maybe heard that little door slowly *slipping closed*. And maybe its bolt sliding back into place. Not a loud clacking noise, but a *dark little whisper*.

And just maybe heard *something else* besides.

Something echoing inside these walls with her.
*Pitter patter. Pitter patter Scritch scratch scritch.*
She tried not to imagine little feet in the darkness.
Little doll feet following after her. About her.
Tried not to imagine she heard the *calliope music* again.
Looping over and over, echoing in the black walls.
As if the walls were somehow *singing* to her.
Walls, she realized, that were *made of stone and not of wood.* Or so she discerned as she stumbled down this dark narrow corridor. The stone walls altogether smooth to the touch. If a deathly cold. As if made of a thick black marble. A thick black marble that revealed to her a *deep red blood-like veining* that glowed in the darkness.

That congregation of black ghosts seemed to push closer now. That pale candlelight guttering, *sizzling*, uncertainly now.

Her wheezing breath turning to ragged mist.

The air colder and colder still. Like a meat locker. Her once *feverish* goose-fleshed skin turning deathly cold, too. *Freezing.*

*The scales even more pronounced in the sinking cold.*
*As if she were turning into a black dragon herself in the darkness.*
The corridor floor also that smooth black marble.
As well as the low corridor ceiling just above her head.
The *deep red blood-like veining* suddenly everywhere.

Emily wished she had brought a coat. Trembling violently, but knowing there really could be *no going back* now. That the mysterious little narrow door back up there in the attic *had slipped closed and had almost certainly locked itself and probably quite disappeared, too.*

*Like a terrible little magic trick. Poof. Just gone.*
And so on she went. *Down and down and down.*
Before rising briefly on a dark narrow stone staircase.
Before descending once more. Even more steeply.
Nearly tripping over her stumbling feet in the dark.
Slipping about on all that cold black marble.

Until she felt certain she was beneath the house, assuming the giant black beast of a house *didn't just continue into the very earth.*

*Didn't just continue into the very pits of hell itself.*
*Albeit a hell encased in cold black marble ice.*

It was then, to her surprise, the low dark corridor opened into a large chamber. The cold black stone marble beneath her echoing feet turning into large square blocks, not unlike black tile.

*Black tile with its own deep red blood-like veining.*

At the very center of the large chamber was a solid black marble table. The solid black marble table was completely smooth and had a black winch and black chain, suggesting it might be lifted into an upright position. Like a black monolith. There were, in addition, four black metal cuffs with tiny medieval-like screws at each corner of the black marble table, suggesting to her a macabre use.

A shallow ivory basin under the table, presumably residing at its foot should the table be lifted into an upright position, fed into a narrow gutter which in turn fed directly into an ivory cistern.

It was not hard to imagine the table upright.

Not hard to imagine a victim cuffed to the table.

Not hard to imagine all that ivory turned red.

Red not unlike the veining in the surrounding marble.

Meanwhile, surrounding the solid black marble sacrificial table like black numbers on a clock were similar black marble tables. Only much narrower. Twelve of them to Emily's silent count.

The pale candle flame guttered, *sizzled*, even more uncertainly. As if *gasping* at all this. As if it might just gutter itself right out.

And Emily silently cursed herself for not having the foresight to bring extra matches. The cold dank air stirring about her.

Stirring about her as if whispering to her now.

Whispering for her to see that each of these twelve surrounding marble tables like numbers on a clock *were not solid at all. At t'all.* Rather, approaching the head table at twelve o'clock, and what she sensed to be due-north, she observed *the narrow grooves of a lid.*

Revealing that it was, indeed, a *sarcophagus.*

Or, in simple layman terms, a large stone coffin.

All twelve of them. Gathered here in the darkness.

Surrounding the solid black marble sacrificial table.

In this deep cold chamber -- that was a *crypt.*

Twelve *sarcophagi* standing in a circle. Like numbers on a clock. The head *sarcophagi* at twelve o'clock, what Emily sensed to be due-north, slightly larger than the others. Though all the coffins appearing to be *uniform* in dimension despite most of them being relatively hidden in the cold darkness beyond the guttering candlelight.

Emily stood quietly over this largest coffin.

This largest stone coffin at twelve o'clock.

Found herself running her hand along its lid grooves.

But finding no obvious way to open the lid itself.

The grooves too narrow. The lid too heavy.

She then ran her hand along the lid itself.
And discovered on the lid an *inscribed symbol*.
She pushed the candle close to the lid, its pale light nictitating, exposing the odd symbol inscribed into the black marble.
Glowing harshly in its own blood-red veining.
An odd symbol she recognized. Surprising herself.
For she had no idea how she knew such a symbol. But it was as if it had *always been there* in her mind. Imprinted, if buried. Buried in a deep dark chamber of her mind, but its *recognition* as instinctive as it would be to yank her hand away from a hot stove even if she'd no concept of a stove or of heat or even of her own hand.
*Did that make any sense? Any sense at all? At t'all?*
Of course it didn't. But the knowledge, it was somehow there in her head all the same as if she'd been born with it. Or as if, perhaps, the peculiar symbol itself were *speaking to her directly*.
For she knew the symbol to be the *Ankh*.
A crucifix-shape, but with a tear-drop loop in place of the upper vertical bar. Meant to symbolize eternal life, death, and rebirth. Also known as the *key of life* according to ancient peoples.
Or so her mind somehow *fetched up for her*.
From this deep dark chamber of her mind.
And it wasn't just on the largest coffin standing here at twelve o'clock, but appeared to be inscribed on each of the coffins.
And not just inscribed, but *stylized*. This *Ankh*.
Stylized in a rather dagger-like *fang* motif.
Meanwhile, hung on the black marble wall just above the largest coffin at twelve o'clock was a black marble medallion with more red-veining, revealing the portraiture *of a black dragon in profile spitting a blast of black fire, its giant dark coriaceous wings splayed in flight, its forked tail curled high above its horned head like a trident, its feet heavily clawed, and that Ankh symbol branded into its scaly black torso as if burned there.*
And the more she stared at the black medallion--
The more Emily intuitively understood, or accepted, it less resembled just a decorative medallion and more a *family crest*.
A family crest down here in this dark cold crypt.
Of the kind one only saw on old castles in Europe.
A family crest with strange rune-like symbols.
Strange rune-like symbols glowing in red-veining.
Strange rune-like symbols which she somehow also intuitively understood, or somehow accepted, were *Slavic* in origin.

Not that she should know any such thing.
But there it was anyway. As if she *should know it*.
As if such things were already a part of her.
There in that deep dark chamber of her mind.
Hiding about in the darkest shadows there.
A congregation of their very own black ghosts.

Even more bizarrely, suggesting she was once more lost in yet another fearsome *fever dream*, she understood, or accepted, she was somehow able to *translate* the strange rune-like *Slavic* symbols.

The translation hissing inside her head:
Hissing in that deep dark voice: Ancient: Wise:
*Hebrews 9:22 Under the law almost everything...*
*Is purified with blood. For without the shedding of blood...*
*There can be no forgiveness of sins.*
Biblical. In this hell of cold black marble ice.
*And what could it all possibly mean?* she wondered.
*This dark scripture? This crypt beneath this dark house?*
*What had she stumbled upon here? Down here?*
*Was it simply a family burial chamber? Or something more?*
*And what something more could it actually be?*

Emily took a slow step back in the darkness, the candle guttering perilously, causing shadows to jump on the black marble walls. As if the occupants of these coffins *were rising from the dead*.

*Pitter patter. Pitter patter. Scritch scratch scritch.*

And for a moment felt herself quite turned around, unable to find the corridor from which she'd entered the chamber. But then suddenly there it was again. The corridor entrance. The exit.

She slipped through it quickly like something might try to follow her to the surface if she dilly-dallied -- *only to find herself not in the corridor but in yet another chamber. Albeit a much smaller chamber.*

A chamber featuring a child-sized *sarcophagus*.

And she instantly felt a most terrible urge to quickly *back away* from this child-sized *sarcophagus*. A most terrible instinctive urge not unlike jerking one's hand away from a hot stove. But Emily, despite this, still found herself moving forward, slowly, ever so slowly, as if she were no longer in control of her own body. Discovered herself leaning, slowly, ever so slowly, over this most mysterious child-sized *sarcophagus* to find that *its marble stone lid was slid halfway down*. Revealing an ivory interior. An ivory interior *that appeared to be empty*.

That appeared to be empty *at first glance*.

Her eyes blinked hard. Twitched really.
Blinked hard. Twitched. In the cold darkness.
Before *seeing* what she at first was *unable to see*.
As white as the ivory interior of this child-sized *sarcophagus*. As white as a freshly fallen snow. *A ghostly alabastrine corpse.*
*Reposed inside the child-sized sarcophagus.*
*Smooth and cold. Statuesque. Nude.*
*As if carved from a block of white marble.*
*Devoid of any blood. Any obvious pigmentation.*
*Save of splay of dark hair she'd mistook for shadows.*
Emily wanted to just run away from it. From this ill-fated *thing*. This *ghostly alabastrine corpse* that appeared to be the *remains* of a poor little girl. Wanted to just run away from this *thing* screaming.
Assuming she could any longer muster a scream.
Her lungs now turned to hard black stones.
Heart *un-beating* in her chest. *As if she were a corpse.*
As if she were somehow only a corpse now herself.
No longer a thing of the living. But a dead thing.
A dead thing moving through this cold darkness.
Through these terrible purgatory shadows.
Wanted to run screaming, if only in her head.
Run screaming for the exit from this awful crypt and scramble her way back through that dark maze to the surface where *the mysterious short narrow door would somehow mercifully be waiting open for her* before scrambling, still screaming, if only in her miserable head, from the dark attic and down the dark narrow staircase and the long narrow dimly-lit plum-colored carpeted hall to her bedroom where she would then slam shut the bedroom door behind her before burying her head into her pillows and scream herself back to sleep.
*Screaming. Screaming.* If only in her head.
Or rather, more likely, scream herself *awake*.
Instead, Emily found herself *pushing closer still*.
Pushing closer still to that *ghostly alabastrine corpse*.
*As if carved from a block of white marble.*
The guttering candlelight exposing small needle-like bones just beneath that cold and smooth statuesque skin before that guttering candlelight *elicited a most horrible gasp from the corpse child. Its sunken eyes popping wide open, revealing pale irises. Pale irises staring blindly at her.*
*Staring blindly at Emily as it now reached for her.*
*As it now reached for her with a bony alabastrine hand.*

*That bony alabastrine hand locking around her wrist like a vice. With a strength she would have never imagined for a child. The motion of which stirred a terrible gust of the cold stale chamber air and blew out the candlelight.*
*Leaving her in a wretched pitch-darkness with it.*
Emily heard herself screaming in that darkness.
*Screaming. Screaming.* If only in her head.
A most dreadful terrified scream. A howling thing.
Born as if from the deepest, darkest nightmare.
*Screaming as the alabastrine corpse came for her.*
*And not only with just that bony alabastrine hand.*
*But with a mouthful of large spiny needle-like teeth.*
*A mouthful of large spiny needle-like teeth missing its front teeth.*
*If not missing a pair of fangs. A pair of long protracting fangs.*
*Fangs that meant to bite her. Bite her and never let go.*
*This undead bloodthirsty thing of the darkness.*

# 22.

EMILY AWOKE CHOKING, fighting for breath, beneath the suddenly harsh light of the Victorian ceiling lamp above her bed. A stained glass, yellow, white, and red, finished in a vintage bronze with a flush mount, turned into a blazing desert sun with halos of yellow, white, and red sunspots, blinding her.

*Sunspots swirling dizzily about with all those awful shadowy black spots that had somehow managed to follow her out of her latest fever dream.*

As if the lamp intended to burn out her retinas.

Whimpering upon failing to manage a proper scream, she buried herself in her bedsheets, damp and smelling of her sickness, but the light was still somehow too harsh. Somehow managing to penetrate those bedsheets. Somehow managing to find her skin.

Threatening to scald it. Burn it to an ashen crisp.

*Ashes to ashes, dust to dust. Ashes, dust. Burn, burn, burn.*

She'd been so terribly cold only just a moment before in that crypt of her latest fever dream *only to find herself thrust from that freezing ice pit into this Hades fire. As if hell itself wasn't any one thing. Not any one thing at all. At t'all. Other than just wanting to burn, burn, burn.*

*Be it the freezing burn of ice. Or of scalding flames.*

"Off," she moaned, eyes shutting. "Turn it off, please."

*Turn it off, please, her mind begged, believing that blazing desert sun of a lamp would turn her skin into that ashen crisp in an instant if she abandoned the bedsheets. Already feeling as if her skin were swelling. Welting.*

Just then that blazing desert sun went black.
As if in answer to her whimpering moans.
With it, the bedroom fell into a gray darkness.
Or so she discerned upon slowly reopening her eyes.
Squinting almost painfully into that gray darkness.
She could feel a dark electricity in the dark gray air.
A dark electricity that seemed to gutter. *Sizzle.*
And realized she had no idea if it was night or day.
Or even if she was actually awake or still asleep.

She could hear that whistle of wind in the eaves and could see the black clouds *hanging even more thickly still* over the house past the long dark curtains. Portending their most terrible black storm. Having gathered so very methodically. Like an advancing army. Perhaps making the question of night or day meaningless in the end.

As if time no longer had any real meaning.
She managed to sit up. Blinking. Twitching really.
For a moment she thought herself alone--
Only to discover a dark figure materializing as if from the gray darkness itself. Appearing at the threshold of the bedroom.
Appearing in the open bedroom doorway.
*Beside a door for which Emily perhaps no longer had a key.*
The gray darkness painting her in stark relief.
This dark figure. A familiar, if peculiar figure in the end.
Her. Clad in her customary long muted black dress.

Her long dark hair featuring a clean middle part and tied back tidily in a simple bun. Presenting a stern and pale face without the hint of make-up or humor. Her razor-thin lips pursed as if in anger, chapped and waxen. Those eyes gray and expressionless.

*As if in perpetual judgement*, she'd once thought.
But no longer believed. Not completely. Not anymore.
Rather, expressionless as if she were in a trance.
A *trance* she'd been in all along. From the very beginning.
A *trance* she sometimes tried to shed. To *un-conjure.*

A *trance* that really wasn't all that much different than all these terrible locks on all these doors and windows. Locks on the outside *and the inside.* A *trance* that served as a prison of its very own.

A *trance* made more obvious to Emily, ironically, by the *haunted expression* lurking there just beneath the surface of this *trance.*

A rather *haunted expression* she'd seen before.
Here and there. Before and then. And again now.

On little sickly Henry. Wobbling on that HUFFY bike behind that Dairy Queen. His laughter sounding to her like tears.

Madelyn. At the back gate leading up into those dark foreboding woods. To that family plot. Down to the playground.

And on that red-headed doll. Offering her that *silver key* in that attic. Staring at her with those dirty blue eyes. *Staring, staring.*

Indeed, a rather *haunted expression* in the end.

Somehow shared by all of them. Henry, Madelyn, and the red-headed doll. *As if the expressions were somehow mirror images of each other*, Emily contemplated, in the augur of the impending storm.

A rather *haunted expression* of a *sad joyful relief.*

Of course, Emily reflected now, *maybe they were not mirror images of each other at t'all,* but only mirrors. *Reflections.* Of her very own hidden emotions. Emotions locked very deeply inside of *her.*

And it was just then Emily heard that grandfather clock begin to gong again somewhere down in the parlor far below her.

*Summoning her. Summoning the both of them, perhaps.*

For the dark figure, Ms. Vivian Dancemore, whispered to her from the threshold shadows: "I was wondering, Miss Emily, if you might care to join me in the parlor for a glass of sherry."

*As if she might finally provide all the answers to all the riddles.*

Before slowly turning and *floating* down the hall.

Down that long plum-colored carpeted hallway. Past that narrow line-up of dimly-flickering bronze scones and toward the steep foyer staircase and the parlor somewhere down far below them.

Where that grandfather clock gonged and gonged.

Chimeric gongs that seemed to put Emily into a trance.

Seemed to put Emily into a trance of her very own.

Assuming she had not been in a trance all along.

And she felt herself rising. *Floating, floating.*

# 23.

EMILY BLINKED, TWITCHED REALLY, to find herself in the parlor. To a final resounding gong. Seated on her customary fuzzy blue armchair. A small fire crackling in the fireplace next to her, its radiating heat feeling especially warm.

Her skin still very tender. Shriveled. Crispy.

She leaned away from the heat only to feel the coldness of the house. The resident coldness of its dark hovering shadows.

Dark hovering shadows undaunted by the dull flickering bulbs of the tiered chandelier and the dark-globed table lamps.

Causing her to lean back toward the flames. As if she'd never find comfort again. As if she'd always be too hot or too cold. Shivering now. Violently. Violently in her delusion. Sickness.

Ms. Vivian Dancemore was perched on the short chenille sofa just opposite her. The crystal-cut sherry decanter and a familiar pair of twinkling faceted sherry glasses sitting on the low marble coffee table with the short gold-trim walnut legs between them.

The sherry sparkles dancing about the parlor.

Twinkling about on all that faded gray wallpaper.

Their own maelstrom of golden fireflies.

It was as those golden fireflies danced and twinkled deliriously about her Ms. Vivian Dancemore eventually murmured:

"We're not alone in this house, Miss Emily."

"Not alone in this house, ma'am," Emily managed.

Unlike the fireflies, their words seemed to pause in the air between them. To just hang there. To *float*. To have a presence.

The golden fireflies fluttering madly about them.

As if drunkenly invigorated by them. Their presence.

"This house, Miss Emily. This house has dragons in its walls," Ms. Vivian Dancemore explained to her, barely audible now.

*This house. In its walls. Dragons. Miss Emily.*

"Dragons. In its walls, ma'am," Emily muttered.

Thinking she'd not heard the woman correctly.

The woman's pale hands fidgeted in her lap.

Her long bony fingers grappling with each other, twisting into bony little knots, suggesting a deep distress for whatever *explanation* might be forthcoming that might somehow dare to explain dragons in the house walls on this most peculiar neither night nor day.

Her bedeviled eyes twitching. *Twitching, twitching.*

"My husband, Alfred, and I bought this house some years ago. Some many years ago," the woman in black said dolefully.

*But as if it were a thing that could perhaps somehow be undone.*

*Could be rid of. If only she'd the strength to do it. As if time would allow it in all its meaninglessness on this most peculiar neither night nor day.*

"We had a nine year old daughter," she said. "Madelyn. Sometimes Maddy. She was a happy child, our daughter. And for a while, this was a happy house. Full of light, if playful mischief."

"Playful mischief, ma'am," Emily said.

"The house came furnished and initially Alfred and I thought such things, such old antique things, were quaint. *Apropos.* Offering a certain nostalgia of a time lost. Of a time long forgotten."

She paused a moment here. *Twitching, twitching.*

"There were such old antique things in the attic, too. A child's things. As if the house were waiting for such a child. As if, perhaps, the house were lonely. Lonely for such sweet innocence."

*Waiting for such a child. Such sweet innocence.*

"I thought about that after the accident."

"After the accident, ma'am," Emily pushed her.

"Yes, after. The idea that maybe the accident was not an accident. That maybe the house could not help itself, Miss Emily."

"I don't understand, ma'am," Emily said.

"It was the dolls that first began to make my skin crawl even before the accident. The way they would silently stare at her. At my child. My Madelyn. And the way she would look at them."

"Look at them, ma'am. The dolls."

"Like they had a secret. My daughter. Them."

"A secret, ma'am. Tell me, ma'am."

"And that cat. Appearing one day in the garden."

"Marbles, ma'am. That cat. Marbles."

"An oily little beast. Slinking around, but always with her. Like an oily little shadow. Sneering and hissing at me. Alfred."

*Slinking around. Always with her. Sneering. Hissing.*

"I've always had trouble sleeping in this house and I thought I could hear them. Madelyn. That oily little beast. The dolls. Moving around in the middle of the long nights. Her soft footsteps. The cat silent as silent could be. Their hard little shuffling feet."

*Pitter patter. Pitter patter. Scritch, scratch, scritch.*

"I'd ask her, Madelyn, what she might be doing in the middle of the night and she would offer me a silly naughty little grin."

Ms. V demonstrated that grin for a moment.

It looked painful on her face. Over-stretched. Morbid-looking. As if being manipulated there by invisible puppet strings.

"*Nothing, mommie...* she'd sing to me, my nine year old daughter, Madelyn, with that silly naughty little grin. *You were just dreaming, mommie. Dreaming, mommie. Dreaming, mommie...*" she'd sing.

And suddenly Emily could see Madelyn.

Could see her clearly in her own mind's eye.

That little white nightie and that eerie little lopsided grin A silly naughty little grin. Whispering in the attic dimness with that lisp. Hair in braids: *The thee was wet a-th wet could be. The thand-ths were dry a-th dry. You could not thee a cloud, be-cuth no cloud was in tha-kie. No bird-th were flying overhead. There were no bird-th to fligh. In a wonderland they lie. Dreaming a-th the day-th go by. Dreaming a-th the thummer die.*"

And the soft hushed warm whisper of her mother's voice, too. Echoing faintly just beneath that child's spooky lisp: "*Sleep, little one, sleep. Dream yourself awake, and all of your dreams will come true.*"

"I often thought I heard her playing in the walls," the woman in the black dress went on grimly. "She'd be in a room with me one moment, then *disappear* from it the next when my back was turned. I'd hear her coming up the hall only to find the hall empty."

She shook her head with the memory.

As if she might somehow rid herself of it, too.

"And I could hear her whispering in these walls. My daughter. As if she were speaking to the very house itself, Miss Emily."

# THE NIGHT SITTER

"And what did she say?" Emily wanted to know.

"Those dolls, and that cat, her only friends, *hovering* ever closer to her," Ms. Vivian Dancemore only said. "Ever closer. Exploring with her the house's long dark corridors. Its cracks and its crevices. Its hidden and secret places. And behind these very walls."

"What's behind these walls, ma'am?" Emily said.

*This house. In its walls. Dragons. Miss Emily.*

"Alfred, my husband, thought I was crazy, of course. He was always traveling for business. He only saw the light and all the playful mischief where I began to see the shadows. Darkness."

The shadows seemed to push on them now.

The shadows that didn't quite feel empty to Emily.

But full of a dark intelligence. Playful or not.

Dark little staring eyes maybe. *Staring, staring.*

*Pitter patter. Pitter patter. Scritch scratch scritch.*

"My husband, Alfred, held me responsible for the *accident. For what happened to the child.* Madelyn. *Our child.* It happened some years ago. Of the kind the mind *never quite completely comprehends.*"

Her gray eyes turned white. Staring blindly.

As if staring back into the past. That distant past.

A distant past not yet undone. *Staring, staring.*

"She'd been gone for days. Madelyn. Our child."

"Gone for days, ma'am," Emily hushed.

"My husband was traveling again and I was fraught with worry, but I could hear her in the walls. Madelyn. Our child."

*I could hear her in the walls. Madelyn. Our child.*

"Whispering. Giggling at all hours of the night."

*Whispering. Giggling. At all hours of the night.*

"Begging me, Miss Emily. Begging me to come find her. She'd always loved to play hide-and-seek, you see. But her begging gradually became less like a game. And more desperate, Miss Emily. As if someone or some-terrible-*thing* were making her play."

"Some-terrible-*thing*, ma'am. Making her."

"And then suddenly, she went horribly silent."

*Horribly silent. Hide-and-seek. Making her play. Some-thing.*

"I found her in the chimney. She'd crawled up there apparently, though I thought it looked like she'd been stuffed inside. Maybe. Fingernails torn to ribbons trying to scrape herself free, leaving her fingers bloody little stubs. Unable to scream, the unforgiving chimney walls too narrow and her poor lungs filled with soot."

*Stuffed inside. Maybe. Fingernails torn to ribbons trying to scrape herself free. Unable to scream. Chimney walls too narrow. Lungs filled with soot.*

*Waiting for such a child. For such sweet innocence.*

Emily glanced at the fireplace now. If out of the corner of her eye. Those flames crackling rather contently. As if laughing.

As those golden fireflies danced and twinkled.

And those dark hovering shadows pushed closer still.

*Pitter patter. Pitter patter. Scritch scratch scritch.*

"We buried her, Alfred and I, in a small quiet plot up in those woods. A place we could visit her. Madelyn. Our child."

*Pitter patter. Pitter patter. Scritch scratch scritch.*

"After we buried her, Alfred, distraught, spent even more time on the road. Traveling. Working. And me alone. Here."

Her pale hands continued to fidget in her lap.

Long bony pale fingers grappling with each other.

Twisting and scraping. Pulling and knotting.

"Alone. Here. In this house, Miss Emily, that was suddenly altogether all too very quiet. Until it wasn't. As it if were *simply holding its breath*, Miss Emily, until I was ready to hear it myself."

*Altogether all too very quiet. Until it wasn't.*
*As if it were simply holding its breath, Miss Emily.*
*Until I was ready to hear it myself.*

"Whispering to me. Imploring my permission."

"Your permission, ma'am. Imploring."

"An invitation of sorts, Miss Emily. I was so very unwell, Miss Emily. Feverish with grief, you understand. And it made such dark, if wonderful promises. And I offered to it my permission."

That morbid-looking grin returned.

Painful-looking. Over-stretched. That grin. As if being manipulated there. Manipulated by those invisible puppet strings.

"She returned to me in the middle of a moonless night. Madelyn. My child. She smelled of the wet earth. A slightly fetid smell of mildew and fungus and of less pleasant things, Miss Emily."

*Returned to me. Moonless night. Madelyn. My child.*
*Slightly fetid smell. Mildew. Fungus. Less pleasant things.*

"But I embraced her. Madelyn. My child. My dear little girl. I bathed her. I loved her. My husband, Alfred, of course, was horrified. He could barely look at her. Refused to touch her."

*My husband. Alfred. Of course. Horrified.*
*He could barely look at her. Refused to touch her.*

"She would sleep all day and disappear into the walls at night. Again. Madelyn. My child. My dear little girl. Giggling and whispering with that *which had whispered to me* such dark, if wonderful promises. To that which is the *soul* of this house. Its dark soul."

"Dark soul, ma'am. I don't understand."

"It wasn't long after she began disappearing out of the house itself. Beyond its walls. Out into the darkness after sun-fall."

*Out of the house. Out into the darkness. After sun-fall.*

"Then a young girl down the street went missing. A child herself. The poor girl taken right from her bedroom as she slept."

*A young girl. Went missing. Taken. As she slept.*

"Madelyn. Our child. She fell into a heavy sleep. For almost a month after the poor girl went missing. Almost a month long."

*Our child. She fell into a heavy sleep. For almost a month.*
*After the poor girl went missing. Almost a month long.*

"When she woke she could no longer tolerate the sunlight and only the weakest of the house lights. Her skin would burn."

"Burn, ma'am." *Burn, burn, burn.*

"We lived in the darkness. With her. Madelyn. Our child. And with that *which lives in the walls*. That and the others around it."

"That, ma'am. The others around it, ma'am."

"My husband, Alfred, held *me* responsible. For the *accident. For what happened to the child. Madelyn. Some years ago,*" she repeated bleakly. "Of the kind the mind *never quite completely comprehends.*"

"Yes, ma'am. But what's in the walls, ma'am?"

*This house. In its walls. Dragons. Miss Emily.*

"Our child lost *only to be found,*" she only said.

Ms. Vivian Dancemore. Eyes turned white.

Staring blindly. Into that distant past.

"It wasn't long after she awoke, Madelyn, our child, two more young children went missing, Miss Emily. A half mile away. Taken from their backyard as they played. Just gone. Vanished. A brother and a sister. The girl was never found despite an exhaustive search. Not a single blonde hair on her head. The brother was found down by the creek. Half-eaten, Miss Emily. Drained of his blood."

*Two more young children. Missing. Miss Emily.*
*Taken from their backyard as they played.*
*Just gone. Vanished. The girl was never found.*
*The brother was found down by the creek.*
*Half-eaten. Drained of his blood.*

"Half-eaten. Drained of his blood, ma'am."

"They were also taken at night, Miss Emily, their father having just called them in for bed. But suddenly *they were just gone.*"

The small fire crackled and hissed loudly.

"We found Madelyn, our child, in the garden after the boy and the girl vanished. On the very night of their disappearance. Bathing in the fountain. Soaked in blood. Black in the moonlight."

*Our child. Soaked in blood. Black in the moonlight.*

"That was almost three decades ago, Miss Emily."

"Soaked in blood. Three decades ago, ma'am."

"We'd no idea such things were happening in other places. No earthly idea what we were dealing with. This was long before all the rumors began. All the horrible rumors of such dreadful things happening in other places. We thought we were all alone. That this was *only happening to us*, Miss Emily. What was happening to her. Madelyn. Our child. What was happening *here* in this dark house."

"What was happening to her, ma'am. Here."

Those white eyes found Emily. Swimming forward.

Large white whorled holes. Those terrible eyes.

"Alfred insisted we lock her in the attic at night."

*Alfred insisted we lock her in the attic at night.*

"I became the first night sitter, Miss Emily."

*I became the first night sitter, Miss Emily.*

"Madelyn. Our child. She slept through winter. A cold winter, that long winter, bringing with it storm after storm of freezing cold wind and rain. The house so very cold. And so very dark."

*Our child. Slept through winter. A cold winter.*

"Alfred became ill. And did not see the spring."

*Alfred became ill. And did not see the spring.*

"I was left alone in the house with her, our child, lost only to be found. And with that *which lives in the walls*. That *which whispered to me* such dark, if wonderful promises. That *which had still not yet fully revealed itself to me*, Miss Emily. And the others around it."

*That which had still not yet fully revealed itself to me.*

*This house. In its walls. Dragons. Miss Emily.*

"But eventually it did so. Not long after Alfred left me. Us. It came to me on one dark and stormy night with howling wind and torrents of angry lashing black rain. From these very walls. It came to me. From the shadows, Miss Emily. Him. Mr. Grayson."

*It came to me. From the shadows. Mr. Grayson.*

"Mr. Grayson, ma'am," Emily repeated quietly in the dimness. "Him, ma'am. From these very walls. From the shadows."

It was then she noticed the cat. Marbles.

That oily little beast. Stepping into the firelight.

Staring at her with its dark green almond-shaped eyes.

And that queer expression of *incurious curiosity*.

Long and fluffy black tail flicking lazily.

A grin creeping at the corners of its mouth.

*We're all mad here. I'm mad. You're mad.*

*How do you know I'm mad?* she moaned in her head.

*You must be… Or you wouldn't have come here.*

That grin grew. That Cheshire grin.

"It is untrue, Miss Emily, what they say about the *undead*," Ms. Vivian Dancemore then hushed as the oily little beast grinned.

Grinned with a mouthful of sharp little teeth.

"Untrue, ma'am. What they say about the undead."

"That the undead are only reanimated corpses. That they have neither breath nor pulse. That they are inhuman creatures."

*Untrue, Miss Emily. The undead. Inhuman creatures.*

"Perhaps this was why I did not fully appreciate her appetites. Her desire to feed made even more ungodly by the simple fact she was forever to be only nine years old. Young. Impetuous."

"Appetites, ma'am. Desire to feed, ma'am."

A black shadow began to slowly grow on the gray-wallpapered wall behind the cat in the firelight. Initially, it appeared to only be a distorted impression of the cat, if a monstrous one at that.

Its head too large. Teeth and claws too sharp.

Its lazily flicking tail appearing as if forked.

But gradually the impression of a cat faded as that black shadow grew in the dancing firelight. Grew larger. Evolving.

*And only too soon no longer resembling a cat at t'all.*

*But a tall man, perhaps. Black suit. Fedora. Cane.*

*And he was not alone.* For in the dark hovering shadows *hiding* all those dark staring eyes, *staring, staring*, Emily convinced herself she could now see the dark silhouettes *of all those creepy-ass dolls themselves. Their tiny shadows rising on the gray-wallpapered walls about her.*

*Becoming more human-like. If too elongated. Unnaturally thin.*

*And yet elegant somehow. These dark shadowy silhouettes.*

*As if their owners could maybe slip through keyholes.*

*As if their owners could maybe slip through the very walls.*

"I kept her locked in the attic at his discretion."

"His discretion, ma'am. Locked in the attic, ma'am."

*It came to me. From the shadows. Mr. Grayson.*

"I kept her locked in the attic. I hired help. The nights being so very long despite the coming of spring. So very long and so very dark that summer, too. Yes, I hired helped. Nanny Hannah."

"Nanny Hannah, ma'am. My predecessor."

"The second night sitter, Miss Emily."

The wind blew harder still outside the black-draped windows. Rising like a scream as it blew gustily through the house eaves.

"But the child was far too clever. Too naughty."

"Far too clever, ma'am. Too naughty."

Screaming. That wind. *Screaming, screaming.*

"There were other incidents. Horrific things in the night. This despite the house rules designed to prevent such a thing."

*Other incidents. Horrific things in the night.*

*Despite the house rules designed to prevent such a thing.*

"And he came back to me from behind the walls."

"Came back to you, ma'am. From behind the walls."

Emily again stared at that cat's black shadow.

*A tall man. Black suit. Fedora. Cane. That shadow.*

"Mr. Grayson, Miss Emily," Ms. Vivian Dancemore sighed to her quietly. "He took her with him this time back into the walls and put her back to sleep. A much deeper sleep. With the others. In the walls. Before retiring himself. To this much deeper sleep."

"A much deeper sleep, ma'am."

"Hibernation, Miss Emily."

"Hibernation, ma'am."

"A curious custom of such creatures, you see. Creatures prone to deep malaise. Creatures who otherwise must feed. Creatures who must navigate eons of time. Decades. Centuries. Eternity."

*Malaise. Eons of time. Decades. Centuries. Eternity.*

"The undead, ma'am," Emily said.

"The undead, Miss Emily," the woman agreed.

*This house. In its walls. Dragons. Miss Emily.*

"But Madelyn, our child, is a restless sleeper, Miss Emily," Ms. Vivian Dancemore hushed darkly, "and her little mind is young and impetuous and cursed. And it has a tendency to wander."

"A tendency to wander, ma'am."

"At night. Midnight to dawn, Miss Emily."

*At night. Midnight to dawn, Miss Emily.*
"I try to deny her. I try to fight her invitation."
*I try to deny her. I try to fight her invitation.*
"But I've grown so very tired. So very weak."
*But I've grown so very tired. So very weak.*
"And she has grown so very restless, indeed."
*And she has grown so very restless, indeed.*
"And her restlessness makes restless the others."
*And her restlessness makes restless the others.*
"For this house has never been quiet for long."
*For this house has never been quiet for long.*
"Yes, Miss Emily, in their slumber their thoughts move slowly like molasses on a cold winter day; and yet, still I find I cannot fight off her invitation. Perhaps I don't wish to any longer fight it."
*And her restlessness makes restless the others.*
"--And though their thoughts move slowly like molasses on a cold winter day, their thoughts are fomenting, too. *Him. The others.* For *they've been watching you, Miss Emily.* And waiting. Yes. Waiting so very, very patiently, my dear girl. And now they *awaken*."
"Watching me, ma'am. Awaken, ma'am."
"Indeed, for you are not here by any accident."
*Indeed, for you are not here by any accident.*
"And neither by coincidence nor serendipity."
*And neither by coincidence nor serendipity.*
"I don't understand, ma'am. Please, ma'am."
Those large white whorled holes grew larger still.
"You are here by invitation, Miss Emily."
*You are here by invitation, Miss Emily.*
"Invitation, ma'am. I still don't understand."
"You soon will, Miss Emily. Oh, you soon must."
Those large white whorled holes blinked. Twitched really. Then the woman's eyes faded back to gray again. Slowly, if very slowly. Filling now with a heavy melancholy. A heavy exhaustion.
*This house. In its walls. Dragons. Miss Emily.*
"And you, ma'am. Are *you* one of them, ma'am?" Emily heard herself ask the woman in black. This peculiar woman in black who disappeared behind her odd bedroom door every morning.
Every morning. Just after the crack of dawn.
Those gray eyes sunk into the woman's skull.
Deeply. Becoming dark little hollow pits.

"I wished to be with her forever, Miss Emily," she finally said, her voice breaking with desperate love and fear. "For eternity, Miss Emily. So she would not have to be alone with him. Them."

*So she would not have to be alone with him. Them.*

"Forever, ma'am. For eternity, ma'am."

"Yes, Miss Emily, as your mother wished not for you. At first *poisoning* you, Miss Emily. And then only by *taking his hand.*"

*At first poisoning you. And then only by taking his hand.*

"So you would not have to be alone with him. Them."

*So you would not have to be alone with him. Them.*

Those dark hovering shadows became even more restless.

Pushing ever closer still. Ever closer still. Ever closer--

*Pitter patter. Pitter patter. Pitter patter pitter patter.*

*Scritch scratch scritch. Scritch scratch scritch scratch scritch.*

And that was when Ms. Vivian Dancemore reached for Emily. Reached for her with a pale bony hand. Grabbing her tightly by the wrist. Only it wasn't her wrist the woman was clutching for.

Rather, it was for Emily's dead mother's watch.

Her dead mother's most treasured possession.

Parisienne. Art Deco. *Much too large for her. That watch. Once upon a time, anyway. Much too large for her little thin nine year old wrist.*

An antique her mother had never removed.

Only to have it removed *from her* postmortem.

*Or so she'd always believed. Or so she'd always told herself.*

Leaving behind a pale ring of skin about her wrist.

A ghostly impression in that casket with her.

*And as Ms. Vivian Dancemore's icy cold hand clutched about her wrist over her dead mother's most treasured possession, as Emily felt those dark hovering shadows pushing ever closer still, ever closer still, ever closer--*

*Pitter patter. Pitter patter. Pitter patter pitter patter.*

*Scritch scratch scritch. Scritch scratch scritch scratch scritch.*

*Her heavy black-spotted feverish eyes reluctantly slipped closed.*

*Slipped closed as if she were being put into a deeper trance.*

It was in this deeper trance, she would find herself tumbled back in time yet again. Not unlike poor Alice plunging down into that rabbit hole.

And it was very deep in this strange rabbit hole--

# 24.

EMILY FOUND HERSELF BACK IN her nine year old body, staring down at her dead mother in that casket in that old church in that small North Carolina farming town. Her grandmother beside her, tightly squeezing her tiny pale hand, telling her *not to fidget*. Her large toady eyes emphasizing the point.
*That antique watch still on her dead mother's wrist.*
Emily blinking heavily. Twitching really.
And suddenly finding herself outside staring at that casket disappearing *down into that open grave*. Down into the cold hard earth of that cemetery above that old church just beyond a short stone wall. The cemetery on a hill overlooking the small farming town. A large pile of earth waiting sheepishly nearby below a tarp next to a small backhoe with a small muddy excavation bucket. The machine waiting *to fill the deep hole. To bury her mother in everlasting darkness.*
*To bury her mother still wearing that antique watch.*
*Despite her own conflicting memory. Her conflicting memory of that watch hanging loosely about her little thin nine year old wrist as she stood there in her itchy new black dress watching her mother being lowered into the ground of that cemetery on the hill beside that old church in that small farming town only a few miles down the road from her grandparents' cozy little farm with all those fireflies. As if both memories could be true. Even as she knew otherwise.*
*Even as she spied him down there by that old church.*
*The mysterious tall man in the long black suit.*

*Standing in the deepest shadows of a cypress tree.*

*His long angular face an ashen gray. His chin razor-sharp below a black fedora tipped very low over his brow. His hair a long pale bone-white. And his eyes gleaming. Gleaming gold. In the shadows of that cypress tree.*

*Not unlike a pair of silently hovering fireflies.*

*His right hand resting on the handle of a black walnut cane. The handle itself carved from alabaster and shaped rather like a long sharp claw.*

*Or, perhaps, an Ankh symbol....* she thought now.

*Stylized in a dagger-like fang motif. Not a long claw at t'all.*

*An ancient symbol of eternal life, death, and rebirth.*

*Also known as the key of life according to ancient peoples.*

*Ancient peoples with dark superstitions nearly lost to time.*

She blinked heavily again with the realization.

Twitched really. *And suddenly found herself on that farm.*

*Suddenly found herself on that cozy little North Carolina farm.*

Inside her grandparents old creaky farmhouse.

In her bedroom that was her father's old bedroom. His childhood bedroom. The man who'd left with only just that single suitcase never to return. Never. *Not for Emily's mother's funeral. His wife. Not even for his own mother's funeral only a couple years later.*

The only father she'd ever really known.

It was an especially cold winter night. This night.

This night Emily *found herself* back inside that old creaky farmhouse. And for some reason she intuitively knew it to be--

The very evening of her eleventh birthday.

Her grandmother had made her a birthday cake. Her grandfather hadn't eaten any. He'd just stared at her from across the dinner table, grimacing angrily, drunkenly, with those rheumy eyes.

*Abomination...* the drunk had said to her.

Had said to her when her grandmother had been washing the dishes later in the kitchen. When her grandmother had been out of the dining room and could not overhear him. *Abomination.*

She mulled over that horrible awful curse of a word in her father's old bedroom on that especially cold winter evening. The cold winter evening of her eleventh birthday after her grandparents had fallen asleep. Mulled over the venom with which he'd said it.

Her grandfather with those rheumy eyes.

Lying in her father's childhood bed, in the heavy country dark, staring out the window at the shimmery reflection of the moonlight on the fresh snow in the fields. Glowing a pale bone-white.

# THE NIGHT SITTER

That word, that curse, echoing in her head: *Abomination. Abomination. Abomination.*
Only to then hear her pediatrician's voice:
Echoing in her head: Offering its own denunciation:
*Getting to the age when we might expect to see changes…*
*Bio-chemical and bio-physiological signifiers…*
*Metamorphosis. A perverted and corrupted puberty…*
*Haven't had any experience in my practice…*
*There is no treatment. No reversal of symptoms…*
*This is a chronic condition. Monstrous…*
*I'll have to report this…* he'd said.

She could feel the wet of confused tears on her cheeks, staring out at that pale bone-white moonlight on that blanket of snow outside that bedroom window. Once her father's window. Her father's window when he was only just a boy. Only a child like she.

*Who or what is the father…* he'd wanted to know.

Her father. The only father she'd ever really known.

Just before he'd left with that single suitcase.

Just before he'd left to never return again.

And that was when she heard in a gentle rise of wintry wind in the eaves outside the window *her dead mother's whispering voice.*

*Sleep, little one, sleep…* her dead mother said softly in that wintry wind. *Dream yourself awake, and all of your dream will come true.*

Emily felt like she was dreaming as she blinked, twitched really, in her little eleven year old body, *to discover her dead mother suddenly sitting at the end of her bed in that old creaky farmhouse in the middle of that cold winter evening of her eleventh birthday two long years after her dead mother had been laid to rest in the cold hard ground of that old cemetery.*

Ashen gray. Her dead mother. Staring at her.

The pale bone-white moonlight twinkling in her eyes.

Eyes that were no longer bright. But muddy.

Muddy. Not unlike that marshy meadow.

*Happy birthday, baby…* she said, the thing sitting now at the end of Emily's bed. The thing purporting to be her dead mother.

Her voice harboring that wintry wind. Cold. Thin.

Emily felt herself recoil when the thing sitting now at the end of the bed purporting to be her dead mother reached for her.

Reached for her with an ashen gray hand.

Her fingers longer than she remembered. Bonier.

But actually not reaching for her at all. *At t'all.*

But dangling for her -- that *antique watch*.

*For your birthday, baby...* the thing sitting now at the end of the bed purporting to be her dead mother said. *For you, my dearest.*

*Parisienne. Art Deco. A most treasured possession.*

*An antique her mother had never removed. Apparently not even in death. Buried with it. That watch. Buried with it into that cold hard ground.*

*Only to return from the dead to give it to her now.*

*As if she were correcting a most horrible breach of etiquette.*

*To give it to her only daughter. On her eleventh birthday.*

*On this especially cold winter night in this old creaky farmhouse.*

*Two long years after she'd been laid to rest in that cold hard ground.*

*A ghost of a memory* forgotten until just this moment.

Emily blinked, twitched really, and her mother's antique watch suddenly hung about her eleven year old wrist. Loosely there.

Her mother, meanwhile, then simply *vanished*.

Simply *vanished* from the end of the bed.

Well, maybe not completely, for Emily, in her little eleven year old body, thought just maybe she saw *shadows moving in the thicket of trees just beyond the moonlit snow-covered field. Two dark shadows.*

*A man. And her mother. Hand-in-hand maybe.*

*The man. A cane. A fedora pulled very low over his brow.*

*Moving her mother through the trees into the blackness beyond.*

*Only to stare back briefly at Emily in the bedroom window.*

*This mysterious man escorting her mother into the blackness.*

*Only to stare back briefly at her with gleaming gold eyes.*

*It was in that moment Emily realized this mysterious man with her mother fresh from the grave was responsible for all things half-remembered, misremembered, forgotten, and misplaced in her fragile little unreliable mind.*

*This mysterious man that seemed more dream than man.*

*First appearing in the corner of that final motel room in that small farming town, sitting there like an apparition in its deepest shadows when her fragile little unreliable mind had been muddled by her mother's terrible poison procured from that white-flowered tree in that marshy meadow. And a man she'd often see again over the passing years. In crowds and around street corners. Sitting in the back of courtrooms. Standing in the rain one night outside her bedroom window during an especially poor foster placement. One where they fed her only hotdogs while they fed their own fat little nasty children steaks and potatoes.*

*Always there without her consciously noticing him.*

*Always hovering at the periphery of her dark little life.*

*As if he were just a part of her very own shadow.*

*As if he were there and not really there at t'all.*
*Walking right there beside her in the sinking cold when she didn't own a proper coat. Humming into her ear and numbing her exhausted mind when she went to bed crying and missed most terribly her dead grandmother.*
*Her dead grandmother who'd left her far too soon.*
*Not unlike her mother. Not unlike her vanishing father.*
*And later when she was missing him. Her Adam.*

Emily, as an eleven year old child, found herself rise from her father's childhood bed and wander that old creaky farmhouse only to find her grandmother awake downstairs in the darkness.

In her flimsy night things. Hair in curlers.

The woman was staring out the front window.

Her large today eyes unblinking, but maybe afraid.

Staring out past their mailbox at a dark ribbon of country road pushing through all that pale bone-white glowing snow.

She was always staring at that road with her large toady eyes as if at any moment she somehow expected to see a *rather terrible something* coming down that road toward their cozy little farm.

*Never show your teeth when you smile…* she'd said.

She'd said in that cemetery on that hill over that slowly lowering casket with Emily's dead mother inside *with that watch.*

*Never show your teeth when you smile…*she'd said.

As if there were anything to smile about.

Before demanding another most peculiar thing:

*From now on, child, we shall call you Emily after my dear late mother… After your great-grandmother. A pious, god-fearing woman.*

Strangely, Emily, even as a child on that night of her eleventh birthday, upon finding her grandmother in that downstairs window staring out at that dark ribbon of country road, and only two short years removed from that cemetery on a hill, discovered *she could no longer place in her own mind her own name. Her name before Emily.*

*Eleanor? Edith? Eileen? Elizabeth? Bethany?*
*It was as if that identity had been completely erased.*
*Completely erased by the dire conviction of her grandmother.*

Her grandmother standing in the window eventually felt Emily's presence in the darkness behind her and turned to her.

*You should be in bed, child. It's late, child…* she said.

As if she didn't know her only granddaughter often wandered the dark house late at night. At sometimes the fields and woods. As if she didn't know Emily felt a kinship with the dark night.

Moving in the shadows like a shadow herself.

It was as she reached down for Emily's tiny pale hand to lead her back up to bed as she had done so many nights before--

On so many long dark nights hours before dawn--

She noticed the antique watch on Emily's tiny wrist.

Hanging loosely about her eleven year old wrist.

*Where did you get that...?* her grandmother hissed at her.

Though her words were less vocalized and more a gasp.

A long, hissing gasp. Escaping out a clenched jaw.

That may have also included the word: *Abomination.*

But it was those large toady eyes that Emily in her eleven year old body on the night of her eleventh birthday fixated on.

How those large toady eyes began to sink deeply.

Began to sink deeply inward. Unblinking. Afraid.

Yes, definitely afraid, if she were being honest about it.

As if the woman were contemplating a ghost.

*A ghost in the unobvious form of an antique watch.*

*Arrived on an eleven year old wrist from beyond the grave.*

*On that cold winter night of her eleventh birthday.*

By the dawn's morning light, her grandmother would be gone from her. A ruptured brain aneurysm that Emily, as a child, would imagine to herself to resemble the sudden twinkling flash of a firefly as that blood vessel in her grandmother's brain exploded.

Leaving her to appear almost as if asleep.

Peacefully asleep in her bed the very next morning. Despite it being almost eight. Almost eight in the morning and well after the rise of the sun even in early January when Emily found her. Emily's grandfather sitting at the kitchen table far below in the gray morning shadows, waiting impatiently for his breakfast like a child himself. Having sent Emily upstairs to fetch her grandmother.

Something Emily had never had to do before.

Feeling a dizzying flutter of panic even then.

The farmhouse so very quiet. Too-quiet.

Her grandmother had looked so very horribly peaceful. Lying there alone in the bed in the darkness behind those still-pulled curtains. Still in her flimsy night things. Her hair in curlers.

It had been her grandmother's large toady eyes that had finally told the truth. The truth of the fatal bleeding in her head.

Those large toady eyes were wide open. Almost as if her very eyes were screaming. The whites filled with a gelid blood.

# THE NIGHT SITTER

Her wrinkly skin cold as snow to the touch.
All this flashed before Emily's eyes now in her eleven year old body as her grandmother stared down at that *ghost of a watch*.
That ghost of a watch. Hanging loosely about her eleven year old wrist. On that cold winter night of her eleventh birthday.
The elegant blue-lacquered hour and minute hands pointing in opposite directions. On that ghost of a watch hanging loosely there about her wrist. Due-north and due-south respectively.
A half hour before the stroke of midnight.
*You will lock me inside the attic one half hour before midnight.*
*You will find the girl in the attic after midnight.*
*You are to be the night sitter, Miss Emily.*
And it was at that moment, somewhere in the distance, Emily heard one long sustained gong of that grandfather clock in the corner of the parlor back in that giant looming beast of a house.
Gonging resoundingly on the half hour.
Something she'd never noticed before, frankly.
The fact it gonged on the half hour. That clock.
Her eyes blinked heavily. Twitched really--
*And she found herself returned to that parlor...*
*To the parlor in that giant looming beast of a house...*
*One half hour before the stroke of midnight...*

# 25.

**RETURNED TO THE PARLOR.** Ms. Vivian Dancemore looming over her from that short chenille sofa. In that giant looming beast of a house. That one long sustained gong still echoing in the old bones of the dark house about them as Ms. Vivian Dancemore loomed over her almost like a bird of prey.

Her pale hands once again fidgeting in her lap.
Long bony pale fingers grappling with each other.
Twisting and scraping. Pulling and knotting.
Dark clicking fingernails reminding Emily of talons.
That antique clock *tick-tocking* in the corner.
*Tick, tock, tick, tock. Tick, tock, tick. Tick, tock.*
Pushing toward that hard stroke of midnight.
Threatening to gobble up the intervening minutes.
Threatening to gobble them up by the mouthfuls.
Pendulum swinging faster and faster still seemingly.
*Tick, tock, tick, tock. Tick, tock, tick. Tick, tock.*

"My mother," Emily hushed to the woman in black before her with that oily beast of a cat still staring at her with its *incurious curiosity* and its Cheshire grin and haunting man-like shadow on the gray-wallpapered wall. Hushed to the woman in black before her with all those dark eyes *staring, staring* at her from the deeper darkness.

"Your mother," the woman in black said.

"Is she *here*? *My mother*?" Emily managed to say.

The question sounding so horribly unreal.

Her mother had always struggled with what was real and what was unreal. What was true and what was only just imagined. Often unable to differentiate between the two. Talking to people, screaming at them. *People who weren't there. People who didn't exist.*

As if shadows were a world unto themselves.

Becoming lost in those shadows. Her mother.

Lost in worlds that did not actually exist.

But perhaps such worlds did exist after all.

Yes, perhaps such worlds did exist, or so Emily was discovering now. *Perhaps they just did at that. Perhaps they actually existed.*

Assuming she wasn't a batshit crazy loon herself.

Then again, perhaps *crazy* was only a relative term. And reality only a perception and *not a reality* at all. *At t'all.* Not in the safe concrete sense that one might otherwise associate with it maybe.

*Perhaps true sanity involved ignoring such a perception.*

*Perhaps true sanity involved denying her supposed reality.*

*Perhaps true sanity involved finally accepting this unreality staring at her from the shadows. Waiting, waiting for her so very patiently to finally embrace it. Waiting, waiting for her to finally accept, in the end, her dark fate.*

*Tick, tock, tick, tock. Tick, tock, tick. Tick, tock.*

"Is she *here*? *My mother*?" Emily said again.

"It sleeps and it wanders," Ms. Vivian Dancemore whispered from the short chenille sofa as the fire crackled and hissed.

*It sleeps and it wanders... Sleeps. Wanders. It.*

"But it's no more your mother than Madelyn is any longer my daughter, Miss Emily. No more than I am who I once was."

*No more your mother than Madelyn is any longer my daughter.*

*No more than I am who I once was... Who I once was.*

The wind outside howled again in the house eaves.

Screaming terribly. That wind. *Screaming, screaming.*

As the brass pendulum swung back and forth.

Back and forth. Faster and faster still seemingly.

Back and forth in the dark body of that antique clock.

The large antique grandfather clock in the corner.

*Tick, tock, tick, tock. Tick, tock, tick. Tick, tock.*

"Even now the darkness consumes *you*, Miss Emily, as it consumed your unfortunate mother once upon a time long ago," Ms. Vivian Dancemore said as the wind *screamed* in the house eaves. As the pendulum swung back and forth and the clock *tick-tocked*.

"Consumed my mother, ma'am. The darkness."

"On a rainy back road in a dark woods, Miss Emily."

*On a rainy back road in a dark woods, Miss Emily.*

"For it was not a car accident that took your mother's parents, Miss Emily. But some-*thing* in the stormy night. Some-*things*."

*But some-thing in the stormy night. Some-things.*

At that was when Emily heard a crack of thunder.

And then the heavy sound of rain. Black rain.

"On a night not unlike this very night, Miss Emily."

"Some-*thing*. Some-*things*, ma'am," Emily said.

"Your mother was home from university for the winter break. A Christmas tree tied to the roof of the car. Freshly cut. The hour late. They'd stopped for a bite of supper to wait out the storm, but the storm was unrelenting. The road dark and very empty."

*Your mother. Home from university. Winter break.*

*The storm. Unrelenting. The road dark and very empty.*

"Perhaps, Miss Emily, my dear, your grandfather thought the car only hit a slippery spot at that bend in that dark and very empty road as the car entered those shadows. As the car flipped."

*As the car entered those shadows. As the car flipped.*

"Perhaps he and your grandmother never truly knew what had really happened. Their quick deaths *sparing* them. Sparing them any knowledge of what was *waiting out there* in that stormy night."

*Waiting out there in that stormy night. Spared them.*

"Your mother was thrown from the car."

*Your mother. Home from university. Winter break.*

*The storm. Unrelenting. The road dark and very empty.*

"Mr. Grayson, he held her hand as she struggled to hold on to her life in those woods. To breathe. He took pity on her. He took pity on your mother, Miss Emily, even while the coven fed."

*He held her hand as she struggled to hold on to her life.*

*Took pity on your mother. Even while the coven fed.*

"He thought her so fair and so beautiful, indeed, your mother, struggling to hold on to her life. To breathe in those stormy woods. Her skin the color of ivory and her mane of hair long and thick and endlessly flowing. A deep sanguine. The hue of fresh blood."

*So fair. So beautiful. Skin the color of ivory. Her mane of hair long and thick and endlessly flowing. A deep sanguine. The hue of fresh blood.*

"Your mother woke the next morning in a hospital nearly ten miles away with no memory of the event. Alone. Afraid."

*Hospital. Nearly ten miles away. Alone. Afraid.*

"And for a while, Mr. Grayson was always there. In the shadows of her life. Watching her. Coveting her. Your mother."

*In the shadows. Watching her. Coveting her. Your mother.*

"Her despair eventually took her into those shadows. To him. Unaware of his role in the death of her parents. Your grandparents. Or unwilling to acknowledge it until it was far too late, Miss Emily. Their shared malaise keeping them together. For a while. The death of her parents. The malaise for creatures of the eternal."

*Her despair eventually took her into those shadows.*
*Their shared malaise keeping them together. For a while.*

"He has a fetish for human women, Miss Emily. Their mortality makes him *feel alive again*. As if he can taste food once more. Feel the wind on his face. Smell the perfume of flowers in the night air," Ms. Vivian Dancemore whispered to Emily, panting softly.

*Unaware of his role in the death of her parents.*
*Or unwilling to acknowledge it until it was far too late.*

"Inexorably," she said, the fire crackling and hissing louder as the black rain fell down the chimney, "she fell in love with him. His long absences from her dreary life only deepening that love."

*Fell in love. Long absences. Only deepening that love.*

"For he was a desire she could never possess even as he possessed her. For he is a thing of the night. Of the shadows."

*A desire she could never possess even as he possessed her.*
*For he is a thing of the night. Of the shadows.*

"Moreover, he infects their minds. Deepens their sorrow. Like a virus, I suppose. And their grief eventually consumes them."

*Deepens their sorrow. Their grief eventually consumes them.*

"Your mother, she tried to move on in his prolonged absences. She married your father. Or the man you knew to be your father before you discovered that man was not your father at all."

*Discovered that man was not your father at all. At t'all.*

"For you are of the shadows yourself, Miss Emily. For you are a product of a tragic union. You are *his* daughter. Progeny."

*A product of a tragic union. His daughter. Progeny.*

"A rare and a most formidable creature, you are, Miss Emily," the woman in black said, her gray eyes turning back to white.

Large white whorled holes. Staring at her.

Staring at her as the others stared. *Staring, staring.*

Those creepy-ass dolls in the shadows. Stirring again.

*Pitter patter. Pitter patter. Pitter patter pitter patter.*
*Scritch scratch scritch. Scritch scratch scritch scratch scritch.*
As the faceted sherry golden fireflies flurried about.
And those dull bulbs of the hanging tiered chandelier and the dark-globed table lamps flickered madly like silent applause.
"A rare and most formidable creature, ma'am."
The wind rising again in the dark eaves. Screaming.
Screaming, that terrible wind. *Screaming, screaming.*
Screaming as the thunder cracked and rumbled.
As that black rain fell harder and harder.
The woman in black nodded solemnly at her.
"You are the offspring of a dragon and a human female. Born *between worlds*. Between the light and the darkness. A *dhampir*."
*Between worlds. The light and the darkness. A dhampir.*
Those dark resident shadows pushing forward again not unlike a creeping black tide. *Threatening to swallow her. To drown her.*
Pulling with them those shadows. Silhouettes.
Those silhouettes lifting on the gray-wallpapered walls.
*Rather human-like. If too elongated. Unnaturally thin.*
*And yet elegant somehow. Those dark shadowy silhouettes.*
*As if their owners could maybe slip through keyholes.*
*As if their owners could maybe slip through the very walls.*
The oily beast of cat still staring with that *incurious curiosity* and its own unnerving shadow. *A tall man, perhaps. Fedora. Cane.*
"He rises from his most recent slumber, his hibernation, Miss Emily, to greet you. To embrace you. To welcome you home."
*He rises from his most recent slumber. His hibernation.*
*To greet you. To embrace you. To welcome you home.*
"For it was his choice for you to be here. In this house. Within these thick dark walls. For the battles to come. The war."
"The battles to come, ma'am. The war."
"The world is sick, Miss Emily. And growing sicker still. The vagaries of man daunted by beast. A beast confined for generations to the deepest of shadows and to the darkest of corners of imagination only to reappear from the haze of black mythology."
"Black mythology, ma'am. Reappear."
*Pitter patter. Pitter patter. Pitter patter pitter patter.*
*Scritch scratch scritch. Scritch scratch scritch scratch scritch.*
"Yes. For the beast has always been there. Hunting. Feeding," Ms. Vivian Dancemore lamented. "From time immemorial."

Her pale hands fidgeted harder in her lap.
Long bony pale fingers grappling with each other.
Twisting and scraping. Pulling and knotting.
Fingernails growing longer, darker, sharper seemingly.
Reminding Emily even more of talons. Claws.

The long dark minute hand on the stately grandfather clock in the corner inching only just moments from midnight now.

Only just moments from joining the hour hand.

Time gobbled up by the mouthfuls. *Gobble, gobble.*

"And as your mother realized, Miss Emily, *causing her to feed unto you that loving poison*, I now accept my decision in this dark house was a most horribly reckless decision fraught with despair."

*My decision in this dark house. Most horribly reckless.*
*Fraught with despair. I now accept. Miss Emily.*

"Now I only feel regret, Miss Emily. Now I only feel a terrible regret for deciding to give unto my child life again. An undead life. An accursed life, Miss Emily, rather than allowing my dear little girl to rest in peace as my Alfred, my husband, would have preferred of me. As my daughter deserved, Miss Emily. But my grief, it was too great in the end, Miss Emily, and the haunted whispers in the walls of this dark grisly house far too convincing. Too seductive."

*An undead life. An accursed life. This dark grisly house.*
*Haunted whispers in the walls. Far too convincing. Seductive.*
*Tick, tock, tick, tock. Tick, tock, tick. Tick, tock.*

"It's most unnatural what I *allowed*. It's most unnatural for life to continue beyond its natural course, Miss Emily," she grieved.

"Yes, ma'am. I suppose it is, ma'am."

"And that is why I am glad you are here."

"And why would that be, ma'am?"

Though unsure she wanted to know the answer.

*Tick, tock, tick, tock. Tick, tock, tick. Tick, tock.*

"A rare and most formidable creature, you are," the woman in black said to her yet again. As if it were its very own curse.

*This house. In its walls. Dragons. Miss Emily.*

"You are more than you suspect. Or perhaps you suspect it already, Miss Emily. What you are. What you are capable of."

*Pitter patter. Pitter patter. Pitter patter pitter patter.*
*Scritch scratch scritch. Scritch scratch scritch scratch scritch.*

"What am I capable of, ma'am? Tell me."

"Dragon-slayer," the woman in black hushed.

The stirring shadows seemed to pull back with this statement. Pull back into the parlor darkness. As if recoiling from it.

As if its mention might invite such a curse.

*Patter pitter. Patter pitter. Patter pitter patter pitter.*

*Scratch scritch scratch. Scratch scritch scratch scritch scratch.*

"Your blood, Miss Emily. He desperately desires it. For himself. For his coven," Ms. Vivian Dancemore hissed at her.

"My blood, ma'am. Why *my* blood, ma'am?"

"You are his only child. Born of his blood. Born of a dragon and a human female. A *dhampir*. And your blood is infected. Infected with the virus. It courses through your veins, Miss Emily."

*Born of a dragon and a human female. A dhampir.*

*Your blood. Infected. Courses through your veins, Miss Emily.*

Emily found herself remembering this same woman with these large white whorled holes for eyes *discouraging* her, not so very long ago, of such a notion. Of such a notion she might be infected.

*Poppycock...* the woman had said to her.

*You're out-of-sorts. You're body clock-- It's still adjusting to working the night...* the woman had insisted. *Throwing off your biorhythms.*

*Fatigue, my dear. Mental indexterity. Malaise.*

The woman had said these things even as she'd known better. And Emily had accepted such explanations even as she'd suspected otherwise. Suspected a much darker truth beneath the surface.

A darker truth slowly being revealed to her now.

*And suddenly Emily could see in her feverish mind's eye little sickly nine year old Henry. Laughing so joyfully as he rode that bike, wobbling around in circles behind that Dairy Queen. Almost painful to listen to. That joyful laughter. For if she closed her eyes, it had almost sounded to her like tears.*

*He had not eaten his banana split that day.*

*Had not eaten it despite it being for his birthday.*

*He'd barely spoken for days afterward. Just sitting in that window again. His bedroom window, staring at the world outside. But no longer waving. And all too soon there had been no one to wave at any longer. No one.*

*For suddenly the pandemic had flowered. The virus.*

*And she sensed the poor little sick boy had felt responsible. As if he had somehow invited the virus by his indiscretion. For suddenly, there were no more children going by on bicycles. Almost as if the entire world outside his bedroom window had somehow contracted his most terrible genetic mutation.*

*Almost as if he'd infected the entire world.*

*Leaving him more alone that ever before. Henry.*

## THE NIGHT SITTER

*It wasn't long after he'd had a terrible relapse.*
*Not long after his condition had flowered malignantly.*
*Only this time there would be no recovery.*
*Almost like he'd simply given up. And hadn't he?*
*Hadn't they whispered around it in so many words as the world outside had come to a skidding halt? When the sky had turned so gray?*
*The sky had still looked blue to her. But not to him.*
*To the poor boy, it had turned gray. Colorless.*
*Gray, colorless, as they had whispered around such things in his bedroom at the end of that long and dark hall far away from the others in the family. A bedroom that had always smelled of him. A moldering, decaying smell.*
*A sickly sweet smell of something slowly dying. As he stared out at that world skidding to a halt. Out at that blue sky turned gray. Colorless.*
*Perhaps she might have told him it was still blue even as it had begun to turn gray and colorless to her, too, as the life had faded from the boy.*
*That poor boy. Henry. After he'd given up.*
*And it was then another memory revealed itself from behind this memory. As if it had been impishly hiding there. Playing hide-and-seek behind it like a mischievous little child. Another memory that took place in the night.*
*Beneath that colorless sky now turned black. Moonless.*
*Black. Moonless. Beyond that bedroom window.*
*Emily. That poor little sickly boy who'd given up. Who had relapsed in a world come so very undone. That poor child whose body was quickly failing him. Whose tired lungs were slowly suffocating him. Drowning him alive. Drowning him alive as his head had pounded mercilessly as if being struck by a malicious sledgehammer. Or stabbed by a fiery-hot poker or maybe, perhaps, a cold blade of ice. Causing him to cry out in pain. Until he could cry no longer, not without choking on all that dark fluid collecting in his lungs. Drowning him.*
*She had not wanted him to suffer any longer. The boy.*
*That was what she told herself. Told herself on that black and moonless night while the rest of the family had been quite fast-asleep. When the poor boy, that sickly boy, had looked up at her with those big blue jaundiced eyes.*
*Gangly. Pale. Head too large. Hair thin. Lips purple.*
*That dark fluid turning his lungs into heavy black stones.*
*Begging her, she'd thought. Begging her to just end it.*
*And she had, hadn't she? Hadn't she done just so?*
*Yes, she could remember smiling at the boy.*
*She could remember showing the poor boy her teeth.*
*And hadn't he, that poor boy, that sickly boy, startled on that black and moonless night when she'd done so. Shown him her teeth in that smile.*

241

*She thought he might have done just that. Startled.*
*Maybe even screamed a little as she'd bitten into his neck.*
*Into his soft and pale flesh. Sinking deeply her teeth.*
*And tasting ambrosia on her probing tongue.*
*The food of gods. The sweetest and most divine of nectars.*
*A thick nectar that had dripped down her parched throat.*
*On that black and moonless night. That night.*
*Screamed a little. The poor boy. That sickly boy.*
*Screamed and cried tears that sounded like laughter.*

*And suddenly it wasn't just Henry in her salivating jaws. But other children. Over a black span of many passing years. Decades maybe. Flashing nauseously before her feverish mind's eye. Other poor sickly little children.*

*Begging for her mercy. Or so she told herself.*
*Or so she'd convinced herself before feeding on them.*
*Before sucking the life from their tender bones.*
*Mercy killings, she'd convinced herself as she'd fed.*

*As she'd fed on their sweet nectar even as she'd somehow managed to wipe the memories clean from her mind until now. Until this stormy night.*

*Even as she'd convinced their families and any authorities the children in her charge had simply gone in their sleep. Had simply passed peacefully.*

*But they had not. Those poor little sickly children.*

*Assignments that Darcey had always reserved specifically for her. Darcey and others like Darcey before Darcey. Sad peculiar arrangements.*

*As if she were perfectly suited for such maladies.*
*As if she were suited for nothing else but such maladies.*

*Almost as if Darcey, and others like Darcey before Darcey, had somehow unconsciously known what Emily was capable of and only unconsciously wanted her thinning out the very weak from the herd. The human herd.*

*Perhaps someone might have finally connected the dots.*
*What she had done over the passing years. Decades maybe*
*But she had always been so very persuasive somehow.*
*Almost as if she were incapable of being blamed.*
*Sure, there'd been the looks. The whispers.*

*Henry's grieving family as his little body had been slowly lowered six feet deep down into the cold hard ground. Other families before that sickly little boy. But those looks and those whispers had remained only just that.*

*Looks. Whispers. With nothing coming of them.*

*Nothing, despite the fact, over time, years, decades maybe, there had been enough victims for anyone who'd cared to look to figure it out. But they hadn't, had they? Somehow she had infected their minds, too. Dissuaded them.*

*Dissuaded them from seeing the terrible truth.*
*Even as she had dissuaded even herself from seeing it.*
*Until now. In this giant looming beast of a house.*
*Of course, not everyone had been dissuaded from seeing her menace. Even as she had somehow dissuaded herself from seeing it. Not everyone, in fact.*
*Though it seemed both like a very long time ago and only just yesterday, Emily could remember her Adam inviting her for Thanksgiving.*
*Thanksgiving at his in-laws country house upstate.*
*Adam. His wife. His little girls. His in-laws.*
*A beautiful spread like something out of the Waltons.*
*Adam's lovely little wife drinking too much wine and cornering Emily in the kitchen at the end of the night. Adam had always fallen under her spell, but not this woman. His wife. She had been able to see through Emily.*
*Had been able to see the monster she actually was.*
*Especially with all that wine in her at the end of the night.*
*She could see how Adam was not Adam around her.*
*How Emily's presence always sent him spiraling down the drain.*
*Down the drain. Into a most terrible malaise. Despair.*
*That she'd managed to do this to him ever since they were children. Feed his depression. His drinking. Drugs for a time. Inviting darkness.*
*His wife was the light. And his cute little girls.*
*How old were they now? His girls? Nine and eleven?*
*She was a part of the nightmare. The past. She. Emily.*
*It had been the last time she and Adam had seen each other.*
*That dreadful Thanksgiving with that beautiful spread.*
*Adam had asked Emily to leave after she'd said some less than flattering things to his wife in front of her parents. In front of Adam and their cute little girls. In front of that wholesome family in that cozy country house upstate.*
*She had disappeared out into the night darkness.*
*Somehow resisting the desperate urge to scream at him he was her family. If not by blood, then by circumstance. Inseparable by neither time nor distance. Nor any cold and heartless earthly convention, either. Her family.*
*A tiny separate universe born of each other.*
*Lost as they otherwise were in a terrible sewer of filth.*
*But, of course, he was no longer lost. Her Adam.*
*He had managed to extricate himself from that sewer.*
*And that had only made her want him more.*
*For him to throw his arms around her once again as he'd done when they were only children in that foster home. And in the years afterward.*
*To whisper in her ear: I'm summer, you're winter.*

*To hold her close to him and to never let her go again.*
*Why had she ever allowed him to let her go?*
*Had it been love? Had she known all along what she was?*
*Had she known all along he could not save her from it?*
*That he could not save her from her dark fate?*
*Had she known she could not protect him from herself?*
*Is that what had brought her here? To this giant dark looming beast of a house at the very edge of the world? To this parlor of awful shadows?*
*To this parlor full of staring, staring dark little eyes?*
*To this seminal moment of her dark life?*
*To this most peculiar woman in black before her now?*
*Staring at her with those large white whorled holes for eyes?*
Those shadows stirred forward again.
Those dark shadows with their dark little eyes.
As her peculiar employer now said to her:
"But as a *dhampir*, born of a dragon and a human female, this virus coursing through your veins adopts a most rare and formidable *adaption*. An *adaptation* unanticipated by man or beast, Miss Emily. For your infected blood becomes a *serum*. A dark miracle."

"A *serum*, ma'am. My infected blood."

"For him, Miss Emily. For them. His coven."

"For him, ma'am. For them. His coven."

"For you are his only child," the woman in black repeated to her. "You are, Miss Emily, his only direct descendant. You."

*For you are his only child. His only direct descendant. You.*
*An adaptation unanticipated by man or beast.*

"Creatures who must feed, Miss Emily. Creatures of the night, Miss Emily, who must feed in order to navigate their eons of time. Decades. Centuries. Eternity. Feed or perish, Miss Emily."

*Creatures who must feed. Feed or perish, Miss Emily.*

"Feed or perish, ma'am," Emily muttered.

"Indeed. For if he fails to feed, our Sire, he will eventually perish. Waste away. And with it, his curse. His coven freed. Including my daughter. Including your very own mother, Miss Emily."

"Freed, ma'am. Is that possible, ma'am?"

"I suppose that depends entirely upon you, Miss Emily."

"Entirely on me, ma'am. This curse, ma'am."

"Yes, for he will attempt to *seduce from you* your infected blood, Miss Emily. To preserve himself. The others. His coven."

*Seduce from you your infected blood, Miss Emily.*

# THE NIGHT SITTER

*Born of a dragon and a human female. A dhampir.*
*Your infected blood. A serum. A dark miracle.*
"He will whisper to you from the walls, Miss Emily. Dark, if wonderful little promises. Dark little invitations, Miss Emily."
*Dark, if wonderful little promises. Dark little invitations.*
"But you mustn't heed his seductions, Miss Emily."
*Pitter patter. Pitter patter. Pitter patter pitter patter.*
*Scritch scratch scritch. Scritch scratch scritch scratch scritch.*
"For while your infected blood, Miss Emily, offers to him and them, his coven, a most desperately desired *serum,* your *saliva,* your rare and most formidable bite, Miss Emily, offers to him a rare and most formidable *venom.* A rare and most formidable *poison.*"
*Your rare and most formidable bite, Miss Emily--*
*Offers to him a rare and most formidable venom. Poison.*
"And why-- *Why* would that be, ma'am?"
"Nature, in her infinite wisdom, providing balance, Miss Emily. Nature, in her infinite wisdom, providing natural order."
*Nature. In her infinite wisdom. Balance. Order.*
"You may end his curse *here* tonight," she revealed.
*Pitter patter. Pitter patter. Pitter patter pitter patter.*
*Scritch scratch scritch. Scritch scratch scritch scratch scritch.*
"His coven will try to protect him," the woman in black softly warned, however, in the heavy parlor dimness as that fire crackled and hissed nearby as the cold whipping wind howled even louder in the house eaves and that black rain pounded down from all those thick black clouds pressing down even harder on the world.
On this dark house *on the very edge of existence.*
The long minute hand only seconds to midnight.
On that large antique grandfather clock in the corner.
*Tick, tock, tick, tock. Tick, tock, tick. Tick, tock.*
"*As will I, Miss Emily, as will I--*" the woman in black mourned. As she fidgeted. Grappled. Twisted. Scraped. Pulled. Knotted.
The long minute hand finally joining the hour hand. Joining it at due-north. Midnight. The large antique grandfather clock gonging. The heavy bellowing midnight gongs echoing in the old bones of the house, causing the dark house to tremble about her.
As Ms. Vivian Dancemore rose above Emily.
Her long black dress sliding down her lean frame.
Pooling below as if reduced to a dark liquid.
Vanishing in the darkness at her feet.

Leaving her standing there in her increasingly agitated state in a familiar little white nightie which had been hiding like a slip.

Her pale hands, grappling, twisting, scraping, pulling, knotting, then began to braid her long and black hair in tangled knots.

Began to braid her hair with those talons. Claws.

Braiding it with white ribbons pulled from that nightie.

That morbid-looking grin returning to her pale face.

Painful-looking. Over-stretched. That grin. As if being manipulated there. Manipulated by those invisible puppet strings.

*As if she were on the precipice of darkly amused laughter.*
*A darkly amused laughter being forced upon her.*
*A darkly amused laughter painful to her.*
*As painful as that horrible morbid-looking grin.*

It was as that darkly amused possessed-laughter finally spilled out from her twisted mouth, the aggrieved woman just managed to whisper, if rather desperately: "To the only people who consistently tell the truth, no matter how difficult it might be to hear--"

"Drunkards and children," Emily finished for her.

Finished for her peculiar employer when her peculiar employer found herself quite unable. Found herself *slipping away.*

*Slipping away. To that painful darkly amused possessed-laughter spilling out from her twisted mouth. From that horrible morbid-looking grin.*

Then suddenly the woman was gone. *Absent.*

And in her place, the child once again. Madelyn.

Those *large white whorled holes for eyes suddenly charcoal gray.* Those charcoal gray eyes capturing the madly spinning speckles of faceted sherry light, gradually turning those gray eyes gleaming gold.

Those gleaming gold eyes twinkling playfully.

Yet filled with their own *incurious curiosity.*

As Madelyn adopted her signature lopsided grin.

And sung in a playful, if teasing melody:

As that antique grandfather clock gonged:

"The-crets, the-crets are no fun..."

"The-crets, the-crets can hurt thumb-one..."

The cat wrapping itself around her legs. Purring.

Her thin legs pale-white beneath that white nightie.

The white nightie billowing like a large white bell.

Billowing even more as she subsequently spun about.

Pirouetting. Head back. White ribbons spinning.

Gold eyes gleaming, as the child hushed:

*"I-th your name really Emily, Emily?"*
*"You daren't not tell the truth…"*
*"You daren't not tell the truth, Emily…"*
The cat blinking languidly as she pirouetted.
Already knowing the answer to come.
The answers to all the riddles. Large and small.
Bored by the simple inevitably of it all.
Even as that infernal little devil of a beast could not look away just in case there might just possibly be a surprise in store.
A dark and rather delicious surprise.
Meanwhile, the child, Madelyn, spun ever faster still. Her pale right hand extending out from her body. Reaching out for Emily. A pale right hand with a host of long sharp black talons. Claws.
No longer simply fingernails. Not at all. *At t'all.*
*"Dan-th with me…"* she whispered to Emily.
*"It-th eethee…"* she whispered to Emily.
That dark laughter bubbling from her thin chest.
Surrounded by a soft hissing chorus of dark laughter.
From the shadows. Dark little eyes staring. *Staring, staring.*
As her lopsided grin became even more lopsided.
More lopsided as Madelyn pirouetted about.
Reaching. Reaching. Reaching out for Emily.
*Dan-th with me… Da-th with us… It-th eethee…*
Somewhere in the darkness above Emily could hear the music box playing. The odd antique music box with that dull glass-topped lid mimicking a red and white circus big-top tent. Its tune like that of an approaching carnival or circus. And again found herself imagining a long train of cars slowly slipping along the rails into a small town in the middle of the country in the middle of a dark night.
*In the middle of a dark night born of a black-clouded day.*
Ferrying clowns and freaks and wild beasts.
Playing at a bright lively tempo, this distant music.
But also seemingly playing at the wrong speed.
Warped and distorted. Stretched like cold taffy.
Into something macabre and unnatural.
Something dark and rather sinister.
And yet, she was certain she could dance to it for all that. *Dan-th.* Her feet already moving beneath her. Turning her head dizzy as the parlor spun around her *as she found herself pirouetting about.*
*Pirouetting about.* Reaching with her own hand.

With her own pale right hand *for those talons.*
Those terrible black talons clicking in the dimness.
Clicking amid the speckles of golden light.
Clicking in the nictitating firelight.
*Dan-th with me… Da-th with us… It-th eethee…*
*Pitter patter. Pitter patter. Pitter patter pitter patter.*
*Scritch scratch scritch. Scritch scratch scritch scratch scritch.*

It would be so easy to just take that offered hand, she decided, as she spun deliriously to that distant ghoulish calliope music.

So easy to just take that open fist of talons.
*And perhaps, just perhaps, be with her mother again.*
She could feel *her.* Her mother. Here.
Here. In this giant looming beast of a house.
Waiting for her. Here. *Waiting, waiting.*

Perhaps, just perhaps, very close by in the dimness of this very sitting room. This very parlor. Here. *Red-headed. Dirty blue eyes.*
Staring at her from the shadows. *Staring, staring.*
Here. Amongst the other creepy-ass little dolls.
Could feel the *inevitably* of it all. This dark fate.
Her dark fate. Here. In the dark walls of this house.
As if it had always been waiting for her. Here.
In this giant looming beast of a house.
*Getting to the age when we might expect to see changes…*
*Bio-chemical and bio-physiological signifiers…*
*Metamorphosis. A perverted or corrupted puberty…*
*Haven't had any experience in my practice…*
*There is no treatment. No reversal of symptoms…*
*This a chronic condition. Monstrous…*
*Sleep, little one, sleep. Dream yourself awake…*
*And all of your dreams will come true.*
Yes, so very *eethee* to take that offered hand.
To *dan-th* off with it into the waiting darkness.

And that was when the child that *really wasn't a child at t'all, the child with that morbid-looking puppet grin spilling out all that darkly amused possessed-laughter,* began to change into *something else entirely.*

Something macabre and unnatural.
Something altogether dark and sinister.
A most horrible transformation. *Metamorphosis.*
The pirouetting becoming a *flinching. A twisting. A morbid dance. Those terrible black talons tearing at its hair. Flesh. Clawing at it.*

## THE NIGHT SITTER

*As if something seemingly in deep struggle with itself.*
*Trying to tear its dark soul to the surface. To liberate it.*
*Head throwing back in a now soundless dark painful laughter. Revealing an elongated jaw, a mouthful of large spiny needle-like teeth, and fangs.*
*Its white-ribboned braids suddenly curved horns.*
*And suddenly, appearing from its thin torso, giant dark coriaceous wings. Splaying wide as it howled, shrieked, and flicked a large spiny coiled tail.*
*A huge fearsome looming beast with gleaming gold eyes.*
*Amid the frenetic tornado of speckled golden firefly light.*
As Emily felt herself *suddenly changing*, too.
Her own skin suddenly feeling far too tight.
Talons forming at the end of her own fingers.
Fingers that turned dark and scaly and prolonged.
As her mouth filled with its own sharp things.
Her jaw jutting out. Elongating. Almost painfully.
A long dark tongue flicking in the musty parlor air.
As gravity released her feet from the parlor floor.
As large veined-appendages spread from her own back.
Stretching and thickening her back muscles. Neck.
Her skin thickening, too. Stretching. Turning scaly.
Those large veined-appendages *lifting her.*
*Lifting her into that frenetic tornado of golden fireflies.*
*As she suddenly could remember in stark grisly detail with appalling horror and craving hunger what had happened out there on that playground.*
*Now. Suddenly. Devoid of any fuzziness or fading.*
*No longer out of order or offered to her only in those brief terrible snatches or glimpses of memory. Neither in a weird kaleidoscope of sheer escalating horror nor in monstrous Rorschach shadows on the cold hard ground.*
*No, suddenly she could remember it all. Clearly.*
*Herself. Lifting. Floating. Changing. Becoming monstrous.*
*Her own terrible gluttony. Her barbarism unrestrained.*
*Alongside the dark terribleness of what the child had become.*
*Ripping and tearing body parts. And feeding. In that pale moonlight in that cold rising wind. In that grim black and white world turned red.*
*Tasting ambrosia on her screaming tongue.*
*The food of gods. The sweetest and most divine of nectars.*
*And not for the first time. Not for the first time.*
*For there had been others. So many others. Children.*
*Over a black span of many passing years. Decades maybe.*
*So many others. So very many others. So many.*

The thing before her was still reaching out for her.
Still reaching our for her in the parlor dimness.
Still reaching out for the thing *she had become*.
The thing that had always been there *inside her*.
There *inside her* waiting patiently. *Waiting, waiting*.
*Dan-th with me… Dan-th with us… It-th eethee…*
*Pitter patter. Pitter patter. Pitter patter pitter patter.*
*Scritch scratch scritch. Scritch scratch scritch scratch scritch.*
And she realized her life had always been a dark jigsaw puzzle with many missing pieces, obfuscating any real perspective.
Those pieces were now available to her.
That dark jigsaw puzzle now falling into place.
In all its grandiose and gruesome horror.
And with it, a *whispering voice* rising. *Rising, rising*.
Rising in the thick black walls of this dark house.
Beneath the shrill scream of the wind in the eaves.
The steady gong of midnight. The calliope music.
The *pitter patter, pitter patter, scritch scratch scritch*.
A dark seductive voice. A foreign voice.
A foreign voice that sounded so very familiar.
As if she'd been waiting to hear it. *Waiting, waiting*.
Waiting to hear it for her entire existence.
Waiting for it to finally speak to her.
Mr. Grayson. Her father. The Sire.

# 26.

**GRAYSON:** Listen to me. Listen to me closely, my dearest girl. Listen to me well. If you would be so amenable. The child's death was only but a lamentable accident. Any suggestion otherwise is only but the grief speaking. Inconsolable. Clamant. This grief of a mother. This grief for her lost child.

I thought I might mollify this insufferable grief.
This grief for something which has been lost.
For something which has been lost forever.
A forever now stretching that grief to eternity.
Immortalizing this grief. This insufferable grief.
For the child will never be the child again.
Not in the mother's eyes. This grieving mother.
For the child has now become something else.
And this something else has not mollified this grief.
My dark mercy offering no mercy at all in the end.
Despite my sincerest of intentions otherwise.
Regrettably. For I am also familiar with grief.
As are you, my dearest girl. As are you.
For you, my dearest girl, it has been a cold blade.
Slicing into you. Offering you pain. Numbness.

For me, it is a *hollowness*. Neither pain nor numbness, inspiring no feeling whatsoever. And it is this lack of feeling that becomes so dismally insufferable. Inconsolable. Clamant. Over eternity.

An existence of being *neither here nor there.*
This *hollowness* that defines my existence. Grief.
At least until the *hunger* returns. A need for *satiation.*
A need to feed, my dearest girl. And to taste.
A rare and sublime pleasure, you see. Tasting.
Proving there is a god. A god unto me. Us.
A god that fills that *hollowness* for a spell.
A god that allows me, us, to sleep. To dream.
To wander quietly amongst the still-living.
To prey, as it were, my dearest girl.

A god that offers me, us, a reminder of the prejudice we must face from a people who would create a virus. A virus to pass silently amongst themselves *in their very own blood.* Knowing that we might once again know mortality should we drink that very blood.

Become *infected* by it. Pass it *amongst ourselves.*

But god always has the last laugh, my dearest girl.

For, my dearest girl, that virus they created to infect their very own blood mutated as you know. And now it *infects them.*

It infects their hubris as well as their flesh.

For they went against the will of god.

For they went against the will of god, and yet--

They believe me, us, the *devil,* you see, my dearest girl. Even as these feeble-minded fools worship a savior who rose from the *dead.* Even as these feeble-minded fools call themselves *the flock.*

But now, perhaps, they will know better.

But now, perhaps, they will see god for what he is.

By what he has wisely created in their midst.

For all his mysterious purposes. This god.

Me. Us. Dragons. My dearest girl.

We live in the darkness so that they might live in the light. We are the shepherds to their feeble-minded flock. We tend to them as black angels on the periphery of their ungraceful existence.

We prevent them from straying. We do.

We keep them in the light by living in the dark.

We suffer eternity for their mortality.

It is our fate, my dearest girl. *Fait accompli.*

And so I counsel you, my dearest girl, you can suffer *their* grief for what feels like forever; or, you can endure our grief, our *hollowness,* for eternity. And when our grief, our *hollowness,* my dearest girl, becomes just too unbearable, you can feed and you can taste.

# THE NIGHT SITTER

The mother. She cannot yet feed. Taste.
Not without the child. Or what is left of the child.
What is left of the child that has not been lost forever. What is left of the child that has not been lost for eternity, you see.
A child that has crossed the threshold from life to undeath. A dark mercy granted unto each one of us. Myself. The others.
The others, my dearest girl. Your family.
Your bloodline. My coven. My brood.
They *walk-eth* from the light into the dark with me.
My companions in this eternal night of dark mercy.
My disciples sharing this grief. This *hollowness*.
A grief immortalized forever. Stretching to eternity.
Nocturnal. Bloodthirsty. Living of the night.
Living of the darkness in their undeath.
Living still to feed. To taste, my dearest girl.
As do I. As must you. *Fait accompli.*
*For you are my only daughter. My only child.*
*But you must choose to do so willingly, my dearest girl.*
*You must take-eth of my hand of your own free volition.*
*My only daughter. My only child. Dhampir.*
*You must now choose the darkness over the light.*
*You've been lost in the shadows. Not knowing who you are.*
*Not knowing what you are. Direly confused. Afraid.*
*Mind conspiring against you. Protecting you. Lying to you.*
*Even as I walked there beside you. A dark promise.*
*A dark promise that you were never alone. Never that.*
*Never alone despite your appetites. Confusion. Fear.*
*That there was a place where you needn't feel any confusion. Fear. Never feel a sense of un-belonging. A place where you would not be the stranger.*
*A place where you'd not be the subject of suspicion.*
*Of confusion. Fear. Of human frailty.*
*A place where you could become who you are.*
*A place where you could become what you are.*
*My dearest girl. My only daughter. My child. Dhampir.*
*A place where you needn't be alone anymore.*
*A place to be your home. For forever. For eternity.*
*A place where you can feed. Taste. Sleep. And dream.*
*For such dreams also fill that insufferable hollowness.*
*We are all waiting for you here. Here in the darkness.*
*But you must choose, my dearest girl. Dhampir.*

*You must now choose the darkness over the light.*
*For it is not a decision that can be made for you.*
*But you have come so very far, my dearest girl. Here.*
*To the very edge of the world where I have waited for you.*
*Where I have waited for you so very patiently. Still--*
*I realize for you this will be a difficult choice. It always is, my dearest girl. Confusion and fear are yokes not easily shrugged off after a lifetime of restraint. Such restraints are stubborn. They dig deeply into the flesh. The mind.*
*They suggest to you that you can never be free of them.*
*They suggest to you that the darkness is curse.*
*A terribly false promise. A land of the lost.*
*That you must offer of it your very soul.*
*And I suppose this is not apocryphal, my dearest girl. My only daughter. My child. Dhampir. I suppose this choice will possess of you the most dreadful of sacrifices. As it did for myself. As it has for the others. Your family.*
*It will possess of you an even greater grief, I fear.*
*An even greater grief for something which will be lost.*
*An even greater grief for something which will be lost forever.*
*A forever that will stretch this greater grief to eternity.*
*Immortalizing this grief. This insufferable grief.*
*Even now I hear this grief gathering in the dark wind.*
*Gathering in the storm brewing outside this house.*
*It will wear a familiar face, my dearest girl. My only daughter. My child. Dhampir. It will speak to your heart. It will speak to your very soul.*
*Listen to me. Listen to me closely, my dearest girl.*
*Listen to me well. For this grief has arrived.*
*A guest, my dearest girl. A guest.*

# 27.

THERE WERE BRIGHT LIGHTS beyond the long thick black drapes drawn over the parlor windows. Suddenly. And incredibly brilliant. Powerful enough to penetrate those long thick black drapes. Set them aglow. A half dozen supernovas, these bright lights on the other side of the long thick black drapes.

Emily found herself blinking. Twitching really.

She could hear the grumble of motorized vehicles. Other machinery. The sound of voices. Many voices. Angry human voices.

All come to this, the very edge of the world.

Surrounding the giant looming beast of a house.

Descending upon it. Preying down upon it.

*Of course, they would come, Miss Emily…* Ms. Vivian Dancemore's voice hushed in her head. *It was a fait accompli the moment he invited us out of the house. Fait accompli the moment blood was shed on that playground. For nothing happens without his consent. Not in this black house.*

*This house is only an extension of him. The Sire.*

*His bones. Skin. Claws. And teeth, Missy Emily.*

*Though I suppose, dear girl, you understand that by now.*

*He invited this moment. This battle, Miss Emily.*

*He invited it as he invited you to join him. Here. Now.*

*I always knew this, dear girl, and I quietly accepted it as I most dutifully extended that dark invitation to you as an extension of him. My master.*

*Even as I prayed you might resist him. The Sire.*

*Despite his invitation. Despite his trust in you.*
*And now here you are. At the precipice of this battle.*
*At the precipice of this war. A war inevitable. Inexorable.*
*The foils of man. The appetites of monsters. Dragons.*
*Predestined to be enemies. To misunderstand each other.*
*Man. A fragile creature. A frightened creature. A mortal creature.*
*Dragons. Beasts born of dark mythology. Hungry beasts. Secretive beasts. Immortal breasts. Conveniently forgotten by man in the dark annals of the past like a cruel nightmare. And certain to be forgotten by man once more when this is finally over. This battle. The other battles soon to come. This war.*
*For man is that fragile creature, is he not, Miss Emily?*
*For man cannot for long stare at such demons in the eye.*
*Not without going insane. Not without losing his humanity.*
*Will you forsake, Miss Emily, your own humanity?*
*Is that the choice he will have you make? The master.*
*I pray not, Miss Emily. I pray not for your sake.*
*I pray not for the sake of my accursed child. The others.*
*I pray not for the sake of myself. And for your own mother.*
*She is here, yes, Miss Emily. Yes. Suffering, my dear girl. Though she is no more your mother than Madelyn is any longer my daughter. It sleeps and it wanders, this thing that presumes to be your mother. And it suffers.*
*Unable to free herself from his claws. From his teeth.*
*Quite as am I. Quite as is my child. Quite as are the others.*
*What decision will you make? What fateful decision?*
*For it cannot be undone once made. It is forever. Eternal.*
*This fateful decision you must make. Now. Alone.*
*For dragons are only immortal if we allow them to be. Only if we allow them to exist in darkness. Dark mythology. But they are every bit as fragile as man when exposed to light, dear girl. When they are dragged out from the cover of their darkness. When they are brought to burn. Burn, burn, burn.*
*For dragons are born of fire and will perish of fire.*
*Will you perish of fire, Miss Emily? Will that be your fate?*
*Look at you. Look at you now, my dear girl.*
*Look at what you've become, Miss Emily.*

Emily blinked again, twitched really, and found herself turning away from the bright lights and angry human noises to contemplate what the child that *really wasn't a child at t'all* had become. The monster. The beast. Eyes gleaming gold. Breathing heavily in the parlor dimness. *Floating* there a foot above the parlor floor.

The fire crackling and hissing noisily.

And revealing to Emily *her own shadow* on the gray-wallpapered parlor walls. Monstrous. Beastly. Floating. *Floating, floating.*

*Floating* there a foot above the parlor floor.

Her own breath laboring in the parlor dimness.

Ms. Vivian Dancemore's voice in her head an echo.

A distant melancholy echo of her in her head given the woman's grisly transformation on this dark stormy night at this, the very edge of the world. *A distant melancholy echo somehow emanating from deep within that monster floating there before her now. Floating there with that most horrible-looking morbid grin as if it could, this monster, perhaps, hear this echo of a voice, too, lost so deeply inside of it. Lost so deeply inside of it, yet somehow still able to communicate to her. To Emily. For now. If only for now.*

*An angel on Emily's shoulder for his devil. Mr. Grayson.*

*Her father. The Sire. The master. Of this giant looming beast of a house. His bones. Skin. Claws. Teeth. This giant looming beast of a house.*

*Or perhaps it was the other way around maybe.*

*Yes, by god, perhaps it was the other way around.*

*Perhaps the echo of this melancholy woman was the devil. And he a dark angel. The master. The Sire. Her father. Inviting her here, to this, the very edge of the world, to mollify her own suffering. To feed. To taste. To dream.*

Emily pondered such things as she realized the antique grandfather clock in the corner was still gonging. Or at least still gonging in the thick dark house walls. Echoing there. *Echoing, echoing.*

Emily felt herself shrinking. Shivering.

Shrinking slowly back into her human self.

Shivering most violently. Terribly. In her sickness.

Her clothing reduced to silly tatters about her.

In this, her dark fate. In this, her *fait accompli*.

Her entire miserable life leading her here.

To this very moment on this dark stormy night.

*The foils of man. The appetites of monsters. Dragons.*

As those gongs echoed endlessly. *Echoing, echoing.*

As if they might echo in the dark walls forever.

And noticed the hour hand and the long minute hand on the clock-face were still conjoined at due-north. As if *frozen at midnight*. With a final dying *tick-tock* sigh fading into all those endless gonging echoes. The grandfather clock's brass pendulum having fallen quite still. Quite still in the dark hollow body of the antique clock.

As if time itself had finally come to a pause.

As if the house were once again holding its breath.

To her further disquiet, Emily noticed her late mother's watch on her wrist, *Parisienne, Art Deco*, was also *stuck at midnight*. The elegant blue-lacquered hour hand and the long minute hand, glowing faintly in the parlor dimness, conjoined at due-north. *Frozen.*

As if time itself had truly lost all its meaning.

In this odd absence of time, Emily found herself peeling open the thick black drapes. Peering out at all those bright lights.

Forced to shield her eyes with a raised hand.

The bright lights burning her eyes. *Burning, burning.*

Bright lights that turned out to be floodlights.

The chorus of angry human voices, the grumble of motorized vehicles and other machinery, a National Guard contingent.

The soldiers dark silhouettes beyond the floodlights and sawhorse barricades and coils of razor wire, their dark silhouettes made somehow blacker still and even more menacing by their inky-black combat gear and their Darth Vader-like protective masks.

Turning their owners from human--

Into something altogether *decidedly less human.*

Something more automaton. As if anything might be required of them. Something requiring but the mind of a machine.

But, of course, Emily knew the real truth.

She'd seen them without their masks at the playground, hadn't she? Their Darth Vader-like masks lifted from their heads.

Almost as if they had been beheaded.

Revealing to her their soft rosy-cheeked faces.

Soft. Rosy-cheeked. Vulnerable. Fragile.

Still, the presence of so many of them here at the very edge of the world was unnerving, facing the giant looming beast of a house. Knowing *what was inside it*. Knowing what was inside it could not be allowed to survive. Knowing that it was *decidedly not human.*

*As was she herself,* Emily accepted woefully.

*Getting to the age where we might expect to see changes…*

*There is no treatment. No reversal of symptoms…*

*This is a chronic condition. Monstrous…*

*Never show your teeth when you smile…*

*I'm summer, you're winter…*

It was just then she noticed one of the automatons remove his Darth Vader-like protective mask behind a coil of razor wire.

One man. Standing off from the others.

Standing rather alone, she thought. This man.

And she knew instantly it was *him*. Her Adam.
Days passing like years. Years passing like days.
Time turning on itself. Stretching. Shrinking.
As it was wont to do even as it now held itself still.
As she stared out at *him*. Her Adam. *There*. Magically.
Well, maybe not magically. Maybe *fait accompli*.

His *clairvoyance* for her had always been downright creepy. Able to read her mind from the very beginning as children, staring at her silently as he had with his large intelligent pale blue eyes. Anticipating her thoughts. Her actions. Her freaking moods. And more.

Yes, that *clairvoyance* could be downright creepy.

Yet also somehow downright comforting.

And it occurred to Emily now as she stared out at him on this dark stormy night, as it had occurred to her before, that perhaps *she* was the *clairvoyant* one. Able to silently communicate her needs and wants to him without speaking. Perhaps across distances.

Perhaps across distances unaffected by time.

Time being rather meaningless in the end.

Their connection, their relationship, a hardass little shiny diamond in the terrible sewer that had always been her life.

A hardass little shiny diamond in the filth.

As if cavalierly discarded by someone who knew not its worth. Or altruistically discarded for only *her* to find maybe. Full of sharp hard edges, but so sparkly in the light. And hiding inside of it a tiny separate universe where anything was possible. Anything.

A tiny separate universe promising infinity.

A young boy who would become her family. Her forever. Not by blood, but by circumstance. Inseparable by neither time nor distance nor any cold and heartless earthly convention, either.

She contemplated on that now as she stared at him.

At that sweet boy who'd now become a man.

*"I'm summer, you're winter," he would tell her. Adam. Whispering softly into her ear. Holding her in the night against his long warm body. As if those poetic words held the key to a lifetime of happiness. But they hadn't. Not with the monster residing within her. The monster that neither he nor she could clearly see. But perhaps could intuitively sense was there. This monster. This winter to his summer. Hiding there inside of her. He had escaped from that monster as it had devoured her. He had a family. A wife. Two young girls. A dog.*

*What was he doing here? On such a dark stormy night?*

*Why had he come for her? Had he done that?*

She could not see him clearly, her Adam, not with the floodlights, but she knew it was him. She knew it was him like one knew a stove was hot when you touched it with your bare hand.

*And she figuratively felt herself jerk back from him not unlike her hand might jerk back from touching a hot stove. The tender flesh scalded.*

She wanted to tell him to flee. Her Adam. *Appearing* before her on this dark stormy night. That there was a terrible danger here for him. Residing here in this giant looming beast of a house.

And she intuited that *he was telling her the same.*

Telling her the same by removing that black mask.

That ugly black automaton *dehumanizing* mask.

As if screaming to her *to flee. To run. Now.*

As if she could. As if she could escape this prison of a house. Then again, perhaps she could do just that. Perhaps. Maybe.

*Yes, Miss Emily, dear girl. Perhaps. Maybe, indeed...* she heard Ms. Vivian Dancemore hush inside her head. *Of course you can.*

Of course she could. And perhaps she must.

*Perhaps she must resist. His dark invitation. Mr. Grayson. Her father. The Sire. The master. Of this black house. Resist it to save her very soul.*

*Resist it to free the others from his most terrible curse.*

*Resist it to save Adam. Her Adam. From him.*

*And thus tame the wretched monster within herself.*

*Assuming this wretched monster could be tamed, of course.*

*But of course it could be tamed. That was the purpose of the virus, was it not? To tame such beasts as she. To return her humanity, if only in death.*

*Was that her choice, then? Death or eternity?*

*Death or damnation? Was her choice that simple? Dire?*

She blinked, twitched really, and suddenly *he was gone.*

Her Adam. Just *disappeared* in a blinding *jarring* instant.

Amid the black rain and a sudden burst of gunfire.

As if he hadn't *just* disappeared, but been *taken.*

*Taken. By a winged-beast in the dark stormy night, perhaps. A howling, shrieking thing in the storm. Taken from the shadowy edge of the armed congregation. Stolen off in the flash of an eye into the surrounding darkness.*

And as the black-clad soldiers stirred even more agitatedly behind the bright floodlights, two huge black tanks with black American flag emblems pushed to the forefront of the contingent.

Those black tanks idled there a long moment before their long ugly gun barrels lifted. And pointed toward the black house.

*Lifted and pointed toward Emily and her window.*

Their muzzles fuming angrily with black smoke, inviting back the terrible black spots before her eyes. *Inviting back that dark oozing fluid into her lungs. Filling them. A pair of black water balloons.*

*The dark fluid rising heavily like a dark wet cement. Threatening to turn her lungs into those black stones. As before. To finally suffocate her.*

Choking, hugging herself, eyes blurry with those terrible black spots spinning dizzily with that maelstrom of golden sherry fireflies spinning about so manically, Emily blinked, twitched really, to find herself suddenly staring closely at the window pane's *solid black steel cross-sections*. Not unlike jail bars in the window before her.

*A small rusted keyhole lock set into that black steel frame.*
*A small rusted keyhole lock Emily hadn't any stupid key for.*
*Trapping her inside this giant looming beast of a house.*

It was then she distinctly heard a terrible hissing rumble of a noise from deep within those black tanks. Before streams of golden fire shot out from those smoking muzzles. Impressively long angry sizzling streams of golden fire. *Like a pair of golden tongues.*

Those golden tongues scorched over the mailbox on its rather crooked post at the end of the driveway, the front flap of that narrow metal box still open, as if the mailbox were sticking out its own tongue. Revealing a dark throat. As if might jump out at the militia gathered before it. Jump out at all of them and bite them.

Swallow them all down its long narrow gullet.

Only to feel the intense heat of those golden tongues.

Only to begin melting beneath them, only too quickly slipping down its rather crooked post like hot black candle wax as the golden tongues then leapt out over the narrow flagstone walkway, turning the slick flagstones to black on this dark stormy night.

Before the horrible golden tongues, roaring quite loudly now, kissed the large dark gothic dollhouse of a Victorian itself.

The flames only *invigorated* by the heavy black rain.

Not unlike a grease fire. These terrible golden flames.

Growing. Sizzling. Hissing. Crackling. Screaming.

Setting ablaze that long and deep wraparound porch, licking at the wrought-iron welcome sign leaning there against the house wall, blackening the gothic-calligraphy and rendering it speechless.

*Luke 10:5 Whatever house you enter,*
*First say: "Peace be to this house."*

The ravenous golden flames then fanning about, torching the dark wood siding. The dark scalloped shingles that only too closely resembled oily reptilian scales. The decorative lattice trim, too, and whimsical brackets, the dentil molding, ornate spandrels, and beaded rails. The steep multi-faceted roof with its series of gables facing in many mysterious directions over that long and deep wraparound porch housing that suspended antique ceiling lantern now swaying in the horribly oppressive heat, exploding, spitting glass in a myriad of directions (the minute shards hitting the old house like grains of sand), discarding off into this dark stormy night the antique ceiling lantern's resident flurry of black and white moths, the moths swirling out into the darkness like thin tissue paper caught on fire, brilliant one moment before fading off into the night the next.

Emily blinked, twitched really, heavily:
And found herself again facing the parlor.
The wall behind her radiating heat. Buckling.
And then burning itself. *Burning, burning.*
The parlor shimmering with the golden flames.
*Found herself facing that black winged-beast.*
*Not unlike the one that had perhaps just taken her Adam.*
Its black-taloned hand still reaching out for her.
Dark laughter bubbling from its scaly chest.
Surrounded by a soft hissing chorus of dark laughter.
From the haunting shadows full of dark little eyes.
Reaching. Reaching out for her. As it growled:
*Dan-th with me... Da-th with us... It-th eethee...*
The black cat nodding at this sentiment.
Nodding in the aura of the ravenous golden flames.
*We're all mad here...* the cat reminding her a final time.
Its dark green almond-shaped eyes twinkling.
Twinkling madly. Flashing with gold.

And Emily found herself *taking that black-taloned hand as that antique grandfather clock held fast. The black-taloned hand taking her own hand and also wrapping about her pale wrist over her mother's antique watch.*

*Her mother's most treasured possession. That watch.*
*Its hour hand and long minute hand stuck at midnight.*

*Queerly frozen as the deep echoes of that antique grandfather clock echoed in the dark walls of the house as the house became engulfed in flames.*

And yet Emily *also felt herself resisting.*

Felt herself resisting the clutch of the black-taloned hand. The cold bony reptilian clutch of it against her pale feverish skin.

Only to feel those parlor shadows fall over her.

Only to then feel tiny hard cold porcelain hands *grabbing* at the rest of her as her heavy black-spotted eyes *fluttered, fluttered.*

Fluttered heavily as if *she were falling even deeper, even deeper still into that trance she'd maybe been in ever since entering the black house.*

*Pitter patter pitter patter. Pitter patter. Pitter patter.*

*Scritch scratch scritch scratch scritch. Scritch scratch scritch.*

Emily blinked, twitched really, heavily:

And found herself in the low and narrow hall.

The low and narrow hall just outside the parlor.

As the dark house burned about her. *Burned, burned.*

Crackling flames crawling along the low ceiling.

Descending the dark and thick wood-paneled walls, then slipping off down the low and narrow hall into the many small rooms offset from it, reminding her a final time of a dollhouse.

A dark maze of a dollhouse. This house.

This black house now burning. *Burning, burning.*

And she imagined the flames hungrily overwhelming the parlor, igniting the plush overstuffed antique furniture, including the short chenille sofa and the fuzzy blue velvet armchair, the pictorial tapestries and landscapes, and the long dark window draperies.

Imagined the parlor becoming a *fiery kiln.* The suffocating collection of antique knickknacks contained within it devoured.

Sculptures. Figurines. Spelter statues. Porcelain bowls.

The dark glass-globed table lamps. Chintz china.

Medallions. Arches. Ovals. Garlands. Wreaths.

And that antique grandfather clock in the corner with its marquetry accented with what she'd believed to be *fleur-de-lis.*

But now knew was not *fleur-de-lis* at all. *At t'all.*

Reducing it all to ash. Every last bit of it.

*Ashes to ashes, dust to dust. Ashes, dust.*

In a thickening black smoke, she moved -- *floated* -- down the low and narrow hall, pulled by the black-taloned hand and all those tiny hard cold porcelain hands grabbing at the rest of her. But the black winged-beast and that coterie of creepy-ass dolls were lost in the thickening black smoke -- or somehow just out of her field of vision. Save for their dark shadows moving on the walls.

Shortly, she found herself passing the newel post of the rising staircase. The steeply rising staircase. As old as the house, the newel post. A carved black walnut. Fluted with ribbed columns.

A playful tendril of flame reached for it, too.

And the old newel post seemed to gasp.

Then offer a dull wounded cracking noise as that black walnut smoldered, producing more black smoke, if a pleasant aroma.

The flames rippled along the front door, too.

The *impossibly impossible* front door to the house.

Guarding this giant looming beast of a *burning* house.

Obsidian black. Thick. Probably oak. That door.

Burning now. That door. *Burning, burning.*

Marbles sat at the top of the stairs. Dark green almond-shaped eyes bulbous. Fur coarse. Standing-up in rigid spikes. Staring down at all the ravenous golden flames and the thick black smoke.

Its tiny mouth opened wide, revealing teeth.

Revealing its sharp little teeth as it howled.

As it howled at all those flames and black smoke.

Howled as the Victorian house *burned, burned.*

The house moaning itself. Shrieking. Bellowing.

As it roasted and sizzled. Bubbled, crackled, popped.

Beset with this most murderous *conflagration.*

A particularly playful flame *reached out* for the cat and Marbles spun away from it, albeit rather maladroitly for the otherwise graceful beast. Stumbling. Tumbling a moment in the darkness.

Before disappearing into the upstairs hall.

Emily blinked, twitched really, heavily:

And suddenly found herself in that upstairs hall.

Floating up the long plum-colored carpet in the narrow dimly-lit hall past its flickering bronze sconces. Some of the sconces popping noisily behind her as the flames overtook them.

Her bedroom already completely aflame.

The bed. The small desk. The wardrobe. *Afire.*

The small plastic bubble TV melting. *Melting, melting.*

Though she thought just maybe she could still hear that President's fuzzy, distorted cartoon-like voice echoing in stereo:

His large beefy fists pounding on the Oval desk:

*"...this undead scourge...these parasitic bloodsuckers..."*

And then Emily was turning the sharp corner into the dark alcove and to the dark narrow staircase leading up to the attic.

The attic door was *ajar.* Waiting for her.

Waiting for her to ascend. *Waiting, waiting.*

She floated up that dark narrow staircase into the waiting attic to find the ceiling *burning, burning.* The ravenous golden flames roaring, the roof caving-in. A fiery beam having landing on one of the dolls. The doll pinned beneath it. Dark glassy eyes burst.

Little black holes staring out sightlessly.

Its little pale porcelain face seared. Blistered.

Melting in some places. *Melting, melting.*

White porcelain drooling onto the attic floor.

The small cot was also *burning, burning.*

The doodles on the near wall reminding Emily of those moths on the porch down below. Reduced to *burning, burning* ashes.

Ashes fluttering madly about the attic. Swirling.

Brilliant one moment, then *fading, fading* the next.

Fading like shooting stars over the wooden rocking horse. The wooden rocking horse rocking rather violently back and forth, back and forth, its springs white-hot and whining terribly as the wooden rocking horse *burned, burned.* The wooden toy chest a bonfire. Toys and games and its other mysterious things *burning, burning.*

And in the small room's furthest corner--

The antique music box on the old steamer trunk.

Its dull glass-topped lid mimicking a red and white circus big-top tent lifted open, but as of yet untouched by the flames.

Just glowing. Red and white. *Glowing, glowing.*

The antique music box singing. *Singing, singing.*

Singing amid the terrible pandemonium.

*Calliope music. But warped and distorted as if being played at the wrong speed. Something macabre and unnatural. Dark and rather sinister.*

*And inside that antique music box that ghoulish spinning carousel of circus animals. Those awful lions, tigers, elephants, monkeys, and zebras.*

*Those awful circus animals with their human faces.*

*Human faces wretched with terrible expressions of agony.*

Spinning on top of that old steamer trunk.

The old steamer trunk in the far corner shadows.

With its thick leather straps and heavy buckles.

The *ghoulish spinning carousel* offering spinning speckles of twinkling golden light about the entire attic. *Spinning, spinning.*

Not unlike a maelstrom of golden fireflies.

Madly chasing about those fading shooting star doodles.

Madly chasing them about as they *faded, faded.*

Faded into nothing at all. To nothing *at t'all*

And that was when she finally noticed the door.

*The short narrow door set into the far wall.*

*It had returned. This short narrow door.*
*Its outline nearly invisible in the firelight shadows.*
*As it slipped shut. This short narrow door.*

And it was in this moment as the door *slipped shut*, she sensed that her escorts -- the black-winged beast and the coterie of creepy-ass dolls with tiny hard cold porcelain hands and the *incurious curious* black cat -- *had passed through it. This short narrow door now slipping shut.* For they were suddenly, suspiciously, absent from the attic around her.

Leaving her here alone. Alone amid the flames.

Sweat drooling down her flushed cheeks.

*Drooling not unlike that tragic doll's melting porcelain.*

She found herself approaching that door with its *nearly invisible outline*, following her *suddenly, suspiciously,* absent escorts, those black spots still spinning in front of her eyes as if shadows of those spinning speckles of twinkling golden light coming from the music box as the endless gongs of that antique grandfather clock striking midnight continued their echo in the dark walls of the house.

The attic an oven against her feverish skin. The fiery-hot poker stabbing again through her brain behind her right eye, making it impossible to think clearly. To maintain coherent thought.

*Floating, floating.* As if in a dream. A nightmare.

But as the flames rose behind her, spitting, roaring, screaming, blocking any hope of escape from the attic, Emily accepted that the short narrow door set into the far wall would be locked.

*This most mysterious door fashioned with a silver knob and a silver keyplate that appeared oversized -- if only because of the truncated size of the door itself. A silver knob and keyplate embellished with more of that cryptic fleur-de-lis that was not fleur-de-lis at t'all. But winged-beasts. Dragons.*

And she found it to be just so. *Locked.* The short narrow door. This magical short narrow door that *appeared* and *disappeared.*

*Locked.* Trapping her with these insatiable flames.

*Locked.* Trapping her in her nightmare that had now *become* her dire reality. And she imagined the *conflagration* overcoming her. Feeding hungrily upon her. Her own flesh melting. Her eyes bubbling and crackling and popping. Small bones roasting and sizzling. Burying her deeply within this giant looming beast of a burning house as it finally collapsed in flames.

Burning, burning. Ashes to ashes, dust to dust.

She tried knocking on the door. Pounding on it.

Her knocks echoing with those deep everlasting gongs.

*You are to please knock on all doors before entering…*

Perhaps hearing the others just beyond the door. The shuffle of tiny hard little porcelain feet, if not that floating monster.

*Pitter patter. Pitter patter. Pitter patter pitter patter.*
*Scritch scratch scritch. Scritch scratch scritch scratch scritch.*

But there was no answer. In fact, the door seemed to be *disappearing* again before her very eyes. Its faint outline *fading away.*

Along with the silver knob. Keyplate. *Fading, fading.*

The *conflagration* roaring with approval. *Spitting, laughing.*

*Spitting, laughing, roaring* as it came for her now.

The last of the ceiling disintegrating. *Falling, falling.*

The dark floorboards *giving-way* beneath her feet.

And that was when she noticed a *flashing silver glint.*

*A flashing silver glint amid all that gesticulating firelight.*

*A flashing silver glint amid the tornado of black spots and the spinning speckles of twinkling golden light. A tinker bell. Glittering on the short narrow door. Seemingly causing that short narrow door to reappear before her.*

*A ghostly reflection. A mirage of a glittering thing.*

*And with it, a voice in the shadows near her. Behind her.*

*A familiar soft warm hushed whisper of a voice.*

Emily turned, her feverish head spinning even more dizzily, to find it sitting there once again. As before. Sitting there. It.

*In the corner shadows as of yet untouched by the flames.*

Sitting in a chair as the flames pushed toward it.

The firelight dancing on its porcelain face.

An elegant chair speaking of French aristocracy. Richly upholstered with chocolate paisley fabric and a crème brulee wood finish and baroque hand-carved details. Hand-carved details vividly detailing wild winged-beast monsters. Indeed, black dragons.

The doll. Red-headed. Dirty blue eyes.

It *seemed to grin* at her. As before. Animate.

Offering to her its sad forlorn-looking grin.

But a grin maybe possessing a *sad joyfulness,* too.

*I thought you might not eat the cookies...* the doll said without actually speaking. This red-headed doll with the dirty blue eyes. *I thought you might resist what had to be done...* it murmured gently to Emily. *But I didn't even have to ask you. I'm not sure I could've asked you, in the end, if I'm being honest with myself. The poison, it works very quickly. Depressing the nervous system. Slowing body functions. Causing first the loss of consciousness. And then respiratory failure. Before eventually, mercifully, death.*

*It's a powerful poison. Potent in small doses. Potent.*

*Nature's own little most terrible awful miracle.*
*Not unlike you, baby. My child. My dearest child.*
*I thought to myself how peaceful you looked slipping into that sleep from which I thought you would never wake. I thought how peaceful I would feel once I joined you. And I let that peaceful sleep fall over me, too.*
*Nowhere left to go… Nowhere left to hide…*
It seemed to grin even harder at her now.
The doll. Its forlorn-looking, if *sadly joyful* grin.
As if relieved this terrible night had finally come.
*Sleep, little one, sleep…* it then whispered to her.
*Dream yourself awake, and all your dreams will come true.*
Its small pale porcelain hands outstretched from its little body, offering to her something glinting like a silver wink amid the shadowy firelight. Amid the tornado of black spots and spinning speckles of twinkling golden light.
The silver key. With its decorative fleur-de-lis bow.
A decorative fleur-de-lis bow that was not fleur-de-lis at t'all.
But a black dragon. In full flight. The winged-beast screaming. Its clawed feet clawing at the air. Its black forked tongue spitting black fire.
Flared black hood framing gold spheroid eyes. Fangs.
Its black nostrils expelling black smoke.
And suddenly the key was in Emily's hand.
Twinkling there in her hand. *As if winking at her.*
As the flames jumped all over that red-headed doll seated on that elegant chair speaking of French aristocracy. The flames consuming the doll.
Its red hair rising. Standing on end. Crackling.
Its small porcelain head turning black. Cratering.
Cratering with a terrible loud cracking noise.
That forlorn-looking, if sadly joyful grin perverted. Warped. Distorted into what appeared through the flames to be a terrible soundless scream.
A terrible soundless scream as that elegant chair speaking of French aristocracy beneath it caught on fire. The chocolate paisley fabric ripping, fluttering, turning black, floating away in tattered pieces. The stuffing beneath it crackling. The crème brulee wood finish roasting. Its heavy varnish bubbling to the surface of the wood, sizzling noisily, before the chair legs simply buckled. Splintering in a gasping heap, producing a showering cloud of tumbling embers. Dumping what was left of the red-headed doll on the floor where what was left of the red-headed doll twisted and contorted in those terrible flames before falling still.
But for a single tiny pale porcelain hand. Lifeless.
Sticking out of the flames. Melting into a white puddle.
Emily blinked, twitched really, heavily:

And found herself in the dark corridor.

In the dark corridor *beyond the short narrow door.*

The short narrow door *slipping shut* behind her. Its bolt sliding back into place. Not a loud clacking noise, but a dark little whisper. *Before the door, its outline nearly invisible now, vanished completely in the dark wall along with the silver key in her hand. The silver key offering to her a final perverse little wink. Before poof. Like magic.* It was just gone, too.

Emily found herself facing that dark narrow corridor *leading into the very walls of the house.* Leading into heavy darkness. Into a heavy coldness undisturbed by the *conflagration* ravaging the house.

*Ravaging the house outside this dark narrow corridor.*
*Unable to burn through the walls of the dark narrow corridor.*
*Walls made not of wood, but of a thick black marble.*
*Along with the corridor floor and the low corridor ceiling above her.*
*A thick black marble glowing with a deep red blood-like veining.*
*A thick black marble that would not conduct heat. Burn.*
*Offering to her a cocoon of sorts. From the flames.*

The long thin white candle and its candlestick holder *with more of the black dragon fleur-de-lis* were waiting on the small shelf. The long white candle already lit for her on this apocalyptic night.

*Sizzling softly.* Pushing back the heavy darkness.

The pale candlelight guttered before her in her trembling right hand as she pushed down the dark narrow corridor, negotiating its sharp corners, descending steeply downward. *Down, down, down.*

*Down, down, down* into the cold waiting darkness.

The pale candlelight guttering even more fervently.

More fervently as she fought to breathe. *Breathe, breathe.*

Her lungs hardening into *black stones* in her chest, offering only reedy wheezes of desperate breath turned to ragged mist in the cold darkness. The air colder and colder still. Like a meat locker.

Emily shivered. Her teeth chattering noisily.

Still too warm, but suddenly too cold, too. Miserable.

Goose-fleshed skin *appearing like scales on her body.*

The black-spots swimming before her exhausted eyes.

The calliope music reverberating in the black marble walls.

Looping over and over and over again. As before.

As if the walls were somehow *singing* to her.

As those heavy bellowing gongs continued to echo.

Continued to echo and echo posthumously even after the presumed demise of the parlor's large antique grandfather clock.

The dark corridor twisting, turning as it proceeded *down, down, down* before rising briefly on that dark narrow stone staircase.

Before descending a final time. Even more steeply.

Emily nearly tripping over her stumbling feet.

Slipping about on all that cold black marble.

Until she felt certain she was beneath the house, assuming the giant black beast of a house *didn't just continue into the very earth.*

*Didn't just continue into the very pits of hell itself.*

*Albeit a hell encased in cold black marble ice.*

It was then, as before, the low dark corridor opened into that large dark chamber. As if from an almost forgotten nightmare.

The cold black marble below her shuffling-echoing feet turning abruptly into large square blocks. Not unlike black title.

*Black tile with its own deep red blood-like veining.*

As for the rest of it, disturbingly, Emily could only fetch such memories from her mind from her first visit into the crypt. For the pale guttering candlelight was *far weaker* on this visit, offering to her *only a few feet of visibility. As if she were moving in a pale spotlight.*

The darkness around her *much darker* than before.

Hiding all the rest of it in a pitch-darkness.

*Including the solid black marble table at the center of the chamber.*

*Completely smooth. With a black winch and black chain.*

*Suggesting the table might be lifted into an upright position.*

*Lifted into an upright position like a black monolith.*

*With four black metal cuffs with tiny medieval-like screws at each corner of the black marble table, suggesting to her a most terrible macabre use.*

*A shallow ivory basin under the black marble table, presumably residing at its very foot should the table be lifted into an upright position. A basin feeding a narrow gutter which in turn fed directly into an ivory cistern.*

*It had not been hard to imagine the table upright.*

*Not hard to imagine a poor victim cuffed to that table.*

*Not hard to imagine all that ivory turned red.*

*Red not unlike the veining in the surrounding marble.*

*And she knew, as well, there were coffins here. Surrounding the sacrificial table like numbers on a clock. Twelve of them in this deep chamber.*

*Stone coffins. Twelve sarcophagi in a large circle.*

*(And another. A smaller coffin. In a smaller chamber.)*

*The largest stone coffin sitting at twelve o'clock due-north.*

*Each of the coffin lids inscribed with a cryptic symbol.*

*Inscribed in more deep red blood-like veining. The Ankh.*

*Crucifix-shaped, but for a tear-drop loop in lieu of an upper vertical bar. An inscription meant to symbolize eternal life, death, and rebirth.*
*Also known as the key of life according to ancient peoples.*
*Ancient peoples with dark superstitions nearly lost to time.*
*And stylized in a rather dagger-like fang motif.*
  *And on the black marble wall just above the largest stone coffin sitting at twelve o'clock due-north, a black marble medallion with more of the red veining, revealing the portraiture of a black dragon in profile spitting a blast black fire. Its giant dark coriaceous wings splayed in flight. And its forked tail curled high above its horned head like a trident. Its feet heavily clawed. And that cabalistic symbol branded into the monster's scaly black torso as if burned there.*
  *The black marble medallion suggesting to her a family crest.*
*Of the kind one only saw on old castles in Europe.*
*A family crest with strange rune-like symbols which she intuitively understood to be Slavic in origin. Not that she should know any such thing.*
*But there it was anyway. As if she should know it.*
*As if such things were already a part of her somehow.*
*There in the deep dark chamber of her own mind.*
*Hiding about in the darkest shadows there.*
*A congregation of black ghosts huddling. Whispering.*
*Ghosts that were willing to translate the cryptic runes for her.*
*Hidden in the pitch-darkness beyond the candlelight.*
*Hebrews 9:22 Under the law almost everything…*
*Is purified with blood. For without the shedding of blood…*
*There can be no forgiveness of sins.*
*Biblical. In this deep cold chamber. This crypt.*
*This crypt beneath this giant looming beast of a house.*
*A giant looming beast of a house burning, burning, burning.*
  Emily found herself contemplating such peculiar otherworldly thoughts as she moved *deeper, deeper* into the dark chamber.
  Slowly pushing forward the weak candlelight aura.
  Only to freeze with a shallow bone-shuddering gasp when the weak candlelight aura suddenly washed over an *ashen-faced figure* appearing from the crypt darkness. *As if conjuring from thin air.*
  Emily blinked, twitched really, heavily:
  To find the ashen-faced figure to be *her mother.*
  *Her mother.* In her mud-stained house dress.
  *Her mother.* Bright blue eyes having gone muddy.
  Muddy. Not unlike that marshy meadow.
  The marshy meadow with that poisonous tree.

Her fingers longer than she remembered. Bonier.
Not unlike the bony limbs of that poisonous tree.
That poisonous tree in that marshy meadow.
Its bony limbs blooming, *blooming, blooming,* with all those white whorled flowers with pink pistils. The flowers perfuming the thick humid marshy air with that faint deadly aroma of apricot.
She could smell the flowers on *her mother* now.
That faint deadly aroma of apricot. Lush and sweet.
Along with maybe the hint of ginger, perhaps.
And it was that hint of ginger that reminded her of Christmas. Her mother baking those holiday frosted ginger cookies.
And that memory slowly melded with others.
With other happy memories of other happy times before Emily *had come to know what she'd come to know -- about herself. Before ghoulish school portraits, visits to pediatricians, and long before the only father she'd ever known had learned to fear her. Had walked out on her and her mother.*
*Before she and her mother had gone on the run.*
*The days passing into nights. Moving in the nights.*
*While the rest of the world was asleep in their warm beds.*
*The money running out. The desolate backroads running out.*
*The world gradually seeming to shrink before them.*
*Nowhere left to go. Nowhere left to hide, her mother had said.*
*Before suddenly they were in that strange marshy meadow.*
*With that small magical apricot-smelling white-flowered tree.*
*And then a final little motel in that small farming town.*
*With that tray of ginger cookies, no less. Frosted.*
*Baked at midnight. Laced with a most terrible poison.*
*Poison from those flowers from that poisonous tree.*
For there had been a time in her life when ginger cookies had not been laced with poison. A time in her life when her dear mother's round eyes had still been bright blue. Alive and crazy, if tainted with a hint of melancholy. But not crazy in a desperate end-of-the-world kind of way. Still crazy with life. Indeed, possibility.
Indeed, possibility, despite the melancholy.
As if the melancholy might somehow be overcome.
Might somehow be overcome in the end.
And suddenly she wanted to embrace *her mother.*
She wanted to embrace *her mother* and blink and twitch and deliver them back to that more innocent time before all this.
Before she'd discovered *the monster within her.*

She wanted to deliver them back and pretend that monster did not exist. As if that monster could be placated. Kept quiet.

As if it could be caged forever inside of her.

*Her mother*, or what purported to be her mother, stared at her now with that familiar forlorn-looking, if *sadly joyful* grin as if able to read her mind before she said to her in a soft hushed warm whisper of a voice from within the pale guttering candlelight: *"Sleep, little one, sleep... Dream yourself awake, and all of your dreams will come true."*

As if to say dreams were still possible after all.

As if to say *everything else* had only been a nightmare.

But then *her mother* faded back into the darkness.

Faded back into the heavy darkness beyond the weak candlelight aura, leaving behind only her forlorn-looking, if *sadly joyful* grin. Frozen there in the blackness. *Illuminated.* A string of fireflies.

A fuzzy golden afterimage. An apparition.

But rather than scattering apart, paling and fading to dark, that forlorn-looking, if *sadly joyful* grin, frozen there, illuminated, a string of fireflies, that fuzzy golden afterimage, that apparition--

Fell crooked. And became rather Cheshire.

And with it, a new owner of that haunting grin.

A new owner who'd first worn that grin. That oily little black beast. Marbles. Emerging wearing that grin in the candlelight. Staring at her with those dark green almond-shaped eyes and that queer expression of *incurious curiosity*. Its long and fluffy black tail flicking lazily. That grin creeping larger at the corners of its mouth.

Revealing that mouthful of sharp little teeth.

*We're all mad here. I'm mad. You're mad...* it might've said.

*How do you know I'm mad?* she might've said back.

*You must be, or you wouldn't have come here...* it grinned.

And with that, the oily little beast was gone, slinking back into the darkness, *but leaving behind its shadow* in the candlelight.

In that pale short-reaching candlelight aura.

The shadow appearing to Emily *almost human-like.*

*A tall man, perhaps. Black suit. Fedora. Cane.*

She blinked, twitched really, heavily:

And that shadow *came to life. No longer just a shadow at all. At t'all.* But a man she'd first seen sitting in a chair in a corner of that motel room in that small farming town. *Just sitting there in its deepest shadows. One long thin leg folded neatly over the other as if he were merely waiting for a bus or train. Dapper in a long black suit. His long angular face an ashen gray.*

*His chin razor sharp beneath a black fedora tipped very low over his brow. His hair a long bone-white beneath it. His eyes gleaming. Gleaming gold.*
*For some reason reminding her of a very old book.*
*Musty pages with just the hint of vanilla.*
*A very old book in which the bad guys maybe, just maybe, weren't so very bad in the end. A very old book in which the bad guys just maybe thrived.*
*She still didn't know why she'd pondered such a thing. Maybe it was the way the tall man in the long black suit had winked at her back then. Beckoning her. A much younger version of herself. To follow him as he'd seemed to float through that small motel room to that motel room door so long ago.*
*Beckoning her to follow him as her mother had died.*
*As her mother had died on that motel room bed.*
*Beckoning her to follow him as he'd softly hissed: Dance with me.*
*Offering back his hand. Ashen with excessively long fingers.*
*His other hand resting on the handle of a black walnut cane. The handle itself carved from alabaster, shaped in what she'd initially believed a long sharp claw, but now knew to be the Ankh. Stylized in a dagger-like fang motif.*
*This tall man who would raise her mother from the dead.*
*This tall man who was her father. Mr. Grayson.*

He winked at her sadly now and offered that same hand. Ashen with excessively long fingers. Offered it to her in that pale short-reaching candlelight aura surrounded by the cold darkness.

And she saw he was not old. Not ancient.

Well, he was these things, of course. *Existentially.*

But this creature she saw staring back at her was also eternally young. Handsome. Preternatural. This creature. Her father.

And suddenly she could understand *her mother*. What *her mother* had seen on the side of that dark road the stormy night her parents had died. The stormy night her own parents had been *taken from her*. Eaten. Consumed. Suddenly she could understand *what it was like to stare into the black abyss and have that black abyss stare back at her.*

To become beguiled by that endless darkness.

That cold and deep and infinite blackness.

Offering neither pain nor numbness. Only *hollowness.*

And from such a black abyss she heard his voice:

Heard his voice as those midnight gongs still echoed:

As that calliope music played, looping over and over again:

In this place where time no longer had any real meaning:

Shrinking: Stretching: Standing still as it did now:

Heard his voice: Heard it softly hissing to her:

*Take-eth of my hand. Walk-eth into the dark with me. Us. My only daughter. My only child. Dhampir. Join me. Us.*

*We are your family and you are now arrived home. Fear not us. Fear not yourself. Fear no longer. You have a place in this world. Here. Forever.*

*Embrace who you are. What you are. Embrace me. Us.*

*Embrace me. Us. My only daughter. My only child. Dhampir.*

*Then prey, feed, taste, sleep, dream, my dearest girl.*

*We live in the darkness. We live in the darkness so that they might live in the light. We are the shepherds to their feeble-minded flock. We tend to them as black angels on the periphery of their ungraceful existence. We prevent them from straying. We do. We keep them in the light by living in the dark.*

*We suffer eternity for their mortality.*

*It is our fate, my dearest girl. Fait accompli.*

And she wondered if maybe he was right, if this was *where* she belonged, and yet, still, in her feverish mind's eye, blinking, twitching really, she could see *little sickly nine year old Henry and all those other children. Over that black span of passing years. Decades maybe.*

*In her salivating jaws. Sucking the life from their tender bones.*

*Feeding on them. Convincing herself it was a dark mercy.*

*Even as she erased such dark memories from her own mind.*

*Pushing the beast back deep inside of her. Deep inside.*

*Pretending the beast did not exist even as the beast prowled at the back of her thoughts. Always there in the shadows. Restless. In the darkness.*

*She thought of little sickly nine year old Henry wobbling around in circles on that bike behind that Dairy Queen. His laughter. Almost painful to listen to. For if she closed her eyes, it had almost sounded to her like tears.*

*She thought of her mother. The Christmases and the frosted ginger cookies before that fateful sojourn to that marshy meadow. How bright blue her eyes had once been. Alive and crazy, if tainted with melancholy. But not crazy in a desperate end-of-the-world kind of way, Still crazy with life. Possibility.*

*As if the melancholy might somehow be overcome.*

*And she thought of Adam. Her Adam. Those nights in his tender arms. Winter to his summer. A tiny separate universe promising infinity.*

*A young boy who would become her family. Her forever. Not by blood, but by circumstance. Inseparable by neither time nor distance nor any cold and heartless earthly convention, either. Or so she'd always needed to believe.*

And despite a desperate part of her wanting to accept it without any reservation, she found herself *backing away* from her father's offered hand. In this pale short-reaching candlelight aura.

"*Adam…*" she then heard herself moan.

Heard herself moan to her father. The Sire.
And again heard his voice softly hissing to her:
*Adam, my dearest girl. Dhampir. As I promised, this moment will possess of you the most dreadful of sacrifices. As it did for myself. As it has for the others. Your family. It will possess of you an even greater grief, I fear.*
*An even greater grief for something which will be lost.*
*An even greater grief for something which will be lost forever.*
*A forever that will stretch this greater grief to eternity.*
*Immortalizing this grief. This insufferable grief.*
*This grief will speak to your very heart. To your very soul.*
*But you must choose, my dearest girl. Dhampir.*
*You must choose the darkness over the light.*
*We are all waiting for you here. Here in the darkness.*
And it was just then, as if *summoned* by her father's very words, a sudden gust of the cold stale chamber air *stirred* heavily:
And *blew out* the pale guttering candlelight.
*Casting the entire chamber in complete pitch-darkness.*
And yet, Emily found, once blind, now she could see.
*Now she could see the others. The coven. Standing silently in all that cold blackness in the midst of their stone coffins. The black lids slid open.*
*Shadowy figures. Ghostly. Undead. Long ashen faces.*
*Not unlike their ghostly portrayals in those childish doodles.*
*Those childish doodles burning back in the attic. Burning, burning.*
*Their collection of eyes gleaming gold like a parade of fireflies.*
*Including Emily's own mother. Red hair. Muddy eyes turned gold.*
*Including a small girl in a familiar little white nightie with white ribbons in her dark braided hair A small girl with a most terrible lopsided smile.*
*A lopsided smile revealing two missing front teeth.*
*Two missing front teeth on her alabastrine countenance.*
*And standing off to the side: Ms. Vivian Dancemore herself.*
*Staring blindly with large white whorled holes for eyes.*
*Staring at the child. The coven. Mr. Grayson. Sire. Master.*
*And yet, her large white whorled holes for eyes also beseeching Emily. Beseeching Emily for what had to be done. For what had to be done here.*
*On this dark stormy night in this terrible crypt.*
But Emily, once blind, could now only truly see in cold black and white what lay in quiet repose on the black marble table at the very center of the large dark chamber. As if he were asleep.
Adam. Her Adam. There. Here. Tonight.
As if he were already dead. Her Adam.

And yet, Emily knew he was not dead even before she saw the cold respiration rising in crystalline vapors from his blue lips.

Adam. Her Adam. There. Here. Tonight.

He was clad only in long black underwear which had the impression of making his soft flushed pink face float in the darkness. His black combat military fatigues folded neatly in a pile nearby, his Darth Vader-like *dehumanizing* mask sitting on top of the pile, black eyes staring at her blindly in the dark. Removed of its soul.

His eyes were closed. Adam. Her Adam.

As if he might never wake again. Her Adam.

His pale-white wrists and ankles, also seemingly floating independent of any body in the darkness, were secured at the four corners of the black marble table by the table's conspicuous four black metal cuffs and their collection of tiny medieval-like screws.

*There was then a dark giggle in the darkness. Madelyn.*

*Little ghostly Madelyn who, with her lopsided smile, began to slowly spin in a playful pirouette before the ashen-faced coven congregated behind her.*

*Head thrown back, braids hung toward the floor, white ribbons dangling. Her bony alabastrine arms outstretched from her willowy little body. Her bony alabastrine hands turning in slow circles in the cold chamber darkness.*

*Turning slow circles as she, in turn, turned in slow circles.*

*Turned in slow circles and hushed in the blackness:*

*"Th-wing... Th-wing... Th-wing..."*

It was then the black marble table began to move. Lift. Lift into an upright *inverted* position. Lifted by its heavy black chain.

That black winch spinning. *Spinning, spinning.*

Turned by a black crank in the nearby shadows.

Turned by Ms. Vivian Dancemore. As if she had no choice in the matter. Her large white whorled holes for eyes screaming.

Screaming most terribly without making a sound.

The black marble table clicking into its final position. Upright. *Inverted. Adam. Her Adam. Suspended upside down in the darkness.*

*Her Adam. Suspended over that shallow ivory basin.*

*A shallow ivory basin which fed into narrow gutter.*

*A narrow gutter which in turn fed directly into an ivory cistern.*

*The ivory cistern framed with black marble blocks decorated with more of that dragon fleur-de-lis etched in that deep red blood-like veining.*

And as those heavy bellowing midnight gongs somehow continued to echo in the black walls of the dark chamber, as the calliope music somehow looped over and over and over again--

Mr. Grayson softly hissed in Emily's ear:
*Now, my dearest girl. Now. Your time has come.*
*Your most dreadful sacrifice. Your most insufferable grief.*
*Now. My only daughter. My only child. Dhampir.*
And just before she might've offered any protest--
*Mr. Grayson gracefully swung his black walnut cane.*
*Gracefully swung his black walnut cane in a neat arc.*
*The handle carved from alabaster and shaped in a dagger-like fang motif slicing through the cold dark chamber air without even a hint of sound.*
*His ghostly excessively long ashen-gray fingers manipulating the cane from the heel. The ferrule. Opposite that handle slicing through the darkness.*
*The handle carved from alabaster and shaped in a dagger-like fang motif making not even a hint of sound as it sliced neatly through Adam's neck.*
*As it neatly severed his jugular veins. Adam. Her Adam.*
*Dark red blood spilling in torrents into the shallow ivory basin.*
*The shallow ivory basin now below him, turning the ivory red before gushing down the narrow gutter and frothing into the waiting ivory cistern.*
*The ivory cistern framed by those black marble blocks decorated with more of that dragon fleur-de-lis etched in that deep red blood-like veining.*
*And then suddenly, not unlike the flurry of black and white moths buzzing madly about the suspended antique ceiling lantern outside on the front porch when she had first arrived as this giant looming beast of a house--*
*The ashen-faced coven descended upon the cistern.*
*Descended upon the fresh pool of dark red blood frothing there.*
*Consuming it. Feasting on it. Devouring that dark red blood.*
*Until all that was left was the bloodstained cistern itself.*
For a moment in this nearly silent mayhem, Emily was certain Adam's eyes had fluttered open if for only a brief moment.
*If for only a brief moment staring at her. Staring, staring.*
*Accusing her maybe. Accusing her of forsaking him.*
*Accusing her of forsaking herself. Of forsaking her humanity.*
*Accusing her of embracing the darkness. The monster.*
Just before his eyes, Adam, her Adam, assuming his eyes were ever really open, *slipped shut for the final time.* Heavily. Inexorably.
His skin taking on the pallor of gray death.
And Emily felt herself screaming. Screaming without making a sound of her own in this cold dark chamber. This crypt.
*Madelyn grinning at her with dark blood smeared on her lips.*
*Dark blood reminding Emily of that putrid red jam.*
*Red jam that had perhaps not been jam at all. At t'all.*

# THE NIGHT SITTER

*As Emily's mother, her mother who'd died in that grim little motel room back in that small farming town, contemplated her with that smile possessing a sad joyfulness. As Ms. Vivian Dancemore, her most peculiar employer, considered her with her most dreadful large white whorled holes for eyes.*

Oh yes, Emily felt herself screaming, *screaming, screaming,* without making a sound until she felt his breath against her ear.

Again. Not unlike a brush of cold wintry wind.

*I can mollify this grief, my dearest girl,* he hushed.
*This insufferable grief for something which has been lost.*
*For something which has otherwise been lost forever.*
*A forever now stretching that grief to eternity.*
*Will you allow me to do that for you, my dearest girl?*
*My only daughter. My only child. Dhampir.*

Emily blinked. Twitched really, heavily.

And softly pleaded: *"Yes, father, sire…"*

Only to blink again. Twitch really, heavily:

To find the black marble table returned to its original horizontal position. *Her Adam lying in a deathly repose upon it.* Bloodless wrists and ankles no longer restrained by the four black metal cuffs.

The coven stood over him. On either side of the black marble table. Heads bowed. Murmuring beneath their collective breath.

A deep monosyllabic murmur. Reverent.

Emily standing at the foot of the marble table.

At Adam's feet. *Her Adam. In his deathly repose.*

Their murmuring rising as the Sire loomed over them.

At the head of the table over Adam's gray corpse.

Their reverent murmuring quickly becoming a frenzy.

Punctuated by the distant heavy bellowing gongs.

And that calliope music looping over and over again.

And just maybe the crackle of those flames.

Those flames somewhere beyond the crypt walls.

The flames burning hungrily. *Burning, burning.*

As Emily witnessed the Sire's own *sad joyful smile.*

*The Sire's own sad joyful smile as he loomed over them all.*

*A sad joyful smile that turned lopsided before his mouth filled with sharp razor blades and a frightening pair of impossibly-long canines. Fangs.*

*Reminding Emily of her grammar school portraits.*

*Of her nine year old self. Two sets. Taken weeks apart.*

*A lopsided grin. A mouthful of tiny sharp-looking teeth in several repeating rows along with a frightening pair of impossibly-long fang-like eyeteeth.*

*Her father, the only father she'd ever known back then, spooked. Unconvinced by her mother's desperate explanations. Afraid of her. Terrified.*
*She felt the terror in her own eyes staring at her father now. Sire. Master. Staring into his black eyes as he winked at her over the black marble table and then sank those impossibly-long fangs deeply into Adam. Her Adam.*
*Sank them deeply into Adam's torn neck. Her Adam.*
*Deeply into him amid the murmuring frenzy of the coven.*
*Including Emily's own mother and Ms. Vivian Dancemore, her most peculiar employer. The woman's eyes still those dreadful large white whorled holes, but her voice in a terrible dark monosyllabic harmony with the coven.*
*Reminding Emily of the woman's morbid grin. The woman's morbid grin back in that parlor up there where the flames now feasted. Devoured.*
*When that pendulum had suddenly fallen so very still.*
*In the dark hollow body of that large antique grandfather clock.*
*Painful-looking. Over-stretched. That morbid grin had been.*
*As if being manipulated there by invisible puppet strings.*
*And she was reminded of what the woman had said in the parlor.*
*Whispering to me... she'd lamented softly. Imploring my permission. An invitation of sorts, Miss Emily. I was so unwell, Miss Emily... Feverish with grief, you understand. And it made such dark, if wonderful promises.*

Emily felt herself grinning now. *Grinning, grinning.*
*As she heard a gasp come from Adam. Her Adam.*
*It was less a draw of air, however, than an exclamation of reluctance. Of unwillingness. Of something desecrated. Made unhallowed. Impure.*
*And she imagined what it must be like to slide into death. Into the warm light only to be awoken to the darkness. To a cold everlasting darkness.*
*To life without death. To, indeed, undeath. To timelessness.*
Still, Emily felt herself grinning. *Grinning, grinning.*
*Grinning as she gave unto her father her own neck.*
*Offering unto him her blood. Offering to him her rarest of gifts.*
*The offspring of a dragon and a human female. She.*
*Born between worlds. Between the light and the darkness.*
*The coven awaiting her. Her family. The Sire.*
*For the battles soon to come. The war. Amid the fires.*
*Lost for so long in the shadows. Not knowing who she was.*
*Not knowing what she was. Direly confused. Afraid.*
*Mind conspiring against her. Protecting her. Lying to her.*
*Even as the Sire walked beside her in dark spirit.*
*A dark promise that she was never alone. Never that.*
*Never alone despite her appetites. Confusion. Fear.*

## THE NIGHT SITTER

*That there was a place where she needn't feel any confusion. Fear. Never feel a sense of un-belonging. A place where she'd never be the stranger.*
*A place where she'd not be the subject of suspicion.*
*Of confusion. Fear. Of human frailty.*
*A place where she could become who she was.*
*A place where she could become what she was.*
*A place where she needn't be alone anymore.*
*A place to be her home. For forever. For eternity.*
*And place where she could taste. Sleep. And dream.*
*A place where she could be with him. Adam. Her Adam.*
*For forever. For eternity. A place of timelessness.*
Yes, Emily felt herself grinning. *Grinning, grinning.*
*Grinning as she felt her father's fangs penetrate into the flesh of her neck. As she felt her serum-rich blood flow onto his dark flicking tongue.*
*As he consumed. Feasted. Devoured her blood.*
*Inoculating him against the virus. A virus created by man.*
*A virus created to destroy the monster in man's midst.*
*Man. Foolish man. Who lived in castles and pretty little villages next to pretty little bubbling streams. Just like in all those ridiculous fairy tales.*
*Man who shunned shadowy creatures. The undesirables.*
*Forcing such creatures, such undesirables, to drearily hunt and to scavenge in cold dark shadows in order to survive. The unwanted. The outcast.*
*Creatures man desired to trick, deceive, defeat, slay.*
*She had always wished for a darker-happier ending to such so-called fairy tales stories. Even as a child. For once, please. Just for once, thank you.*
*An end to this endless lineage of immoral allegory.*
*And here, now, perhaps she could finally have it. Finally.*
*Offering unto her father her blood so that he might not perish.*
*Not be tricked, deceived, defeated, slayed by foolish man.*
*That he might offer this elixir to the coven so it might not perish.*
*Her family. Her family in the shadows. In the darkness. Here.*
*Including Adam. Her Adam. Just now born to a new life.*
*An undead life. To forever. Eternity. Timelessness.*
*A life they would share together. Adam. Her Adam and she.*
Yes, Emily felt herself grinning. *Grinning, grinning.*
*Grinning as she felt her father's fangs penetrate into the flesh of her neck. And not just take something from her. But offer unto her something.*
*Offering unto her immortal life. Eternity. Forever.*
*Dismissing from her mortality. And waking fully the dragon.*
And she felt her feet lifting. *Lifting, floating.*

Her feet rising above the black marble floor.
Felt herself *changing* once again. Becoming beastly.
Her skin suddenly feeling far too tight.
Talons forming at the end of her own fingers.
Fingers that turned dark and scaly and prolonged.
As her mouth filled with its own sharp things.
Her jaw jutting out. Elongating. Almost painfully.
A long dark tongue flicking in the dark cold crypt air.
Large veined-appendages spreading from her back.
Stretching, thickening her back muscles. Neck.
Her skin thickening, too. Stretching. Turning scaly.
Those large veined-appendages *lifting her.*
*Lifting her* in the cold dark chamber blackness.
*Lifting her* toward the cold black marble ceiling.

Her lungs no longer congested with that wet black cement, no longer hardening into those horrendous black stones, but expanding mightily, tugging in the *suddenly delicious* dark cold crypt air, making dizzy her head. Not from fever, but in a drunken ecstasy.

Meanwhile, the coven *lifted* around her. *Floating.*

*Transforming. Becoming those winged-beasts of her dream. Black dragons with curved horns, large spiny coiled tails, and giant dark coriaceous wings.*

*Huge fearsome looming beasts with flared black hoods.*
*Flared black hoods framing gold spheroid eyes.*
*Lifting. Rising. Floating. Around her. Now.*
*Including her mother. Red hair flowing like lava fire.*
*Including Adam. Her Adam. Flinching. Twisting. Screaming.*
*Talons tearing at its hair. Flesh. Clawing at it.*
*As if something seemingly in deep struggle with itself.*
*Trying to tear its dark soul to the surface. To liberate it.*

*Head throwing back in a soundless dark and painful laughter. Revealing an elongated jaw of his own. A mouthful of large spiny needle-like teeth.*

*And fangs. Dagger-like fangs. Descending. Glistening.*

"*Adam,*" she said to him. It. "*My Adam.*"

Her voice no longer sounding like her own. But of a shrieking thing. A monstrous thing. A thing becoming of the night.

"*Em…*" he said to her. It. Adam. Her Adam.

*Floating* there before her in the dark cold crypt air.

His voice no longer sounding like his own. It's voice. But of a desperate and tortured thing. A thing becoming of the night.

Reaching for her with a black-taloned hand.

The black-taloned hand of a monstrous beast.
She accepted his hand. Adam. Her Adam.
*And suddenly they were flying like a dark wind with Mr. Grayson. Or what had become of Mr. Grayson. Her father. Sire. Master.*
*For he'd become before his coven, his bloodline, an inconceivably enormous black silhouette. An almost invisible thing in the cold dark chamber blackness. A black shadow in unanimity with the very curtain of darkness itself.*
*But for a pair of large spheroid eyes gleaming gold.*
*And his breath. Its breath. A shadow of black fire.*
*A shadow of black fire that led the coven from the crypt.*
*A coterie of dark wind gathering into its own black storm.*
*Vivian remained behind in the dark bowels of the crypt even as her only daughter, Madelyn, sometimes Maddy, joined this fomenting black storm, those large white whorled holes for eyes still silently beseeching Emily as she and Adam, her Adam, or what she and her Adam had now become, flew in that dark wind in that black storm through the cold black marble corridors from the crypt and into the giant looming beast of a burning house. Burning, burning.*
*Following their Sire. Their family. The coven.*
*Following them. Dancing with them. Through the flames.*
*Moving as if made of air. The blackest of air.*
*Rising through the chimney of that giant looming beast of a burning house out into the dark stormy night. Thunder shaking the earth below and nocturnal sky about them as the black rain pounded down from the heavens above.*
*The house now engulfed in a breathtaking fiery pyre.*
*The terrible flames leaping, roaring, exploding, screaming.*
*Everything combustible burning, burning, burning.*
*If not those cold black marble corridor walls leading down from that attic, down, down into the crypt below. All that cold black marble scorched, revealing a most awesome thing seemingly rising in the midst of all those flames.*
*Rising as that giant looming beast of a house collapsed.*
*A giant black dagger-like fang in the dark stormy night.*
*A giant black dagger-like fang rising amid the terrible flames below and circled by dark monstrous-looking shapes rendered their very own black silhouettes against the dark stormy night at this, the very edge of the world, but a pale-white against the flames and bright floodlights of the gathered militia.*
*Winged-beasts. Howling. Shrieking. The coven.*
*As somewhere down below, too, in the midst of all those flames that large cast iron bell, its mounting shaped like a sleek black dragon, rung. Large black clapper striking hard the interior of that black bell over and over again.*
*No longer soundless, but sounding of the rapture itself.*

*A clarion call to the dark monstrous-looking shapes.*
*These many winged-beasts. Howling. Shrieking.*
*Howling. Shrieking. Before descending upon the gathered militia.*
*The gathered militia standing like sheep in the dark storm in their inky-black combat gear and their silly Darth Vader-like protective masks.*
*Standing like sheep behind their coils of razor wire.*
*Their silly black tanks with black American flag emblems spraying golden fire in all directions in a hysteria of fear and desperation, but only managing to catch their own terrified personnel and motorized vehicles on fire.*
*Burning, burning, burning as the winged-beasts darted through the flames and descended down upon them for the slaughter. Feasting. Gorging.*
*An inconceivably enormous black silhouette preventing any hope of retreat for the terrorized sheep panicking wildly before it. An almost invisible thing. A black shadow in unanimity with the very curtain of darkness itself.*
*But for a pair of large spheroid eyes gleaming gold.*
*And its breath. A shadow of black fire.*
*Forcing the sheep back to the slaughter. To death.*
*A bloody mayhem in this dark stormy night.*
*A bloody mayhem on this, the very edge of the world.*

Meanwhile, as the carnage continued far below, and somehow appearing less gruesome from their altitude far above it, more like a swirling swarm of golden fireflies dancing about in the black storm, and everything else reduced to shadows and concealed in the night, Emily and Adam *ascended* through the storm past the black rain and deafening cracks of thunder, *their black-taloned hands still clasped together* as they rose through the thick blanket of black storm clouds pushing down heavily on the world, the black storm clouds superheated with electricity, crackling and snapping, producing jagged streaks of angry white lightning striking. Angry white lightening that managed to illuminate for *brief snatches that carnage down far below. Illuminating all that blood, and painting the winged-beasts in a pale-white stark relief.*

But then suddenly that was all left behind them.

Suddenly, they were exiting the black storm clouds.

Suddenly, Emily and Adam, her Adam, or what her Adam had now become, were rising above all those black storm clouds.

The thunder only distant soft booming echo.

The white lightning only making the black clouds glow.

Making the black clouds glow a soft pulsating white.

And there in the heavens below a blanket of bright stars, there in the sudden silence with the storm muted below them--

Emily and her Adam stared at each other.

Stared at each other, stared at what each other had become, as they slowly spun around and around and around and around. Black in the darkness. Pale-white against the large watchful moon.

Tightly holding each other in their arms not unlike when they were only children. When they had no one but each other.

His summer to her winter. Adam. Her Adam.

*But that was no longer true, she realized now, as they slowly spun around and around and around and around in the darkness and the moonlight.*

*He was now cold to the touch. Adam. Her Adam.*

*His pale blue eyes, that had always stared at her with such unconditional love as they'd lay there face-to-face, nose-to-nose, in bed as children in the quiet darkness beneath the bedsheets, suddenly large white whorled holes.*

*His once pale blue eyes that reminded her of--*

*Of little sickly Henry. His big blue jaundiced eyes.*

*Staring forlornly out his bedroom window. Those blue eyes.*

*Forlornly as that blue sky had turned gray. Colorless.*

*As little sickly Henry had given up on this world.*

*Just before she'd shown the poor boy her teeth.*

*She remembered how he'd startled when she'd finally done so.*

*Maybe even screamed a little as she'd bitten into his neck.*

*Into his soft and pale flesh. Sinking deeply her teeth.*

*And how the color had faded from his eyes. Little sickly Henry.*

*Just like Adam now. Her Adam. His eyes turned white.*

*Large white whorled holes staring back at her with love, and yet beseeching her. Silently beseeching her in the darkness and the moonlight.*

*Screaming at her. Screaming at her without making a sound.*

*Screaming at her without making a sound even as he still loved her.*

*Just as that poor boy had maybe still loved her. Perhaps.*

"Adam..." *she said. Her voice a moaning growl.*

"Em..." *he said. A shrieking thing. A monstrous thing.*

*A thing now lost. Lost in a terrible malaise. Despair.*

*She reflected how she'd always seemed to invite for him darkness.*

*She reflected it was the reason why she'd often run from him.*

*To spare him. To save him. From her. From the monster.*

*How his wife had always been the light. His cute little girls.*

*How old were they now? Adam's girls? Nine and eleven?*

*He had a family. Even a dog maybe. Perhaps. Her Adam.*

*And she felt him changing once again in her arms.*

*Felt him changing back to Adam. Her Adam.*

*Here. So far above the earth. The storm. The mayhem.*
*Shivering in the terrible cold altitude as he became human again.*
*And she felt herself shivering as she did the very same.*
*As she became human again in her Adam's arms.*

*But, of course, it was only an awkward fumbling. Not unlike when they were only silly children fumbling in the dark beneath those bedsheets.*

*Awkward because not unlike their burgeoning adolescence back then, there was no turning back from what they'd now become. Monsters. Dragons.*

*Immortal. Undead. No longer human at all. At t'all.*
*Even as their innocence tried desperately to reassert itself.*
*An innocence now dead for eternity. An innocence now lost.*
*In the end, she had cursed him with her undying love.*
*In the end, she had not spared him at all. At t'all. Her Adam.*

*And so they kissed. They kissed a final time. Or what felt to them like a final time. A final kiss. And in the embrace of that final kiss, they fell.*

*They fell from the peaceful heavens in each other's arms, in the embrace of that final kiss, still spinning slowly around and around and around.*

*They fell back down through the black storm clouds.*
*The bellowing thunder and the streaks of white lightning.*
*They fell with the black rain. Falling, falling, falling.*

*They never broke their embrace even as they fell toward the giant looming beast of a house burning, burning, burning below. They only held tighter still to each other as they fell heavily into the roaring flames leaping to meet them.*

*For dragons are born of fire and will perish of fire.*

# 28.

EMILY BLINKED, TWITCHED REALLY, heavily, and found herself not fallen in Adam's arms into the fiery cauldron of that black house being cremated in the black storm, but somehow staring into a weak pale guttering candlelight.

*Found herself returned to the cold dark chamber.*
*Found herself once again in the cold dark crypt.*

Her mother's watch on her wrist *frozen* at midnight.

The distant heavy bellowing gongs of that large antique grandfather clock *echoing* in the dark house walls. As before. The looping calliope music of that strange antique music box *singing*.

And the black house protesting as it *burned, burned, burned* outside the cold marble walls of the cold dark chamber. Crypt.

Burning amid the distant crackle of flames.

Protesting as if it might still *shrug off those flames*.

This giant looming beast of a house. This black house.

As if it might still survive the fiery conflagration.

Meanwhile, here in the cold dark chamber, in this deep crypt, as the weak pale candlelight guttered even more fervently still, Emily felt that virus surging through her veins again. As before.

Her lungs hardening into *black stones* in her chest, offering only reedy wheezes of desperate breath turned to ragged mist in the cold darkness. The air colder and colder still. Like a meat locker.

Emily shivered. Her teeth chattering noisily.

Her head pounding. That ice pick again stabbing into the back of her neck. Or rather, maybe, that fiery-hot poker. Her skin feverish. Too warm, and yet too cold, too, as that invisible blade stabbed through her spine into her very brain behind her right eye, making it impossible to think clearly. To maintain coherent thought.

Goose-fleshed skin *appearing like scales on her body*.

The black spots swimming before her exhausted eyes.

It was into this tornado of black spots *swirling, swirling* about in the weak pale candlelight aura, *her mother* appeared. As before.

*Her mother*. In her mud-stained house dress.

*Her mother*. Bright blue eyes having gone muddy.

Muddy. Not unlike that marshy meadow.

The marshy meadow with that poisonous tree.

*Her mother*. Speaking to her in that soft hushed warm whisper of a voice: Behind that forlorn-looking, *sadly joyful* grin in this cold dark crypt beneath this burning house: *Sleep, little one, sleep… Dream yourself awake, and all of your dreams will come true.* As before.

As if to say dreams were still possible after all.

As if to say *everything else* had only been a nightmare.

As if to say that perhaps Emily was the *clairvoyant* one after all. *And that while she'd maybe had a glimpse at one possible outcome, one possible fate, she had yet to make her choice. She had yet to make her decision.*

And again heard Ms. Vivian Dancemore's voice:

Her hushed voice in the parlor earlier that very night:

*Will you perish of fire, Miss Emily? Will that be your fate?*

*Will you forsake, Miss Emily, your own humanity?*

*Now I only feel regret, Miss Emily. Its most unnatural what I did. It's most unnatural for life to continue beyond its natural course, Miss Emily.*

*This house. In its walls. Dragons. Miss Emily.*

Emily blinked, twitched really, heavily:

To find *her mother* fading back into the darkness.

Fading back into the heavy darkness beyond the weak candlelight aura, leaving behind only her forlorn-looking, if *sadly joyful* grin. Frozen there in the blackness. *Illuminated*. A string of fireflies.

A fuzzy golden afterimage. An apparition.

But rather than scattering apart, paling and fading to dark, that forlorn-looking, if *sadly joyful* grin, frozen there, illuminated, a string of fireflies, that fuzzy golden afterimage, that apparition--

Fell crooked. And became rather Cheshire. As before.

And with it, a new owner of that haunting grin.

A new owner who'd first worn that grin. That oily little black beast. Marbles. Emerging wearing that grin in the candlelight. Staring at her with those dark green almond-shaped eyes and that queer expression of *incurious curiosity*. Its long and fluffy black tail flicking lazily. That grin creeping larger at the corners of its mouth.

Revealing that mouthful of sharp little teeth.

*We're all mad here. I'm mad. You're mad...* it might've said.

*How do you know I'm mad?* she might've said back.

*You must be, or you wouldn't have come here...* it grinned.

And with that, the oily little beast was gone, slinking back into the darkness, *but leaving behind its shadow* in the candlelight.

In that pale short-reaching candlelight aura.

The shadow appearing to her *almost human-like*.

*A tall man. Black suit. Fedora. Cane.* As before.

She blinked, twitched really, heavily:

And that shadow *came to life* before her eyes.

Mr. Grayson. Her father. Sire. Master.

As before. Winking at her sadly. And offering to her his hand. Ashen. Excessively long fingers. Offering it to her in the weak pale short-reaching candlelight aura surrounded by cold darkness.

Here. Where time no longer had any real meaning.

Shrinking. Stretching. *Standing still as it did now.*

And again heard his voice: Here: Now: As before:

Heard her father's voice softly hissing to her:

*Take-eth of my hand. Walk-eth into the dark with me. Us.*

*My only daughter. My only child. Dhampir. Join me. Us.*

*We are your family and you are now arrived home. Fear not us. Fear not yourself. Fear no longer. You have a place in this world. Here. Forever.*

*Embrace who you are. What you are. Embrace me. Us.*

*Embrace me. Us. My only daughter. My only child. Dhampir.*

*Then prey, feed, taste, sleep, dream, my dearest girl.*

*We live in the darkness. We live in the darkness so that they might live in the light. We are the shepherds to their feeble-minded flock. We tend to them as black angels on the periphery of their ungraceful existence. We prevent them from straying. We do. We keep them in the light by living in the dark.*

*We suffer eternity for their mortality.*

*It is our fate, my dearest girl. Fait accompli.*

And yet, she found herself *backing away* from his hand offered to her in this weak pale short-reaching candlelight aura. Found herself *backing away* from him. Here. Now. Hesitating. As before.

"*Adam…*" she then heard herself moan.

Heard herself moan to her father. The Sire.

And again heard his voice softly hissing to her:

*Adam, my dearest girl. Dhampir. As I promised, this moment will possess of you the most dreadful of sacrifices. As it did for myself. As it has for the others. Your family. It will possess of you an even greater grief, I fear.*

*An even greater grief for something which will be lost.*

*An even greater grief for something which will be lost forever.*

*A forever that will stretch this greater grief to eternity.*

*Immortalizing this grief. This insufferable grief.*

*This grief will speak to your very heart. To your very soul.*

*But you must choose, my dearest girl. Dhampir.*

*You must choose the darkness over the light.*

*We are all waiting for you here. Here in the darkness.*

And it was just then, as if *summoned* by her father's very words, a sudden gust of the cold stale chamber air *stirred* heavily:

And *blew out* the pale guttering candlelight.

*Casting the entire chamber in complete pitch-darkness.*

*And yet, Emily found, once blind, now she could see. As before.*

*Now she could see the others. The coven. Standing silently in all that cold blackness in the midst of their stone coffins. The black lids slid open.*

*Shadowy figures. Ghostly. Undead. Long ashen faces.*

*Not unlike their ghostly portrayals in those childish doodles.*

*Those childish doodles burning back in the attic. Burning, burning.*

*Their collection of eyes gleaming gold like a parade of fireflies.*

*Including Emily's own mother. Red hair. Muddy eyes turned gold.*

*Including a small girl in a familiar little white nightie with white ribbons in her dark braided hair. A small girl with a most terrible lopsided smile.*

*A lopsided smile revealing two missing front teeth.*

*Two missing front teeth on her alabastrine countenance.*

*And standing off to the side: Ms. Vivian Dancemore herself.*

*Staring blindly with large white whorled holes for eyes. As before.*

*Staring at the child. The coven. Mr. Grayson. Sire. Master.*

*And yet, her large white whorled holes for eyes also beseeching Emily. Beseeching Emily for what had to be done. For what had to be done here.*

*On this dark stormy night in this terrible crypt.*

And as Emily, once blind, stared at Adam, her Adam, lying in quiet repose, as if he were asleep, on that black marble table at the very center of the pitch-dark chamber, as before, *Ms. Vivian Dancemore's large white whorled holes for eyes now gravely reminded of her:*

# THE NIGHT SITTER

*Born of a dragon and a human female. A dhampir.*
*Your blood. Infected. Courses through your veins, Miss Emily.*
*Your infected blood becomes a serum. A dark miracle.*
*But you mustn't heed his seductions, Miss Emily…*
*For while your infected blood, Miss Emily, offers to him and them, his coven, a most desperately desired serum, your saliva, your rare and most formidable bite, Miss Emily, offers to him a rare and most formidable venom.*
*A rare and most formidable poison.*
*Nature, in her infinite wisdom, providing balance.*
*Nature, in her infinite wisdom, providing natural order.*
Emily blinked, twitched really, heavily:
*And heard a dark giggle in the darkness. As before. Madelyn.*
*Little ghostly Madelyn who, with her lopsided grin, began to slowly spin in a playful pirouette before the ashen-faced coven congregated behind her.*
*Head thrown back, braids hung toward the floor, white ribbons dangling. Her bony alabastrine arms outstretched from her willowy little body. Her bony alabastrine hands turning slow circles in the cold chamber darkness.*
*Turning slow circles as she, in turn, turned in slow circles.*
*Turned in slow circles and hushed in the blackness:*
*"Th-wing… Th-wing… Th-wing…"*
It was then the black marble table began to move. Lift. Lift into an upright *inverted* position. Lifted by its heavy black chain.
That black winch spinning. *Spinning, spinning.*
Turned by a black crank in the nearby shadows.
Turned by Ms. Vivian Dancemore. As if she had no choice in the matter. Her large white whorled holes for eyes screaming.
Screaming most terribly without making a sound.
The black marble table clicking into its final position. Upright. *Inverted. Adam. Her Adam. Suspended upside down in the darkness.*
*Her Adam. Suspended over that shallow ivory basin.*
*A shallow ivory basin which fed into a narrow gutter.*
*A narrow gutter which in turn fed directly into an ivory cistern.*
*The ivory cistern framed with black marble blocks decorated with more of that dragon fleur-de-lis etched in that deep red blood-like veining.*
And as those heavy bellowing midnight gongs somehow continued to echo in the black walls of the dark chamber as the calliope music somehow looped over and over and over again--
Mr. Grayson softly hissed in Emily's ear:
Softly hissed in Emily's ear as he'd done before:
*Now, my dearest girl. Now. Your time has come.*

*Your most dreadful sacrifice. Your most insufferable grief.*
*Now. My only daughter. My only child. Dhampir.*

Emily heard herself *this time*, at that very moment, *cry out* in the cold chamber darkness. Cry out loudly in dire protest just as--

Mr. Grayson gracefully swung his black walnut cane.

*The handle carved from alabaster and shaped in a dagger-like fang motif. Making not even a hint of sound as it sliced through the darkness.*

*His ghostly excessively long ashen-gray fingers manipulating the cane from the heel. The ferrule. Opposite the handle slicing through the darkness.*

*Intending for the deadly handle to slice through Adam's neck.*

*To sever Adam's jugulars. This dagger-like fang motif.*

Yes, Emily heard herself cry out in the cold chamber darkness and found herself moving as if made of the dark air itself, deftly intercepting the black walnut cane in mid-arc before the deadly handle could make contact with Adam's neck. Grabbing the cane and snapping it as if it were a twig.

*Eliciting a collective gasp from the ashen-faced coven.*

In this moment, Emily was certain Adam's eyes fluttered open if for only a brief moment. *Staring, staring* at her. Her Adam.

*His summer to her eternal winter. Adam. Her Adam.*

*Staring at her with such love. With the warmth of his arms.*

*Arms that had once held her so very close to his warm body. So very close to his warm body when the only thing she'd ever known was the cold.*

*Their relationship, a hardass little shiny diamond.*

*A hardass little shiny diamond found in a world of shit.*

*As if cavalierly discarded by someone who knew not its worth. Or altruistically discarded for only her to find maybe. Hiding inside of it a tiny separate universe where anything was possible. Anything. Anything at t'all.*

*A tiny separate universe promising its own infinity.*

And as his eyes, Adam, her Adam, assuming his eyes were ever actually open, slipped shut again -- Emily blinked, twitched really, heavily, and softly hushed to her father in the darkness:

Her feet no longer on the black marble floor:

Lifting as she slowly lifted: As she began to *float*:

"*Spare him, father, sire, and I will spare you...*"

Her voice no longer sounding like her own. But of a shrieking thing. A monstrous thing. A thing becoming of the night.

*Her words were met with the Sire's sad joyful smile.*

*A sad joyful smile offering a most desperate dark love.*

*A sad joyful smile that turned lopsided before his mouth filled with sharp razor blades and a frightening pair of impossibly-long canines. Fangs.*

And Emily felt herself grinning. *Grinning, grinning.*
*Grinning as she gave unto her father her own neck. As before.*
*Offering unto him her own blood. Her serum-rich blood.*
*Grinning as she felt her father's fangs penetrate into the flesh of her neck.*
*As she felt her serum-rich blood flow onto his dark flicking tongue.*
*A blood rich with a serum born of the virus in her body.*
*The offspring of a dragon and a human female. She.*
*A rare and most formidable creature. She.*
*A virus designed to pass amongst the still-living.*
*To pass amongst the still-living in their very own blood.*
*Knowing the preying undead might once again know mortality should they drink from that very blood and become infected by it. This pathogen.*
*Not anticipating a rare and most formidable creature such as she.*
*And suddenly accepting of where she'd gotten this virus. As if there could be any doubt. For quite suddenly she could taste it again. On her very lips.*
*As if it had never left her lips. That boy a rotten apple. Mealy.*
*Sour-tasting for his otherwise sweetest and most divine of nectars.*
*Sour-tasting for his ambrosia on her dark probing tongue.*
*Sour-tasting for the food of gods. His blood. That boy.*
*Henry. Offering her a dark mercy, perhaps, of his very own as she offered to him that very thing. Or so she'd told herself on that black and moonless night while the rest of his family had slept. When that poor boy had looked up at her with those big blue jaundiced eyes. Gangly and pale. Head too large. Hair thin. Lips purple. Suffocating on all that dark fluid in his lungs. Drowning him as his head pounded mercilessly as if being struck by a sledgehammer.*
*Begging her, she'd thought. Begging her to just end it.*
*Having gone downhill so very quickly after his birthday gift.*
*His birthday gift from her. Their terrible little secret.*
*Dairy Queen. Wobbling around on that bicycle.*
*She'd never heard him laugh. Let alone laugh so joyfully like that.*
*It was almost painful to listen to. That joyful laughter.*
*For if she closed her eyes, it had almost sounded to her like tears.*
*Wobbling around on that bicycle behind the restaurant.*
*In the fresh air with all those kids who'd disappeared not long after from outside his bedroom window when the world had come so very undone.*
*For suddenly the pandemic had flowered. The virus.*
*The boy destined for six feet down into that cold black hole.*
*In a dreary rain amid a congregation of old and fresh graves.*
*Beneath an audience of red cedar trees with wind-twisted trunks.*
*In the cemetery beside that deep river at the far corner of town.*

*Six feet down into that cold black hole not long after she'd snuck him out of his house while the rest of his family had been gone at the movies.*
*The family suspecting only his inherited condition.*
*The family suspecting only his immunodeficiency disorder.*
*Making him particularly susceptible to respiratory infections.*
*The family always so very careful around the boy. So very careful.*
*The boy who was never to leave the house. Not ever.*
*Emily never telling them of what she had done. Lying to them.*
*But medical authorities insisting the boy be tested for the virus.*
*And yet the boy testing negative just before he died. Negative.*
*Emily testing negative herself. The rest of the family, too.*
*Still, she'd known the dark truth, hadn't she? Known it even as she convinced herself not to heed that growing chorus of rumors suggesting the tests were all too often unreliable. Wonky. Especially in those earliest of days.*
*She'd known the truth because she'd tasted it on her lips.*
*And fretting over how long it would be before she'd fall sick. Only to have two long weeks slowly pass by in that tiny shot-hole motel apartment.*
*That veritable rat's nest with stained threadbare carpet and tattered curtains and the mini-fridge with a noisy compressor screeching to life every hour of the freaking night and day beneath that filthy window staring-out toward that desolate drive-in theater next door with all that trash blowing around in endless circles. The trash grimly unable to escape the wretched theater's rusty chain-link fence in a rather miserable waltz of the discarded and the forgotten.*
*Two long weeks without any symptoms. Seemingly.*
*She had believed herself spared. If that was the right word.*
*Poor sickly Henry's own little dark mercy unanswered.*
*But apparently the virus had been inside her after all. Apparently it had been hiding in there. Just waiting. Just waiting to flower malignantly. Just waiting for her to enter this dark black house. As if the virus were clairvoyant, too. This awful pathogen. That boy a rotten apple. A most rotten apple.*
*A magic wishing apple…* Emily mused drearily.
*One bite and all her dreams would come true.*

Which made her think of her late grandmother. A strict woman with large toady eyes. Often unblinking. Full of reprimand.

Her late grandmother's voice now in her ear:

Reprimanding her with that litany of aphorisms: Reprimanding her for just perhaps the final time: Her voice *fading, fading*:

*Never groom yourself in public.*
*Keep covered your cleavage and posterior.*
*Always maintain good posture.*

*Be humble about your accomplishments.*
*Always speak in a quiet polite tone.*
*Always remember your please and thank yous.*
*Always be kind and courteous and decent.*
*Refrain from impure thoughts and behavior.*
*Watch your table manners and your cocktails.*
*Treat others as you would like to be treated.*
*The covetous man is always in want.*
*The unwanting soul sees what's hidden.*
*And the ever-wanting soul sees only what it wants.*
*Tempt not the devil to whisper into your ear.*
*Never show your teeth when you smile…*
But that was exactly what she did now.
Her mouth full of terrible sharp things. Fangs.
She smiled. And embraced that *desperate dark love.*
*Embraced it as she embraced her father. Sire. Master.*
And just before she sunk her own fangs into his sinewy ashen neck as her father sank his fangs into her neck, she felt them come for her in the dark. Felt the rush of stale dark air as they came for her. Her family. The coven.

*His coven will try to protect him--* Ms. Vivian Dancemore had promised her, her most peculiar employer. *As will I, Miss Emily, as will I--*

But they were too late. Her family. The coven. Perhaps their minds muddled by a long hibernation and hunger. Perhaps only that in the end.

As for her father-- Sire-- Master-- As for him--

Emily sensed his own clairvoyance just before her own fangs sunk into his sinewy ashen neck. Sensed his own clairvoyance like a field of cold dark electricity. Sensed his unquestionable anticipation of what she intended to do.

But not fighting it. Not fighting her. Simply acquiescing.

To his only daughter. His only child. Dhampir.

Allowing her fangs to sink into his sinewy ashen neck.

Allowing her rare and most formidable bite.

Allowing her saliva, her venom, to poison his very own dark bloodstream. Allowing fate to decide his own fate after enduring time immemorial.

Acquiescing to her. Acquiescing to the hollowness.

The hollowness which had defined his existence for so long.

Acquiescing to this terrible lack of feeling that had become so dismally insufferable. Inconsolable. Clamant. Over eternity. An existence of being neither here nor there. At least until the hunger returned. A need for satiation. A need to feed. And to taste. A rare and sublime pleasure, you see. Tasting.

Proving there was a god. A god unto him. Them.

*A god that filled that hollowness for a spell.*
*A god that allowed him to sleep. Dream. This god.*
*To wander quietly amongst the still-living.*
*And to prey. As it were. For time immemorial.*

*Yes, Emily felt her father's acquiescence as her fangs sunk into his sinewy ashen neck. Allowing fate to decide whether or not her serum-rich blood flowing onto his dark flicking tongue would define this dark stormy night or if the venom of her rare and most formidable bite would finally end his grief.*

*An immortalized grief stretching that grief to eternity.*

*Allowing fate to decide his fate. The coven's fate. Her fate.*

*Fait accompli. Here. Now. In this black place beneath this giant looming beast of a house. Flames roaring above. Burning, burning, burning.*

*The heavy bellowing gongs of the large antique grandfather clock still echoing, echoing, echoing, while the calliope music sang in the burning walls.*

*And in the midst of this she heard their shrill screams.*

*The coven. Her family. As they came for her. Here. Now.*

*As they came for her in the darkness. Tooth and claw.*

*As her most peculiar employer had promised her they would do.*

*And then she heard his scream. Her father. Sire. Master.*

*A scream that sounded like the cold whipping wind in the eaves of the giant looming beast of a house. A howling scream that felt like it would burst her very eardrums. Shaking the giant burning black house around her.*

*Shaking the black house at its very foundations.*

*As if that black house might somehow rise into the night.*

*Might somehow escape into this terrible dark storm.*

*She felt her fangs sink deeper into what now felt like a corpse.*

*A corpse turned stony with deepening rigor mortis before then turning rotten. Not unlike a rotten apple. Mealy. The sweet-sour taste of death.*

*And as that howling scream turned to fading echo--*

*Her father, Sire, Master, turned to nothing in her mouth.*

*To ash. Ashes to ashes, dust to dust. Ashes, dust.*

*Like a swarm of black butterflies dispersing into the darkness along with the coven. Her family. Ashes to ashes, dust to dust. Ashes, dust.*

*Including her mother. Including Madelyn, the child.*

*Including Ms. Vivian Dancemore, her most peculiar employer.*

*To ash. Ashes to ashes, dust to dust. Ashes, dust.*

After which, as the swarm of black butterflies *dispersed* into the chamber darkness, Emily found herself alone. With him.

Alone with Adam. Her Adam. *Here. Now.*

As the cold black marble walls began to burn.

*Began to burn for suddenly they were only wood and not cold black marble at all. At t'all. Burning, burning, burning with the large black house.*
*Burning as the flames pushed down the narrow corridor.*
*Pushed down the narrow corridor into the cold dark chamber.*

Adam, her Adam, awoken from his deep stupor. His pale blue eyes growing wide, bulbous, with a bloodcurdling fear as his upside down gaze digested her. Digested her bathed in the firelight.

For she was no longer Emily. Not his Emily.

*For she had changed. Become the monster. The monster in the flesh before him. Her Adam. The monster before his horrified disbelieving gaze.*

*As if something from a most terrible dream. Nightmare.*

Adam, her poor Adam, screamed with terror as she freed him from the black marble table. As she gathered him into her arms. As she *flew* him out of that cold dark crypt *through the flames*. Exiting out the back of that giant looming beast of house *burning, burning, burning*. The conflagration reducing the once proud black house to ashes.

*Ashes to ashes, dust to dust. Ashes, dust.*

She flew him low through the beautiful garden.

The beautiful garden now also in flames.

Flew him low *as to not be detected by the militia* over the meandering crushed stone path through the flames as those flames hungrily consumed the maze of tall thick hedges and the colorful plants of all kinds now *screaming, burning* in the dark stormy night.

Roses, lavender, delphinium, citrus-hued daylilies, purple alliums. Among the more wild-looking things. Some plants ordered in their neat little rows and others crowded more lushly together as if perhaps springing organically from an untamed meadow.

Flew him low past the trained vines and climbers climbing the walls. Past the trees and trellises and small arbors and draping wisteria blooms *screaming, burning* in the dark stormy night.

Flew him low past the wooden benches and marble birdbaths with bubbling fountains and that fish pond in the southwest corner with black water offering blinding flashes of large, pale, rather carnivorous-looking fish now boiling as if in a pool of hot oil.

And then over the now *burning* gazebo.

The gazebo leaning. Collapsing in a fiery heap.

And then finally they were *eclipsing* the tall wrought iron fence with its thick iron bars and those terrible sharp-looking spikes.

Following the crushed stone path *as it turned to dirt and ascended* into those thick dark waiting woods behind the burning house.

*Those thick dark woods full of ghosts maybe.*
*And for a moment Emily believed she saw a flash of silver.*
*A flash of silver in the dark trees below. A bicycle.*
*And Henry, too. Sitting on that bicycle in the dark trees.*
*Laughing that joyful laugh that sounded to her like tears.*
*Eyeballs turned white. No longer jaundiced or blue.*
*Seeing without seeing. Shouting without making a sound.*
*Laughing soundless tears that would sound like joy.*

And then they were flying low over the crest of the hill of the dark bewitching woods, moving over the brief clearing from which jagged teeth rose from a wild intertwined patch of pigweed and bull thistle. Jagged teeth which were actually *stone grave markers.*

It was then they left the dark woods behind.

Rising high into the dark stormy night.

And far above the small playground on the other side of those woods, the playground growing smaller and smaller still as she flew Adam higher and higher still into the dark stormy night.

The small abandoned playground still surrounded by fluttering yellow caution tape. Appearing like a crime scene. Its brief parking lot blocked off by sawhorses and a large PARKED CLOSED sign. A swing set, jungle gym, and slide frozen in the darkness over a bed of dirty sand as if it all were trying to blend into the shadows.

To hide from this awful world come so undone.

Emily held Adam, her Adam, closer to her.

And shrieked and howled in the dark stormy night.

Shrieked and hollowed as Adam screamed.

Adam. Her Adam. In her embrace.

# 29.

IT WAS A COZY COUNTRY HOUSE upstate. The nearest neighbor was nearly a mile up the road. There was a small barn and an empty overgrown pasture and a dark little fishing pond. The small barn sat on the other side of the pasture from the country house and *Emily floated with Adam through an open door into its hayloft*. The open door being of the sliding barn door variety and *a good fifteen off the ground*. Its hinges quite badly rusted as if the door hadn't been shut in ages. Perhaps not since fresh hay might've been tossed through it from a horse-drawn wagon in much simpler times.

Much simpler times now long ago past.

Assuming time wasn't meaningless here, too.

There was no hay in the hayloft now, however.

Only long planks of old rotting floorboards.

While the black rain fell in sheets outside the hayloft, the wind causing the old barn to creak and moan, only to shudder with each punctuation of thunder, Emily released her embrace of Adam. Her Adam. Placing him down in a dark corner of the old hayloft.

Their presence disturbed an owl in the rafters.

The owl fluttered about noisily, especially for an owl, before it fled out into the dark stormy night. Its oval head turning one hundred eighty degrees to stare back at her with frightful eyes.

To stare back at the thing she'd *become*.

The monster. The beast. The dragon-thing.

A creature unlike anything it had ever seen.
Before it disappeared into the heavy darkness.
Into that storm, leaving them alone in the barn.
Emily stepped back from Adam now. Her Adam.
Stepped back from him in the dark corner. Stepped back from him and fully into the storm-light. A dark terrible thing.
Adam was no longer screaming. Just staring.
Staring with his own frightful eyes just like that owl.
And probably assuming he was only dreaming.
That what stood before him could not possibly be real. That it could only be a thing of the imagination. Of a nightmare. No matter what rumors he'd heard or been told or could imagine.
And under her Adam's most frightful stare--
Emily felt herself *changing*. Shrugging off the beast.
Large veined-appendages no longer spreading from her back. Fading in the storm-light like fragile cotton candy on the tongue as the talons faded from the end of her fingers, too. Fingers no longer dark and scaly and prolonged. Her mouth no longer filled with its own sharp things, either. Her jaw no longer jutting out. Elongated. Almost painfully. Her long dark flicking tongue receding.
Her body shrinking back into its human-self.
Shrinking back into Emily. Her Emily. His Emily.
As the wind howled. The thunder bellowed.
And Emily and Adam silently stared at each other in the empty hayloft of that barn, the cozy country house on the other side of that empty overgrown pasture. A cozy country house that belonged to Adam's in-laws. The very same cozy country house where Emily had spent that Thanksgiving with Adam and his family.
In what seemed like a century ago now.
Yet also seemed somehow like only yesterday.
*Adam. His wife. His little girls. His in-laws.*
*A beautiful spread like something out of the Waltons.*
*Adam's lovely little wife drinking too much wine and cornering Emily in the kitchen at the end of the night. Adam could always fall under her spell, but not this woman. His wife. She had been able to see through Emily.*
*Had been able to see the monster Emily actually was.*
*Especially with all that wine in her at the end of the night.*
*She could see how Adam was not Adam around her.*
*How Emily's presence always sent him spiraling down the drain.*
*Down the drain. Into a most terrible malaise. Despair.*

*Something Emily had managed to do to him ever since they were children. Feed his depression. His drinking. Drugs for a time. Inviting darkness.*

*His wife was the light. And his cute little girls. How old were they now, those little girls? Nine and eleven maybe? And what were their names?*

*Why couldn't she remember their names? Those little girls?*

*Had she known their names at that dreadful Thanksgiving?*

*It had been the last time she and Adam had seen each other.*

*(Until he'd shown up outside the giant looming beast of a house.)*

*Adam had asked Emily to leave after she'd said some less than flattering things to his wife in front of her parents. In front of Adam and their cute little girls. In front of that wholesome family in this cozy country house upstate.*

*She had disappeared out into the night darkness.*

*Somehow resisting the desperate urge to scream at him he was her family. If not by blood, then by circumstance. Inseparable by neither time nor distance. Nor any cold and heartless earthly convention, either. Her family.*

*A tiny separate universe born of each other.*

*Lost as they otherwise were in a terrible sewer of filth.*

*But, of course, he was no longer lost. Her Adam.*

*He had managed to extricate himself from that sewer.*

*And that had only made her want him more.*

*For him to throw his arms around her once again as he'd done when they were only children in that foster home. And in the years afterward.*

*To whisper in her ear: I'm summer, you're winter.*

*To hold her close to him and to never let her go again.*

*But she had let him go, hadn't she? Yes, she had. Out of love.*

*For she'd known all along what she was. The monster.*

*Yes, she had. Even as she'd been unable to admit it to herself.*

*Known all along he could not save her from what she was.*

*Known she could not protect him from herself maybe.*

*That he could not save her from her dark fate.*

And yet, here they were, *together again*. In the midst of this terrible storm with his family hidden away in that cozy country house right now. Hidden away from this world come so very undone.

Emily could sense as much. His family there.

His little girls. Nine and eleven. His wife. In-laws.

Perhaps she'd known all along they were here. Being *clairvoyant* like she was. Able to read his mind as she was wont to do.

Perhaps this was why she'd brought him here.

Of course this was the reason she'd brought him here.

But there was another reason, too. *Fait accompli.*

And she found herself shivering before him now. Adam. Her Adam. But not from sickness. *Not from the virus.* Perhaps her serum-rich blood, the blood of a creature *born of a dragon and a human female,* had always had the ability to overcome the virus. Perhaps Ms. Vivian Dancemore had been correct all along. Perhaps the virus itself had not been the root of her discomfort *at t'all.* Her illness.

*Fatigue, dear...*she'd said. *Mental indexterity. Malaise.*
*Working the night. Throwing off her biorhythms.*
*Pulling her out-of-sorts. Dark little euphemisms in the end.*
*For really what she'd been saying was that the root of her disarrangement was Emily herself. The monster inside of her she could not control.*
*And any other explanation, tragically, just poppycock.*

Which made *what had to be done* now more important than ever. Which made *what had to be done* now absolutely imperative.

Or so Emily contemplated dreadfully as she stood before Adam. Her Adam. Stood before him shivering so desperately.

Stood before him completely nude. Her Adam.

Completely nude. The poor remnants of her clothes dismissed in her *monstrous transformation* and in the dark storm of this night.

It felt good to stand before him *completely nude.*

Completely exposed to him. Her Adam.

And she saw he was shivering, too. Violently.

And in his pale trembling hands she saw *he held a rather familiar-looking wooden mallet and one long wooden wicket. Rather familiar-looking for a most obvious reason. The reason being they belonged to a croquet set.*

*An antique croquet set in a garden now burning.*
*Behind a giant looming beast of a house now burning.*
*The wooden wickets staggered neatly about a small croquet lawn ready for a game, if slightly warped with age and weather. A lawn now burning.*
*The mallets stored in a wooden stand beneath a fig tree now burning. The mallets hung from wooden pegs and the balls tucked in a narrows wooden sleeve between them, the old mallets and the balls dimpled and chipped here and there, rather pleasantly so, and nearly faded of their original colorful stripes.*
*Red, orange, green, yellow, and blue.*
*Strangely, however, one mallet had been missing.*
*An empty slot with a faded black stripe.*
*Its black ball, dimpled and chipped, tucked in that narrow wooden sleeve with the other balls. Abandoned there with the more colorful balls.*
*Red, orange, green, yellow, and blue.*
*And she imagined those colors in the flames.*

*Imagined them as she saw in those flames a memory she'd dismissed from her fragile mind. A memory of how that black mallet had disappeared.*

*How it had disappeared from that wooden stand beneath that fig tree now burning beside that small croquet lawn now burning with those wooden wickets staggered neatly about the lawn and ready for game that would never be played. Burning in the storm. Ashes to ashes, dust to dust. Ashes, dust.*

*Yes, she saw in those flames a shimmering memory.*

*A memory of herself taking that black mallet and one long wooden wicket. Taking them up to her bedroom in that giant looming beast of a house.*

*Staring at herself in that vanity mirror in her bedroom.*

*Wondering if she could still see her reflection in the cold flat glass.*

*Contemplating the mallet and that sharp wooden wicket.*

*Storing them beneath her bed even as she dismissed the odd memory from her fragile mind. The odd memory that hid in the darkness of her mind with all the other memories she had dismissed over time. Terrible memories.*

*Terrible memories wrapped in patinas of dark mercy.*

*All those children over that black span of so many passing years.*

*Sickly children. Some not so sickly maybe. Most horribly.*

*Sucking the life from their tender little bones. Her.*

*Her. The monster. The beast she had hidden from herself.*

*Even as she'd suspected its presence. There. Here.*

Emily blinked, twitched really, heavily:

And, completely nude before the only man she had ever really loved, shivering harder than ever, tears spilling from her eyes, asked him, Adam, her Adam, without speaking, to do a dark mercy.

Knowing it was her *fait accompli* to be *here* with him, Adam, her Adam, tonight for this final terrible act begun with her own mother in that final little motel room in that small farming town.

In what seemed more than a century ago now.

And yet also seemed somehow like only yesterday.

And it was then Adam, her Adam, spoke to *her* without speaking. Spoke to her with fear still in his voice, but also with a desperate love born from a shared life once lived in a terrible sewer.

A shared life. A hardass little shiny diamond.

Hiding inside of it a tiny separate universe.

A tiny separate universe where anything was possible.

Where anything had seemed possible back then.

A tiny separate universe promising happiness.

Or if not happiness, then survival. A way to survive.

Yes, he spoke her now. Adam. Her Adam.

Spoke to her without speaking in that old hayloft.

As she stood before him in the storm-light.

*I saw what you did, Em-- I thought I was dreaming, but I saw what you did in that giant looming beast of a house. In that dark crypt, Em.*

*I saw what you did for me. For us, Em. I did, Em.*

*I think you wanted me to see what you did. And what you are.*

*I think perhaps you always wanted me to see what you are even when you couldn't always see it yourself, Em. And perhaps I could always see it. Maybe even back then. Maybe even before you could really see it yourself, Em.*

*You're winter to my summer. How so very terribly cold you always felt in my arms. How you so desperately seemed to want to melt in my arms. How so desperately I wanted you to do so. To melt. To just melt in my arms and to stay there forever. How desperately I wanted that for you. For us, Em.*

And suddenly Adam, her Adam, was wrapping his arms about her pale nude shivering body now as that black storm raged.

*The black mallet and wicket set aside in the dark corner.*

And then they were making love. *Here. Now.*

*Fumbling and awkward like when they were just kids.*

*Stealing the breath from their lungs in the midst of the hayloft.*

*Adam staring at her with such tender and unconditional love. Embracing her in the warmth of his arms. Holding her so close to his warm body.*

*Their relationship, a hardass little shiny diamond.*

*A hardass little shiny diamond found in a world of shit.*

*Hiding inside of it a tiny separate universe. This diamond.*

*A tiny separate universe promising its own infinity.*

*And she felt herself melting in his arms as they made love.*

*Felt herself melting into him. Into his warm body as Adam, her Adam, then reached for that black mallet. Wicket. Reached for them with tears spilling down his flushed trembling pale cheeks as all that black rain fell and lightning scorched the dark bruised sky and thunder bellowed most miserably.*

*And as he reached for that black mallet and wicket--*

Emily found herself staring out at that feral storm.

Found herself staring out at that feral storm before slowly closing her eyes with relief as Adam, her Adam, somehow still managing to embrace her in the warmth of his arms, employed that black mallet to drive that long wooden wicket into her. The long wooden wicket, that long wooden stake, slicing cleanly into her neck and offering unto her the familiar sensation of an ice pick.

The blade passing through her spine into her very brain behind her right eye. Her head throbbing as the pain of that slicing blade radiated down a highway of nerves into her thin arms, making tiny splinters in her fingers.

## THE NIGHT SITTER

*But her splintery fingers only too soon falling numb on this terrible dark stormy night before that splintery numbness climbed into all the rest of her.*
*And it was in this bed of splintery numbness she fell asleep.*
*Fell asleep in a paradox of pain and nothingness.*
*Emily embraced it, slipping into it as if slipping into a warm bath. As if such a thing might actually exist for her. A warm drowning water.*
*Gratefully drowning in it. This welcoming sleep.*
*And she felt those numbing splinters begin to fade.*
*Begin to fade as that warm drowning water embraced her, too.*
*Embraced her, too, as her own mother might've once done.*
*As her father had once done. The only father she'd ever known.*
*A father who'd walked out that front door and disappeared.*
*Disappeared. A single suitcase on a cold and blustery winter day.*
*Not returning for his wife's funeral. Emily's mother.*
*Not returning for his own mother's funeral. Her grandmother.*
*Gone for so long now. So very long. Her disappearing father.*
*Large soft brown eyes. A hollow dimple in his right cheek.*
*His beard mimicking an evening shadow by the very end of the day, tickly when he tucked her into bed at night before he was suddenly just gone.*
*Gone so very long now. Not unlike her grandmother.*
*Large toady eyes. Unblinking. Full of reprimand.*
*But always certainly having the best of intentions for her.*
*Even as she must have known what dark fate was to come.*
*Yes, Emily embraced the warm drowning water. So warm.*
*As warm as his own arms. Adam. Her Adam.*
*The only boy she'd ever loved or who'd ever loved her.*
*Yes, Emily embraced it as Adam embraced her.*
*As he drove that long wooden wicket into her.*
*Yes, she embraced it. Embraced death.*

# 30.

ONLY IT WAS NOT DEATH that was embracing Emily back. Not death at all. *At t'all.* Rather, as the warm drowning water receded, it left her in a most peculiar *stasis.* Neither in the light of the living nor in the darkness of the dead.

But in a shadowy state not unlike *hibernation.*
And she thought of her father. Sire. Master.
His whispering voice rising. *Rising, rising.*
Rising in the thick black walls of that house.
That black house where his coven slumbered below.
Slumbered below in their black marble coffins.
That black house now burned to the ground.
Ashes to ashes, dust to dust. Ashes, dust.

Yes, Emily found herself neither living nor dead. But, frankly, in a most peculiar *stasis.* That long wooden wicket driven by Adam through her neck, spine, and into her very brain leaving her in *suspended animation.* But though her *slumbering* mind was muddled, moving slowly like molasses on a cold winter day, still she had *awareness.* A peculiar *clairvoyance* for events in the outside world. A *clairvoyance* that registered in her muddled mind like a clouded dream.

Disjointed. This dream. Full of puzzle pieces.
Not unlike the dark jigsaw puzzle of her life.
And not unlike the dark jigsaw puzzle of her life, these puzzle pieces slowly began to fall into place for her in this slumber.

And she knew herself to be below ground.

Beneath the old barn of the cozy country house.

The cozy country house of Adam's in-laws. The cozy country house where Emily had spent Thanksgiving with Adam and his in-laws. With Adam's wife and his two little girls. A family.

The cozy country house where Adam, his wife, two little girls, and his in-laws now attempted to find safe harbor from the world. From this world come so very undone. So terribly undone.

For this cozy country house, Emily *dreamt* in her most peculiar *stasis*, sat on the near outskirts of a small Mayberry-like town.

The township itself was situated in a verdant green valley surrounded by farmland and woods. It was an isolated town with only one road leading into the valley from the world beyond.

A road now guarded by local National Guard.

A road now subject to strict Martial Law.

And this presented a silver lining of sorts. This isolation. For, in effect, once the town sick were identified and quarantined--

Life in the town went back to normal. More or less.

The diner re-opening. The corner grocery store.

The local bar. The mill. The one-room schoolhouse.

The town was self-sustaining and it became rather easy for the townspeople to disregard the world beyond their little town. And yet, of course, it was important for this Mayberry-like town not to become too comfortable in this new atmosphere of normal.

For it wasn't only *The Reaper Virus* out there.

Out there beyond the local National Guard contingent.

There were things in the night. Terrible flying things.

Things the awful virus had been created to defeat.

Things undeterred by Martial Law roadblocks.

And such terrible flying things in the night were the reason for Emily's continued existence. *Here.* Beneath the ground. Beneath the old barn. A purpose for her in this world come so undone.

She would watch over Adam and his family. *Here.* In this time of peril. *Intuitively* understanding, even in her slumber, Adam would release her from this *stasis* should these terrible flying things, these howling, shrieking winged-beasts, suddenly appear, as they eventually would, in the night sky above the cozy country house.

Release her by *removing* the long wooden wicket.

For she was the Night Sitter. The protector.

For Adam. His wife. Two little girls. His in-laws.

Still, she would occasionally need to feed. Adam was aware of this need. To feed. To taste. This *hunger*. A need for *satiation*.

A burden she made clear to him *even from* her slumber. Speaking to him without speaking. Echoing her father's own words.

*For I am also familiar with grief...* he'd said.

Her father. Sire. Master. Mr. Grayson.

*As are you, my dearest girl. As are you.*

*For you, my dearest girl, it has been a cold blade.*

*Slicing into you. Offering you pain. Numbness.*

*For me, it is a hollowness...* he'd continued. *Neither pain nor numbness, inspiring no feeling whatsoever. And it is this lack of feeling that becomes so dismally insufferable. Inconsolable. Clamant. Over eternity.*

*An existence of being neither here nor there.*

*This hollowness that defines my existence. Grief.*

*At least until the hunger returns. A need for satiation.*

*A need to feed, my dearest girl. And to taste.*

*A rare and sublime pleasure, you see. Tasting.*

*Proving there is a god. A god unto me. Us.*

*A god that fills that hollowness for a spell.*

*A god that allows me, us, to sleep. To dream.*

*To wander quietly amongst the still-living.*

*To prey, as it were, my dearest girl.*

Yes, she would occasionally need to feed. To feed beyond the woods and township, perhaps. *To wander quietly amongst the still-living. To prey, as it were. To taste. To fill the hollowness for a spell. A hollowness she now felt, if she were being honest with herself, since Adam had driven that long wooden wicket into her. A hollowness that had replaced the cold blade.*

*Fatigue. Mental indexterity. Malaise. Hollowness.*

*Dismally insufferable. Inconsolable. Clamant. Eternal.*

But in the meantime, she would sleep. *Dream.*

And as she dreamt, she found more puzzle pieces.

So many more dark disjointed jigsaw puzzle pieces.

Revealing themselves in her clouded dream.

Offering more than one jigsaw puzzle in the end.

Offering to her more than one dream seemingly.

Further clouding her most peculiar slumber.

One such dark jigsaw puzzle of a dream invited to her mind a mysterious, if a hauntingly glorious tableau. Emily soaring in serene passage in the night above a black blanket of storm clouds. In dark flight with the coven. Black silhouettes in the dark night sky around her but pale-white against the moon. Her father near her. Sire. Master. That moon staring down at them. Like a giant pale-white eye. A giant unblinking pale-white eye *as if belonging to god Himself. Or at least a god maybe. A god with an incurious curiosity for such events below.*

And with a howl and a shriek in the stillness--

Emily, her father, and the coven, terrible flying things, terrible winged-beasts, *descended* through the black blanket of storm clouds. *Down, down, down upon the dark land below. To satiate their hunger. To feed. To taste. Living in the darkness so their prey might live in the light. Shepherds to their feeble-minded flock. Tending to them as black angels on the periphery of their ungraceful existence. Preventing them from straying. Keeping them in the light by forever living in the dark. Suffering eternity for their mortality.*

And yet, this was only one dream.

Only one dark jigsaw puzzle of a dream.

For there were others in her most peculiar slumber.

Including a dark jigsaw puzzle of a dream--

In which she and her Adam *had perished in that conflagration* after embracing in a final kiss and falling in the embrace of that final kiss *in each other's arms* from the peaceful night heavens. Spinning slowly around and around and around as they fell back *down, down, down* through the black storm clouds, streaks of white lightning, and bellowing thunder. Falling with all that black rain *down into the conflagration of that giant looming beast of a house burning, burning, burning far below. Never breaking their embrace. Never. Only holding on to each other tighter and tighter still as they fell into those roaring-leaping flames. Perishing there in each other's arms. Dying there. Amid those hungry flames. Perishing of fire.*

*Perishing of fire as the fire stripped the beast of their souls.*

*Leaving only their naked souls. Amid those flames.*

*The flames turning to a glorious golden light. A golden light inviting them into another eternity. An eternity they could share together. Forever. An eternity devoid of flying-winged beasts and of blood, if not sacrifice maybe.*

And yet as this dark jigsaw puzzle of a dream dissolved in her most peculiar slumber, she found herself in yet another dream.

Found herself in quite yet another dream still.

Found herself back in that final little motel room.

That final little motel room in that small farming town.

The shades tightly drawn over the window. A single bed and a little kitchenette with a two-burner stove and a tiny oven.

Her mother in that mud-stained house dress.

Humming to herself. A dark melancholy hymn.

And baking. Baking a tray of ginger cookies in the tiny oven in that final little motel in that small farming town. Baking as expressionless tears stained her pale cheeks. Humming a dark melancholy hymn as she then frosted those still-warm ginger cookies.

And Emily feeling *her little nine year old self* yawning with terrible exhaustion after all their running on all those dark nights with suddenly *nowhere left in this big shrinking world to go*. A softly-buzzing digital clock beside the single bed reading midnight. Midnight.

*Perhaps even frozen. That clock. Frozen at midnight.*

And little nine year old Emily, despite yawning with her terrible exhaustion, being unable to sleep, sensing this final little motel in this small farming town was finally, finally, the end of the shrinking road for them. Evidenced by her mother's manic baking.

Her mother's manic baking at midnight, no less.

A tray of ginger cookies, no less. Frosted.

Her mother's favorite. Emily's, too, perhaps.

Cookies her mother had baked them every Christmas.

Her mother turned to her now even as she scraped the cookies off the cooking tray and placed them neatly on a platter.

On a platter with a vase of white flowers.

Large white whorled flowers with pink pistils.

Large white whorled flowers taken from a small magical apricot-smelling white-flowered tree in a large marshy meadow.

The flowers still smelling faintly of apricot.

As the cookies smelled so strongly of ginger.

Her mother speaking without speaking. Wearing that lopsided smile, bright blue eyes gone muddy. And yet still Emily could hear her. A wistful serene voice despite her expressionless tears:

Heard her even as her lips refused to move:

*I thought you might not eat the cookies...* she said without speaking a word. Without her lips moving. Just staring at her with her bright blue eyes gone muddy. *I thought you might resist what had to be done. But I didn't even have to ask you. I'm not sure I could've asked you, in the end, if I'm being honest with myself. The poison, it works very quickly. Depressing the nervous system. Slowing body functions. Causing first the loss of consciousness. And then respiratory failure. Before eventually, mercifully, death.*

It was as her mother spoke to her without speaking Emily noticed a blender on the counter beside that tiny oven. Into which her mother had stuffed some of those white flowers, stems and all.

Reducing them to a very fine white powder.

A very fine white powder now in those cookies.
*It's a powerful poison. Potent in small doses. Potent.*
*Nature's own little most terrible awful miracle.*
*I thought to myself how peaceful you looked slipping into that sleep from which I thought you would never wake. I thought how peaceful I would feel once I joined you. And while you slept, I ate a cookie. And then another.*
*Just as you had done before you'd fallen into that sleep.*
*And I let that peaceful sleep fall over me, too.*
*Not pills, baby. Not an overdose. Just poison, baby.*
*Not what you were later told to spare you the ugly truth.*
*A truth your grandmother thought would devastate you.*
*That I meant to take both of us. Together, baby.*

And that was when Emily noticed in the bathroom mirror: the single bed against the opposite wall. Her mother lying there on top of the bedsheets. Little nine year old Emily lying beside her.

*Emily now separate from her little nine year old self.*
*Her little nine year old self now lying there beside her mother.*

Their eyes closed. Sleeping that peaceful sleep.

Frosting still on their fingers. Waxen lips.

And in the *ether* of this dream, Emily heard her mother's voice again: A soft hushed warm whisper of a voice: Her mother:

*Sleep, little one, sleep…* that soft hushed warm whisper of a voice said. *Dream yourself awake, and all of your dreams will come true.*

Something she'd hushed to her, her mother, as little nine year old Emily had fallen asleep after eating those frosted ginger cookies. Fallen into a deep sleep from which she was never supposed to wake. From which her mother was never supposed to wake.

But then something very odd happened.

Something very wonderful, actually. *Unlike before.*

In that final little motel room as dawn colored the sky.

Colored the sky over that small farming town.

Turning the sky from black to purple to soft pink.

*Emily's mother woke. And then gently shook awake her daughter. Rousing her little nine year old daughter from that terrible poison that ostensibly had not been administered correctly. Fate having other plans for them.*

*Fate having other plans for them in this dream.*

*In this odd, if most wonderful dream. Unlike before.*

*Emily suddenly finding herself back in her little nine year old body as her mother then embraced her. Embraced her daughter in her arms. Holding her so very close to her bosom. Telling her everything would be all right now.*

*Humming a soft hymn that was no longer melancholy.*
*Humming a soft hymn that was no longer dark, but hopeful.*
*Hopeful as a dark shadow slipped out quietly from that final little motel room in that small farming town. Slipped out quietly beneath the door.*
*And just as this dark shadow slipped out quietly--*
*Emily realized, as she'd been roused awake, then embraced by her mother, this dark apparition had been sitting in the corner of the room--*
*A dark apparition of a man with gleaming gold eyes.*
*A dark apparition of a man now gone. Vanished.*
*Vanishing with the night beneath that motel room door.*
*And little nine year old Emily sighed gratefully and sunk deeper into her mother's arms. So very deeply as her mother softly hummed into her ear.*

It was a dark jigsaw puzzle of a dream she would return to often in this, her most peculiar slumber here below ground.

Beneath the old barn of the cozy country house.

The cozy country house of Adam's in-laws. The cozy country house where Emily had spent Thanksgiving with Adam and his in-laws. With Adam's wife and his two little girls. A family.

In a town isolated from a world come so terribly undone.

But not safely isolated. Not from things in the night.

For such terrible flying things in the night were the reason for her continued existence. *Here.* Beneath the ground. Beneath the old barn. A purpose for her in this world come so terribly undone.

For she was the Night Sitter. The protector.

She would watch over Adam and his family. *Here.* In this time of peril. *Intuitively* understanding, even in her slumber, Adam would release her from this *stasis* should these terrible flying things, these howling, shrieking winged-beasts, suddenly appear, as they eventually would, in the night sky above this cozy country house.

Yes, she was the Night Sitter. The protector.

Unless this was all a dream, too. Yet another dream.

Yet another dark jigsaw puzzle of a dream.

A dream in which there were rumors the government had *captured* some of these beasts with more rumors that the dark blood of such beasts perhaps offered the opportunity for a vaccine.

A vaccine against the virus, if not the beasts.

If not their hunger. Their need to feed. To taste.

Emily felt herself embracing all of these *dreams*.

Finding an odd comfort in these *dreams*. Dreams of flying with her coven. Her family. Her father. Sire. Master. Dreams of perishing with Adam. Her Adam. In the conflagration of that giant looming beast of a house. Dreams of waking with her mother from that terrible poison. In her mother's arms as her mother softly hummed to her a hopeful tune. Despite a world come so very undone.

Her mother had always struggled with what was real and what was unreal. What was true and what was only just imagined. Often unable to differentiate between the two. Talking to people, screaming at them. *People who weren't there. People who didn't exit.*

As if shadows were a world unto themselves.

Becoming lost in those shadows. Her mother.

Lost in worlds that did not actually exist.

But perhaps such worlds did exist after all.

Perhaps they just did at that. Perhaps the shadows, or in Emily's peculiar case, dreams, were portals to other worlds that actually existed. *Actually existed, more or less, after all. These shadowy worlds.*

*Assuming she wasn't a batshit crazy loon herself.*

Emily took comfort in this. The idea her *dreams* might not just be dreams, but places of refuge. *And their reality, as she'd always defined reality,* not very important in the end. Not at all. *Not at t'all.*

Yes, she considered such a delicious thought.

Such a delicious idea her fate might be a myriad one.

Where all things were possible *simultaneously.*

Time no longer having any real meaning *at t'all.*

Her mother's watch still frozen. At midnight.

The blue-lacquered hour and minute hands standstill at twelve o'clock. The watch hands and small Art Deco numbers housed in a 14K white gold case with a unique red tone enamel pattern.

*An antique her mother had never removed. Only to remove it from herself postmortem. In her undeath. As a birthday gift for her only daughter.*

Still frozen at midnight on her pale wrist as if time might never move forward again. Still frozen at midnight even now as Emily found herself *entombed* below ground. Below the old barn.

Below the old barn on the other side of that empty overgrown pasture from the cozy country house with Adam's family.

*Entombed* in a cold root cellar full of cobwebs.

*Entombed* there in an old steamer trunk in the dark.

One with thick leather straps and heavy buckles.

*Not unlike the old steamer trunk* with its own thick leather straps and heavy buckles she'd found *in the attic of that giant looming beast of a house.* In the far corner of that attic where the roof slanted low.

And not unlike that old steamer trunk--
There sat above her in the dark of the root cellar--
On top of her very own old steamer trunk--
*An antique music box with a dull glass-topped lid mimicking a red and white circus big-top tent. Not unlike that antique music box in that attic.*
*And suddenly she could remember Adam placing it there.*
*Adam. Her Adam. This antique music box above her now.*
*And suddenly she could remember more besides. She could remember that her father, the only father she'd ever known, the father who'd walked out on her and her mother, not returning for her mother's funeral, or even for his very own mother's funeral, had given her such an antique music box on her birthday only weeks before walking out that door on a cold and blustery winter day.*
*Perhaps, just maybe, just this very antique music box.*
*Well, not perhaps. Not maybe. Not that at t'all.*
*For suddenly she could also remember how she'd taken this antique music box with her when she and her mother had gone on the run. Had treasured this antique music box through those most terrible hard years in foster care.*
*How she'd given it to Adam's girls last Thanksgiving.*
*Given it to them as an early Christmas present.*
*Only to then dismiss this antique music box from her mind.*
*Erasing it from her mind along with so many memories.*
*This, of course, didn't explain how this very antique music box had ended up in that giant looming beast of a house. Didn't explain that at t'all. But she had no doubt it had somehow followed her there to that black house.*
*Had no doubt the answer would soon be made known to her.*
*Along with an explanation for this old steamer trunk maybe.*
*And she listened to it now. Entombed in the root cellar.*
*Listened to it play for her in the cold and the dark.*
*Her Adam having put it down here to keep her company.*
Calliope music. Like that of an approaching carnival or circus. And again found herself imagining a long train of cars slowly slipping along the rails into a small town in the middle of the country in the middle of a dark night. *With shimmering moonlight, perhaps.*
Ferrying clowns and freaks and wild beasts.
Big-top tents and kettle corn and funnel cakes.
Fried pickles and strange foreign meats on sticks.
Booths featuring games of chance and skill.
Balloons, banners, and clouds of confetti.
But rather than played at a bright lively tempo as was the tradition of such music, carnival or circus music, playing at the wrong

speed. As it had done before. Warped and distorted. Stretched like cold taffy. As if she were hearing it from beneath dark water.

Its tune unnaturally slowed down. Perverted.

Into something macabre and unnatural.

Something dark and rather sinister.

Its dull glass-topped lid mimicking a red and white circus big-top tent open, revealing a spinning carousel inside. A spinning carousel of circus animals. Lions, tigers, elephants, monkeys, and zebras. The circus animals having adopted grisly human faces.

*Human faces wretched with terrible expressions of agony.*

Spinning on top of this old steamer trunk.

This old steamer trunk in which she was *entombed*.

With thick leather straps and heavy buckles.

The *ghoulish spinning carousel* offering spinning speckles of twinkling golden light about the cold dark cellar. *Spinning, spinning.*

Like a maelstrom of golden fireflies.

Reminding her of her grandparents' farm.

*Chasing such flying critters down there in North Carolina on hot muggy summer nights, the long grass pleasantly cool beneath her bare feet as she toted about a mason jar with tiny holes punched in the tin lid, gleefully snatching and stuffing those little flying critters by the handful into the jar until it blinked and glowed with the golden light emitting from their tiny translucent bottoms.*

She'd then sit beneath a large oak tree in the dark. Her back to its trunk. There at the very outskirts of the property. Just inside the wooden split-rail fence. And peer closely into the mason jar. Twisting it this way and then that way. Peering at all those beetles fluttering about. Those trapped soft-bellied fluttering beetles.

Blinking and glowing inside the thick glass.

Resisting the urge to shake the jar. To make those buggers really dance. To make them all suddenly glow at once. To make them all light-up in the heavy darkness. And cast her completely in their *soft golden light*. As if she were somehow in the jar with them.

As if she were somehow *glowing herself.*

Resisting the urge even as she knew she'd not be able to resist the urge forever. Knowing she'd eventually shake that jar. Knowing she was helpless to stop herself. It being the reason she'd collected the bugs in the first place. Needing to be swallowed by all that *soft golden light*. To feel as if she were *imbued with her very own light.*

If only for but a brief, if glorious moment.

Imbued with a most *magical golden light*.

And not lost in all that darkness.
*And felt her eyes glow with a magical golden light now.*
*Felt them glow with a gleaming gold in the old steamer trunk.*
*Here. Now. In the cold dark root cellar below the old barn.*
*Below the old barn on the other side of that empty overgrown pasture from the cozy country house with Adam's family. With Adam's family.*
*And then suddenly she was inside that warm cozy country house.*
*Inside the upstairs bedroom Adam's two young girls shared.*
*Nine and eleven. Adam's two young sweet little girls.*
*Yes, she found herself inside their bedroom with all their things as the two young girls slept. There was a bunk bed, but the girls had decided to crawl into the same bed. The lower bunk. Sleeping very close together. The curtains tightly drawn over the lone bedroom window. The window boarded. A feeble attempt to protect the two young girls from the dangers out there in the nighttime.*
*Yes, she suddenly found herself watching over them.*
*Watching over the two young girls as they slept fitfully.*
*(A dog sleeping at their feet. Their dog. An eye half-open.)*
*Found herself on a dark shelf on a dark wall as she held vigil.*
*Found herself inside the porcelain body of a China doll.*
*A red-headed doll. A red-headed doll with dirty blue eyes.*
*Emily had always looked so much like her mother after all.*
*Her own hair red, long and tangled. Eyes dirty blue.*
*Meanwhile, there were other porcelain China dolls on her dark shelf and other dark shelves around her in this bedroom the two young girls shared.*

The dolls sitting quietly in their neat little rows.
Their dark eyes closed as if asleep. These dolls.
Their porcelain faces rather too human-like.
Their skin tinted in order to resemble flesh.
If still a ghostly pale for all that nonsense.
With deftly painted cheeks, lips, and eyebrows.
And what appeared to be real human hair.
Though maybe it was only just mohair.
*Yes, she suddenly found herself inside one of these dolls.*
*Suddenly found herself watching over the two young girls.*
*The Night Sitter. The protector. Here. Now.*
*And yet not really knowing if she was really here. Or if this was still just yet another dream. Still just yet another dark jigsaw puzzle of a refuge.*

The dolls sitting quietly in their neat little rows.
Sitting quietly like they'd been here forever.
Like they'd maybe been here for all of eternity.

# THE NIGHT SITTER

*As if maybe all her dreams, all her memories, were now immingling in her mind. Unwilling to remain separate from each other. But rather, perhaps, representative of only just one giant dark crazy jigsaw puzzle in the end.*
*One giant looming beast of a dark jigsaw puzzle.*
*A dark jigsaw puzzle refusing to make any lucid sense.*
*Despite her fragile mind's desperate attempt to reconcile it.*
*Reality as she'd always defined it not very important in the end.*
*Reality only a perception and not a reality at all. At t'all.*
*The dark jigsaw puzzle pieces hopelessly existing in disarray.*
*Implacably confused in her muddled slumbering mind.*
*In a place where time truly no longer had any real meaning.*
*Here. Now. In her deep sleep. Stasis. Hibernation.*
Meanwhile, she could also see black butterflies in the night sky above the cozy country house and over the empty overgrown pasture, dark little fishing pond, and old barn. *Swarming, swarming.*
*Could see them in her deep sleep. Stasis. Hibernation.*
Black silhouettes against the dark night.
Pale-white against a shimmering moonlight.
*Little black butterflies like so many black ashes.*
*Swirling black ashes. Ashes to ashes, dust to dust. Ashes, dust.*
And wondered if she hadn't perhaps died after all when Adam had *stabbed* her with that long sharp wooden wicket. And wondered if maybe these scattered dark jigsaw puzzle pieces were only her life pulling apart at the seams before the final dark curtain fell.

That maybe Adam, her dear Adam, had burned her remains in a fiery hot bonfire in that empty overgrown pasture beside the cozy country house. And these black butterflies her own ashes.
*Ashes to ashes. Dust to dust. Ashes, dust.*
*For dragons are born of fire and will perish of fire.*
*Will you perish of fire, Miss Emily? Will that be your fate?*
She asked this of herself now. And wondered.
Wondered in this most peculiar slumber.
Darkness. Light. Fate. *Fait accompli.*

## ABOUT THE AUTHOR

Russell Gilwee is a novelist and screenwriter. He lives in Northern California with his wife, Lauraleen, and their goldendoodle, Sophie. He is busy at work on his next novel and several film projects.

Printed in Great Britain
by Amazon